DINOSAUR
SUMMER

GREG BEAR

DINOSAUR
SUMMER

Illustrations by Tony DiTerlizzi

ASPECT®

WARNER BOOKS

A Time Warner Company

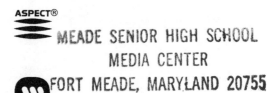

Aspect® name and logo are registered trademarks of Warner Books, Inc.

Warner Books, Inc., 1271 Avenue of the Americas, New York, NY 10020
Visit our Web site at http://warnerbooks.com

 A Time Warner Company

Printed in the United States of America
First Printing: February 1998
10 9 8 7 6 5 4 3 2 1

Library of Congress Cataloging-in-Publication Data

Bear, Greg
    Dinosaur summer / Greg Bear.
       p. cm.
    ISBN 0-446-52098-5
    I. Title.
PS3552.E157D56   1998
813'.54—dc21   97-12318
                                             CIP

Book design and composition by L&G McRee

For all who have brought dinosaurs back to life—
paleontologists, explorers, artists, moviemakers, animators, writers,
and young minds everywhere.

—G.B.

The illustrations herein are dedicated with much admiration and
respect to my mother and father, who allowed me to paint
Tyrannosaurus Rex
on my bedroom wall when I was nine years old.
And for Ray Strassburger, my fifth-grade teacher, who knew a seed
when he saw one.

—T.D.

Acknowledgments

My special thanks go to Phil Currie, Michael Ryan, and the staff of the Royal Tyrrell Museum in Drumheller, Alberta, Canada; to Karen Anderson, Kathleen Alcala, and Astrid Anderson Bear; and to my children, Erik and Alexandra, both of whom contributed animal ideas and listened to portions of the manuscript.

I owe a debt of gratitude as well to Ray Harryhausen, for partaking of this adventure; to Ron Borst and George E. Turner for information on Merian C. Cooper and Ernest Schoedsack; to Bill Warren; and to Dan Garrett, for enthusiastic footwork in Los Angeles.

I thank also the estate of Sir Arthur Conan Doyle, for keeping his works alive and available.

I cannot begin to list all the other artists, paleontologists, authors, animators, etc.; instead, I reemphasize the dedication.

—G. B.

I would like to thank Charlie McGrady at CM Studio for supplying the wonderful dinosaur models used in the paintings for this book.

I would also like to thank William Stout for his warm support and inspiration, and for bringing dinos back to life in my imagination via his delicious art. Thank you, thank you, thank you.

—T. D.

DINOSAUR
SUMMER

BOOK

ONE

June 1947

Chapter One

On the last day of school, after walking to the old brownstone building on 85th where they had an apartment, Peter's father told him that they would be going away for a few months. Peter gave him a squint that said, *What, again?*

The mailbox in the lobby was empty. Peter had been hoping for a letter from his mother. She had not written in a month.

They walked up the three flights of stairs in the hallway that always smelled of old shoes and mice—the polite word for rats—and his father said, "You think I'm going to take you to North Dakota or Mississippi or someplace, don't you?"

"It's happened," Peter said.

Anthony Belzoni gave his son a shocked look. "Would I do that to you—more than once?"

Sad that there had been no letter in the box and that school was over, Peter was in no mood for his father's banter, but he tried to sound upbeat. "We could go to Florida," he said hopefully. He loved Florida, especially the Everglades. His father had sold two articles to *Holiday* on travel for wealthy folks in the Everglades and resorts in the Keys, and they had lived well for several months after Anthony had been paid—promptly, for once.

"Florida," Anthony said. "I'll keep it in mind." At the end of the dark hallway, a window let in sky-blue light that shone from the old, scuffed floors like moonglow on a faraway desert. The ceiling's patchy Lincrusta Walton tiles reminded Peter of a puzzle left unfinished by giants. "Did we stay here the whole year, instead of moving?"

"Yes," Peter said grudgingly. "Until now."

"So, what did you think of Challenger High?"

"Better than last year." In fact, it was the best school he had attended, another reason to want to stay.

"Do you know who Professor Challenger was?"

"Of course," Peter said. "He found living dinosaurs."

They reached the door and Peter took out his key and unlocked the deadbolt. Often enough, Peter came home alone, returning to an empty apartment. The door opened with a shuddering scrape. The apartment was warm and stuffy and quiet, like the inside of a pillow. Peter dumped his book bag on the swaybacked couch and opened a window to let in some air from the brick-lined shaft.

"I've been saving something to show you," Anthony said from the kitchen.

"What?" Peter asked without enthusiasm.

"First, I have a confession to make."

Peter narrowed his eyes. "What sort of confession?"

"I got a telegram from your mother. Last week. I didn't bother to tell you—"

"Why?" Peter asked.

"It was addressed to me." Anthony returned to the front room and pulled the crumpled piece of paper from his shirt pocket. "She's worried about you. Summer's here. She thinks you're going to catch polio in all these crowds. She forbids you to swim in municipal pools."

There had been talk of a bad polio season in the newspapers and at school for months. Everyone was worried about putting their children together with other children.

Peter had hoped his mother might have sent a message inviting him to come to Chicago for a visit. "Oh," he said.

"She's practically ordering me to get you out of town. It's not a bad idea."

"Oh," Peter said, numb.

"And then, there's the prodigy," Anthony said, stepping back into the kitchen. He assumed a thick and generally faithful Bela Lugosi accent. "A sign looming over us both, like a . . . like a—"

"Forewarning," Peter said pessimistically.

"An auspice," Anthony countered cheerfully, switching to a kindly but menacing Boris Karloff lisp. He rattled the cans, one or two of which would probably be dinner. "Like a red sky at night." *Red sky at night, sailor's delight.*

"A *portent*," Peter said. Peter delighted in words, though he had a difficult time putting them together into narratives. His father, on the other hand, preferred living facts, yet could spin a yarn— or write a compelling piece of journalism—as easily as he breathed.

More cans rattled, then he heard Anthony dig into the bag of onions. That meant the canned goods were not up to expectations. Dinner would be fried onions and macaroni, not Peter's favorite. He missed good cooking.

"Why does it have to be a portent?" Anthony asked, standing in the kitchen doorway and tossing an onion in one hand.

"A foreboding," Peter continued. "An omen." He realized he sounded angry.

The slightest breath of warm wind ruffled the curtains at the window.

"Really." Anthony let the onion lie where it fell in his palm, balanced by his long, agile fingers.

Peter did not want to cry. He was fifteen and he had sworn that nothing would ever make him cry once he had reached twelve, but he had broken that vow several times since in private.

"You're angry because she didn't ask you to come to Chicago, and because there's no letter for you," Anthony said.

Peter turned away. "Show me your prodigy," he said.

"Your mother never did write letters, even when I was in Sicily."

"Just show me," Peter said too loudly.

Anthony looked down at the onion and pulled back a dry brown shred. Black dust sifted to the worn, faded carpet. "This one's rotten," he said. "You know about pizza? I ate my first pizza in

Sicily. There's a restaurant called Nunzio's about six blocks from here where they serve them."

"We don't have any *money*," Peter said.

"Which shall it be first, the prodigy, or a pizza at Nunzio's?"

Peter realized his father was not kidding. Some other kids at school—the ones whose parents had money, whose fathers had regular jobs and could afford to take their families out to eat; fathers who still had wives, and kids who still had mothers living with them—had mentioned eating pizzas. "The omen," Peter said, staring out the window at the brick wall, waiting until his father wasn't looking to wipe his eyes. "Then pizza."

His father put a hand on his shoulder and Peter remembered how light Anthony's step was, like a cat. His father was tall and lean and had a long nose and walked silently, just like a cat.

"Come with me," Anthony said. They went past the kitchen, down a hall that led to a small bedroom behind the kitchen and the cramped white-tiled bathroom. The sound of groaning pipes followed them.

Peter slept on the couch in the living room and Anthony had a single bed in the small bedroom. This was not a bad apartment, Peter knew. It was certainly better than the one they had lived in last year in Chicago. That had been a real dump. But the brownstone building was old and dark and in warm weather the hallways smelled, and sometimes men peed in the lobby at night. Peter would have loved to live in the country, where, if people peed on the grass or on a tree, it didn't smell for days.

They entered the bedroom. A bright polished steel camera lay disassembled on a blue oilcloth on the narrow unmade bed. Clothes hung on the back of the tiny desk chair like the shed skin of a ghost. Books had been stacked in random piles under the window and against the wall. Two battered cardboard boxes in the one corner carried polished slabs of rock with beautiful patterns. The heavy rocks had burst the seams.

Some months ago, in the worst of his anger and boredom, after drinking half a bottle of Scotch, Anthony had carved a rude poem with his pocketknife in the plaster wall above the dresser. He had later covered it with a framed Monet print. Anthony was often an angry man; it was one of the reasons Peter's mother had left him. Left *them*.

Anthony tapped the wooden door above the bedstead. In the building's better days, the door had once concealed a dumbwaiter—a small elevator between floors. It had been painted over so many times that it had been glued shut. Peter had once tried opening it when his father was out, and could not.

Now, Anthony tapped it with his graceful hands and spread his fingers wide like a magician. "Voilà," he said. The small door opened with a staccato racket that vibrated the wall and tilted a picture of his father's Army buddies.

Behind lay an empty shaft. The elevator was either in the basement or had vanished long ago. There were no ropes to pull to bring it up.

"Maybe it's not a dumbwaiter at all. Maybe it was a laundry chute," Anthony said. Peter was not impressed.

"What's in there that's so great?" Peter asked.

"Have you been dreaming of large animals?" Anthony asked with a funny catch in his voice.

"No," Peter said.

"I have. Sleeping right here, in this bed, I've dreamed of very large animals with scaly skin and huge teeth and the biggest smiles."

Peter wondered what else his father had dreamed about, on those nights he came home and drank himself to sleep. He sniffed. "Why should I dream about them, just because you do?"

"Peter, my lad, loosen up. This is a real marvel." Anthony reached to the back of the shaft and pulled on a board. The board came away with a small squeak, revealing smooth dark stone beyond. Anthony put the board aside. He lifted a flashlight off the shelf beside the bed, bumped its end against the palm of his hand, and switched it on. "Where we're going this summer means I'll make enough money for us to live comfortably for at least a year."

"What about Mom?" Peter asked.

"Her, too," Anthony said a little stiffly. "Look." He handed Peter the flashlight and Peter shined it into the shaft, playing the beam over the dark slab of stone. A ghostly plume of cool air descended

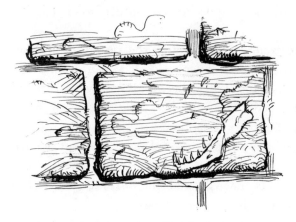

the shaft. Outside, the building was covered with soot, dark gray or almost black; here, the stone looked freshly cut, a rich dusty chocolate like the color of a high-priced lawyer's suit. *Like the lawyer Mother hired.*

The light caught a black shape pressed flat in the stone, a long irregular wedge with something sticking up out of it.

Peter's eyes widened. "It's a *jaw*," he said. He got up onto the bed, knees sinking into the feather pillow, not bothering to remove his shoes. Anthony did not care about the shoes. Leaning into the shaft so that he could see all the way down, three floors, and all the way up, five more floors, Peter touched the dark thing embedded in the brownstone. "It's got teeth . . . like shark teeth."

"It's not a shark," Anthony said. "There are lots of fossils in brownstone. Brownstone is a kind of sandstone." Before the war, his father had worked as an apprentice coal and oil geologist in Pennsylvania. "Connecticut, late Triassic. A long time ago, animals died and washed down rivers until they settled into the sand and mud. They became fossils. I've heard of a bridge made of brownstone blocks that contains most of a dinosaur."

"A *dinosaur?*" Peter asked in disbelief.

"An old one. Not like the ones you see in circuses. Or rather, used to see."

"Wow," Peter said, and meant it, all his bad mood fled. "What kind is this?"

"I'm not sure," Anthony said. "Maybe a small meat-eater. Look at the serrations on that tooth. Like a steak knife."

"Whoever left it there, when they built this place, was *crazy,*" Peter said.

"You know," Anthony said, "I've wondered about that. Fossils must have fetched a pretty penny when this building was made. But a stone mason, someone cutting and fitting all these blocks of stone, he sees this and shows it to the foreman, and the foreman tells the owner, and the owner, maybe he's superstitious . . . he thinks this building needs a guardian, something to protect it. He thinks maybe it's a dragon in the rock. So he says, 'Everything's numbered and I don't want to have you cut a new piece. Put it up and leave it there.' And everybody shrugs and they set the block in place and leave it. The owner, he remembers where the block is, makes a note on the blue-prints. He comes back after the building is done, finds the room, looks into the dumbwaiter shaft, pulls out this board . . . And there it is."

Anthony smiled with great satisfaction. "I found it one night last week when I was bored. I couldn't sleep for all the dreams. I dug with my penknife at the paint around the door. Maybe I thought I'd crawl up into some pretty lady's bedroom. When I looked inside, I saw where a board in the back had been pulled loose. I tugged on it . . . voilà. The board has been loose all this time."

"It's great," Peter said thoughtfully. "A building full of fossils."

"Maybe. We don't know there are any others."

"A whole riverbed full of skeletons," Peter said, his mind racing. "Maybe there was a flood and they all piled up, and there are dozens of them all around here, inside the stones."

"That would be fun," Anthony agreed.

Then Peter remembered. "So how is this an omen?"

Anthony sat on the edge of the bed. "The day after I found this, I got two letters, one from the Muir Society and another from *National Geographic*. You remember I sent my photos to Gilbert Hovey Grosvenor. He's the editor. He liked them, and he knows the director of the Muir Society. Conservationists."

"Yeah," Peter said. "So what do they want?"

"They want me—us—to work with Lotto Gluck and Vince Shellabarger."

Peter knew those names. He tried to remember . . .

"Stick in your mind, don't they?" Anthony asked, his grin bigger than ever. "They used to be famous. Every boy in America knew who they were—hell, maybe the whole world."

Peter wrinkled his brow. He climbed off the bed, and the flash-light slipped from his fingers. As he bent to pick it up, he said, "Circus Lothar!"

"You got it. The last dinosaur circus. They're going to shut 'er down in a few days. Have a final performance. Grosvenor wants pictures and an article. I asked if you could come with me, as an assistant. They said sure, gives the angle some family polish. It's the big time, Peter."

"Jeez," Peter said, at a loss for any other word. His chest felt hollow and his mouth dry. Anthony pulled a chair out from the tiny desk and sat on it, and Peter sat on the edge of the bed, careful not to upset the oilcloth and all the pieces of the Leica spread there.

"Well, are you coming?" Anthony asked.

Peter shot him a quick frown. "When?"

"That means yes?"

"*When?*"

"First, we get packed. Then we take a train to Boston."

"And then?"

"We see the circus's last performance."

"That will take a couple of months?"

Anthony looked away with an odd smile. He was keeping something to himself. "If it all works out, we'll have lots more work. And if it doesn't—well, at least we're likely to get a trip to Florida. That's where Gluck keeps the circus's headquarters.

"One more thing," Anthony said, lightly squeezing Peter's upper arm. "You're going to write it down. They might take your story and print it."

Peter opened and closed his mouth like a fish. "In *National Geographic?*"

"Sure, why not?"

Peter swallowed a lump.

"Enough of a prodigy for you?" Anthony asked.

It meant work for his father, who had had no work for six months. It meant regular meals and a place to go this summer—maybe Florida—rather than staying in the apartment day after day, watching his father try to stay away from the bottle, waiting for a letter from his mother and an invitation to come visit her and Grandma.

It meant a lot.

Peter got off the bed and hugged his father, feeling so many things, all at once, that tears came to his eyes.

"That's fine," Anthony said, letting the hug last as long as it should, between two strong men, father and son. He put his hand on Peter's chest and pushed him gently back, then thumped him lightly. "I told you it would all work out. Your mother just didn't believe in me."

"Can I call her and tell her?"

Anthony frowned. "She'll want money right away," he said.

Peter felt the familiar pang. "I won't mention the money. I'll just say you've got work."

"*We've* got work," Anthony corrected. "The perfect summer job. And it gets us out of town."

"There's something more," Peter said.

Anthony fiddled with the camera parts, eyes down.

"What is it?"

Anthony smiled slyly and said, "I've learned to keep quiet about things that might never happen." His brow furrowed. "You can trust me and go along without asking too many questions, or you can live the kind of life your mother wants you to live: safe and snug and dull as dishwater."

Peter examined his father's eyes. He was painfully serious.

"Are we a team?" Anthony asked.

Peter felt a small shiver creep up his back. He resented this kind of emotional blackmail, but then again, his curiosity had been piqued. Peter had never thought of himself as terribly brave, but he was curious to a fault.

He also wanted to please his father; please this difficult, lean man, who had lived through so much and yet sometimes seemed more of a child than his son. It hurt to feel need for Anthony's approval; there had been times when relying on Anthony was like leaning on the wind. But there it was.

"A team," Peter said.

"My lad," Anthony said solemnly, and they shook hands.

Chapter Two

When his head was clear, free of emotional clouds, as it was now, standing on the platform waiting for the train to Boston, a traveling and uprooted life with his father was better than a rooted life with a mother who, it seemed, had no place for him. "When I get a job and Grandma is feeling better," she had written a year ago, "you can come and live with us. But right now the apartment is just too small, and we don't have much money, Peter."

Peter rubbed his nose. Whenever he thought about these things, his nose itched. Anthony put his hand on Peter's shoulder. "Five minutes," he said, "and you'll be inside a dining car slugging back cocoa and doing real damage to a grilled cheese sandwich."

Penn Station was not very crowded at one o'clock in the afternoon. Outside, the city was hot and humid, but below ground, surrounded by dirt and concrete, the air was still cool. People waited on concrete platforms for the big, sleek stainless steel train cars to roll in behind their pounding diesel engines, dragging gusts of hot air strong enough to blow your hat off, if you were wearing one. Most of the men and all of the women wore hats. The men wore seersucker suits and panamas, homburgs, and fedoras. The women wore calf-length summer skirts and jackets and felt pillboxes, round-brims, and toques. Peter's mother had sold hats in Chicago before she met Anthony. Some of the women's hats were decorated with satin ribbon, sweeps of veil, even fake fruit; a few sported long pheasant plumes that made them look like marmosets.

Anthony wore an old rumpled corduroy jacket and wool slacks, too warm for the weather but that was all he had, and no hat.

They had packed up their belongings and moved out of the apartment. Their address, for the next three months, would be a post office box. They were staking everything, it seemed to Peter, on the generosity of *National Geographic*.

He was still puzzling over what he had done the night they had gone out for pizza. They had walked to Nunzio's, a loud and cheerful place with red checked tablecloths. His father had drunk a bottle of Chianti, to celebrate, he said, and they had shared a very large pie, almost as big as their table, covered with tomato sauce and cheese. Peter had eaten more than his fill and they had strolled home through the quiet side streets. Anthony was slightly drunk and was telling Peter about his work on oil rigs in 1939. He had hated every minute of it, he said, but still, there was the excitement and the camaraderie of the men all working together, and there had been the regular paycheck.

"I was in a straitjacket," Anthony had said, putting his arm around Peter's shoulders. "Every hour was misery. Best damned thing that ever happened to me. But the war came . . . That was miserable, too. Also the best damned thing that ever happened to me."

Peter had helped his father up the stairs and into bed, and then had sat on the threadbare couch in the front room for a while, his head buzzing. About one in the morning, he had clapped his hands down hard on his knees and walked into the kitchen, grinding his molars so loudly he wondered if Anthony could hear. He had looked under the kitchen sink, pulled out a box of empty whiskey bottles, and carried them down the stairs. Then he had hefted the box to his shoulder and walked half a block to the entrance of an alley. And in the alley, surrounded by wooden crates and garbage cans, he had pulled the bottles from the box, one at a time, and flung them against a brick wall. There had been fifteen of them, and on the fourteenth bottle, an old woman had leaned out of a third story window and shouted at him, "All right, all right! You've made your point! Now get on home and let us sleep!"

He had stared up at the lighted window, the last bottle in his hand. Then he had put the bottle gently and silently down on the concrete, wiped his hands on his pant legs, and returned to the apartment.

The train arrived, little different from any of the other steel monsters that had hauled Peter and his father all over the Midwest and the East and the South in search of work. They climbed aboard and found their seats and Anthony slung their luggage into the overhead and strapped it in. Peter sat beside the long high window and examined the station's brick wall through smudges of fingerprints and hair oil.

As the train pulled out of the station and daylight flooded the car, Anthony asked, "Did you say good-bye to Millie Caldwell?" Millie Caldwell was a girl in his class. She and Peter had gone to the movies a couple of times and Peter thought she was more than a little nice to talk to.

Peter nodded. Millie was in love with a varsity football player, a college boy; she liked rugged, adventurous men. She had told him, on their last movie outing, "I really go for men who like to get in trouble." Millie Caldwell's eyes had gleamed at the thought. "I prefer the growl of a tiger to the lick of a lapdog. You're just too tame for me, Peter." Millie Caldwell wanted someone like Anthony, Peter realized . . . not for the first time.

"Did you tell her what you're doing?"

Peter shook his head. "It's a secret, isn't it?"

"Just checking," Anthony said, and for a moment, Peter's stomach soured.

"I don't think I'll ever see her again," he said. "We'll come back and live someplace else, I mean."

"A nicer place, maybe," Anthony said.

"Maybe," Peter said.

"Let's go eat," Anthony said, and they walked toward the rear of the train, where the dining car was. The food was pretty good and Anthony bought him all he could eat. After sipping steaming cocoa from a thick, heavy cup, he ate three grilled cheese sandwiches with fried tomatoes on the side and drank two glasses of cold, rich milk. Anthony ate a BLT and drank a glass of beer, then two cups of coffee. He took out his Leica and aimed through the window, snapping a few pictures of hilly suburban neighborhoods where all the returned vets lived in long lines of cookie-cutter brown and gray and white houses. Finally they reached the countryside, gray under June's overcast skies. Thick green elm trees raced past the windows.

"We'll get into Boston late this evening," Anthony said. "We'll stay in a big, fancy hotel, and then tomorrow, we'll shop for traveling gear and go see the circus and meet Gluck and Shellabarger."

Peter wondered why they would need traveling gear. He swallowed his last gulp of milk, wiped his mouth on the napkin, and said, "Dad, what if they decide they don't want the article? What will happen to us?"

Anthony gave him a stern look.

"Mom would say it was practical to worry about such things," Peter said primly.

"Your mother never lived a peaceful day in her life," Anthony said. His face reddened. "She worries all the time."

Peter stared back at him, biting his lip.

"Sorry," Anthony said.

"What will we do if it doesn't work out?"

"I'll get a job in a camera store in Boston," Anthony said. "You can help me sell cheap Japanese cameras to folks who don't know any better. All right?"

Things were getting off to a mixed start. Peter realized this was his fault—in part, at least. He tried to think of something to say that would put things right again. "It was right not to tell Mom. She would have worried. She would think the circus was a dangerous place to work."

Anthony said, "Mm hmm." He was studying a woman sitting two tables behind Peter, on the other side of the train.

"Dad . . ."

"Mm hmm?"

"Do you think I worry too much—like Mom?"

Anthony curled his lip casually and squinted out the window.

"Sometimes it's best to look an adventure right in the eye and not back down, not even blink. Never let life see you're afraid."

That sounded like someone in a book talking. Much of his father's life could have come straight out of a book. A veteran of the campaigns in Italy, wounded twice, assigned to help motion picture director John Huston make documentaries of the fighting, Anthony Belzoni had survived the war with a scarred arm and chest, two Purple Hearts, a broken marriage, and his beloved Leica, "Not made in Canada. Made in Germany."

Peter could hardly imagine what his father had been through and survived.

"I'm with you, Dad," Peter said. The words sounded forced and a little awkward, but they seemed to do the trick.

"I never doubted that, Peter," Anthony said with a big smile. "How about starting that journal?"

Peter loved words. He had read his mother's old *Merriam Webster's Dictionary* almost from cover to cover. It was one of the few things he had of hers. She never used it and so had given it to him when she left Chicago to go to Grandmother's and live. But when it came to stringing one word after another . . .

With a sigh, he took out his new black notebook and a fountain pen. He spent more time than was strictly necessary filling the pen from a bottle of Quink. Then he tapped his chin and hummed until Anthony gave him a stern look, and finally applied nib to paper.

Today we left New York for Boston. My father saw the Lothar Gluck Dinosaur Circus before the war, but I've never seen it. I am really very excited, but sometimes I think too much and don't know how to feel.

My father thinks on his feet, and he's smarter than almost anyone, but sometimes he leaps before he looks. I'll have to watch out for both of us.

Writing this took Peter half an hour.

They arrived in Boston after seven o'clock at night and took a taxi to the hotel. A smiling, wizened porter carried their bags up to the room. After giving the old man a whole dollar for a tip, Anthony fell onto the bed and began snoring. Anthony could fall asleep instantly wherever he was; he had learned that trick in the Army. Peter had to settle down and get used to his surroundings first.

The hotel room was a marvel. Peter had never slept in such a fancy bed. Even with his father sprawled across half, there was more than enough room. The furniture was dark maple. Original works of art hung on all the walls—mostly paintings of flowers, but pretty. The bathroom was a radiance of white marble, with a huge clawfoot tub and glittering brass faucets and shower head.

Peter tried the shower. The stinging spray of steaming hot water felt wonderful. He rubbed himself vigorously with a soft white towel that seemed as big as a bedsheet. He had neglected to place the cloth curtain inside the tub, however, and got water all over the floor. He wiped it up with the big towel and then settled into bed beside his father to read the book they had bought at the Strand the day before.

Peter could not read on trains or in cars. It made him queasy. Writing in the notebook had been bad enough. He had been waiting for this moment, however, to open the thick, heavy book with all of its pictures: *The Lost World,* by Sir George Edward Challenger, as told to Sir Arthur Conan Doyle. Doyle had written the Sherlock Holmes books and many novels. Peter had read *The Lost World* when he had been eight or nine. Now he had his own copy instead of one from a library, and this one was the deluxe illustrated edition. The bookseller at the Strand had told them it had been out of print for more than five years. People were not very interested in dinosaurs anymore.

Peter scanned the glossy pictures first. He flipped past portraits of the explorers and their Indian guides, stiffly posed in the fashion of 1912, and stopped when he came to a sepia-toned picture of an overgrown marsh with a lake beyond. Looming over the lake were the highland mesas that formed a barrier to the wind on the northern edge of El Grande, the Grand Tepui.

Like most young people, he had grown up hearing about El Grande, biggest of Venezuela's ancient sandstone plateaus. Twenty miles north of Brazil's Monte Roraima, El Grande rose as high as eight thousand feet above the Gran Sabana, and stretched eighty-five miles from end to end. This was the last place on Earth where dinosaurs still lived.

He read the text beneath the picture:

> *The Lake of the Serpents, as seen from the south. The mountains in the distance squat atop the Grand Tepui, plateaus piled upon plateaus, and protect the entire elevated region from the cold northerly winds. They are more than fifty miles away, yet visible on this remarkably clear day. Between the Lake of the Serpents and the southern end of the Grand Tepui lies the south-central lake, called the Lake of Butterflies, or Lake Akuena. In all, there are six lakes on the Grand Tepui, the largest of them being the Lago Centrale, or Central Lake, which connects with the Lake of the Serpents by a narrow strait.*

Peter was a quick reader, and in the next hour he re-lived the 1912 journey of Edward Challenger and his crew and Indian porters up the Caroní River to the Grand Tepui, called Kahu Hidi by the Indians. They were blocked by mile-high falls and impenetrable rapids, and had to circle around to the Pico Poco, the "little mountain," where an ancient overgrown Indian switchback trail allowed them and a few burros to climb six thousand feet. They arrived at the top of Pico Poco, which was only a mile or so wide, but level with the Grand Tepui. The gap between Pico Poco and the Grand Tepui, at its narrowest, was one hundred feet. Challenger ordered the construction of a rope bridge . . .

Peter read through to the chapter that described the rock maze on the southern end of El Grande, and the swamp beyond the maze, where lurked huge crocodile-like animals with heads longer than a man was tall and teeth over eight inches long. "Yet far more dangerous and enchanting than these fresh-water Krakens," Challenger wrote, "are the cobra-necked, turtle-bodied saurians of Lake Akuena, supposed by some to be *plesiosaurs*. Though less than a fourth the size of the largest crocodilians, they are as vicious as the fabled *piranha*. They sit on the shores of the lake and hoot and chirp maddeningly throughout the dark, wet nights, hideous sirens inviting their victims to join in fatal reptilian play. They allow no rest, no thoughts but of death and rubbery hooded necks and broad grinning mouths full of slashing teeth . . . "

Peter rubbed his eyes. It was nine o'clock. He was hungry again despite their supper on the train. Traveling always sharpened his appetite. He leaned across the bed and shook his father's shoulder. "Dad."

"Mmmfgk."

"Dad?"

"Huh?" Anthony jerked his head up from the pillow and stared owlishly around the room.

"Are you hungry?"

His head flopped back. "You want to try room service?"

Peter grinned.

"How about a steak . . . rare? One for each of us, and baked potatoes with sour cream and chives. I'll have a glass of wine and you'll have a cola."

"That would be terrific," Peter said.

Anthony dialed the phone for room service and pointed to the book. The cover was stamped with the gruesome image of a black-and-white-and-green-feathered *Stratoraptor velox* in its native rain forest. "Like to run into one of those?"

"No, sir," Peter said. "Nor an *Altovenator*. But I'd like to see both of them in the wild." But his father was talking to someone in the kitchen, ordering their steaks. When he finished, he put down the phone and grinned wolfishly at his son.

"They don't take kindly to nosy *Norteamericanos* down there. Not anymore."

"Why not? What happened?" Peter asked.

"It's a long story . . . "

"We have time," Peter said.

"It's a tragedy, really," Anthony said. "Professor Challenger followed in the footsteps of half a dozen explorers—like Shomburgk and Maple White—but he was the first to actually make his way to the top of El Grande and live to tell about it. That began the big dinosaur craze. Everybody sent teams into El Grande and started catching dinos and exporting them for zoos and circuses. Things got out of hand, of course, and some animals started getting scarce.

"It was high time that somebody with good sense stepped in. In 1924, the Muir Society told First Lady Grace Coolidge—Calvin's wife—that bringing down all those animals, just to put them in zoos—or letting big game hunters journey in and shoot them—just didn't make sense. President Coolidge had a son who loved dinosaurs. The boy was sick, dying actually, and before he died, he asked his father to help save the animals on the tepui. Like me, ol' Silent Cal had a soft spot for his son, made even softer by knowing the boy wasn't going to be around much longer . . .

"So Coolidge put pressure on the Venezuelan dictator, Juan Vicente Gómez. The next U.S. president, Herbert Hoover, kept up the pressure because he and Coolidge were friends. That was before Black Monday brought on the Depression.

"The Muir Society wanted to turn El Grande into a nature preserve. But Gómez got angry. He didn't like gringos telling him what to do. Instead, he stopped letting *anybody* go in there.

"Then there are the Indians. They think of El Grande as a sacred place, and send their warriors and future chiefs there to prove themselves. The army doesn't like that, because the tribes get uppity when heroes lead them, and that makes trouble.

"The Venezuelan army still guards the place. Gómez is gone, but they let in only two or three people each year, Latin American scientists mostly, and they won't let them carry guns. Well, of course, without guns, a lot of them die.

"Meanwhile, up north, most of the circuses and zoos didn't know how to take care of the dinosaurs they had. They lost them and couldn't get replacements. The only circus that kept its animals alive and healthy was Circus Lothar, and they're just about broke."

Their dinner arrived on a rolling cart pushed by a tall, smiling black man in a white jacket. Everything was covered by silver trays. The steaks were grilled to perfection, thick and rare.

Peter loved hearing his father speak. His precise diction, like an actor's, and his pleasant if somewhat clipped tone reminded him of the times when they had lived together with his mother, and Anthony had read newspapers and magazines to him before dinner.

"Dad, who's the fiercest predator on this planet?" Peter asked as they finished the last cooling, still-succulent bites of beef. He wiped a dribble of juice from his chin.

"The butcher who sliced up this steer, I suppose," Anthony said.

"You don't think *people* are?"

"*Some* people," Anthony said. "Not me. If I had to shoot my own cow to eat meat, I'd become a vegetarian."

"Isn't that hypocritical?" Peter asked. He fluffed his pillow and lay back on the bed.

"Sure," Anthony said. He tapped his fork on the plate and got up to roll the cart to the door. "Dollars to donuts a carnivorous dinosaur is a whole lot more honest than any human being."

"Better dressed, too," Peter said.

"Yeah, well, we'll take care of that tomorrow morning. It's time we get some serious sleep. We're due at the circus to meet Gluck and Shellabarger at three p.m. And the last, gala performance starts at seven."

Anthony opened the door and pushed the cart outside.

Chapter Three

They went shopping as soon as the stores opened, taking a taxi to a men's clothier, then walking down the street with their parcels to a big camping and Army surplus store. In a couple of hours, they had dungarees, light wool coats and khaki jackets, new lightweight cotton underwear, two pairs of hiking boots apiece and six pairs of wool socks, bush hats, two new belts, two all-purpose hunting knives and two pocketknives, and two compasses. Peter had never owned a knife before and immediately wanted to find a stick and test the blades, but Anthony said they barely had time to get to the circus.

Peter did not ask why they needed all the rugged clothing, and his father did not volunteer any information. Anthony wandered up and down the aisles, filling his basket with item after item. He treated it as a long-delayed and well-deserved shopping spree, all on the tab of the National Geographic Society. Peter realized they could never carry all this stuff, and challenged Anthony: "What are we going to do with five kerosene lamps? Or with a box of tent stakes?" Usually, his father relented with a smile, and Peter put the items back on the shelf. On a few items, Anthony simply said, "Keep it. We'll need it."

• • •

At two-thirty, four miles outside the city, the green and white taxi dropped them off by a railway siding on the edge of a broad field covered with long, wet, trampled grass. Anthony paid the driver and they stepped out. The driver removed their luggage and bags of new clothes, then tipped his cap with a sly smile, the same kind of smile he might have given to two gentlemen being dropped off in a red-light district. The taxi rumbled away and they stood for a moment on the edge of the field.

A long line of flatcars, Pullmans, and boxcars pushed up beside a concrete loading platform. Across the field, a big top had been erected, and two connected smaller tents formed the wings of a Y. North of the tents, a gray awning sheltered five large diesel generators that coughed smoke into the afternoon sky. Four long trucks were parked alongside the generators, and roustabouts busily loaded and unloaded equipment from the rear and side doors of their trailers. Three wide white searchlights sat dark like big blind eyes between the siding and the big top.

From around the eastern tent paced a dozen horses on a jaunt with their grooms. Concession carts and a few game booths stood unattended and sad beside the path to the big top. Peter did not see any dinosaurs.

A banner sagged wearily over the ticket booths near the closest wing of the tents. On the banner, in vivid green letters adorned with painted scales and feathers, stretched the name CIRCUS LOTHAR, and below that, in smaller letters, LOTHAR GLUCK'S DINOSAUR CIRCUS, and on a second banner below that, Beasts from the Edge of Time!

Peter had not been to a circus since he was five years old, and he remembered only a confusion of bright colors, large cages with bored-looking animals, a huge woman in a frilly dress, and a clown in a spotlight with a bouquet of flowers. This circus, he saw immediately, was different.

A few big drops of rain pattered from the gray sky. "Gluck hasn't made money in more than six years," Anthony said as he popped a tattered black umbrella over their heads. "I guess the public's gotten tired of hearing about dino disasters. Thirty of them died of worms at the World's Fair. Big disgrace. Cruelty to animals. Before that, in 1935, a venator got loose in a circus in Havana and killed twenty people. The newspapers blamed everybody in the business. So Lothar Gluck is at the end of his rope, through no fault of his own."

They walked past the concession stands and the sideshow tent to the ticket booth. A husky bearded attendant who might have doubled as a strongman checked them against a list and nodded permission for them to go in.

Immediately, they stepped from mud onto dry sawdust and the air went from warm and moist to dry and musty with a sharp smell that made Peter wrinkle his nose. He had smelled horses on his uncle's ranch in Kentucky and cows in a dairy barn, but he had never smelled anything like this. Then he remembered visiting a big pet shop in Chicago and the rich sour odor of parrots and macaws. This was more primal, alarming; it stirred deep memories.

Peter wondered if it was actually the *smell* that kept people away from the circus.

They came to the cages, eight of them arranged in two rows on either side of the end of the first tent. Most were covered with tarps. Whatever was inside the cages was quiet and still. Ahead, through a canvas flap furled and tied to a crossbar between two poles, Peter saw the third ring under the big main tent, and bleachers in shadow beyond. A man and woman were riding a dappled gray gelding around the small ring, taking turns standing on its back and leaping off as the other leaped on. No music, no sounds but the pounding hoofs and the grunts and comments of the performers. The man wore loose pants and a white shirt and the woman nicely filled out what looked like a black swimsuit.

Of course, Anthony noticed her. Peter noticed her as well.

As they walked between the cages, a tall powerful-looking man ducked under a lifted cut in the canvas. "You the photographer?" he asked in a voice stuck somewhere between black velvet and gravel.

"And writer," Anthony said.

"I'm Vince Shellabarger."

"This is my son, Peter. He's my assistant." Anthony and Shellabarger shook hands, and then the big dinosaur trainer turned to Peter and glowered down at him. His judgmental sea-green eyes glinted with bits of turquoise. Straight white-blond hair stretched thin over his brown scalp. He had a long chiseled jaw and prominent cheekbones, a solid barrel gut and broad heavy shoulders. A brilliantly white shirt strained across his chest. Gray curly chest hair billowed over the V in his shirt and thick biceps threatened to rip the rolled-up sleeves. For a moment, he scared Peter.

"Hello, Peter," Shellabarger said. He stuck out his hand and smiled warmly. Suddenly Peter was no longer afraid, but proud to shake hands with the man.

"Is anybody else here?" Anthony asked.

"Not yet. We're having a last supper sort of thing at five. I thought I'd introduce you to the animals before the show. Mr. Gluck—Lotto to his friends—is around someplace. Let me see if he's free."

"How big's the crowd going to be?" Anthony asked.

"How the hell should I know?" Shellabarger said.

Shellabarger left them by the third ring and went off looking for Gluck. They watched the man and woman and the horse, practicing over and over again the same leap, the man running up a ramp and jumping onto the horse and around the ring and then off, the woman leaping back on. Standing on the horse's back, the woman glanced at them as she passed, then jerked her head away as if she had made a mistake and no one had been there after all.

"You think the horse gets bored?" Anthony asked, tracking the woman with his eyes.

"Probably. Why aren't they training with a dinosaur?" Peter asked.

Anthony laughed. "Just wait," he said.

Shellabarger returned a few minutes later. "Lotto's on the squawk box. He says he'll join us later. Come on." Shellabarger stomped ahead, his big black-booted feet kicking up flakes of sawdust. He took them to the other end of the side tent, by the first cage on the right, and thumped the tarpaulin with his knuckles. Something inside harrumphed and squeaked.

"Don't be fooled by their pretty eyes," Shellabarger said. "They don't think like bears or big cats, or like any mammal." Shellabarger lifted the canvas cover. Inside the cage, a leggy creature as tall as a man lifted its smooth flexible neck and puffed out its throat below a toothless pointed jaw. A long naked tail twitched like a cat's, with a slow horizontal curl at the end. It seemed to be covered with brown and gray fur, but as it stalked forward, neck bobbing, and squeaked again, then whistled, Peter saw the fur was really a fine down of primitive feathers. Its eyes gleamed a beautiful golden color, mottled with rich chocolate specks, and the inside of its mouth and tongue was lavender.

Instead of wings it had long agile three-clawed hands. The claws gripped the bars and it angled its head to peer at Shellabarger.

"This is Dip," the trainer said. "He's not a bird or an avisaur—he's a real dinosaur. A plains struthio. Scientists call him a ratite mesotherm." He twisted his mouth in distaste. "I like the Indian names better. Does it look like a *sadashe tonoro,* or like a *Neostruthiomimus planensis?*"

Peter grinned.

"Yeah," Shellabarger said. "His mate's in the trailer outside. Her name's Casso. They were brought out by the last expedition in 1928. Gluck bought them from Wonder World Ohio in 1937. They were in sad shape. Damned fools didn't know what to feed them."

"What do you feed them?" Peter asked.

Shellabarger smiled craftily. "They like possums and bugs and lizards and chickens—and eggs, of course. Other circuses and zoos used to feed them strictly meat and eggs. But . . . " He put his hand between the bars of the cage. The struthio twisted his head, examined the hand as if it might be tasty, and pecked the fingers lightly. Peter was afraid he might have bitten the trainer, but Shellabarger laughed and pulled his hand back unbloodied. "We've known each other a long time. Casso's eggs, by the way, are infertile. Always have been. So far, I've never gotten any dino to make babies away from El Grande, more's the pity."

"What else do they eat?" Peter persisted.

The trainer bent over and whispered in Peter's ear: "They're omnivores. They love nuts and berries. Casso will do anything for a peanut."

Shellabarger winked to show this was their secret. They walked to the next cage, considerably larger than the first in the row, and pulled on a rope that lifted the canvas cover. "Good afternoon, Sammy," he murmured. Inside the cage, lying on its side, a massive, brown-spotted green body lifted one elephantine foreleg in the air, then rolled toward the small visitors, coming to rest on both forelegs, with hind legs splayed out behind. He tipped forward an ornate crest, swung his head to one side, and regarded them with a beady little black eye. His stomach rose and fell with a deep rumble. Sammy's aspect was already formidable, but as a final touch, he sported a bent, forward-jutting horn on his rhinoceros nose.

"Sammy's a *Centrosaurus*," Shellabarger said. "A real survivor. A true older dinosaur, not very evolved. His breed's been around for about seventy million years. Sammy's small for his type, but fossil centrosaurs are even smaller. When I was a lad and visited southern El Grande, I saw centrosaurs in herds of hundreds, some of the big females thirty-five feet long. Sammy's been with us since the beginning, and he still acts like a youngster. Don't you, Sam?" Shellabarger grabbed hay from a bale, pulled a eucalyptus leaf from another box, and tied them up with a long green blade of grass. Sammy's beak opened and a rasping parrot tongue poked out. He rolled over a little more, stretched out his beak, and took the wad from Shellabarger. The centrosaur whistled softly through his nose.

All around Sammy's crest, reddish-brown knobs stuck out like studs on a dog's collar. Spots of dark green and fleshy pink covered the crest to just behind the prominent bony ridges surrounding his eyes.

"He looks placid now," Shellabarger said, "but Sammy gave me fits when I was younger. Liked to step on toes."

"Do the dinosaurs live a long time?" Anthony asked.

"We've got one old carnivore here, Dagger, a venator—he's in the trailer now, we don't take him out until the show—he's thirty-seven or thirty-eight, probably. He was a youngster when I plucked him off the plateau thirty years ago. Herbivores live about three times longer than the carnivores. So Sammy could live to be ninety or more."

"You seem to like them all," Peter said.

"Well," Shellabarger said, "I like some, and some like me." He drew up one corner of his lips and lowered his eyebrow in a half grimace.

The size of the *Centrosaurus* stunned Peter. He had never seen a dinosaur up close—only in pictures—and Sammy's bulk was both bigger, in some ways, and smaller, than he had imagined. Bigger, because if Sammy got loose, he could certainly smash up most of the circus, and smaller, because he could not tear apart a city.

Peter wondered how big Dagger the venator was.

"There's Lotto now," Shellabarger said, nodding toward the juncture of the two tents. "You'll meet the rest of the beasts soon enough."

Lothar Gluck was a short plump man with a pale face and red cheeks and thin graying brown hair. He wore an expensive suit that refused to fit properly. His short stubby nose and florid lips reminded Peter of Charles Laughton, but Gluck's features seemed more dissipated, as if in his youth he might have been a handsome man.

"Lotto, this is Anthony Belzoni and his son, Peter," Shellabarger introduced. Gluck stuck out a thick pale hand, and Anthony shook it first as Gluck murmured certain standard phrases, "Pleasssed to meet you, delighted, yesss . . ." Then he came to Peter. Gluck's hand felt soft and slightly damp, like bread dough. He kept glancing over his shoulder, as if expecting someone else to arrive.

Though he was a U.S. citizen—and had been since 1913—Lothar Gluck still spoke with a German accent. He hung on to many of his s's as he said them, as if unwilling to let his words loose.

"Sso, Mr. Shellabarger hass given you a small tour?" Gluck asked.

"We've seen a few of the animals," Anthony said. "It's a thrill to get this close, isn't it, Peter?"

Gluck focused on Peter, sized him up, and smiled sunnily. "Esspecially for a youngsster. I have built my career on thrilling young folks with the beassts."

Peter felt he was expected to say something. "They're great," he said. "I mean, they're *big*."

"Both great *and* big," Gluck said. "Sssome bigger than others."

He cast a sad, glassy eye on Sammy. "Will Ssammy be performing tonight?"

"He wouldn't miss it," Shellabarger said.

"Sammy was the first dinosssaur I brought down from El Grande. I first went up the rivers to the tepuis when I was thirty-one yearss old, in the expedition of Colonel Fawcett himself. He ordered me to take Sammy and two other beassts down the Caroní, back to civilization. Colonel Fawcett stayed behind, and was never seen again. After Professor Challenger, he was the greatest explorer of that region . . . But then, Challenger wass a dynamo, a genius, and something of a monsssster himself."

"Cardozo was better," Shellabarger said. "He knew his stuff."

"If you get the impression I am waiting for somebody," Gluck said, glancing over his shoulder again, "I am. The producers, Mr. Cooper and Mr. Schoedsack, and their photographer, O'Brien, should be here soon. They are going to film the circus tonight."

"We always enjoy publicity," Shellabarger said dryly.

Lotto waved his plump hand. Three gold rings glittered on his thick fingers. "I think we may alsso have John Ford. He has always been a loyal patron. They will arrive in time for dinner, I hope. Already the movie truckss are here." Gluck turned to Peter again. "Shall we take a look at more beassts? It is wonderful, the way Vince has with them . . . "

Gluck accompanied them to one more cage. At the end of the row, near the entrance to the tent, a large, sluggish animal stood asleep on its four pillarlike legs. Heavily armored, the tail tipped with a large ball of bone, with spikes poking from its sides and shorter spikes in rows along its back; even its eyelids were covered with plates of bone. It looked like a cross between a horned toad and a Sherman tank and was longer than Sammy, almost thirty-one feet.

"This is Sheila," Shellabarger said to Anthony and Peter. "Sheila's a southern ankylosaur."

Peter bent over to examine the underpinnings of the cage. Big curved steel shock absorbers were mounted on each wheel axle and the cage rolled on truck tires.

"Vince, she seems to sleep all the time," Gluck said. "Whenever I look at her."

"I doubt Sheila knows the difference between being asleep and awake. She's not asleep, exactly. She's just got her eyes shut."

Anthony stepped forward and was surprised by a sudden swing of the tail against the cage. The ball of bone made a hideous whack against the bars and they all jumped back. The ankylosaur opened her small brown eyes, blinked with translucent membranes, opened her beaked mouth, stretched her neck, and made a shrill clucking noise, like a huge bass chicken.

"You startled her," Shellabarger said, grinning. "See, not exactly asleep." Anthony had almost dropped his camera. He looked at Peter with chagrin.

"You big lummox," Shellabarger said to the animal. Sheila clucked again, swung her head slowly back and forth, and rasped her big side spikes against the bars, making a fierce racket. "Just about the only fun she has is walking around the ring. She's a good platform. Just wait."

"Let us see the titan," Gluck said.

Shellabarger shook his head firmly. "Not when there's a show to do," he said. "She's as sensitive as a wild horse."

Gluck looked irritated, but shrugged; Shellabarger was master of the beasts.

"Titan?" Peter asked.

"*Aepyornis titan,*" Gluck said proudly. "We call her Mrs. Birdqueen."

"Our young visitor hasn't seen the show yet, and you haven't done much publicity lately, Lotto," Shellabarger said. "Let it be a surprise for him."

Chapter Four

A crowd of bigwigs and celebrities stood around outside the tent, most dressed in gray suits and fedoras and smoking cigars and cigarettes. Two seemed out of place, standing a few yards apart from the rest: a thin young man, balding prematurely, and a grandfatherly-looking fellow with a pleasant but discerning expression. Their suits were almost slick with wear. The thin young man seemed to have inherited his clothes from an ancient male ancestor, they gleamed so at knees and elbows.

Gluck waded in among the celebrities, shaking hands, smiling, enthusing about this or that. Behind the men, Peter saw three women preening and displaying their cigarettes in long thin holders. Their high heels, sheer gowns, and fur coats seemed odd on the sawdust floor. One of them glanced at Peter, looked away, glanced back, and smiled. They were heart-stoppingly beautiful.

Anthony, Peter, and Shellabarger followed Gluck. Shellabarger knew the men in good suits, and he nodded and shook hands with them, introducing them in turn to Peter and Anthony. "This is Merian Cooper," he said. "Coop did *King Kong,* what, ten years ago?"

"Fourteen," Cooper said with a thick Southern accent. He was plump, middle-aged, of medium height. At first, he did not seem very impressive—but then Peter caught his direct gaze.

"You made *Kong?*" Peter asked, suddenly awed.

"You betcha. OBie, over there, created our big ape." Cooper pointed to the older man in the worn suit. "Some of our dinosaurs we put together from footage we shot for *Plateau.* The public, bless 'em, didn't much like the mix."

"I saw it last year," Peter said. "I thought it was great."

"A good story has some staying power . . ." Cooper said with a shrug and a grin. "But it damned near broke us. Ever since *Kong,* Monte thinks I'm a jinx. He refuses to work with me."

Peter wondered who Monte was, but they moved on. Shellabarger steered them toward Gluck, who was standing next to the grandfatherly fellow. They and the balding young man were in conversation with a tall, slender fellow with a thick stand of wiry salt-and-pepper hair. "Monte, may I introduce our writer and sstill photographer, from the *National Geographic,* Anthony Belzoni, and his son, Peter . . . My friends, thiss is the great director Ernest Schoedsack. Everyone calls him Monte."

"Only if I say so," Schoedsack said gloomily, and then gave a small smile. "Glad to meet you." He had a tall, square head. His ears stuck out on each side like handles and he looked half blind; he wore very thick glasses. "This is O'Brien, my camera and effects man. And this is . . . "

"Ray," the balding young man said, quickly catching that Schoedsack had forgotten his name. "Ray Harryhausen."

Peter and Anthony shook hands all around. Schoedsack took Gluck aside and Anthony struck up a conversation with O'Brien and Harryhausen.

Peter tuned in first to what Gluck and Schoedsack were murmuring.

"Last time we went in there, to make *Plateau,* we lost a plane and three men. Damned near lost OBie when a boat went the wrong way down a rapids. That Caroní is a bitch of a river, Lotto."

"Don't I know it," Gluck said.

Peter felt his neck hairs tingle.

O'Brien and Harryhausen examined Anthony's Leica. O'Brien described a new portable 35-millimeter movie camera and the newest Technicolor film stock. "Whole thing weighs less than thirty pounds."

"Sounds like a good dance partner," Anthony said pleasantly. "Hope I'll be able to squeeze a few snaps in between."

"This isn't my strong suit, y'know," O'Brien confided, shaking his head. "Oh, I'm good; I've been filming live action since before *Kong*, but Ray and I have been hoping we could get enough money together to try again."

"Try what again?" Peter asked.

"A fantasy film," O'Brien said. He pulled a wry face. "All this focus on real animals. Not that I don't like dinosaurs. They're swell. I put some of my own together for *Creation*."

Harryhausen chuckled. In a soft, deep voice, he said, "We've been put in the shade by real life."

"Yeah," O'Brien said. "But it was sound killed that old beast, not live dinosaurs. Silent movies aren't worth the gun-cotton they're printed on."

"Nitrocellulose," Harryhausen explained to Peter.

"Oh," Peter said.

Harryhausen smiled. At first glance, his face and expression seemed affable, even simple—sympathetically angled eyebrows, quick smile, a low-key manner. But when Harryhausen looked directly at him, Peter sensed keen intelligence, real determination—and almost infinite patience.

"Ray would like to animate things we've never seen before, creatures from Venus and Mars, Greek gods and fire-breathing dragons. But dinosaurs spoiled the public for any of our imaginary monsters." O'Brien raised his hands in resignation.

"Fickle," Anthony commiserated.

"At least we've got work," Harryhausen said softly.

"Yeah, moviemaking is about the public's dreams, not our own," O'Brien said with a sigh.

A long table and folding chairs had been set up in the center ring of the big top. The dinner was brief, not very lavish, but at the end, everybody toasted everybody else. Peter toasted with a glass of milk. Looking around the table, he realized with a creeping numbness that his father and he were sitting with half a dozen circus performers, a ringmaster, a dinosaur trainer, and Lotto Gluck himself.

John Ford sat at one end flanked by Merian Cooper and Ernest Schoedsack; to the right of Cooper were Willis O'Brien and Ray Harryhausen, three beautiful actresses—one blonde, one brunette, and one redhead—and . . . he had come back around the table to Anthony and himself. Anthony was deep in conversation with the redhead, the one who had smiled at Peter. She wasn't much older than Peter, either.

Ford, a pleasant but ordinary-looking man with thinning hair and round horn-rim glasses, stood to deliver his personal toast and wishes for the expedition.

"Damn, I wish I was going with you," he said, aiming his glass around the table. His other hand clutched and worried a napkin.

Peter looked at Anthony. "Going where?" he whispered.

Anthony held his fingers to his lips.

"When I was just breaking into movies, I read about the explorers following after Challenger. I remember the newsreels of Roy Chapman Andrews. Andrews divided his time between El Grande and the Flaming Hills in Mongolia. Monte, you ran into Roy once, didn't you?"

"That grandstanding S.O.B.," Schoedsack said. Behind his goggling glasses, he seemed perpetually irritated.

"He coulda made a hell of a lot of omelets," Ford said. "Some of them would have been pretty tough, of course."

Harryhausen leaned across the table and said to Peter, "Andrews found fossil dinosaur eggs in Mongolia and real eggs on El Grande."

"Oh," Peter said, realizing he had a lot to catch up on.

"I remember the headlines when Colonel Fawcett went missing. Lotto, you knew Fawcett personally."

"Another prima donna," Gluck said under his breath.

"I heard that," Ford said. "Well, it takes one to know one."

"Too right," Gluck said. He mopped his face with a handkerchief and took another swig of wine. Then he looked down at the table sadly.

"And who could forget Jimmie Angel cracking up his airplane on El Grande and having to walk thirty miles to the bridge at Pico Poco? That was *after* it was supposed to be closed . . . I wanted to make a movie of that, even had Gary Cooper set for the part, but the studios were kinda cold on the idea, and other things came along." His eyes sparkled as he turned toward O'Brien. "OBie, you've been itching for years now to make another monkey movie."

Everybody around the table but Schoedsack laughed. OBie shook his head wryly.

"Well, I tell you what. Get these dinos into retirement"—he paused, then glanced around the table, smiling—"down in Tampa. Bring me back some great scenes, well blocked and with lots of drama, like you did for *Kong* but in color, and we'll make that monkey movie. Only this time, the ape'll be smaller so it'll cost less. I'll even rope in Monte."

"Never again," Schoedsack vowed darkly.

Shellabarger got up and said he must excuse himself. The circus performers—including the ringmaster and the man and woman who had practiced with the horse—stood up with him. Everybody had to get dressed and ready for the final show, which would begin in an hour.

As the table was cleared, the guests milled about. The ringmaster's assistant ushered everybody out. The tent was to be closed to bring in the performing cages. "Wouldn't want any of the animals to find you here!" the assistant said with a wolfish smile.

"My beassts," Gluck said sadly, standing beside the ring, one hand on a guy wire. "All right, we go to the third tent. Come, we have photographers and newspaper people to talk to."

The crowd of reporters in the third tent was not what Gluck had hoped for. There were only five, and two of those were from the society pages hoping to snag interviews with the actresses and Ford. Nobody seemed much interested in Gluck himself. He walked from group to group with a hangdog expression.

Peter had a chance to talk with Harryhausen some more. The actresses aside, Harryhausen was the closest in age to Peter—twenty-seven.

"How long have you been a moviemaker?" Peter asked.

"Just a few years," Harryhausen said. "Haven't had the chance to do much yet. How about you?"

Peter shook his head. "I'm a writer, I suppose."

"Is that what you want to be?" Harryhausen asked, catching the uncertainty in his voice.

"I suppose," Peter repeated. In a quiet rush, Peter said, "What's all this secrecy? Mr. Ford seems to know something, and my dad— he's holding something back, too. What are we going to do?"

Harryhausen made a face and held up his hands. "Damned if I know. We're going to follow the animals south to Tampa and make a movie about the trip, is what I've been told. I don't dare hope for anything more."

The big top opened forty minutes later and they entered to take their seats in the front rows beside the center ring. The public was allowed in, and after half an hour, the big top bleachers were only three-quarters filled. Anthony leaned over to Peter and whispered, "What's *wrong* with Americans these days? Doesn't *anything* get them excited?"

Clearly, his father was worried. If the last performance of the last dinosaur circus was not a sellout, standing room only, then who could tell what Mr. Grosvenor might think back in Washington, D.C.? Maybe he'd cancel the whole article, photos and all.

Large cages with thick black bars had been erected at each side of the center ring and two smaller cages had been placed in each of the outside rings. Steel-bar tunnels covered with tarps led from the side tent into the cages. One of the tunnels stood over fifteen feet high.

Outside, a wind started to blow and the canvas of the big top flapped and snapped, letting in little gusts. Peter could smell fresh air and rain. The crowd seemed expectant and cheerful. Big spotlights switched on and the ringmaster came into the center ring, followed by his assistant.

The ringmaster's name was Karl Flagg. He stood ramrod straight in his red coat and high black hat and black jodhpurs, a thick black belt cinching in his stomach, broad shoulders tapering without interruption past his nonexistent waist to his knees. He looked imposing in the ring, but at the dinner Peter had noticed that Flagg was only a little taller than he.

"Ladies and Gentlemen!" The ringmaster's voice boomed through the tent without help from a loudspeaker. The audience quieted. "You are here to witness an historic performance, a performance of

which we are all immensely proud. Tonight, we will show you some of the most wonderful and terrifying animals on Earth, and with sadness in our hearts . . . we will bid them farewell.

"Lothar Gluck's Dinosaur Circus first performed on this very date two decades ago, in 1927 . . . and quickly grew to be the biggest dinosaur circus in North America, Europe, and Asia. We have performed for presidents and prime ministers, kings and queens . . . celebrities and tyrants!

"Tonight, ladies and gentlemen, for your delight, and yours alone, and for the *Very. Final. Performance!* Lothar Gluck presents . . .

"Animals from the edge of time!

"Beasts transported at great peril from the fabled and horrifying Lost World of El Grande, the last of their kind!

"Performing . . .

"In CIRCUS LOTHAR . . .

"Lothar Gluck's world-renowned DINOSAUR CIRCUS!"

The tarps were rolled back from the caged runways and spots swung to highlight an animal running toward the two cages in the center ring. Peter saw that it was Dip, the male *Struthiomimus* that had pecked at Shellabarger's hand. Simultaneously, a clown in a ridiculous green dragon suit with broad floppy red wings jumped and stumbled into the ring and slapped up against the cage door. The door swung open as the clown stared at Dip in stupefaction. The ostrichlike dinosaur pushed at the door with his three-clawed hands, pulled his head back on his long neck, and stepped through.

Another clown dressed as a mighty hunter—oversize pith helmet, a gun six feet long, floppy jodhpurs—ran from the opposite side of the ring. He aimed the gun not at Dip, who scratched his jaw idly with one claw, but at the dragon clown. The dragon shrieked, ran away, and was pursued by the hunter. As the hunter ran past Dip, the *Struthiomimus* neatly lanced out with his jaws and plucked the helmet from the clown's head. A big wad of brilliant red hair spilled out, and the hunter heaped unintelligible abuse on the animal. The struthio deftly flipped the hat out of the ring.

The hunter lifted his rifle, peered down the sights, and took a long time to aim, wriggling his butt and jiggling the barrel up and down. The struthio stepped forward and just as deftly pulled the gun from the hunter's grasp, broke it in half, and tossed it aside. The hunter leaped into the air, arms and legs akimbo, and fled. Dip followed with casual swiftness, head and neck bobbing, eyeing the audience in the bleachers.

As the hunter and struthio circled, a third clown rolled a popcorn cart into the ring. The hunter stopped, bought a bag of popcorn, and began to eat as the struthio caught up. Dip squawked harshly and the hunter turned and trembled, shaking popcorn all over. The struthio pecked eagerly at the fallen kernels. The hunter mouthed a white-rimmed O of surprise and offered the long-necked animal the bag, leering knowingly at the audience. The struthio stuck his head in the bag—and the clown shoved the bag higher with a flourish. The bag stuck. Dip shook his head from side to side (but did not pull the bag away with his claws) and made more squawking sounds. The audience roared with laughter.

The hunter was taking aim with the recovered, reassembled gun when the dragon clown sneaked up from behind and gave him a sound kick in the pants. The gun went off with a loud bang, shooting powdery white smoke and more popcorn. The struthio jumped and shook the bag loose, then chased all three clowns off-stage. The lights dimmed.

The audience laughed and applauded, but Peter wriggled on the bench restlessly. He was waiting for the real show to begin. He didn't think dinosaurs were anything to laugh at.

Anthony stood just outside the center ring, camera in hand, waiting to snap a good picture of the action.

Flagg the ringmaster returned to the center ring and the lights narrowed to intense white circles around him and the open door of the cage. Dip chased the hunter clown around the perimeter outside the ring. As the hunter passed, Peter saw with some surprise that it was Shellabarger.

"You!" Flagg shouted. "You left this door open! Somebody could get hurt! We're going to have really *big* animals in this cage!"

Ashamed, the hunter sidled up to the cage door, big shoes slapping, but before he could close it, the struthio pushed it shut. At the clang of steel meeting steel, the hunter jumped and shivered all over, nerves clearly shot, and the struthio nudged him none too gently out of the ring.

"Well, we've finally had enough of *that*," the ringmaster said, and Peter agreed.

"The drama of life on Earth," the ringmaster said, "is full of surprises. Beginning thousands of years ago, we found the mysterious bones of extinct animals, turned to rock in the soil—and we tried to piece together the history of what Earth was like, millions of years before humans walked the planet. We were even more surprised to discover living examples and close relatives of these extinct animals in South America. But the greatest surprise of all was that we could *communicate* with these animals, train them, make them our companions—and in some cases, our implacable foes. What could be more surprising than the mystery of ancient life meeting modern man . . . Ladies and gentlemen, Lothar Gluck presents . . . THE CAVALCADE OF LIFE IN TIME!"

The runways to the now-empty cages pulled back.

Ray Harryhausen leaned over and whispered to Peter, "Not the way I'd run this railroad."

"What would you do?" Peter asked.

"Bring out the big animals right away. Show the danger," Harryhausen said. "Tell a story that makes some sort of sense. Then have an elephant fight a venator." He grinned mischievously.

Three beautiful dapple gray horses ran around the ring. The struthio Dip ran after them, followed by his mate, Casso. In turn, the man and woman who had been riding joined the procession around all three rings. The man was dressed in a sleek white outfit, and the woman in a tight glittering ruby red suit, arms and legs bare and holes cut out of her midriff and back. Peter instantly fell in love with her.

Next came the ankylosaur, Sheila, a huge, lumbering presence that immediately drew enthusiastic *ohs* and *ahs* from the crowd. The horses passed her on each side, and the struthios leaped up and over her, deftly avoiding the spikes along her back. The crowd applauded wildly.

Harryhausen approved of the spectacle. "Much better," he said.

Now two elephants joined the procession, and the animals and man and woman ran around the rings and passed the lumbering ankylosaur twice. The struthios paused, then stepped back and forth in perfect synchronization, as if dancing. The ankylosaur stopped dead, seeming as stubborn as a mule, and Shellabarger appeared, holding a rod with a blunt steel hook. He poked the ankylosaur and urged her into the center ring. She lifted her feet, gave a deep-throated quavering cry, like a gigantic baby, and twitched the massive bony tip of her tail, as if to warn against these indignities. But in she went, and came to a stop between the cages. The struthios ended their dance. They leaped as one into the ring onto the ankylosaur's broad armored back and stood blinking and pirouetting prettily.

Shellabarger locked a big iron ring and short anchored chain around the ankylosaur's tail, just above the ball of bone, and returned to the perimeter. The man and woman mounted the horses and the horses broke into a canter around the center ring. The woman got to her feet, arms out, and on the second horse the man also stood. The struthios swung their heads around, craned their necks, leaped down from Sheila's back, and ran after the horses.

"Watch this," Harryhausen said.

"You've seen it before?" Peter asked.

"Of course!" Harryhausen said. "Wouldn't miss it for anything. It's been a few years, though."

"I thought you didn't like it!"

Harryhausen scoffed. "I love this show. I'd just do it differently."

The struthios caught up with the horses and riders and both riders leaped onto one horse, just as Dip bounded up a ramp onto the back of the abandoned horse. The horse whinnied and shook its head but kept to its course. The woman climbed onto the man's back, and with hands clenched, he hoisted her onto his shoulders.

The audience applauded loudly, and the procession—man and woman on one horse, Dip riding the second, and his mate Casso following—circled the ring and the cages quickly.

Lights switched on and burned bright circles in the outer rings, showing more clowns juggling, and the horses returned to the side tent, followed by the unmounted struthio. Roustabouts rolled the runways out again and connected them with loud clangs to the cages in the center ring.

From the opposite side tent came a sound like a huge hoarse wolf howling. The lights briefly played on the opening to the tent, but nothing was there. The ringmaster shouted for someone to watch the cages.

"This is more like it," Harryhausen enthused, grinning broadly. Peter wondered if something had gone wrong.

All the lights in the tent went out. The hoarse roar sounded again. Peter's neck hair prickled.

The ringmaster's voice boomed out in the dark.

"From earliest times, life has hungered after life, and animals have become mortal enemies. We shudder to think of becoming food—all our lives, all our memories, reduced to lunch or dinner—how horrible! Yet in nature, we are all food eventually . . . That is the rule."

Again the roar, fierce yet almost plaintive.

"Hunger and death . . . The *predator* . . . and its prey!"

The lights came on again, dazzling Peter's eyes. In the center ring, two large animals faced each other with thick iron bars between—Sammy the *Centrosaurus,* whom they had met earlier, and something large and beautiful and nightmarish, a sleek brown and yellow demon with flashing emerald eyes, marked along its sides by slashes of white. It stood on two tensed legs, muscles corded beneath smooth scaled flesh. Its three-toed feet scratched the dirt beneath the iron cage, reminding Peter of a monstrous chicken. The beast's long tail swished back and forth stiffly, its tip slapping the bars behind, making the entire cage shudder. Along its neck and over its head rose two ridges of long, stiff, flat scales tipped with red, as if dipped in blood. Two long arms stretched from its trunk, ending in three expressive curling dactyls with black scimitar claws.

Peter stared at the beast's snout and jaws and wanted to run. The crowd seemed to feel the same way—he could smell the tension in the air and heard their abrupt gasps, even from those who had seen this animal before. Harryhausen dug his fingers into the bench seat. From where they sat, fifteen yards away, Peter could smell the rich iguana-parrot scent and something sharper, described so vividly in Challenger and Doyle's book that he could recall the words now:

> *It was the odor of a killing thing that wanted our blood, our meat, our bones; less a flow of atoms through the still air than a spiritual miasma, a sickly breath out of the rotting tropical regions of Hell . . .*

The pictures he had seen could conjure bad dreams, but none did the animal justice. For the first time in his young life, Peter felt distinctly mortal and unsure of where he stood in the great scheme of things, or whether indeed he even liked that scheme.

Flagg the ringmaster had worked with this animal for two decades, yet did not approach the cage any closer than he had to. His voice, admirably enough, lost none of its sureness as he announced, "*Altovenator ferox,* the ferocious hunter on high, by no means the largest of the predators of ancient times . . . and by no means the smallest . . . See how he observes what might be a week-long feast, a plant-eating *Centrosaurus.* The swift and hungry meets the slow and armored, and who can say how the match would end? As meat-eaters, where do your sympathies lie?"

Peter measured the venator using the ringmaster as reference. Fourteen feet high, when reared back he scraped the upper bars of the cage. Peter's eye swept from tip of snout, past gaping mouth, vibrating wattle pendulous from its neck, green eyes ringed with vivid blue, a surprisingly narrow and swift-looking trunk still as thick as a bull in the middle, past broad haunch and along the stiff-

ened tail like a partly frozen snake . . . Twenty-four feet long. The
venator was deeply irritated to be among all these people, in plain
view of a prey that could never be brought down.

"And now . . . a man who has spent most of his life hunting and
training dinosaurs, who knows more about these incredible animals
than any man on Earth! Ladies and gentlemen, our supreme Master
of Beasts, *Vincent Shellabarger!*"

Shellabarger entered the ring in splendid tailored khaki jodhpurs
and dark brown coat, with a flat-brimmed campaign hat. This time
he carried only a short whip. The ringmaster backed out of the ring
and Shellabarger stepped into the spotlight.

"Behold the venator," he said, pronouncing it veh-NAY-tor. "Its
scientific name speaks for itself. It is the *hunter.* We've worked
together for thirty years now and I have a healthy respect for him—
but he has no respect for me at all.

"Smell the promise of death in the air! Hang on to your children,
feel your legs tense with terror! The venator is a killer from a special world, not a world frozen in time, filled with throwbacks and
sluggish lizards, as we once imagined dinosaurs to be, but a living
and fertile and vital world that can support even such a swift, a
ruthless, a ravenous and intelligent hunter as this. I introduce you
to Dagger, the name we have given to *him.*"

Shellabarger approached the cage. He turned and glared judg-
mentally at the audience. "Do you expect a show of animals
jumping through hoops and sitting on boxes, batting at my puny
whip? Dagger the venator recognizes no master, refuses to be
trained, waits only for the day—perhaps not far off—when he will
escape his cage and hunt again, with a top speed of twenty-four
miles an hour—faster than you or I can run—across the cloud-
shadowed grassland and cool rain forests of El Grande, all that he
loves and knows, all that he desires . . .

"Except perhaps to sink his jaws into *me,* to crack my head like
an egg!"

The crowd sucked in its breath disapprovingly. Peter gulped,
looked around for his father and found him with camera practically
glued to his face, standing in shadows less than ten feet from the
cage. Much too close, Peter thought.

"We can well believe that Dagger wants to take revenge for his capture, his imprisonment—for all these long years away from the clouds and forests of El Grande."

Shellabarger strode across the ring to the cage containing Sammy the centrosaur and opened the broad, high door. The centrosaur trotted through the door, swinging his head slowly from side to side as he approached Shellabarger. Sammy lifted his beaked snout and squalled his disapproval at being once again placed so near the venator. Shellabarger tapped the long forward-curved nose horn with the stock of his whip, and Sammy turned toward him, mouth open. The trainer shoved something from his pocket into Sammy's mouth, and the centrosaur closed his eyes in ecstasy, lifted his snout, and gave a nasal bullish snort.

"Sammy has learned to live among us and accept our generosity. But in a dinosaur's life, as in the lives of men, there are stages, and the time has come for endings. Never again will these animals perform for the simple pleasure of a human audience."

A rustling sound from outside the ring attracted Peter's attention. Three brilliantly plumed birds the size of turkeys, with long feathered tails, flapped across the ring. One landed on the centrosaur's frill, the other on his nose. Sammy did not seem to mind. The birds spread their wings two yards wide, twisted their heads, and opened their mouths to reveal rows of small white teeth. These were the famous toothed birds, Peter realized, smallest of the avisaurs, unique to the tepuis, the only ones of their kind in captivity. Red and green, with shiny black backs and white-fringed black tails, these descendants of *Archaeopteryx,* christened *Eoavis* by Maple White, plucked treats from Shellabarger's fingers and lifted their fleshy feathered tails.

"Pretty little cousins of *Stratoraptor,*" Harryhausen said. "What I'd give to see one of *those!* Biggest bird that ever lived . . ."

Peter nodded, but without conviction.

"All that these animals have taught us," Shellabarger went on, "all that we have learned of the true nature of the past, we owe to a fluke of nature unparalleled in Earth's history: the Grand Tepui. Because of the majestic isolation of this mighty plateau, we can observe directly the evolution of reptilian lizard into dinosaur,

dinosaur into bird, bird into the tiniest and most beautiful of jewels, as well as into the fiercest predators of all, the *Totenadlers* or death eagles sacred to the Pepon and Camaracota Indians . . . Only on the Grand Tepui. Compare the venator to this fabled and seldom-seen beast, never captured . . . imagine the animal that made the brave, foolhardy, and indomitable Professor Challenger wish he had never been born . . ."

Peter made the comparison. Dagger the venator looked fierce enough.

The toothed birds flapped their wings and leaped a short distance from Sammy's nose to the outspread and gloved hands of the trainer.

Flagg the ringmaster returned. In the outer rings, Peter saw, clowns and roustabouts were making preparations for another act. Dagger turned restlessly in his cage, stiff tail banging the bars, eyes sweeping the crowd. The venator opened his mouth, showing his crimson tongue and rows of wicked serrated teeth. The beast's throat pulsed and for a moment, Peter thought the venator had picked him out of the crowd personally. The beast cocked his massive sleek head to one side, spotlight glinting from his eyes and scales, as if asking Peter a question: *Are you as strong and savage as I?*

Then Dagger gave a hideous screech, followed by a thuttering bellow like a roaring lion trying to drown out a diesel truck. He lifted his head and clawed wildly at the cage, lifting first one leg, then the other. He leaned back on his tail, braced his head against the rear of the cage, balanced for a second, then marched his clawed feet up the bars, kicking at them like a furious cat. Both legs flexed against the bars, claws curling, as if trying to push the cage down. Then the venator's tail gave way and he fell ponderously on one side and lay there for a moment, chest heaving.

As Dagger rolled over and pushed himself up with slender but strong forelimbs, Shellabarger quickly guided Sammy back into the second cage. The *Centrosaurus* went all too willingly, and thumped down the caged runway out of the spotlights, out of sight, into the side tent.

The ringmaster took over as Shellabarger approached the venator cage.

"Ladies and gentlemen, observe the fury of raw nature!" Flagg called. The venator's screeches and banging almost drowned him out, but couldn't hide the quaver in his voice.

Shellabarger seemed to have suddenly lost interest in the audience. He circled the cage with chin in hand, studying this new problem intently.

Anthony stood outside the ring, camera poised, observing the situation calmly. Peter knew his father was waiting for a key shot, a frozen fraction of time that summed the relationship between the trainer and his beast. Peter hoped that shot wouldn't include somebody being eaten.

Shellabarger suddenly kicked the cage with all his might. The venator started back and pulled his jaw into his neck and chest. Then he thrust his head and neck forward with the speed of a striking snake and the heavy jaws *whacked* shut like clapped two-by-fours just a couple of yards from Shellabarger's head. Shellabarger held his ground and the venator swung around again, tail slamming the cage's bars like a giant's stick against a picket fence.

Shellabarger turned halfway like a bullfighter tempting a charge and the venator swiveled with blinding speed, driving up against the cage, cramming the side of his head against the bars and pushing his forelimbs between, clawed dactyls spread. The beast made no sound this time but a grunt of expelled air.

The cage swayed a few inches toward Shellabarger, and the audience rose as one, ready to escape. Indeed, several men had already taken to their heels and were rushing for the exits.

Shellabarger's arm narrowly escaped a swipe from Dagger's left claw. The breeze from the beast's arm wafted the campaign hat from the trainer's head and sent it falling toward the sawdust. Shellabarger stepped away from the cage slowly and deliberately, bent to pick up the hat, and turned to face the venator, this time from a safer distance. The dinosaur fell back and the cage swung upright with squeals of scraping metal.

The ringmaster's patter had ceased. Clearly, this hadn't happened in some time, if ever. Flagg examined the audience and the animal, and decided to say nothing—neither to assure the audience that they were safe, for perhaps they weren't, nor to describe what was happening, for no words were necessary. The band's music sounded tinny and hollow, like a radio heard through a bad dream.

Shellabarger made low throaty noises at the venator, staring directly into his brilliant emerald eyes. The venator sidled back. Peter saw blood on the side of the animal's head, trickling down to his shoulders. A glassy ribbon of slaver oozed between his teeth and swung like a pendulum from his jaw.

The acts in the side rings had stopped. The entire tent was filled with people watching this drama of will versus wild, and Peter, to his dismay, suddenly felt a sharp sympathy for the venator. *Never allowed to run free, never allowed to hunt live animals, brought night after night into this cramped prison, not knowing his freedom is just weeks away . . .*

Peter almost wished Dagger could knock the cage down and run wild, grab a few complacent members of the audience, shake them, snap their necks—

He looked at Harryhausen. The cameraman was on his feet, body arched forward, eyes gleaming. He glanced down at Peter. "Do you feel it?" he asked.

Peter nodded.

Harryhausen's hands formed fists. "He must *hate* that man," he said.

Peter looked at the center ring. Five or six roustabouts stood ready to reinforce the cage with wooden beams. The venator seemed suddenly to lose interest in the whole affair. He clawed the ground, lifted his head to sniff the air, then raised his left arm and delicately scratched the bleeding spot on his head, as if judging the damage. Shellabarger took a deep draft of air and walked along the side of the cage to the runway. Dagger turned slowly, then bent over, bringing his tail level with his head and neck, and ambled down the runway and out of the tent.

The ringmaster nodded his relief to Lotto Gluck, who stood in the shadows on the edge of the center ring. Harryhausen sat down and folded his arms.

"Fantastic," he said.

For Peter, the rest of the acts passed quickly. Even the twelve-foot-high *Aepyornis titan,* dragging a wagon with an elephant on it, seemed uninteresting.

The venator had looked at *him.* Peter had sensed the wildness and pent-up fury. He felt as if he had stared into the throat of a tornado and just barely escaped.

As the tent lights came up and the people filed out, Anthony joined Peter and Harryhausen. "Gluck's asked Peter and me to sleep here tonight in his Pullman," Anthony said. "He wants me to shoot the final tear-down tomorrow."

"OBie and I are going back to Boston for the night," Harryhausen said, eyeing the departing celebrities. Ford and O'Brien were talking, Schoedsack and Gluck listening, a tight square in the milling throng of overdressed humans. "I'll be glad to be out of this crowd." He turned and shook hands with Anthony and Peter. "See you in Tampa."

Harryhausen went off to stand beside O'Brien.

"He's a regular guy," Anthony said. "Most movie folks are something else. I'd like to see John Huston go up against that Cooper fellow in a ring, bare knuckles, nine rounds . . ."

Peter's exhaustion suddenly hit him. "We need to rest," he said.

"Ever the practical fellow," Anthony chided. They left the tent and crossed the path to the sidetrack, where Gluck's Pullman waited. Summer twilight still lingered.

"Where's the venator kept?" Peter asked.

"In a big trailer across the field. They won't roll the animals onto the flatcars until the morning."

A high screech rose into the night. A few yards away, a roustabout swore.

"So," Anthony persisted, "what did you think?"

"It was wonderful," Peter said. "It was awful."

"Good," Anthony said. "Write it down before you go to sleep."

The train cars were each painted with animal skins or camouflage patterns: scales, long multicolored feathers, zebra stripes and leopard spots. The largest car of all, which carried Dagger, bore the distinctive brown and yellow colors and white stripes of the venator. Equipment was already being loaded as Anthony and Peter approached, and flashlight beams played back and forth beneath the clear, star-gloried sky. They passed a steady line of roustabouts packing up the paraphernalia into train cars, carrying rolls of thick ropes over their shoulders or slung between two men, iron bars and beams and collapsed sections of cages, welding equipment, and piles of other stuff Peter was too tired to identify.

Gluck's train car had been hooked to the very end of the train. It was the only one without camouflage, a long shiny dark red and green Pullman divided into four rooms.

They climbed the iron steps and knocked on the door. Gluck's Brazilian valet, Joey, let them in. "How was the show?" he asked them, smiling. He did not really need to ask.

"Great," Peter said.

"Tough to believe it's the last one," Anthony said.

Anthony and Peter were to sleep in the parlor, at the forward end, on couches made up as beds. Pictures covered the walls: lineups of the members of expeditions; cages filled with animals— lions and tigers, zebras and quaggas, as well as dinosaurs and avisaurs; celebrities who had seen the circus; performers in costume, and many smiling women in sleek, low-cut gowns. Peter scanned the photographs sleepily and spotted a tight row of framed glossies: Gluck standing beside Franklin Delano Roosevelt, a second picture with him and Josef Stalin, and a third with Adolph Hitler.

Gluck stood in the door to the parlor and puffed a cigar. The rank smoke stung Peter's eyes. The circus owner seemed agitated, talkative, sad.

"Did you get ssome good picturess?" he asked Anthony.

"Six rolls," Anthony said. "I think some will do."

"Ssome *will do*," Gluck repeated ironically, shaking his head. "Young fellowss, this was the last night of the best part of my life. The very best part. Do you think Shellabarger had his little dust-up with the venator for my benefit?"

"Doesn't he do that every show?" Anthony asked.

Gluck shook his head, eyes wide. "Oh, no-ooo," he said. "Thiss was special. This was a farewell, maybe jusst for me." Gluck lifted his cigar with a theatrical gesture, peering at it critically. "Maybe if he had done it more often, we would still have regular crowds. Of course, we might not have a *trainer* anymore . . ."

A loud shave-and-a-haircut rap sounded on the parlor door.

Gluck turned. "Yess, John," he roared. "I know your knock anywhere. Come in. I've been expecting you."

Peter wondered if John Ford had come to the car to visit, but it was not the director. A small, dapper man with a broad forehead and close-cut jet-black hair swung the cherrywood door open, entered the Pullman, brandished a long cigar, and grinned at Gluck. He wore a beautifully tailored striped suit. A brass-tipped ebony cane hung from his elegantly manicured forefinger.

"Quite a show, Lotto," he said in a pleasant tenor. "*Quite* . . . a . . . show."

"John Ringling North," Gluck said, "may I introduce Anthony Belzoni and his son, Peter?"

"Part of this whole movie scheme?" North asked, his eyes sharp.

"Magazine, sir," Anthony said. "*National Geographic.*"

"Ah. Always sad to see a great show fold," North said. He tapped his cane lightly on the carpeted floor. "Well, Lotto, you got my offer."

"I have," Gluck replied with a nod.

"It's a reasonable offer, you old bandit," North said. "I'll take everything—the rig, the transportation, the Tampa base—your remaining acts and employees, though God knows they need pruning. I'll even take old Baruma. She'll make quite an attraction."

A recent picture of Baruma stood on Gluck's desk. "Lotto Gluck's fabled sauropod, Baruma, now over sixty feet in length," read a caption clipped from a newspaper and pressed against the glass below the photograph.

"We haven't toured her in ten years," Gluck said, taking a seat at a round table set with a Tiffany lamp and a brass ashtray.

"I'll turn the Tampa base into a fairground," North said. "Bring easterners down for the winter, and old Baruma can drag Gargy around in his cage. Won't that be a fine sight?"

Peter looked up at Anthony. Anthony leaned over and whispered in his ear, *"Gargantua."* Then Peter knew who John Ringling North was: the owner of Ringling Brothers, Barnum and Bailey Circus. Gargantua was his giant and temperamental gorilla.

"It will be, but only if you own it," Gluck said sadly.

North approached the table and tapped his cigar into the ashtray. "I had a wonderful dinner this evening. Oh, not here—sorry to have missed the event. In Boston." His face fairly glowed for an instant at the memory. Suddenly, without warning, his eyes turned steely and his voice took an edge.

"Dammit, Lotto, you haven't made money from this outfit in seven years—"

"Six," Gluck corrected him mildly.

"And you never toured the big gardens—why, you're not even in Boston Gardens tonight. You could have recouped some of your losses!"

Lotto's thick pale face assumed a look both wistful and proud. "For once I will tell you a trade secret, John. Madison Square Garden is a concrete nightmare. It is heated by steam and it is cramped and hard. The stalls down below are humid and the air is bad. There iss no room around the stage to walk the animals, and they musst all be brought up at the lassst minute, through many changes of temperature. My animals are like fine wines. If I had taken them in there, I would have lost all of them years ago—as you did, John. As you did."

North stood silent for a moment. "The Cincinnati fire in '42 took the better part of my dinos," he said quietly. "But I saw they were a lost cause even then. The public doesn't mind leaky canvas and buckets of rain, they don't mind dust and noise and mosquitoes, but . . . they hate to be eaten. They hate to be dinner. Havana was the real end. Bad news and disaster everywhere." North turned to Peter. "You aren't old enough to remember it all, boy. Some called it Challenger's curse. Preachers called the dinos abominations. It's bad press to claim Darwin is a fool and dinos and other extinct animals never existed, and then along comes Challenger . . ."

"Yes, yes," Gluck said. "Spare me, John. You smell money in it somewhere."

John Ringling North shook his head. "Lotto, I'll lose my shirt for at least two years. I've already got debts coming out of my ears."

"My life, my life," Gluck murmured, and delicately wiped a tear from one eye with a pudgy finger.

North admired this gesture with the proper respect: a parsimonious smile. "Final offer, old friend," he said.

"You will not have the beasts," Gluck said softly.

North's gaze sharpened. "Rumors . . . " he murmured. "True?"

"Except of course for old Baruma. She will stay in Tampa."

Anthony would not return Peter's look. Silence for several seconds, as North and Gluck stared at each other, one-time adversaries, as ruthless as they ever came; and then:

"What would I do with them, anyway?" North said, examining his cigar. "Put them out to pasture? Got enough horses and elephants freeloading already."

"One last thing," Gluck said, and stood.

"What?" North asked.

"You will park my Pullman permanently at the headquarters, and I will come and stay whenever I wish, for as long as I wish."

"Of course." North waved the cigar at this trifle.

"And you will listen to everything Vince Shellabarger tells you, about keeping Baruma alive and healthy. No touring for her, no Madison Square Garden, no steam heat—okay?"

"Done." He waved the cigar again and winked at Peter.

"Then she is all yours: a dinosaur circus with only one dinosaur. And I keep my collection of memorabilia, of posters and artifactss, paintings and photo albums and costumes."

"It's a fine collection," North said. "I'd be proud to add it to my own. I'd even up the deal a little."

"I will *keep* my collection," Gluck insisted.

North tapped his cane sharply on the floor of the railroad car, smiled like the very devil, and said, "Done."

Gluck and North shook hands.

Joey came out with a bottle and several glasses on a tray. North stayed for a few minutes to share a brandy with Gluck and Anthony and regale them all with tales of the fine dinner he had had.

Finally, after Gluck's brandy ran out, and Peter felt himself drifting into an exhausted gray haze, North left and he was able to climb into the made-up couch-bed. The couch's dark red tuck-and-roll leather squeaked beneath the stiff clean sheets. After spreading out his equipment on an end table, Anthony lay down in his clothes across from his son. He planned to rise at dawn and shoot a roll or two of film.

Joey turned out the lights.

Before Peter could get to sleep, another knock sounded on the cherrywood door. Joey came out in his robe, muttering in Portuguese, and answered it. Two men in gray hats and long black coats entered the car and stood restlessly until Gluck came out in his pajamas to see them.

Anthony stared at Peter from his couch opposite. Only the porch light had been turned on. Gluck and the two men conferred for several minutes in low voices. Peter heard several words, and a name: "quarantine restrictions waived," and "Truman." Gluck clapped his hands and laughed and said, loudly enough, "Jolly! Joll-eee."

The two men left and Joey closed the door behind them. Gluck grinned at Peter and Anthony in the dark, then retired to his bedroom without saying a word.

Peter, so exhausted just minutes before, was now wide awake. Anthony grinned at him, then rolled over and pulled up the blanket around his neck.

"Father!" Peter whispered loudly.

"Yeah?"

"Who was that?"

"Some men, Peter. Just making plans."

Peter knew by his tone that Anthony would not tell him any more. He stared up at the shadows on the ornate ceiling, listening to the the roustabouts still working in the darkness, hammering and pulling and singing.

CIRCUS
LOTHAR
DINOSAURS!
LOTHAR
GLUCK'S
DINOSAUR
CIRCUS
WITH DINO-TRAINER
VINCE
BEASTS FROM THE
TIME!

Chapter Five

So ended the days of the last dinosaur circus.

For the last time, the tents had been folded and tied and shoved into wooden racks in their trucks, the bleachers collapsed and rolled into the boxcars, the animals in their cages and trailers pushed along the platform onto the flatcars and covered with canvas, the concession stands and cook shack dismantled and hauled away. Anthony had gotten his pictures, and by nine o'clock the train began rolling.

Most of the roustabouts seemed to think they were going to Tampa. Peter looked out the window intently, hoping to catch glimpses of the cars ahead as they rounded a curve. He had not slept well.

Whenever Peter let his mind explore the possibilities, he got the willies. He looked at the sun and frowned. They were going into Boston, not heading south.

After a breakfast of bacon and eggs, prepared and served by Joey, Peter took out his notebook and wrote down what he had seen.

I know Sammy the centrosaur gets out and chews grass, but Dagger the venator is never free. They can never let him out to wander. No cage is big enough for him to run around in. It's worse than any tiger or polar bear. By now he's probably gone mad. That makes me sad.

I enjoyed meeting Mr. O'Brien. He's old—but he looks strong, like an old boxer. Ray Harryhausen is a nice fellow. He doesn't treat me like a kid.

Poking the eraser tip against his chin, Peter looked out the window at the passing backs of brick and stone buildings, fish processing plants, canneries.

Maybe Father has been sworn to secrecy, but I wish he would trust me. Who else knows, I wonder? What do they know?

The train passed through a switching yard and was diverted to a long wharf beside an austere black-hulled freighter. As the train came to a jerking halt, wheels squealing and brakes hissing, Peter saw that the ship bore the name S.S. *Libertad* on its bow and across its stern. Its home port was Caracas.

Caracas was in Venezuela.

Joey stood by the parlor window as Gluck finished some last-minute bookkeeping on a pull-down oak desk in the corner. "I'd sure like to go south again," the valet said with a mischievous grin. "It gets cold up here in the winter." He turned his black eyes on Peter. "You ever been down by the equator?"

Peter shook his head.

"You will think you were never cold in your entire life. Heat will fill you like a big mug of hot tea and insects will cover you day and night. You have to watch for poisonous snakes. They're as common as cracks in a city sidewalk; especially the parrot snake, big and green. It floats along with the river and attacks anything that comes near. Deadly poisonous. And then there are the ants. Some ants make their cities in trees, and if you bump that tree, they send armies out to swarm you. Make you wish you'd never been born. Ants are the real bosses of the forests. They can be big, and the worst of them are called *veintecuatros* because if they bite you, you have twenty-four hours to decide whether to live or die."

Gluck looked up from his checks and records. "Joey, don't sscare the boy," he said dryly. "None of uss was ever bitten."

Joey raised his eyebrows. "Last time we were in the forest, I brushed ants out of Mr. Gluck's sleeping bag every night," he said in an undertone, winking. "Big ants. And when you go swimming or dip your hand in the water to cool off—look out for the *caribe!* Some folks call them *piranha.*"

"There are no *caribe* or *piranha* in the Caroní," Gluck said with a smile. Clearly, he appreciated the showmanship Joey was demonstrating.

"But the tepui is better," Joey continued, "for it is cooler. High up, and covered with clouds. Not as many insects as on the *sabana,* but what there are, you watch out for . . . Mosquitoes big as starlings and biting flies like hot needles zuzzing through the air!"

"He exaggerates," Gluck called from across the parlor.

"Not much," Joey said.

Peter stared at them in shock, speechless. He turned to look at Anthony, who was gathering his camera equipment.

"I thought we were going to Tampa," he said. Joey laughed and slapped his knees.

Anthony raised his brows innocently. "They're going to unload the animals. Want to come see?"

"Where *are* we going, Father?" Peter asked as they walked alongside the brightly colored animal cars.

"I thought you would have figured it out by now," Anthony said. "Did they tell you?"

"They told me to be prepared. And I'm still keeping my mouth shut until we're on that ship—if we ever get aboard. We've been disappointed before. I'll let Cooper and Schoedsack confirm things."

Peter clenched his fists.

They met Harryhausen and O'Brien near the biggest train car. The dismantled cages from the center ring had been mounted on a huge wooden pallet. A big rolling crane on its own tracks had straddled the train, lowering on thick steel cables a hook almost as big as Peter. Stevedores—dockside workers, big and brawny and wearing sweat-stained T-shirts—joined with the circus roustabouts to strut and tell stories, waiting for the action to begin. Anthony wandered off to take pictures of the men.

"What do you know about this?" Peter whispered to Harryhausen.

Harryhausen said, "OBie says we may have more work than we thought—for several months, at least. Monte and Coop—Mr. Schoedsack and Mr. Cooper—didn't want the newspapers to know until it was a sure thing. Whatever *it* is."

O'Brien's camera crew and several reporters and newsreel photographers were also waiting. Harryhausen introduced them to the two-man crew: Caleb Shawmut and Stony Osborne. Shawmut stood little more than five feet tall, and with his round grizzled blond head and short jaw, resembled a pugnacious bulldog. Osborne was dark and lean and intense and seldom said anything.

Osborne complained about giving up the lease on his apartment in Los Angeles. "Took the goddamned airplane," he said. "Last minute flight. My first time. Got sick in the little bag. This better be good, OBie!"

O'Brien warned the newsreel men to stay out of his sight lines. Harryhausen drew diagrams on a big sketch pad and pointed out camera positions. Shawmut and Osborne efficiently laid steel track for the dolly.

Anthony surveyed the shadows and bright sky, then took his Leica up and down the length of the *Libertad* for the sixth time that morning.

"Your dad's particular," O'Brien said.

"He just wants to know where to be when the action begins," Peter said.

"Me, too," O'Brien said. "Only I've got two guys behind big hunks of metal. Not very flexible once we're set up." O'Brien watched the brawny stevedores with a grin. "They remind me of boxers," he said. "Used to do a little boxing. I was a wild one when I was a boy. How about you? You give your daddy a rough time?"

"No," Peter said.

"How's he going to know what it's like to be a dad?"

O'Brien's tone was jocular, but beneath the banter lay something large and distant and sad. Peter felt uneasy, but Anthony, passing on another foray close to the train, heard OBie's question and laughed. "Peter's my mainstay," he called. "He keeps me out of trouble."

OBie gave Peter a respectful, amused look. "So maybe you're the dad?"

Peter grinned and gave a little nod.

"They're going to unload the venator first," Harryhausen said. "They think he'll stay calm if he can't see what's happening." While they waited for the cables to be rigged, he took up the sketch pad and began drawing the venator and the roustabouts. Peter looked over his shoulder. In the drawing, the venator was busting out of the cage, toothy jaws gaping, big clawed toes spread wide, scattering panicked workmen in all directions.

Peter looked at the cage, then at Dagger's train car, which was quiet. "I hope you're wrong about that," he said to Harryhausen, pointing to the sketch.

"If *I* were in charge, things would be a lot more exciting," Harryhausen admitted. "Do you draw?"

"A little. I'm not very good."

"Takes practice. OBie and I sketch a lot. We could teach you."

"Sure," Peter said, his spirits lifting a little.

A man with a forklift unloaded big flat black iron plates one by one from the forward end of the venator's car. The plates were lined up along a steel scaffolding that led to the cage, and Peter realized this was another assembly of the runway that had guided the venator into the center ring. He admired the flexible design. The circus workers had had years of experience, perfecting the handling of these animals—even the venator.

Anthony stopped his pacing and focused his camera on the cage. "They're going to hang his breakfast from the top bars," he told Peter.

O'Brien gave the signal and one big Mitchell camera on a heavy tripod whirred, running on power from a small crate full of car batteries.

A roustabout entered the cage with a stepladder and strung chunks of beef from the bars on the inside of the runway. He and two others lifted and hung a whole haunch from the top of the cage. As they folded the ladder to leave, another roustabout made a move as if he were going to slam the cage door and lock it. The men inside stretched out their thumbs in unison, poked them between the first two fingers of their fists, and thrust them defiantly at the other. The workers laughed.

"Cut," O'Brien yelled, disgusted. "Hey, guys, this is a family film, okay?"

Harryhausen put away his drawing of the rampant venator and sat on the seat behind the big camera mounted on the dolly. Shawmut and Osborne prepared to push him along the steel tracks.

Out of nowhere, startling Peter, Shellabarger appeared, clutching a cup of coffee and frowning at the commotion. Gluck walked beside the train with hands pushed deep into his pockets. He wore a dark blue suit and vest.

"Looks like we're taking your babies back home, Lotto," Shellabarger said.

"Yess," Gluck replied, shaking his head. "I give them to you now. They're all yours until you set them free."

Peter felt the sweat bead under his arms and on his back.

O'Brien shouted, "Slate it, *rolling!*"

The right-hand door on the big car rumbled open. Peering into the gap where the iron plates covering the runway did not quite meet the car, Peter saw a quick brown motion. The car rocked slightly, then the ramp bowed under a heavy weight. They all heard a low chuff and snort.

"Blowing out the morning boogers," Shellabarger said. "I do the same thing myself—don't you?"

Peter forced a grin.

"Maybe it wantss some of your coffee, Vince," Gluck suggested.

Eight men with hook-tipped wooden poles lined up along the runway. Harryhausen sat behind the camera as Shawmut and Osborne rolled it smoothly toward the ramp and runway. The camera panned the length of the runway to take in the expectant roustabouts and the cage sitting on the loading pallet. "Not very exciting, all covered like that," O'Brien commented.

Everybody's eyes followed the progress of the venator as it walked down the steel-sheeted runway. Ropes holding the pieces of meat snapped one after another. Peter could hear Dagger's big jaws crunching and chewing, then, near the cage, the top of the runway banged.

Shellabarger wryly lifted the corner of one lip and mimed the big beast leaning his head back to jerk at the piece of meat. Shellabarger's nose bumped his flattened hand, representing the top of the runway. Peter nodded, then turned back. Anthony had positioned himself beside the cage, his camera lens poking into a gap between the plywood sheets covering the cage.

"He's in," Shellabarger said, tapping out a cigarette from a box. He stared at the cigarette with a disgusted frown, and then at Peter. "I only smoke when we're transferring the animals."

"All right," shouted Rob Keller, the chief roustabout. "Close him off and shut the car door." The door rumbled and clanged. Two men climbed to the top of the cage and secured the hook. The cage vibrated once but the venator seemed quiet.

A man in a black coat and pants, wearing a broad-brimmed white officer's hat set with gold stars and braid, strolled toward the assembly, hands gripped behind his back.

"I am *Capitan* Ippolito," he said to the group. "Who is *Señor* Shellabarger? *Señor* Gluck?"

"I'm Shellabarger."

"The loading is going well?" Ippolito's long brown face and dark, amused eyes took them all in quickly, judging and cataloging his passengers.

"Fine so far," Shellabarger said.

"I am still expecting clearance from your Department of State. Have the officials arrived yet?"

"Haven't seen them," Shellabarger said. "Mr. Gluck tells me we got our verbal OKs last night."

"You have been in the hold to look over the work our men did last night?"

"Everything's shipshape," Shellabarger said.

"Good," Captain Ippolito said. "You know these animals better than I. But if there is a storm, some difficulties, or we have to wait in port a week or so—not unusual in Venezuela—all will still be well?"

Gluck stepped forward. "Your concern is undersstandable, *Capitan,* but I believe all iss in order."

Ippolito leaned his head to one side, politely neutral.

The big crane's motor began reeling in the slack on the cable to the venator cage. The hook tugged at the cables and the cage shuddered on its pallet. The venator's two tons did not seem to bother the crane or its motor in the least. The pallet rose flat and smooth and from inside the cage came an almost comic snort of query.

"For a moment, just like itss coussins," Gluck said, smiling. "It flies."

The cage was twenty feet from the ground when the venator decided to get upset. It paced back and forth, making the big cage sway on the end of the cable. The swaying agitated the beast even more and it made a staccato screeching sound, then a deep-throated bellow. The plywood covering the cage bent outward and Peter heard that unforgettable racket of tail banging against bars.

The crane operator quickened the lift. The cage seemed to soar over their heads, swaying a yard back and forth now, above the level of the ship's gunwale. The venator screamed like a furious woman. More staccato protests followed like the cawing of a monstrous crow.

Peter saw Harryhausen elevate the lens of the big camera, focusing on the swaying cage.

Gluck wiped his brow with a handkerchief.

Shellabarger sniffed and watched the cage come into position above the hatch to the number one hold. The plywood ten feet up on one side of the cage suddenly splintered and a long brown and yellow arm thrust through, claws snatching at the air. As the cage was lowered into the hold, the arm continued to seek for something to kill, to vent the animal's rage.

Men shouted inside the hold, but Shellabarger appeared unconcerned. "He's fought that cage for fifteen years," he muttered. "Once he's stowed, the rest will be a piece of cake."

For a moment, there was little going on that interested Anthony. He stood by Peter. "Looks like its really going to happen," he said.

"What's going to happen?" Peter asked, his voice cracking. "What are we going to do?"

Anthony put his hand on Peter's shoulder. "Grosvenor came up with an idea. 'Close the circus down,' he told Gluck, 'and I'll get the Muir Society to pay you to take the dinosaurs back.'" Anthony puffed out his chest and stuck his fingers in his suspenders— though he was not wearing suspenders—just like a posturing bigwig. "Everybody makes money, everybody's happy."

"Back to the Grand Tepui?"

Anthony nodded. "Ford heard about it. He told Cooper and Schoedsack. They all thought it was a swell idea, so they approached the government. They have a lot of muscle in Washington, I guess. The State Department wasn't too keen about the idea, but Cooper told everybody to get ready anyway. And to keep it secret. I'm sorry, Peter. It isn't that I don't trust you."

"I didn't say anything to Mom," Peter said.

"I just didn't want to get your hopes up if it all fell through. Maybe I was wrong not to tell you everything."

"You were wrong," Peter said.

Anthony accepted this with a slow nod. "The sticky part is getting the Venezuelans to go along. It's dicey down there now. But I guess *el Presidente* Betancourt likes movies. He's agreed—but he and the army generals don't see eye-to-eye."

"It's going to be dangerous . . . isn't it?" Peter asked again.

"It could be," Anthony said. "If we aren't careful."

Peter stared at him, full of one question he could not ask.

Anthony solemnly asked it for him. "So why take my only son along? Because . . . We're not actually going to set foot on the Grand Tepui itself. There's the Pico Poco, on the southern end."

Harryhausen, eavesdropping to one side, ambled closer.

Anthony continued: "We take the old Indian switchback trail the hunters and entrepreneurs carved into a road in 1913. The old motorized steel bridge is still there. We swing it across to El Grande and let the dinosaurs return to the Lost World. We take our pictures and get paid like kings. And then we go home. And you get a little experience of the world you can't get in New York."

"Jeez," Peter said. He had always loved reading about dinosaurs and about the Grand Tepui. Going there would be something special in any man's life. But going there with a circus, with live dinosaurs . . .

His father was brave—that was a given. But Peter had always preferred home and a good book to rugged adventures. A hiking trip with Anthony was like going on safari with a restless cheetah. Anthony always outdistanced him in a few minutes, then doubled back and tapped his foot impatiently. Peter preferred to study things slowly and carefully.

"Is it really going to happen?" Harryhausen asked. He seemed to be feeling the same qualms as Peter.

Anthony said, "Keep your fingers crossed." He clapped Peter on the shoulder, then lifted his camera and walked off to snap more pictures.

"I didn't bargain on making a long trip," Harryhausen confessed. "I'm not an explorer. I like my monsters to sit on a table and do what I tell them to, one frame at a time."

Peter tried to put on a bluster. "You don't think it's exciting, going to El Grande?"

"Maybe too exciting," Harryhausen said.

Two black cars, a hump-backed green De Soto and a long black Packard, drove up as Sammy the centrosaur was being led down the ramp from his train car and into his cage for loading. The struthios, Dip and Casso, and the avisaurs had already been put aboard. Shellabarger had ridden alongside the *Aepyornis* in its cage, soothing her with his voice. He returned with the empty platform to the dockside and stepped off, eyes on two men in long black coats and gray hats, who stood by the De Soto. They looked like the men who had come to the train the night before. Ippolito watched from the wing of the ship's bridge, leaning on the rail.

The two men walked over to the Packard.

Schoedsack and Cooper stepped out of the Packard and conferred with them, took a sheath of papers, and carried them to Shellabarger and O'Brien. Schoedsack held the papers just a couple of inches from his thick glasses, flipping them back crisply. Cooper guided him. Peter stood beside Harryhausen near the dolly.

"It's go all the way," Schoedsack said. "Foggy bottom has no objections."

"Give our regards to Carl Denham," one of the men from the State Department called to Cooper. They smiled and got into the green De Soto.

"Yaaah!" Cooper said, waving his hand at them.

Schoedsack turned to O'Brien. "You heard what Ford said. Get a story for us, something we can really fly with . . ."

"Indians, dinosaurs, rivers, jungles, mountains," O'Brien said. "What more can an audience ask for?"

"We'll be getting the rushes on the circus tomorrow," Schoedsack said. "You'll be under way by then. I'll radio you, tell you what they're like."

"They'll be good," O'Brien said evenly.

"Well, it's in your hands now," Cooper said. He shook hands with O'Brien and watched the centrosaur's cage being lifted into the hold. "Remember, if anything happens to you—"

"I'll be fine," O'Brien said. He waved Cooper and Schoedsack back into the Packard and slammed the door on them. "You're just jealous," he said, leaning on the doorframe.

"I'd give my eyeteeth to be on that ship with you," Cooper drawled. Schoedsack grunted agreement and looked longingly through his thick glasses at the *Libertad*.

"You've got lots of responsibilities," O'Brien said with a twinkle in his eye. "Movies to produce . . . airlines to run . . . government committees . . . no time for big adventure."

"Don't rub it in." Schoedsack winced, leaned back in his seat, and waved. "Anything's easier than making movies in a studio nowadays." O'Brien closed the door with a solid *thunk*. The big black car rumbled down the pier. O'Brien walked past them, shaking his head. "Monte and Coop won't let us have all the fun, believe me."

"Which cage do you want to ride?" Anthony asked Peter.

"Huh?" Peter swiveled to face his father.

"Just fooling. We should get our bags aboard now." Anthony looked Peter over. "You look pensive."

"I still think we should call Mom," Peter said, eyes lowered. "Let her know we're leaving the country, at least."

"If we do, she won't let you go," Anthony said, two thin lines forming beside his lips. It had always been a bone of contention between his mother and father that when she did spend time with Peter, she coddled him. Anthony always expected him to pull his own weight, and that had started any number of fights before his mother and father had parted.

Peter thought of the caged venator and of the big black ship with its hold full of wild animals. He had never been at sea before. He wondered if he would get seasick. Worse things could happen.

Anthony watched him intently, the lines still present at the corners of his lips.

Peter took a deep breath. "Let's go," he said.

"My lad," Anthony said.

That night, wrapped tightly in blankets in his narrow bunk in the small, neat ship's cabin, Peter wrote:

My stomach still hurts. Maybe I am a coward.

My father and I explored the ship all afternoon while the animals were being stowed and the cages locked down. The captain and crew ignored us and got ready for the voyage. I am just getting used to what it feels like to be aboard a ship. The deck is steady enough but not as steady as land. When another big freighter went to sea and passed our pier, the ship rocked a little. Tomorrow we'll be going to sea ourselves.

Loading all the animals took a long time because some of the cages aren't strong enough to be lifted. The venator cage and the centrosaur cage are strong enough, but the ankylosaur cage needed to have new braces welded to the sides and bottom, I guess because the ankylosaur is heavier than she is strong. I mean the cage was lighter on the sides because Sheila doesn't rush the bars like the venator, or butt them as Sammy sometimes does. That meant the animals had to be transferred to wooden pens on the wharf while the welders went to work.

Father took some pictures looking over the side of the ship. The ankylosaur turned and turned in her pen as the arc welders flashed and hissed and snapped. She must have thought there were some very funny animals that she could hear but not see.

OBie and Ray Harryhausen spent the day exploring the ship, when they weren't stowing their cameras and other stuff as it arrived. Mr. O'Brien (all his friends call him OBie, with a capital O and B) seems to be a nice man but sometimes a little sad. His face lights up when he sees the animals, and he stares at them with such concentration.

The ship is clean but a little old, rusty in places. The engines are big, though Dad says they aren't nearly as big as the engines in an ocean liner like the Queen Mary. *Dad was on the* Queen Mary *during the war. It was hit by a big wave and nearly capsized, he says.*

The ship's insides are painted white and green and everything smells of fried food and diesel oil and bilge and other things I can't identify—some really funny smells that I will never forget, but not unpleasant. All together, it smells like a big iron ship, Dad says.

There is lots of polished brass on the bridge. The captain takes pride in his ship. This evening, at dinner, he said he had served on much larger ships in the war. He had two ships sunk from under him by German submarines, one off the coast of New York, the other off Florida. His English is fine, but I'd like to learn to speak Spanish.

On the ship, the sailors speak Spanish and Portuguese, and some know German and French. Most speak at least a little English.

Our cabin is amidships, two decks below the bridge, with a porthole on the starboard side. I'm talking like a sailor already! We're about twenty feet above the water. It's dark outside now. The provisions have been loaded, including the meat, hay, and alfalfa, and all the expedition supplies. (Is that too many commas? Father says commas slow things down.)

The captain told OBie that we had received clearance from Venezuela to put into Boca Grande, on the south side of the Orinoco Delta. We should be there in less than a week. It's not hurricane season and the weather should be good.

Shellabarger did not have much to say at dinner. He was quiet, but he had a fierce, angry look. He didn't come out of his cabin when we gathered on deck this evening after dark to talk about the day.

I guess I'm looking forward to tomorrow. I feel a little better now. Writing helps. Dad's getting great pictures and I like OBie and Ray Harryhausen a lot. I've always wanted to learn how to draw.

Peter put down the fountain pen and looked at the pages he had covered. Except in school, he had never strung so many words together in one sitting.

Chapter Six

The *Libertad* was not designed to comfort landlubbers. At sea, she would roll thirty degrees, then slow her roll, give an alarming shudder, and right herself, continuing over to the other side until she shuddered again: back and forth, hour after hour, over the dead calm sea.

Anthony, OBie, and Harryhausen were seasick after a few hours; Peter, to his surprise, joined Vince Shellabarger in feeling chipper.

The sky was clear from horizon to horizon and the sun warmed the ship's decks until they were almost too hot to walk on barefoot. Still, Peter reveled in the sensation of strolling from end to end of this little world, smelling the paint, the oil, the salt water, the warm and pure air. The dull steady pounding of the engine vibrated the deck, and any interruption of this reassuring rhythm seemed ominous. It was so totally unlike New York that he might have been carried to another planet.

He leaned over the wooden rail on the starboard wing of the bridge, using his hands to block his peripheral vision until he couldn't see the ship, and became one of the seagulls that wheeled and glided beside him.

Anthony recovered from his seasickness by the second day, but after a few quick turns around the ship with the Leica, there wasn't much left to do except remain vigilant. "If the ship sinks, or if a dinosaur escapes, I'll get some good shots," he told Peter.

Peter played shuffleboard and Ping-Pong with Harryhausen, burly, sandy-haired Rob Keller, who was in charge of the roustabouts and reported directly to Shellabarger, and Osborne from the camera crew. Keller and his men would travel with them all the way to the Pico Poco, to provide whatever was needed for the care and confinement of the animals.

Ping-Pong on the rolling ship was a real challenge. Harryhausen and Keller played a few games, and then Harryhausen handed his paddle over to Peter. Peter played against Osborne and quickly whacked two balls over the side. Harryhausen and Keller joined them at the rail to see if they could spot the balls in the flat sea. "If we roll far enough, I'll just pluck them out and we'll play another game," Harryhausen said.

It was at this point that Harryhausen insisted Peter call him "Ray." "Anything else makes me feel ancient, like C. B. De Mille," he said, eyes crinkling.

The roustabouts and camera crew ran around the ship to keep in shape, or read paperback books on the few deck chairs, or hung out with the sailors, trying to pick up information about the ports they would be seeing. Sailors knew a lot of things that Peter found fascinating. Anthony warned him against some of those things.

There were four other passengers, a middle-aged British lady named Mrs. Cantwell and her traveling companion, a thin, pretty young woman named Fiona, and two Venezuelan men who wore white suits on deck and did not speak to anybody. Anthony said the two men worked for an American oil company as translators.

"The *anglos* way back in the 'teens came down to see dinosaurs," Shellabarger explained at dinner on the second night, "and found oil instead."

"Is oil made from old dinosaurs?" Peter asked.

"No," Anthony said. "Ancient sea plants, like algae, not dinosaurs."

The ship rolled back and forth as dessert was served. The stewards wore white. Captain Ippolito insisted on all the amenities, to "keep up morale," as he said, "and because it is part of tradition."

"She's a well-run ship," OBie said as he joined them at the long table, "though exuberant. She wallows like a whale in heat."

At that moment, the ship rolled a little farther than usual, and the larger of the two oil company men tipped backward in his chair. He grabbed hold of the tablecloth and pulled everything off the table as he fell: plates, bowls of food, pitchers of water, all came crashing down around him. He was a portly fellow, and while everyone hung on to their tables for dear life, he rolled through the food, eyes wild, shouting curses in Spanish and bumping against chair legs.

Mercifully, Captain Ippolito leaned over, stuck out his arm, and stopped him. The poor man grabbed the captain with a desperate squeal, and the engineer and first mate helped him to his feet, apologizing profusely.

"She is top-heavy," Ippolito explained, looking around the cabin for support. "As *Señor* O'Brien says, exuberant."

"Dear me," exclaimed the English woman.

The steward dabbed with a towel at the stains of gravy, milk, and red wine on the portly translator's white suit. With a grimace, the large man pushed away the solicitous hands and stalked out of the mess, lurching against the door and almost slipping again with another roll to starboard.

Afterward, on the main deck, Ray and OBie and Anthony fell into helpless laughter. Peter couldn't help joining them, though he felt sorry for the man.

"He could have h-h-hurt himself," Anthony said to Ray, trying to keep a straight face. "Aren't you ashamed?"

Ray straightened and lifted his chin. "I have *nothing* to say," he intoned with great dignity, imitating Oliver Hardy.

"It's been a umpty-ump years since I've been rocked to sleep at night," OBie said. "This ship should be condemned!"

"Do you think *he'll* sleep well?" Anthony asked.

They all doubled over, faces red, laughing so hard.

Ray tugged his lips down with two fingers to keep from smiling. "Poor man," he said, and tears of laughter filled his eyes. They managed to keep solemn faces for about a second, and then began roaring and cackling all over again.

"We're all sick, cruel human beings," OBie said, shaking his head and wiping his eyes.

Shellabarger stepped out of his cabin to stare at the ocean and the stars. He caught the tail end of the laughter, but did not seem in a mood to have the joke explained.

"How are the animals?" Ray asked him.

"Sammy sleeps most of the time," Shellabarger said. "Most of them are eating all right, but Sheila is seasick. Has my sympathy, I'll tell you. Dagger just stands in his cage, rocking from leg to leg, staring at whoever's in the hold. The sailors won't go down there. We'll have to keep our own watch at night, just in case something breaks loose."

Keller came from below to join them. "I hope we don't have any rough weather," he said. He pulled a bottle of whiskey from his pocket, passing it around. OBie and Ray refused. Anthony took a swig. Shellabarger waited for him to be done, then took the bottle, wiped it on his sleeve, took a deep swallow himself, and threw it overboard.

"Hey!" Keller shouted, rushing to the rail and tracking the bottle as it soared into the ocean and vanished. "We can't get that kind of stuff where we're going!"

"I'll need all the sober help I can get," Shellabarger said. "So far, we've been lucky. But things aren't going to get any easier."

Keller grumbled and shook his head, but the roustabout knew better than to cross the trainer.

The next morning, Shellabarger invited Anthony and Peter to come down to the hold and inspect the animals. It was too dark in the hold for Anthony to get any decent pictures, but he took the camera anyway. Shellabarger's attitude had softened since the night before, and he even smiled at Peter as they walked along the catwalk between the forward hold and amidships.

Peter made out the square bulks of covered cages below, dimly lit by incandescent bulbs at the same level as the catwalk. He recognized the large venator cage, the *Aepyornis* cage, and the cage that contained the struthios. Shadows hid the rest, farther aft in the cavernous hold.

"I check on 'em every couple of hours," Shellabarger said, gripping a ladder and swinging out from the catwalk. He deftly clambered down to the bottom of the hold. Anthony let Peter go next.

Shellabarger led them between the cages. The hold smelled terrible. "We bring hoses down each evening to wash the shit into the gutters," he said. "The captain doesn't want it in the bilge, and I don't blame him. We haul the slop up in barrels and dump it overboard. Keeps the seagulls off our tail." He grinned and pulled a flashlight from his pocket. The light's yellow beam played over the tarps. Nearby, something made faint *gurking* noises. Heavy feet slapped ponderously.

"Sheila's still feeling poorly," Shellabarger said. He raised the corner of the tarp and aimed the beam into her cage. Peter and Anthony peered around the trainer to get a glimpse of the ankylosaur. She lay on her huge stomach, legs doubled up beneath her, almost hidden by the brown spikes and great folds of armored skin. Sheila raised her head and *gurked* again, stretching her beaked jaws wide.

"Ever seen a dinosaur throw up?" Shellabarger asked Peter.

Peter shook his head.

"It isn't pretty," Shellabarger said. "Though better the herbivores than the venator. Funny that Sheila's the only one who's sick. I was hoping Dagger would get a little under the weather. Be easier to handle."

"Is he acting up?" Anthony asked.

"No," Shellabarger said. He pulled his lips back in an expression Peter couldn't read. "Conserving his energy."

"What are you feeding him?" Peter asked.

"Shall we go look?" Shellabarger invited. "Sheila's going to spend this trip sleeping and throwing up. She hasn't eaten much . . . " He dropped the tarp and Peter and Anthony followed him on the steel-plated deck between the cages. The smell grew worse, sharp and strong enough to make Peter want to gag. A thick yellow fluid with massed black and white curds poured across the deck as the ship rolled. Peter narrowly missed stepping into the middle of the flow.

They came to the venator's cage. Shellabarger untied a rope near the cage and raised the tarp like a curtain. Inside, the venator lifted his head and blinked. His skin glimmered in the flashlight beam.

Shellabarger looked on the dinosaur with lifted chin and thinned lips. His jaw muscles worked for a moment as if he were chewing tobacco, and then he turned to Peter and Anthony and said, "You going to write about the changes on El Grande? No one's said much about them."

"Changes?" Anthony asked.

"Yeah." Shellabarger tied off the cord. "The clefts closing. Everything mixing up like a big old stew."

"That's not exactly news," Anthony said.

The venator gazed steadily at the trainer, his only motion the steady rise and fall of his breast, flushed slightly pink in the heat.

"You can't understand El Grande without knowing about the old divisions. For tens of millions, maybe hundreds of millions of years, El Grande used to be cut up into three parts. There used to be a cleft north of the Lago Centrale, and another just south of it, each about a hundred feet across, like the present gap between Pico Poco and El Grande. Nothing crossed over but flying birds and insects. Just after Challenger arrived in 1912 came the first quake. In the north lived the therapsids and the suchids—mammal-like reptiles and crocodilians. They weren't seen in the southern portions of El Grande until after the earthquake. In 1917, another quake, and the second cleft collapsed, and the central region started to spill south, too. Avisaurs and small mammals invaded the realm of the venators and other dinosaurs, along with the therapsids and suchids. Now it's a big stew pot. Who knows what other kinds of competition and change are going on? In just thirty years . . . what a laboratory the Grand Tepui becomes."

Shellabarger held up his hand, palm toward Dagger, as if signing "peace." "Dagger's one mean fancy *pachuco,* but his kind can't compete with the death eagles. I figure in a few more years, the venators will die out and the death eagles will take over. I wonder if he knows what he's going home to."

The venator had eyes only for Shellabarger. It did not even look at Anthony or Peter. Shellabarger kept them well back from the thick steel bars. "Couldn't train him, couldn't tame him, and you know what? He's my favorite. Humans are perverse bastards, don't you think?"

"He's fascinating," Anthony said. "Like looking at your own personal death."

"Yeah," Shellabarger said. "Audiences would have stopped coming to Lotto's circus years ago if it hadn't been for the venator. Elephants are great, but lions and tigers make us shiver . . . And the venator is scarier than any tiger ever born."

Peter's eyes had adapted to the darkness. He examined the venator from ten feet away, through the bars of the cage, feeling the hair on his neck prickle. The animal's throat wattle flicked as if trying to rid itself of a fly, and his ribs swelled and subsided with slow, steady respiration. The venator's breath smelled thick and sour-sweet, like an ancient slaughterhouse.

Shellabarger turned to look at Peter. "I envy you, Tony."

"Why?" Anthony asked.

"Years ago, I wanted a son so I could teach him about the circus. How to know and care for the animals. Have him follow on after I was gone. I've lived a lot longer than I thought I would. Between this beast and a half dozen others, I was sure I'd be crushed or bitten in half by now. I never had a son, and I've outlived the circus. So what's to pass on?"

Peter stepped forward. "I'd like to learn," he said.

Anthony stared at Peter, brows lifted.

Shellabarger studied Peter for several seconds. The venator's warm stench surrounded them. "What's the first thing to know?" he asked quietly.

Peter felt his lungs catch and his shoulders stiffen. He had never liked direct challenges from older people, whether they were teachers or people on the street.

"What they like to eat," Peter said.

Shellabarger angled his head away but kept his slitted eyes on Peter's. "You have to know what they need to be. Animals remember, but they don't exactly *think*. Life is one long *sensation* for them."

"Oh," Peter said.

"What does Dagger need?" Shellabarger asked.

Peter glanced at the animal. The venator still had his eyes fixed on Shellabarger.

"You," Peter said.

Shellabarger gave a rueful snort of laughter. He looked away from Peter. "Does he have any other chores on this voyage?" he asked Anthony.

"Not for the moment," Anthony said. "If you want him, he's yours."

"You'll have to hose down the shit," the trainer warned. He looked at Anthony curiously. "Is it okay if I use a few good old Anglo-Saxon words in front of the boy?"

Anthony grinned and shook his head. "I guess you will whether I want it or not."

"Maybe," Shellabarger admitted. "You'll have to hose down this . . . this *muck* and climb into the cage and feed Sammy and Sheila with your own hands. You'll have to scrub and curry the struthios and spend an hour each day with the toothed birds. They get lonely and they like someone to talk to them and fluff their feathers."

Peter found it harder and harder to breathe. The air seemed rank and gelatinous and his eyes burned. His body couldn't decide whether to be excited or terrified.

"You up for that?" Shellabarger asked him.

"Yeah," he said. He felt a little dizzy.

"Then you'll be my apprentice," Shellabarger said.

"Thanks," Peter said, gulping. He looked at his father, who was still grinning, and then swung his head around to see Dagger.

Dagger watched *him* now, with the same steady, needful glare he had reserved for the trainer. His throat flexed and he blew a glob from his nose through the bars to the deck. The glob landed squarely between Peter's shoes.

"You have his blessing," Shellabarger told Peter. "All right, let's get to it."

For the next five days, as the *Libertad* passed down the coast of the United States, skirted Florida and Cuba, and made its way through the Antilles, Peter worked with Shellabarger from seven in the morning to dinnertime, and for an hour each evening after dinner. Shellabarger found him a pair of gum boots in the circus boxes, a couple of sizes too large, but they kept his shoes from getting ruined. Shellabarger also supplied him with a pair of rubber gloves. "This stuff really does nasty things to your skin," he explained as a bucket of slop was being hauled out of the hold to be dumped overboard. "It's worse than guano. But if your ma keeps a garden, it's fabulous. Shall we ship it to her?"

Peter smiled wanly, but did not want to explain that his mother and father were divorced. The thought of his mother, immaculately dressed in a cotton gabardine suit, getting a big drum full of this nauseating green and yellow liquid . . .

"She doesn't garden," he said.

"The clowns do a little gardening when we spend a few months in Tampa," Shellabarger said. He cleared his throat. "Used to. Flowers and tomatoes and stuff. Dinosaur . . . muck . . . makes them pop right out of the ground, sweet and juicy." He smacked his lips.

Peter could not figure Shellabarger. Sometimes he was as nasty as could be, as if sitting under a dark cloud. The venator made him nasty. They would glare at each other, and Shellabarger would begin stomping around the hold, shouting orders and getting even more particular about Peter's work.

The sailors did not come into the hold, but Captain Ippolito ventured down a few times. The captain once saw Shellabarger staring down the venator. Ippolito said to Peter, "Between them both, they have enough evil eyes to kill a city. I would not stand between them, not for a million dollars."

Peter hated cleaning the slop, but he enjoyed feeding Sammy and tending Sheila. Sammy was "less vicious by far than a rhino," according to Shellabarger, "but you still have to watch him." Sammy took a shine to Peter and was careful not to tread on the boy when he was in the cage. Peter had a chance to wash the centrosaur twice, and the big animal rolled his eyes in sheer delight as the rough bristle brush was pushed, laden with soapy water, over his tough, horny hide. Peter loved to feel the hide, almost hard as rock, and feel the weight of the huge animal as Sammy shifted his feet with the roll of the ship. Shellabarger warned him to keep a watchful eye out in case the ship rolled more than usual, and then, to scramble up on Sammy's back if the big animal missed his step and slammed against the cage.

In the cage, Sammy could angle himself from corner to corner, but he could not turn around, and if his straw wasn't changed regularly, he would get sores on his hoof pads and between his nails.

"We're all going to be glad to be on dry land again, aren't we?" Peter asked the centrosaur. Sammy closed his eyes and lifted his broad, heavy shield to be scrubbed on the nape of his neck.

Peter brought mineral salts from a big steel drum in the circus store room to Sheila. The spiky, heavily armored animal moved very little, usually spending the day lying half on her side, spikes wedged between the plywood deck of the cage and the bars just beyond. She drank the mineral salts mixed with water from a big bucket, sucking the water through her tough, turtle-like beak.

The ankylosaur's droppings were big as baseballs, and just as round and solid. After evening cleanup on the fourth day out, Shellabarger found a baseball bat and they took a bucket of Sheila's refuse and went to the stern. There, Ray and OBie and Anthony joined them for a game of dungball. The droppings hit the bat with a solid whack and flew out over the rail to vanish into the *Libertad*'s broad wake.

"Dino dung and the national pastime . . . who'da thunk it?" OBie asked. He grinned as another round ball of dung flew out over the ocean.

"I'da thunked it," Ray said, handing the bat to Shellabarger. Peter played catcher until he complained about being on the receiving end of so much shit. Anthony made a face and Shellabarger held up his hands and said he was keeping *his* language clean.

"Hey," OBie said, "I'm the Irishman here. That should be my line."

They tried to explain to Peter the joke about the Italian and the Irishman, but they couldn't clean it up and make it funny, so Peter had to piece it together for himself later that evening. Even then, it wasn't very funny.

Ray began teaching him to draw in the evening after what Peter called his "dino-chores" were done. Peter had sketched enough to be able to block out forms and put them together; Ray showed him how to compose a picture, find the lines of action, make sure things in the picture "know about each other." He explained that a picture has its own weight that tugs the eye from one side to the other, or swings it around in a spiral.

"Understand the animals, the people," Ray said, quickly sketching a man crouching as some dark shadow loomed behind him. The shadow became a huge cave bear. Peter, much more crudely, sketched a man standing with his hands in his pockets. In front of him cowered a little mouse.

Ray looked at it and shook his head. "Not bad," he said. "Where's the action, though?"

"The mouse is really afraid," Peter said.

Ray laughed, then turned the page on his pad and began sketching an ancient Hindu temple.

"You want to be a writer, like your father?" Ray asked again.

"Yeah," Peter said.

"Really?"

Peter drew some long dark lines with his pencil. "I don't know I'll be as good as he is," he said.

"I know a writer, back in Los Angeles. Known him since we were boys. Writing is his whole life. All he talks about is writing."

"Is he good?" Peter asked.

"Pretty good," Ray said. "He says you have to do what you love, or you're going to end up dead inside, a grotesque, like someone in a Sherwood Anderson story."

"Hm," Peter said.

"So, what do you love?" Ray asked.

"I don't know," Peter said.

"Better find out," Ray said.

Peter went to sleep each night dead tired, still a little smelly even after multiple lavings of the ship's brutal hand soap. He did not care. He was ecstatic just to be one of the guys.

Peter spent the third day with the struthios. Anthony came

down to see how his son was progressing with the dinosaurs. Shellabarger patiently explained how the struthios thought.

"They're dumber than ostriches, but smarter than possums, and what they lose in brains, they more than make up for with body smarts. Watch." Shellabarger picked up a piece of dried cob corn and tossed it through the bars of the cage. Even though the female had her back to them, she sensed the cob coming, turned with lightning speed and grace, and snatched it out of the air. She deftly turned it with her rough tongue and stripped its kernels in a few seconds, then spit the cob back at them.

"Don't get behind the male or he'll eviscerate you," Shellabarger said. "You know what that means?"

"He'll gut me," Peter said.

"Yeah. He won't mean to, it'll just happen. The female's not so touchy, but she's still heavy. She's broken my foot twice in the twenty years we've been together, and believe me, she's much too proud to apologize."

Anthony got a concerned look. "Hey," he said, "in these cages, are you sure it's safe? With the ship rolling the way it does?"

"Who said anything about it being safe?" Shellabarger said. "If he watches himself, he'll survive."

"That's a bit callous, don't you think?" Anthony asked testily. Peter gave a little laugh, but Anthony did not see the humor.

"He's done everything like a pro without getting hurt. He's a smart kid."

"I'm okay, Dad," Peter said. "I watch myself."

Anthony gripped Peter's shoulder. "Make sure you watch *every-thing.*"

Peter entered the cage with Casso, the female struthio, and used a wide-toothed curry comb to groom her fine, tiny feathers. He noticed that the feathers rose from the ends of small scales with central ridges; though not as developed as the feathers in birds or avisaurs, they were still recognizably heading in the same evolutionary direction.

Other than reaching back with her long arms to make sure where he was, poking him in the thigh with a thick black claw, Casso kept still, eyes wide and black in the darkness of the upper hold.

"I think she wants to see the sun," Peter called to Shellabarger, who was across the hold, stuffing herbs into the ankylosaur's beak.

Shellabarger grunted. "It *is* damned dark down here. I suppose we could open the hatch covers, as long as the weather's good . . . I'll ask the captain."

Peter finished the grooming and walked on the perimeter of the hold to the ankylosaur's cage, giving a wide berth to the venator. Dagger stood on both legs, tail poking through the bars, and angled his head to watch Peter with heavy-lidded eyes. One claw on his right forelimb—his right *manus,* Ray called it—rose and fell as if marking time.

"How's Sheila?" Peter asked, entering the ankylosaur's cage and standing behind Shellabarger.

"Not good," Shellabarger said. "All this rocking. Damned ship." He held up a fistful of herbs, then poked them at her beak. "She's always been the most delicate." She turned her head aside and the trainer thrust his thumb at the hinge of her jaw. She flinched and involuntarily her jaw opened. Shellabarger quickly stuffed the herbs in and she chewed on them halfheartedly, making small grunting noises.

Captain Ippolito agreed to open the hatch covers over the forward hold, and for several hours on the fourth day, all the animals enjoyed a peek at the sky and a rolling reacquaintance with the sun. Ray came down into the hold with Anthony. Anthony took quick photographs as the sun shone down on the dinosaurs, and Ray sat on a stool by a bulkhead and sketched his favorites, the venator and Sammy the centrosaur.

He gave Peter a small sketch pad and a box of No. 2 pencils. When the morning's chores were done, Shellabarger left them in the hold while he climbed topside to smoke a cigarette. Ray showed Peter how to loosen up and draw from the elbow and shoulder, not from the wrist. "Look at things as they are," he said. "Not as you want them to be. And remember . . . everything has its own kind of life. Even a rock." The ship ended its roll to one side and shuddered underneath them. "Even *Libertad,*" he said with a grin.

"The animals are going to be a lot happier on land," Peter said.

"Won't we all," Ray said.

Peter took a second stool and sat in front of Sheila's cage, drawing a portrait from the front.

"You'll be home soon, girl," Peter said. She watched him through her small, rheumy eyes, unhappy, understanding nothing. Ray joined him as Anthony came back from photographing the venator, and they all listened to Sheila's labored breathing.

"Doesn't sound good," Anthony said. "Not that I'm an expert on sick dinosaurs." He looked down at Peter's drawing. It was rough, but it had a strong sense of light and shade, and the animal's dim eye had been captured nicely. "Pretty good, don't you think?" he asked Ray.

"Ask me in a month," Ray said. Then he allowed, "It's a good start."

That night, Shellabarger banged on their stateroom door. "Peter, come with me," he said from the other side. Peter had almost been asleep. He dressed quickly and his father asked him if he could tag along. "Sure, I guess," Peter said, not used to giving his father permission.

Shellabarger led the way to the forward hold. The sea had grown rougher since sunset and the ship was now shuddering strongly at the end of each roll. The animals were very nervous, particularly the struthios, who made loud shrieks and clawed at the bars of their cage. They swung their heads back and forth on snaking necks, eyes wide, jaws gaping, tongues poked out.

Shellabarger walked around their cage. "Never mind them," he said. "They're just raising hell."

Anthony and Peter followed him to Sheila's cage. She had fallen over on her side, her back propped against the bars. Rivulets of blood seeped out from under her. "She's torqued some spikes and opened up her hide," Shellabarger said. "But that's not the worst. She has an impacted bowel. Hasn't defecated for a day and a half."

Peter thought of the large pellets they had used as baseballs. Sheila's eyes were closed and her underside spasmed at the end of each slow breath.

"I keep telling her we're taking her home," Shellabarger said softly. "But it's no good. She's too dumb and too sick to care."

"Can we roll her over?" Peter asked.

"Not without a winch. I could rig some block and tackle . . . We have a harness for that sort of thing, but we'd bust the cage if we fastened it to the upper bars. The captain would have a fit if we asked him to rig a boom at night, with the weather getting worse . . ."

Sheila craned her neck and gave a gravelly sigh.

"I hate to lose her, but that's what's happening," Shellabarger said. "And it isn't just the ship rolling and her being on her side . . . She doesn't feel she belongs."

"Can you blame her?" Anthony asked.

Ray and OBie and Keller came down into the hold. Shawmut and Osborne followed, eyes big as they looked over the dark, covered cages.

They stood around Sheila's cage, each offering a different scheme for how to rig a harness and get the old dinosaur upright again, and each idea went down to defeat as a major problem was found.

They sat up all that night, each taking turns to bring water or herbs. Exhausted and sad, at four in the morning—by the tolling of the ship's bell—Peter wandered off to be by himself. Anthony found him sitting against the aft bulkhead.

"Blaming yourself?" Anthony asked, sitting beside him.

"They're supposed to be going *home*," Peter said. "I didn't think any of them would die."

From across the hold, they heard a gunshot, and then Shellabarger cursing. OBie and Ray found them and told them the news. The trainer had put Sheila out of her misery. She was still dying—it took ankylosaurs a long time to know that their time was up.

OBie had tears on his cheeks. Ray shook his head, his sketch pad tucked under one arm.

"Keller bought another bottle of whiskey from the crew," OBie said, sitting beside them. He wiped his eyes on a handkerchief. "He gave it to Vince and Vince took it back to his room."

Ray slumped against the bulkhead last and they all sat in silence, thinking about the big animal's death.

"What'll they do with the body?" Peter asked. "Will they dump it at sea?"

"I'll call the society in the morning," Anthony said. "I'm sure the Smithsonian or some other institution will want it . . . There aren't that many dinosaurs that we can just dump poor Sheila at sea."

After a few minutes, they stood up together. OBie said, "I'm going to Vince's cabin and share a drink, talk him through it . . ." He looked around the group. "Anybody coming with me?"

They all said they would. Then they shook hands. It was a funny response, Peter thought, but it made them all feel better. It made them feel less like a bunch of people sharing a ship with some animals and more like a team with a single, real goal.

Peter and Anthony passed the venator's cage. Shellabarger had lowered the tarps for the night, but they heard Dagger scrape his claws on the bottom of the cage as they passed. Peter could almost feel the venator's attention.

"Do you think he blames us?" Peter asked his father, nodding at the covered cage.

"Odd idea," Anthony said. "I don't see how he can."

Peter was not so sure.

Chapter Seven

The coast of Venezuela appeared the next day, a line of dark green on the horizon, mounted by towering white thunderheads. The sun beat down on the deck, making the white surfaces unbearably brilliant, but a cooling wind blew and it was pleasant in shade. The ship rolled less than usual and OBie and Ray and Anthony prevailed upon the captain to let a few of the smaller animals run around in the sun. An enclosure was built around the number two hatch from the lumber of scrap pallets. The ship's crew then rigged a small boom and brought up the struthios and avisaurs. The avisaurs stayed in their cages, but spread their wings at the touch of sun and preened themselves. Peter had established quite a rapport with the four bird-lizards, and he scratched their necks through the bars of the cage, all the time keeping an eye out for their toothy jaws, which could draw blood with even a friendly nip.

The struthios pranced about on the deck, dipping their necks and investigating all the nooks and crannies available to them. They walked very much like ostriches, lifting their legs delicately, three clawed toes curled under on the lifted foot and splayed flat on the grounded foot.

Shellabarger walked with the struthios for a while, wearing dark aviator glasses and a cloth cap. To Peter he seemed older, most of

the enthusiasm gone out of him. But as the afternoon wore on and they had to gather up the dinosaurs, the chase seemed to enliven the trainer. They managed to guide each struthio back into its cage and the boom delivered them safely back into the hold, where Keller and his men tied them down again.

That evening, Peter fed the avisaurs seeds and scraps of ground meat and helped Shellabarger and Ray inspect the *Aepyornis*'s claws for fungus. Shellabarger painted the claws with a smelly purple concoction.

"I didn't know keeping animals was so much work," Peter said, watching from outside the cage.

Mrs. Birdqueen jerked her foot vigorously. Shellabarger grunted and continued painting.

"I thought dinosaurs were really tough . . . You know, monsters." He didn't *really* think that, but he wanted to give Shellabarger something to react against. He hated to see Shellabarger gloomy. The trainer shrugged but took his bait.

"In their own place, they're a lot tougher than we are. In Chicago or New York, I might feel tough, but on El Grande, none of us is going to be very tough. These beasts will be back in their element. Then we'll see them shine."

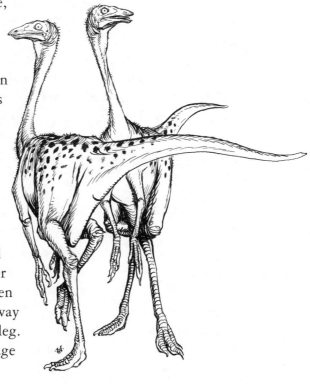

"Dad says we'll be in port tomorrow evening."

The *Aepyornis* stared down at them with her beady black eyes, then pushed Shellabarger away with a casual flip of her leg. He came out of her cage with the brush and bottle, rubbing his back where he had bumped against the bars. "Had enough, eh, Mrs. Birdqueen?"

She shook her head vigorously. A cloud of neck feathers swirled through the air.

"Molting," Shellabarger said. Ray sneezed.

They passed Trinidad early that morning, just after sunrise.

Libertad glided through the broad muddy outfall of the Orinoco River miles from shore. The water took on a brownish color and bits of log and scraps of vegetation drifted past. Anthony and Peter watched from the bow; OBie and Ray and the film crew were setting up some shots for their arrival. Captain Ippolito estimated they would be in the river's broad mouth by fourteen hundred hours: two o'clock in the afternoon.

The rest of the dinosaurs seemed to be doing well enough.

The cage with Sheila's body lay in the hold, covered with canvas. Shellabarger had been on the radio for hours but had not been able to get any offers from museums; none were willing to move five tons of decaying dinosaur so many thousands of miles. Anthony had tried the night before to get the National Geographic Society and the Muir Society to take charge of the ankylosaur, but with so little time to make preparations, and with more important work to do— getting the living dinosaurs up to El Grande—the directors of both organizations decided against mounting any effort.

"The captain says there have been heavy rains on the highlands," Anthony said. "The Orinoco's running deep. The rains will have lifted the Caroní, too. We'll have to fight a strong, steady current upriver."

Peter unfolded a pocket map his father had brought along and studied the length of both rivers. The Orinoco was immense, flowing through the middle of Venezuela and cutting it in half; the Caroní joined it about one hundred and twenty miles from where the Orinoco met the sea. Peter drew his finger down the Caroní, into the brown spaces of the Guiana Highlands.

At noon, Shellabarger came from the bridge, where he had been on the radio to New York, Boston, Chicago, and even Miami. "No one will take her," he murmured, staring gloomily out over the muddy water. "I even called Trujillo's people in the Dominican Republic. He's supposed to be nuts about dinosaurs. But he bought all he wanted back in the thirties, and they're dead now. He's lost interest."

If something was not arranged soon, Ippolito said, it would be best to dump the body at sea before they journeyed up the Orinoco. The captain warned that there would be no place to store the body in San Félix or Puerto Ordaz, and that no one in either town was interested in dead dinosaurs. "They have thirty years' worth of dead dinosaurs to put in their museums—not to mention their town squares, their hotels, and their bars."

The captain climbed down into the hold to check the temperature. He pursed his lips unhappily and said, "We have maybe a day before it bloats and fills the whole cage and we have to dump it overboard, cage and all."

Shellabarger rubbed his grizzled chin. "All right," he said quietly. "We bury her at sea."

The water was calm enough now that rigging a boom presented little problem. The boom swung out over the open hold and heavy cables were attached to three points on the cage's thick bottom bars. Shellabarger and Keller rode the cage up out of the hold, getting off as it drew level with the deck. OBie and Ray used their portable camera to capture it all from the port side.

The boom swung the cage out over the water. Rob Keller had undone the cage door and tied a rope to a winch cable, which drew taught. The cage tilted. Sheila's head, neck, and side spikes continued to hold her in place; the cage tilted forty-five, fifty, sixty degrees.

With a sudden ugly snapping of her spikes, Sheila's body slid ponderously out of the cage and into the ocean. She nosed in with surprising grace and very little spray and sank out of sight.

Peter and Anthony went aft with Ray and OBie to see if the big animal rose to the surface, but she remained hidden in the ocean depths. "Some oil tanker is sure going to get a surprise in a few days," Ray said.

They observed a moment of silence.

As they walked forward, OBie said, "Tony, you used to work with Standard Oil people up north. What are they like down here?"

Anthony shook his head. "Never met any, personally. They're calling their Venezuelan operation Creole Oil. They might be real helpful . . . Or they might not."

From the *Libertad*'s bridge, Anthony and Peter watched their progress into Boca Grande—the broad, muddy mouth of the Orinoco. The captain had sent his first mate down to the bow with a crew of five men to scrutinize the water ahead and take soundings; he guided the ship with nervous glances along both distant banks.

"Big trees float down here sometimes," he told Anthony, who was taking notes and snapping pictures. "Fifteen, twenty meters long. Put big dents in my ship, maybe even break the rudder or jam the screws. Snags, mudbanks, sandbanks, thick river grass . . . " He took off his hat and combed his fingers through his shiny black hair. "I am always nervous in the river."

Little shantytowns lined the banks every few miles, or bigger whitewashed buildings surrounded by shacks. Mostly, however, there was flat mud and wetlands and broad expanses of jungle. Big birds with flame-colored wings filled the skies, landing to fish in the shallows less than fifty yards from the channel the ship was following.

Peter tended the animals with the roustabouts that afternoon while Shellabarger and OBie confirmed advance preparations on the radiotelephone. Peter, Rob Keller, and Keller's second, Arnie Kasem, rolled a side of beef from the ship's cold locker, heaved it over the side into the hold, cut it up, and tossed the pieces into the venator's cage. Peter watched the animal bend over and lift one twenty-pound chunk, fling it back, spraying a drizzle of watery blood, and snatch it out of the air. Dagger gave it several noisy chomps, bones and all, and swallowed it with that now familiar, still hideous sucking noise.

"Good fellow," Keller murmured, and grinned at Peter. The animal's steel and gold eyes followed their movements with cold interest and no gratitude. "Think he'll get even with old Vince before he runs off into the jungle?"

Peter blinked, shocked that the head roustabout would express that thought so boldly.

Keller chuckled. The venator grabbed another chunk and sucked it down. "Just like that," Keller said, turning his hands and forearms into big jaws, clapping his palms just inches from Peter's face. "That'd be fun to watch, hm?"

"He's *joking*," said Arnie Kasem, at twenty-four the youngest of the roustabouts. Kasem wiped his bloody hands on a filthy rag. "Don't mind him."

Keller swabbed up the bits of fat and blood and squeezed the mop into a bucket.

"No need for that," Peter said. "We're going to hose it all down in an hour."

Keller glared at him and continued swabbing. "Dagger likes a clean cage and a clean floor right after meals," he said. "He won't go after me when the time comes, because I take care of him."

Arnie Kasem followed Peter over to Sammy's cage. They rolled bales of alfalfa and some bundles of Shellabarger's special herbs up to the cage on pushcarts. The centrosaur rubbed the cage noisily with his horn-studded shield.

"Think they'll miss getting regular meals?" Kasem asked. "There's no meal ticket in the wild."

Peter liked Kasem. Strong, soft-spoken, and not very smart, Arnie Kasem had stayed quiet much of the trip, and only now seemed willing to talk with Peter, or anybody but his fellow roustabouts.

Ray came down to watch the feeding of the struthios, sketching the process quickly.

When they were done, Keller climbed up the ladder with most of the roustabouts, but Kasem and Ray stayed with Peter in the shadowy hold. They sat on a crate and listened to the sounds of the animals echoing in the dark spaces. Sammy's stomach made great liquid glurps as he digested his alfalfa.

"We're privileged," Ray said.

Kasem chuckled. "Listening to dinosaurs burp isn't much of a privilege."

"This is my first big adventure," Ray confided. "I've spent most of my life in California trying to get work in movies, making unreal things look real. I wasn't sure about all this at first, but now I feel privileged . . . just to be here."

"Oh," Kasem said. He rubbed his nose. "Yeah."

The venator chuffed behind the bars of his covered cage, and Kasem gave Peter an odd, scared look, as if he had just seen a ghost.

Chapter Eight

———◆———

Despite the captain's misgivings, the river was broad and deep enough to take them easily into Puerto Ordaz. There, the *Libertad* pulled alongside an old, half rotten wooden dock, beside a single rusted tanker that looked as if it had been there for twenty years. Pilings for a new series of piers were being pounded into the river bottom a hundred yards south of where they tied up, and stacks of fresh lumber lay in dirt yards waiting to be erected into warehouses.

On the bridge, Anthony said, "Oil's coming out of every port now, I guess."

"This is just a trickle compared to the gulf," Ippolito said. "But there are railways across the river at Palùa, and towns going up all over where the rivers mingle. Soon there will be iron—there is much iron west of here—and even aluminum."

OBie smiled. "Think the tourists will ever come back to see dinosaurs?"

"Puerto Ordaz was the gateway to El Grande for years," Ippolito said. "I think the visitors will prefer iron and aluminum. And maybe gold and diamonds, too."

Shellabarger came onto the bridge, the skin under his eyes dark with lack of sleep. He had lost weight in the last couple of days.

"I've been in the radio shack," Shellabarger said. "The

Venezuelan Army's up in arms about some of Monte Schoedsack's advance people going to Pico Poco, they say without the necessary permits. The Army colonel in charge of the area around El Grande says he'll shoot any more trespassers. We got the permits from Caracas, though—Coop confirmed that in Washington." He shook his head in dismay. "God save me from little tyrants."

A jeep and two dark green trucks roared out onto the dock and parked. Five soldiers in shiny black helmets emerged from the jeep and the rear of one truck. They slung their rifles and stood in a line along the dock.

"We must be very polite here," Ippolito warned in a low voice. "The Betancourt junta is fragmenting. The Gallegos government is having a dispute with the Army and it does not look good. I think where you will be going, the Army will be in charge and will not listen to Caracas."

OBie's face suddenly brightened. "Well, if it's going to be a war, I *know* we'll have company," he said.

"Who?" Shellabarger asked, glaring at him.

"Monte and Coop will come south just to get in the thick of a good fight," OBie said.

"So who's the good guy and who's the bad guy?" Ray asked.

"Around here," Anthony said, "the Army's mostly bad."

Ippolito frowned. "I have warned you, *señors*. You have been reading too many *Norteamericanos* newspapers."

The air of Puerto Ordaz was thick with the smell of petroleum. A long rainbow slick flowed north from the docks, dappled by big drops of rain. A few miles away, a bright torch blazed in the late afternoon sky like a candle planted on the jungle's endless green tablecloth: natural gas burning off from a wellhead. Rain fell in curtains from thick black clouds within the hour, and still the torch burned, lighting up the bottoms of the clouds with a ghastly yellow-orange glow.

Ippolito was in great haste to unload the animals and head downriver to the sea. He did not trust the river in the rainy season and did not want to be associated with *Norteamericanos* who were arguing with the Army.

Shellabarger was just as eager to get his beasts out of the hold. First, however, he wanted to go into town and make sure the boats that would take the animals to the rail station at San Pedro de las Bocas had been built and were ready.

Anthony, Peter, and Ray accompanied him. Keller and OBie stayed behind to make sure the animals weren't unceremoniously dumped on the docks. As they walked down the dock, the soldiers in shiny black helmets stared at them impassively. Nobody said a word.

Puerto Ordaz had indeed been the gateway to El Grande. Once, it had grown to ten thousand people, serving the hunters and scientists and hardy tourists who traveled up the Caroní to the foot of Pico Poco. Indians had come from all over the Orinoco and Amazon basin, from as far west as Peru, looking for work, mingling their tribal cultures and languages, and forming new political coalitions.

After dictator Juan Vicente Gómez had succumbed to pressure from the United States and closed El Grande, Puerto Ordaz had withered. The Indian coalitions had disintegrated. Dozens of wood and whitewashed plastered brick buildings still stood empty along the muddy streets, many crumpled under the onslaught of ants and termites.

Away from the main streets, shantytowns were taking on new life, however, as oil workers and miners moved in. Many gold and diamond fortune hunters kept their families in Puerto Ordaz, and a few of the businesses along the main street bustled, their feeble yellow electric lights gleaming in the gray twilight and the frequent swirling brooms of warm rain.

In the town square, weathered dinosaur skeletons decorated an overgrown park. Benches had been made out of huge sauropod ribs, and Shellabarger led them past an outdoor bullring that had once seen the slaughter of dozens of animals like Sammy. The ring's ticket booth and round entrance was now barred by a half circle of the forbidding skulls of the ceratopsians that had died there. Their lower jaws had been removed, and their shields lay flat in the dirt, horns pointed outward, as if still defending the young and the females.

Ray stood by the skulls for a moment, chin in hand, lost in

thought. "Did you ever see a dinosaur fight here?" he asked Shellabarger.

"Yes, to my shame," Shellabarger said.

Shellabarger walked them to a boatyard on the other side of the town. There, in the humid darkness, they met with a short, fat man in a yellow rain slicker. He smiled and assured Shellabarger that the big flat-bottom boats were ready.

"They are very tough, very sturdy," he said in Spanish. On the ship, Peter had picked up enough Spanish to understand most of what was said. "Yet just the right size to be loaded on train cars at San Pedro de las Bocas. I have followed the specifications of *señors* Grosvenor and Schoedsack . . . through their agent, *Señor* Wetherford."

Wetherford, they had learned, was waiting for them at San Pedro de las Bocas. It was Wetherford who had had the run-in with the Army, after scouting the trails and working with President Gallegos's engineers on Pico Poco.

"Show the boats to me," Shellabarger said. The owner waddled into his office and came back with diagrams, which he happily unrolled in the drizzle. Small drops of rain speckled the paper.

"The boats themselves, I mean," Shellabarger said.

The man's face fell. "It is dark, *señor,*" he murmured.

"I want to see them now," Shellabarger said.

The man grudgingly brought a kerosene lantern from his brightly lighted shack and led them through the mud to the water's edge. There, in five big hangar-like sheds, the river boats sat on broad chocks, deserted by the craftsmen for the day, surrounded by scraps of lumber and piles of shavings and tables covered with tools.

Three scruffy, skinny dogs whined around their legs and the fat man shooed them away gently with his foot. He whispered affectionately to the thin animals while Shellabarger circled the boats, then took a workman's ladder and climbed up into one.

Shellabarger took the lantern and walked from stem to stern. The boats were each about forty feet long, fifteen feet wide across the beam, with flat bottoms and blunt prows and squared-off sterns. A single cubical cabin perched aft like a guardhouse.

"We do very good work," the boatyard owner said. "We work for Creole Oil and the U.S. Steel. The motors, they are new, they arrived a week ago, and have just been mounted from their crates. Big, fine diesel engines, very expensive!"

Shellabarger climbed down, handed the man his lantern, and said, "We'll need them launched and down by the *Libertad* tomorrow morning. Captain Ippolito's anxious to be on his way."

"*Sí, perfecto, señor!* At dawn, I will begin."

As they walked back to the docks, Shellabarger pulled a pistol from his pocket and showed it to Anthony and Ray. "You were a soldier," he said to Anthony. "You ever use one of these?"

Anthony looked over the glittering long-barreled gun with a blank expression. Peter knew his father did not like guns. "No," he said. "I used an M-1."

"Gold and diamonds attract all sorts of freaks, and the Caroní up to the railhead is thick with them. When we go upriver, there could be riffraff who'll shoot us just for fun. And there's always the Army, of course." He glanced around, shadows from a tavern's blinking sign swinging across his gaunt face. "This is a sad place now. You teach your son how to shoot?"

"No," Anthony said, jaw clenching. "I had enough shooting to last me a lifetime."

Peter glanced between them, then looked at Ray. Ray gave a little shrug.

"You ever fire a gun?" Shellabarger asked the cameraman.

"Just blanks," Ray said.

Shellabarger shook his head sadly. "I've not had to shoot a man in twenty years."

The next morning came an unexpected delay. More soldiers arrived in two more trucks, and a small, wiry, very dignified officer asked to inspect the animals on the *Libertad*. Peter was in town with OBie and Ray, trying to buy some wooden boards for laying between the cages, and when they returned, only a truck and four soldiers remained. Shellabarger was livid.

"I have never had to deal with such arrogant sons of bitches in my entire life," Shellabarger said. "They're forcing us to keep the animals on the ship another day while they get word back from Caracas. They ignored our permits and paperwork."

The day passed slowly, and by late afternoon, still without word from the officer in charge, Shellabarger was fit to be tied. He stormed back and forth on the deck. Ippolito watched him stoically, arms folded, nodding now and then whether or not the trainer said anything.

The presence of the soldiers seemed to have aroused dark and unpleasant memories in Anthony. He sat in their cabin on his bunk, arms wrapped around one drawn-up knee, smoking a cigarette he had borrowed from Shellabarger. The air in the cabin was hot and close and the smoke did not make things any better. Anthony rarely smoked. "If we get stopped here and they send us back, it's all over," he said. "We'll lose everything." He looked at Peter, face drawn, white lines around his lips. "Your ma will have me pegged exactly right."

"We'll be fine," Peter said.

Anthony smirked. For a moment, his face seemed to show that he had forgotten they were father and son, with any special bond; Peter was just another guy in the cabin. "That sounds so damn optimistic," Anthony said bitterly. "How in hell do you know?"

Peter was taken aback. "I'm just hoping," he said.

Anthony took a deep drag on his cigarette. "Hope away."

Peter went topside, angry and confused. No word had come by the time dark fell, and Anthony came thumping up a ship's ladder to the port wing of the bridge, where Peter leaned on the rail, breathing the cooling air off the river. "Vince and I are going into town. Ray and OBie are cleaning their cameras. You want to come?"

Peter looked at his father's tense features and wondered if he would ever know this man. "Sure," he said. In truth, Peter was bored out of his head.

"We're going to get drunk," Anthony said as they joined the trainer on the dock. "You can have one or two beers, but I'll rely on you to guide us back to the ship if we're completely blotto."

Peter remembered the trainer throwing the bottle overboard on the *Libertad*. He also remembered Shellabarger taking another bottle from Keller (according to OBie) and going to his room to drink it alone. Alcohol was a puzzle. "All right," he said.

"Have you ever been drunk?" Shellabarger asked Peter.

"No," Peter said.

"Good," Shellabarger said. "Don't start. It's a bad habit, but we sorely need to blow off steam."

"All right," Peter said in what he hoped was a worldly tone, and followed them into town.

A light drizzle fogged the air and softened the few red and white lights from cantina windows on the muddy main street. Anthony and the trainer strolled from one run-down bar to another, looking for the perfect combination of qualities necessary to a "one hundred percent rivertown dive."

Peter tried not to stare at the rough, ragged men who sat at worn wooden and metal tables, bleary exhaustion in their eyes and dull determination in the set of their faces. They cradled their glasses in callused thick-fingered hands, their nails black with dirt, dirt up to their elbows and caked around their rolled up sleeves. In most of the bars, one or two tired-looking women in lacy black dresses sat with mannish postures on stools or near tables, soft eyes turning from man to man like moths searching for a flame.

The rain drummed heavily and they settled on a cantina near the old arena. It resembled all the others except for flyspecked pictures of matadors and horned dinosaurs that covered one wall. Anthony and Shellabarger ordered whiskey and Peter took a glass of watery beer and they sat at a small wooden table, crowded together in the damp air, surrounded by the odors of rank cigars and sweet whiskey, mildew and unwashed men.

The first few drinks, Anthony and Shellabarger said little. On the third round, Anthony asked Shellabarger if he had ever served in the U.S. Army.

"Never," Shellabarger said. "Too young for the first war, too old for the second."

"Orders and uniforms," Anthony said. His father was not good at holding his liquor, Peter knew; if he did not get fractious, he became sleepy. So far, his eyes burned intensely. "You feel like a part of something. Very secure. Then somebody above you screws up and friends die. It's all a sham. Everybody's in it for themselves. You do your best to get out alive."

Shellabarger drained his glass. They called for a bottle. It was not cheap.

"Don't flash your money," the trainer warned Anthony. "We don't need trouble."

"Right," Anthony said thickly, and studiously concealed the few bills in his thin wallet.

"I like working with animals," Shellabarger said. "You always know where you stand. Like 'em or don't, you can never trust 'em. Black jaguars are the meanest things on Earth. Worse than old Dagger. I trained them for a few years before I signed on with Lotto." He gave Peter a slow, confidential wink. "Damnedest thing, a dinosaur eye. Older and better than ours. Cats can't see in color. Lots of mammals gave up color for black and white back when we were all skulking around in the bushes at night. Dinosaurs see very well in color. Never needed to give it up. Birds, too. Masters of day and night." He raised his hand off the table a few inches. "Our great-great-umpty-ump-great-grand-daddies were little shrew things no bigger than possums. The dinosaurs hunted us down and munched us." He tapped his white-haired temple. "Back in our little shrew brains, we dream about scampering through the brush, hiding in holes or in trees, waiting for the sharp-eyed eaters to grab us. Seeing dinos makes us want to run and hide."

"Whole life you've been with dinosaurs," Anthony said. "Better than people."

"Sometimes," Shellabarger agreed. "But people . . ." He leaned over the table. "People don't try to bite you in half." He nodded decisively and leaned back.

"Sometimes they do," Anthony said.

"With guns?"

"With divorce," Anthony said, and Shellabarger laughed.

"I've been married twice," the trainer said. "Circus women both times. Both jealous of my animals."

"I was a real problem for Peter's mother after the war," Anthony said.

For a moment, the beer had made Peter feel pleasantly in tune with his father and the trainer, but mention of his mother brought on a cold clarity. "Father," Peter said, rolling his eyes.

"It's the truth," Anthony said, working on his fifth drink. "I wanted to be a writer and a photographer. Peter's mother didn't approve. We married young and Peter came along. I trained to be a geologist and make lots of money working for the oil companies. Security. She gave me a lot, so I gave up my dreams. But after the war . . . seeing men die. Really rubs it in. You got to do it before you're dirt."

Peter stared down at the table.

"When I came home, I took up photography again," Anthony concluded. "Money became a problem."

Shellabarger belched into his fist and apologized.

"We're disgusting," Anthony said. "Let's go before we embarrass ourselves. But first—let's hear your story."

"My story," Shellabarger said, spreading his hands on the table.

"Okay, let's hear your story," Anthony repeated.

"Nah," Shellabarger said. He glared at the dinosaurs and matadors lined up on the wall. "Maybe I'll save it for a book."

Peter walked between Shellabarger and his father on the way back to the ship. They paused before the staring half circle of centrosaur skulls in front of the arena. Shellabarger swayed as he contemplated their eyeless sockets.

"That's my story," he said quietly, pointing at the skulls.

Anthony bit his lower lip and shook his head. "Damned shame," he said.

"Yeah," Shellabarger said. "I hope we can make up for it."

On the road to the dock, Shellabarger and Anthony found a large horned beetle crawling through oil-smirched grass. They got down on their hands and knees to see it up close. Peter stood with his hands in his pockets, looking nervously around in the dark. They could all be robbed and he did not think Anthony and the trainer were in any shape to defend themselves.

"How does he move all those legs?" Anthony asked Shellabarger.

"Concentration," Shellabarger said. "All the time. It's all a bug can do. That's why they're not very smart."

"You ever train a bug?" Anthony asked.

"Nope," Shellabarger said.

"Start with this one."

"I don't have anything he wants," Shellabarger said.

"Train him with kindness."

"All right. He does a trick, I won't step on him. He'll learn fast."

Anthony cackled and got to his feet.

"We're embarrassing the boy," he whispered to Shellabarger.

"He understands," Shellabarger said. Both men put their arms around Peter's shoulders and leaned on him. His knees almost buckled under the weight. "Don't you?"

"Sure," Peter said, helping them up the gangway to the ship.

From the bridge, a sailor shouted something in hoarse Portuguese. Anthony looked up, squinting at the bright lights shining on the forecastle. More men lined the decks, pointing toward town. Peter turned and saw a large fire burning to the south, thick billows of smoke with orange bellies rising and twisting toward the dark overcast.

"It's the boatyard," OBie shouted on the main deck. "That's our boats!"

Anthony shook his head and made a growling noise, trying to shake off the effects of the booze. Shellabarger turned without hesitation and lurched down the gangway, but slumped at the end as he stumbled. Hanging from the rail, he righted himself. Peter and Anthony joined him on the dock, and Ray, OBie, Keller, and Shawmut pounded down the gangway after them.

The boatyard was in chaos. Men from all around the town hauled hoses from old trucks and attached them to water pumps on the backs of other old trucks. A single dilapidated red fire engine, its paint peeling and faded by the tropical sun, stood by the gate to the boatyard, surrounded by hapless firemen who were doing nothing to help.

Peter and Ray helped pull hoses from the pumping trucks near the river to the fire. Four of the big sheds were ablaze and the roofs had collapsed. The plump boatyard owner, Jiménez, stood in a puddle of water from the leaking hoses, mopping his forehead with a broad, twisted handkerchief, hands wringing the cloth into tighter twists and knots. He shouted at the volunteers in Spanish, then saw Shellabarger walking along the perimeter of the fire and ran to walk beside him. Shellabarger stared at the blazing outlines of boats under the collapsed roofs, eyes wide with drunken shock and disbelief.

"The boats, *señor!*" Jiménez called.

"How many are in there?" Shellabarger demanded.

"I saw some men in dark clothes, *señor.* Four or five men with cans of petrol. My guards, I do not know where they went—I was about to go to my house to sleep—"

"Are those all our boats?" Shellabarger shouted.

Jiménez flung his hands in the air. "You are not to be worried, *señor!* Your boats, I put them in the river yesterday. They are a kilometer from here, *señor!* You are very lucky. These are boats belonging to Creole Oil. I hauled them up for repair this afternoon."

Shellabarger's legs folded until he squatted on the dirt, a slow, almost studied collapse. "My God," he said softly. Anthony stood beside him, hand on Peter's arm, his grip tight. Then Shellabarger rose and they set to work again.

The fire burned bright even in the drizzle. All the sheds had collapsed and the hoses were leaking more water than they shot from their nozzles, arcs of fine mist soaking Anthony and Peter and Ray as they tried to help maneuver them. The spray from the hose nozzles was as ineffectual against the blazing sheds as the sputtering drizzle.

After an hour, they all gathered by the gate. Jiménez paced and gestured helplessly around them. The boatyard owner seemed alternately half crazy with grief and jubilant. "Your boats, they were brand new, my prizes, with beautiful engines," he said to OBie and Shellabarger. "These are old boats. But what will I tell the oilmen? Who would want to burn boats? Where will my men work now? My father owned this yard. I have inherited it from him! Who will work for me now?"

The crew crept back to the *Libertad* as dawn broke in the east. Anthony and Shellabarger still had a hard time walking straight.

Peter could tell the trainer was furious with himself. With each lurch and stumble, Shellabarger barked, "Goddamn me. Never again. I swear, never again."

Anthony was equally but quietly contrite.

"We were lucky this time," he muttered to Peter. "But what about tomorrow?"

The next morning, two officers in crisp khakis with broad black belts and shiny black helmets came to the *Libertad* and conferred with an exhausted, hungover Shellabarger and crisp, proper Captain Ippolito. The permits had checked out in Caracas, they said; the expedition had permission to proceed upriver to El Grande.

Shellabarger huddled with Anthony, OBie, and Ray in his cabin. His face was red and puffy and his eyes seemed ready to start out of their sockets. "Jiménez says he thinks some soldiers burned his sheds," the trainer said. "The local troops don't want the Indians in an uproar about El Grande, and they really don't care what Caracas thinks." He lifted one corner of his mouth in a half smirk and shook his head. "We need to make a decision now. Creole Oil takes care of both sides here, the Army and the Betancourt government, so nobody would want to burn *their* boats. That was a bad mistake. But somebody is willing to do some pretty desperate things to stop us. Do we give up and go back, or do we go on?"

"Will Ippolito take us back?" OBie asked.

"I haven't asked. I don't know if this should make up our minds one way or the other, but . . . if we go back, the animals will die. They need to get out of the ship."

OBie glanced apprehensively at Ray and Anthony. Clearly, for him, physical danger was not the most important factor here. Peter saw that OBie, too, regarded this expedition as his last chance. "Then we have to go on," OBie said.

"No other way," Ray agreed softly.

Anthony stared down at the floor, then lifted his gaze to meet Peter's.

"We have to go on," Peter agreed. He could not bear the thought of all the animals ending up like Sheila. Besides, the fire in the boatyard had been kind of exciting—terrifying and beautiful all at once. And other than a few blisters on his hands from the rough hoses, he had come out of it unhurt.

"We all agree, then," Shellabarger said, more cheerful.

"We agree," Anthony said, but his eyes were full of doubts.

The tension seemed to break. Ray closed his eyes and took a deep breath.

"I'd hate to have lost those boats," OBie said, grinning broadly all around. "Jack Ford would have had a fit. And Monte would have never let me hear the end of it!"

They spent their last few hours on the ship. Anthony laid out their clothes and taught Peter how to make up a backpack. He rubbed his temples and scowled.

"It is the age of alcohol, Peter. Red eyes and puffy red noses and hangovers. Being drunk is just about the only time a man can convince himself he's not a fool. Stands to reason that's when he's the biggest fool of all. We were lucky. Very, very lucky."

"Could you have done anything more?" Peter asked. He hated to see his father being so hard on himself.

"My lad," Anthony said somberly, "we were sitting ducks. Drunk ducks. No excuses. No more drinking."

Peter tied his bedroll and looked around the cabin. "How dangerous is it going to get?"

Anthony finished stuffing his pack and flopped on the lower bunk. He rubbed his temples and frowned. "I didn't think it would be this dangerous when I brought you. You know what kind of danger I'm talking about?"

"Not dinosaurs."

"Right."

"Will they try to kill us?"

Anthony snorted and wiped his nose with a handkerchief. "It could be a lot rougher on the river and in the jungle than I thought, long before we get to El Grande."

Peter thought this over. "I don't want to go back," he said.

Anthony chewed his lower lip and fingered his camera where it lay on the blanket. "A father is responsible for keeping his child healthy."

"I'm not a child."

Anthony gave a short laugh. "I don't want to put you in any danger."

"But you brought me here and you knew there would be *some* danger." Peter's level of irritation was rising rapidly. This seemed pointless to him. He had made *his* decision.

"I wanted to balance out your experience. Until now, you were never outside the United States. You need to see what the world is all about."

"The world is dangerous," Peter said. "Are you going to send me back?" He thrust out his chin and crossed his arms.

Anthony thumped his fist on the bed. He sat up and rubbed his hands on his knees. Peter thought, *Five nervous gestures in just a couple of minutes.*

"Do you wish you hadn't brought me?" Peter asked, his voice sharp.

"Yes," Anthony said. "But . . ."

"I haven't done anything stupid or wrong," Peter said in a rush. "I learned how to tend the dinosaurs . . . the animals. Vince—Mr. Shellabarger—thinks I'm doing well. I could learn to shoot—"

Anthony gave him a stern look. "I don't want you to ever have to learn to shoot people."

"I meant animals, dangerous . . . things. Animals," Peter said. The words started to pour out of him; he was frustrated and afraid—afraid of going, but horrified at the thought of being forbidden to go, of being sent back home. "I know you want me not to have to go through what you did, in the war. But I need to grow up sometime, and that means I have to face things as they are."

Anthony regarded him through narrowed eyes. Why was it he always felt that Anthony was weighing him, judging him? Peter resented this, and stared right back at him.

"I want to stay with you and go to El Grande."

"Can you possibly conceive of how cruel human beings can be?" Anthony asked.

Peter sucked in his breath before answering, to give himself an instant to think. "I probably can't," he said.

"I can. Shellabarger can. We've both had to face bad people, or people stuck in bad situations. What I'm saying, Peter, is that I'm not sure I want you to have to grow up that much, that fast."

"Huh?"

"Never mind," Anthony said. "I won't send you back. Not yet. But I reserve the right to do so, if and when I judge . . . that things are getting too dicey. Okay?"

Peter did not answer.

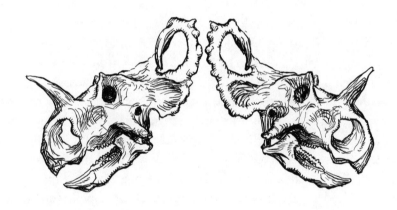

Chapter Nine

The dinosaurs were unloaded by noon. It was an operation of some delicacy—lifting each cage from the hold, swinging it out over the starboard side of the *Libertad,* away from the dock, and then lowering it onto one of the five wooden river barges.

Shellabarger supervised the unloading, trying to be everywhere at once. Where the cages did not cover the decks of the barges, steel drums filled with diesel fuel, food, and water for the humans and the animals were arranged in rows, tied down with thick jute ropes. The motion picture cameras and film cans were loaded on the last barge, packed in great black trunks that OBie hoped were waterproof. Ray used the portable camera to record their departure.

The sun chose this day to beam down in full tropical force and the heat was intense. Everybody was soaked in sweat by ten, and by one o'clock, as the barge engines started, Peter could hardly think straight. The sun seemed to actively hate him; its brightness and heat lay on his head like a hot brick.

Peter felt as if everything he drank went directly from his stomach to his sweat glands. Rivers of sweat rolled off him. The town of Puerto Ordaz drew its water pretty nearly untreated from the Caroní. Anthony had brought along water purification tablets. He thought they might be able to drink the water safely at El

Grande, but certainly not where they were now. He dropped a tablet into each of their canteens.

Anthony took quick shots from the boat and the dock, then rode a motorboat with Peter out to the third barge, which carried Sammy and the avisaurs. Sammy was none too happy with this new floating platform, and let out mournful groans and grunts as the barge rocked in the river.

The best pilots on the river, Jiménez had told them, were Indians. Each barge had an Indian pilot hired by Jiménez. They sat on padded stools within small cabins at the rear of the barges. The pilot of the third boat, a short, skinny fellow only a few years older than Peter, introduced himself as Billie. He spoke English very well.

Shellabarger finished his inspection, accompanying Jiménez on his own motorboat, leaping up on each barge, examining the tie-downs and the cage chocks, peeking under the tarps to see how his beasts were doing. He shouted as he passed the third barge, "They know they're going home. They remember!"

OBie, Ray, and the roustabouts and camera crew took their own boat rides from the dock and clambered onto the barges. Ray and OBie joined Anthony and Peter on the third barge.

They began the journey to the station at San Pedro de las Bocas at two o'clock, late, but Shellabarger had expected to have to tie up at night several times during the upriver journey. The diesel motors were powerful, but they couldn't push the barges faster than ten miles an hour, and the river flowed at three miles an hour.

Anthony and Peter stood on the bow as the barges moved toward the middle of the river and the deeper water.

"No more iceboxes," Anthony said to Peter. "No more fresh food, unless we find fruit or fish on the way."

"Not much chance of that until we get up near El Grande," OBie said, making his way carefully around Sammy's big cage, "and even then, I don't think Shellabarger will take time for us to hunt for bananas. Food isn't that easy to find in these jungles."

"Tell us what it's like," Peter said.

OBie stared philosophically at the barges forming a long line up the river, their engines chugging in unison, laying intertwined trails of black diesel exhaust above the water. The air was still and the exhaust hung behind them for minutes before dissipating.

"It's been years," he said. "I haven't been there since we shot jungle footage for *Kong.* That was after Gómez shut down the tepuis, and we didn't get to El Grande that time. But all the way up to the canyon and the falls, it's green and beautiful. There are bugs everywhere—butterflies, midges, no-see-ums, flies, biting bugs, and crawling bugs. It rains a lot, and I don't think it'll get any hotter than this, but on El Grande . . . "

He shook himself. "I won't spoil it by telling you ahead of time," he said. "Just believe me, you'll never forget it."

Behind them, half a mile downriver, Captain Ippolito blew the whistle on the *Libertad.* Peter watched the ship work itself into the deep channel and head back for the open sea.

Billie responded by blatting their barge's horn. The other barges followed suit, the Indian pilots grinning at one another.

Peter sat in the shade of Sammy's cage, gaze fixed on the green eastern shore of the Caroní. He felt as if he had been hypnotized. Only a month ago, he had been in New York, wondering what he would be doing this summer . . .

Shellabarger yelled at them from the first boat. "Anthony! OBie! We're going to put in for the night about a mile ahead." He waved the map Jiménez had given him. "There's a little cove where we can tie up our boats out of the current. I'll want a watch set up . . . Jiménez says there are bandits even this far south, trying to steal from the diamond miners."

The cove nestled under an overhang of huge trees, just barely big enough to hold all five barges. A line of creosoted wooden piles from an old dock served to tie up the barges. Anthony and Peter and Ray jumped from the third barge to the shore and walked a few yards into the jungle, but much beyond that it was impenetrable. Peter kept looking for the deadly *veintecuatros,* the twenty-four-hour ants, but saw none. He did see enough mosquitoes and flies to keep him occupied swatting and brushing at his clothes.

"How about a little yellow fever?" Ray asked testily, turning over his palm to reveal a mosquito he had just squashed. A red smear on his skin showed it had already drawn blood.

"Nature's little creatures of the air feed all the fish," Anthony said with mock piety, and crossed himself, then swatted at a cloud of gnats. "And we'll be feeding them."

"Is it true, male mosquitoes don't bite?" OBie asked from the barge as he stretched out a plank for them to climb back aboard.

"I think so," Peter said.

"The harmless male," OBie said regretfully. "He doesn't know all the finer arts."

Peter watched a small fly land on his hand. It did not look like a mosquito so he did not smash it. Then a needle-stab of pain shot up his wrist. He swatted at the fly but missed, and a small drop of blood welled from his pierced skin.

"The little black flies, they are hell," Billie said, putting on a worn jacket. "They are called *jejenes*." He pulled a netted cap down over his face and the back of his neck, tucking the net into his collar. Peter envied him; but at least they had havelocks hanging behind their hats to keep sun and insects off their necks, and mosquito nets for when they slept.

They set up a small steel cookstove on the second barge. The pilots insisted the gringos cook their meals first, and stood by their cabins, each of them wearing their netted caps.

Keller served as cook. "I used to cook in the Navy," he said. "My food never killed anybody, so I'm qualified."

Gathering around the stove, swatting at *jejenes,* they ate cups of soup and canned beef. The venator let out a roar just after nightfall, scaring dark fogs of birds out of the jungle all around. They rose with pumping twitters and flapping wings into the twilight and swung about in a cloud to another, less disturbing part of the river.

On the first barge, Shellabarger fed the big predator one of the five sides of beef they had left. "In a day or two, the raw meat's going to go bad," the trainer said, watching Keller and Kasem slip the beef into the venator's cage. Under the tarp, the dinosaur swung about, making the boat pitch and roll in the water. Chewing, crunching, and sucking sounds followed, and Shellabarger backed away, hands on hips. "Dagger won't mind," Keller added. "He's always liked it a little gamy."

Dark came on quickly. Shellabarger suggested they turn in early, for they would head out on the river again at dawn. The five pilots stood by the cookstoves, waiting for their beans to cook, and Billie read Spanish- and Portuguese-language newspapers to the others.

Anthony and Peter rigged their sleeping rolls and mosquito nets. Peter was exhausted. He crawled into the sleeping bag and gazed up through the netting at the dark clouds and brilliance of stars. The last things he heard were Billie's voice, saying prayers in Spanish, and Shellabarger murmuring softly to the struthios.

In the morning, Peter was covered with welts from the *jejenes*. Anthony's skin seemed tougher and his welts did not show as much, but he still itched and swore under his breath.

"Adventure," OBie said, "is nine tenths misery and one tenth disaster."

Ray suffered as badly as Peter. "I feel a little woozy," he said.

"Yellow fever," Peter suggested.

"You're a pal," Ray said, grimacing.

"Or malaria," OBie added, helping untie the barge from the piling.

"Malaria does not come on so soon," Billie said from the cabin. He smiled, showing even yellow teeth, and started the engine on number three.

Peter shared binoculars with his father and studied the forest. The forest took on more meaningful detail the longer Peter observed it. At first, it had seemed a mass of rolling green foliage and brown vines and creepers, dotted at random by white, yellow, and red flowers. The flies had kept him from paying much atten- tion to individual plants and trees near the shore, but here, in the middle of the river, the flies were less bothersome. Now he made out trees strangled by cages of vines, trees that seemed to thrive at different altitudes and brightnesses of sunlight within the canopy. In places the river had changed course recently and undercut the banks, revealing a cutaway of the forest interior, gloomy and bare beneath an almost opaque lid of thick foliage.

OBie was chatting with Billie, and Ray sat sketching on the bow. Sammy had fallen quiet after the boats set out. When Peter lifted the tarp to let air flow through the cage, the big centrosaur, hunkered on his belly with legs half underneath, blinked at him with translucent membranes, but did not lift his head. "Soon, fella," Peter whispered.

Occasional *curiaras*—dugout canoes—slid past the barges, heading downriver, piloted by scrawny brown men with impassive faces half hidden by broad floppy hats. Piles of dirt filled the middle of the dugouts, and in the rear, one or two men sat holding big rifles, hats tilted back. They glared fiercely at anyone who dared to notice.

"Diamonds," Billie said from behind the wheel. "One or two diamonds a day, little ones, for industry. Not for ladies' rings. They are slim pickings around here. But everybody is hopeful . . . diamonds, or maybe gold."

"They look pretty wild," Ray said.

"And hungry," OBie added. "They might be interested in our food."

The jungle gave way to a broad stretch of grassland and Anthony took out his camera, giving Peter a poke in the ribs. Peter, who had been dozing, lifted his head. "Huh?"

Ray Harryhausen

Anthony pointed. "Thar she blows," he said.

The northwestern escarpment of El Grande rose in the distance, an immense black mass with a projecting silhouette like the prow of an ancient galleon. Gray and white billows capped the prow, and the rest of the massive tepui fell back in the shadows of rank after rank of thick dark clouds, filling the horizon. The sun gleaming against the brilliant green and yellow grassland and the gloom of El Grande beyond made a striking contrast—cheer and tropical splendor against mystery and danger.

"Eighty-five miles from end to end," OBie said reverently. "Eight thousand feet high at this end, the highest point. With six big lakes and who knows how many little lakes and swamps."

"Fabulous," Ray said. He grinned at OBie and Peter. The thrill was returning—a real sense of adventure that had been damped by the soldiers and the fire. "Lord, it's *huge*."

"Wait'll we get closer." OBie stuck his thumbs in his pockets like a proud papa and winked at Peter. "Takes me back to when I was young."

"It looks like a monster all by itself," Anthony said. Peter looked at him to see what he was thinking, whether he was seriously considering sending Peter back now.

"The ship's gone, Dad," Peter said softly, squinting at his father.

"There's an airstrip up ahead," Anthony said, but with a slight smile. He put his hand on Peter's shoulder and squeezed. "Impressed?"

Peter nodded and turned the binoculars on El Grande. He could see a long, thin waterfall descending in a bright silver thread from a shelf of clouds hiding the upper third of the galleon's prow. "Will you look at that!" he said, and handed the glasses to Anthony.

Anthony peered through them. "It's falling from about five thousand feet," he said. "Straight down."

"That's Raleigh Falls," OBie said. "The folks here call it Bolívar. There's a higher one in Challenger Canyon. Jimmie Angel saw that one first. He called it Jorge Washington Falls. He picked a smaller one on Auyan Tepui to name after himself."

Peter looked at the five boats with their precariously balanced cages. Despite the *jejenes* and the mosquitoes, he was really enjoying himself. He doubted that any other *Norteamericano* boy had seen what he was seeing—at least not since the 1920s.

"Ten kilometers to San Pedro de las Bocas," Billie said. Tall trees and jungle rose on the left bank again, blocking much of their view of El Grande. More of the big flame-winged water birds clustered in shallows on the southern bank, and the river took a gradual turn to the northeast, toward the highlands. Peter went to the cabin.

"Shouldn't there be falls or rapids or something?" he asked Billie.

Billie nodded. "Farther up. Little ones we will climb, but the big ones, they are beyond San Pedro. Big rapids, many falls."

"Have you been up here a lot?" Peter asked. He felt like talking and was afraid Ray and OBie would get tired of him if he chattered.

"Not a lot," Billie said. "Only by canoe above San Pedro. A few miles up the rapids—then the flies and the mosquitoes, they are too much. You will be glad to take a train."

"Yeah," Peter said. "Do you know anybody who went to El Grande?"

"Yes," Billie said, his smile suddenly vanishing. "My father. He was full-blooded Makritare. We have been going up there for thousands of years. We climb up the old trail on Pico Poco, and sling a rope, and climb across . . ." Billie raised his arms and made hand-over-hand motions, then got a distant look in his eye. "Especially if we want to be chief, or to have many beautiful wives and become great warriors."

Peter nodded.

"My father went there two months before I was born. He did not come back."

"Oh," Peter said. "I'm sorry."

Billie shrugged. "I am proud of him."

Peter wondered how much Billie had really wanted to go, if he had been stopped by just the flies. *Maybe I just don't know how bad the flies can get,* Peter thought. Then he remembered that the Army had restricted access to the tepui, especially to Indians.

Billie saw the look in Peter's eyes and turned away to examine the river, jaws clenched. "In my father's day, there were no prospectors and diamond hunters and not so many thieves on the river. He had to worry about other tribes—the Arecuna, perhaps, or the Camaracotas. But they did not have guns. The soldiers have guns."

They anchored in a stretch of still water and fed the animals as darkness approached. They had seen more dugouts, but so far, no one had offered any resistance, or even harsh words, to the strange barges moving steadily upriver. Billie thought that by now, nearly everybody on the river knew about the dinosaurs. OBie asked Billie to join their group around the cookstove. "If you don't mind beans," he said.

They were about to eat when the venator decided once again to protest. He did not move enough to rock the barge on which his cage rested, but he let out a peevish, ear-splitting shriek nevertheless.

Howler monkeys in the jungle began a ragged chorus of angry whoops.

"He is the Challenger," Billie said.

OBie, Ray, and Anthony traded looks and OBie stirred the pot, then ladled up black beans for each. "You mean like the professor," he said.

"No." Billie gave them a quizzical look. "The one who challenges. He asks questions only ghosts can answer."

Ray lifted his eyebrows and grinned. "True enough," he said.

Billie stared across the dark waters to the other boats and their cages. "Perhaps a Challenger like him ate my father," he said, as if this were a matter of merely casual discussion.

"He damn near ate Shellabarger, before he was captured," OBie said. "He was just a youngster then. Less than eight feet high. In his gangly youth."

"I am proud to be near them," Billie said. "More Indians will come to see them."

Quietly, they ate their beans.

Chapter Ten

San Pedro de las Bocas was a bigger town than Peter had expected. With many whitewashed stone and brick buildings, an imposing railway station made of local granite and sandstone, and a wharf with a big if somewhat rusted steel crane, it had been built ten years before to accommodate the miners and oil explorers on the north side of the river. OBie, Keller, and Shellabarger inspected the crane, which had been built to lift heavy mining equipment from boats on the river and transfer them to the railway cars. Within an hour of their arrival, the cages were lifted from the barges and loaded on a train with twelve flatbed cars. By three o'clock, the barges themselves were hoisted from the river. Anthony and Ray recorded the transfer, which went smoothly enough.

The stationmaster, a tall, lean man with leathery skin and deepset eyes, wore an ancient ragged leather hat and a threadbare white pinstripe suit. He told them that the advance crew had arrived three weeks before with five trucks. He spoke very good English. His family, he said, was descended from English settlers in British Guiana.

"I think your man, who is supposed to greet you, he is in town now drinking. He will be here soon. I come to welcome you personally." He smiled at all this activity—and all the money he was doubtless being paid. "The oil, it is slow up here now, only a trickle. The engineers say El Grande is too heavy, it squeezes everything south."

"They only left one man?" Shellabarger asked.

"They needed every able-bodied fellow at the railhead. So they told me . . . " He smiled slyly, then stared at the cages in concern.

The animals were putting up a great fuss. Sammy in particular seemed out of sorts and gave out bugle-like bellows every few minutes, startling the railroad workers. They laughed and shook their heads, vowing not to be frightened again, but each time, Sammy made them jump.

"It'll be a six-hour ride or more, but we won't leave today," OBie said, wiping sweat from his reddened forehead.

By late afternoon, the barges were lashed down, one to each car. As OBie had suspected, the train's engineer refused to set out with dusk so close, and so they pitched their tents beside the train. Shellabarger did not want them to go into town. He did not trust the prospectors and diamond miners and all their associated hangers-on to leave the train alone. "We'll need to stand watch all night," he said wearily.

Wetherford, the representative of the advance party, showed up just before nightfall: a short young Englishman in slacks and a baggy white shirt stained with food and jungle green. He seemed a little under the weather.

"The beer here is terrible" was the first thing he said to Shellabarger, before they shook hands. "Made from tree sap, of all the bloody things. Anteater piss, I call it. James Wetherford." He extended his hand and Shellabarger gave it a perfunctory shake.

The trainer looked him over angrily. "You're the only one here?" he asked.

"Yes. I've been down with some fever." He leaned to one side to see around Shellabarger. "Also, I got in an argument with some soldiers, with a bloody colonel no less, and the Mendez woman, *Doña* Catalina, decided it would be better for me to stay here to meet you. They're here representing Caracas—Betancourt and Gallegos. I see the cars are loaded. Everything's ready to go?"

"You're drunk. You've been drunk for days," Shellabarger said. "Who's paying you?"

"Mr. Schoedsack. Why?"

"Because if Lotto Gluck were paying you, I'd fire you right here and now."

"Well," Wetherford said owlishly. "I'm spared that, aren't I?"

Peter kept the irony of this remonstration to himself.

OBie and Ray took advantage of the golden light of late afternoon, shooting views of the train and the town. They also filmed Shellabarger inspecting the cars. He had done this job to his satisfaction earlier, but OBie asked him to do it again. The trainer's demeanor before the whirring camera was a little wooden.

"Vince, for a man who's been in showbiz so long, you're stiff as a board," OBie said.

Shellabarger shrugged. "I'm not going to be in showbiz much longer."

Wetherford stood to one side, a crooked smile on his face. "If anybody needs me," he said, "I'm right here."

Peter's main memory of that night was that ants were everywhere. Small red ants and large black ants crawled in lines along the dirt and up the walls of the buildings. They crawled into his sleeping bag, where he found them waggling their antennae and lifting their fierce mandibles. Billie reassured him that these were just town ants, not *veintecuatros,* but they still nipped him pretty good.

He used this opportunity to write in his journal, something he had been neglecting. He recorded the important events of the day, but not his thoughts about men and alcohol. He did not think that *National Geographic* would be very interested.

At four in the morning, Anthony roused him for his share of the watch and they got up in the warm stillness beneath an unblinking haze of stars. Ray had preceded them and he showed them how to use rush brooms to brush ant trails away from the tracks and the train cars. "Wouldn't want Dagger to get swarmed, would we?" Ray asked with a big yawn.

With first light, Shellabarger joined Anthony and Peter and the others awoke to the smell of coffee brewed in a big steel jug by the stationmaster. The roustabouts and film crew gathered around. Billie and the four other pilots joined them with seven large, fresh catfish, which were soon gutted and fried for breakfast. The strong black coffee, syrupy with sugar, made Peter buzz with happy anxiousness to get going, to get to work, and the catfish, served with cassava bread broken from large flat wheels, tasted better than any breakfast he remembered eating in years.

They boarded the train and everybody swung their hats and cheered as they pulled out of the station of San Pedro de las Bocas. The engineer tugged a raucous squeal from the engine's steam whistle. The animals in their tied-down cages replied with a chorus of bellows and screams and the monkeys in the jungle howled in turn. It sounded energetic and chaotic and cheerful. The strong coffee made everything seem cheery to Peter.

They all sat on old wooden seats in one dusty passenger car, jostled back and forth on the irregular tracks. At times the train seemed to crawl, especially around curves; OBie said you never knew when a tree might have gone down and blocked the tracks. He leaned back over his seat to where the roustabouts were playing poker and said, "You boys good with axes?"

Kasem hid his hand, rolled his eyes, and jerked his thumb at Shellabarger. "He's the boss man. If you want us to build a bridge, tell him, and he'll tell us."

Shawmut and Osborne laughed. "We'll do the bridge building," said Shawmut. "You guys just cut the logs."

The jungle presented an unbroken wall on either side of the tracks, comprised of all manner of palms, some standing on tall stilts rooted in the floor, and kapok trees, rising above the forest with thick round green crowns. Giant ferns pushed out fronds to brush the windows of the passenger car. Peter saw many other trees he could not identify, and Anthony, looking quickly through a guidebook, shook his head and grinned. "The leaf shapes change depending on whether a tree is old or young . . . We need a botanist!"

He did manage to identify a huge saman tree, spreading over its section of forest like a giant's umbrella.

"Grandfather of the forest," OBie said. "Glad to see vigor in old age. There's hope for us fogies yet."

The train's passage disturbed hordes of squirrel monkeys, which rushed off through the canopy, and Peter saw several green parrots and one macaw, bright red with blue markings.

Shellabarger sat slumped in his seat, snoring after his vigil during the night. He had kept watch the longest. Behind him, face pale in the green light from the jungle, Wetherford stared out the windows at nothing in particular, lips puckered as if about to whistle.

The train began its long climb. With frequent tenor blasts on the steam whistle, it dragged its line of cars along the rock edge of the Caroní, past a broad, foaming set of falls. Mist rose in clouds and drifted across the tracks and forest, wetting the glass and swirling in through the open windows.

Three hours into the journey, the train crossed a log trestle bridge over a tributary feeding into the Caroní. The tributary tumbled white and slick green and black over rocks two hundred feet below the laboring train. There would be many more such rushing tributaries and trestle bridges the next few miles.

Shellabarger came awake and went to the rear to look out over the flatcars. When he returned, he lit up a cigar he had bought in Puerto Ordaz. The smoke swirling through the car smelled worse than old tires burning, but Peter did not dare complain.

"Lots of plants and small animals here come from the tepuis, particularly from El Grande," Shellabarger said. "Bugs, flowers, orchids—hardwoods—nuts no white man's ever tasted. Worth a hell of a lot more than gold. Someday, somebody's going to see the value."

"A bit hypocritical for a *circus* man, don't you think?" Wetherford inquired, leaning forward to rest his elbows on the back of the next seat. He surveyed Shellabarger coolly.

"Guilty as charged," Shellabarger said, unruffled. Wetherford seemed to rank somewhere behind the ants in his estimation, not worth being impolite to. The Englishman did not appear to be bothered by this.

"Yes, well, at least you're trying to make amends."

"So," Anthony said, "what is your line of work, Mr. Wetherford?"

"Guilty, myself, truly guilty," Wetherford said. "Until recently I worked as a secretary for Creole Oil. Mr. Shellabarger, have you a fag to spare?"

Shellabarger handed him a pack of cigarettes and he took two. "Blessings of the New World, tobacco," Wetherford said, lighting up. "Or better yet, revenge. And a match?"

They reached a leveling out of the landscape and the jungle thinned, giving way to broad expanses of grassland. Anthony and OBie pored over a map and agreed that they were now on a lava ledge that had risen up beneath El Grande and pushed it several hundred feet higher, "Hundreds of millions of years ago," Anthony said.

Wetherford leaned over the map with a cigarette dangling from his lips. He puffed several times and narrowed his eyes against the smoke, then plucked away the cigarette and said, "Recent thinking says it could have been over a billion years ago."

"You're a geologist?" Anthony asked.

"I listened to the oil men. When they left, I stayed, because . . . you see"—he waved the cigarette with self-conscious style—"they were ever so much smarter than me."

"The plateaus of El Grande are cut through with lava flows, like marbling in ice cream," Anthony said. "Some of it seeped out to form caps, and erosion has worked all the way around them, like big mushrooms."

"All true, and wonderful stuff," Wetherford said. "You worked for oil men, too, eh?"

Anthony smiled. "Guilty as charged."

Peter did not know whether to like the Englishman or not. He stared out the left side of the train at El Grande, now so huge a presence that it blocked the sky to the east. Ledges in the escarpment supported whole forests, rising in narrow terraces to the clouds.

Billie walked forward, staring out the windows at the scattering of trees along the relatively barren highlands. He sat down next to Peter. "Look outside," he said quietly, and waved at the window on the left side, then made a graceful flip of the hand toward the front of the train.

Peter looked but saw nothing.

"There," Billie said. Peter suddenly spotted a lone naked brown man just yards below the window, with a neatly cut bowl of black hair, standing in tall grass, carrying a gourd, a black bag, and a bow. The man watched the train pass, then dropped to his knees and vanished. Billie smiled at Peter. "More, soon," he said.

"I'll bet Monte and Coop are both at Uruyen," OBie said. Uruyen was the closest airstrip, about eight miles from the railhead. "I'll bet they've flown in to meet us. That would be grand."

They reached the railhead after six hours. Shellabarger paced for the last hour, sick with worry about the dinosaurs. "They've gone hours without water, much longer than I planned," he said. As soon as the train had stopped, they all disembarked from the passenger car. Shellabarger ordered the roustabouts to bring barrels of water up from the last car, which carried their supplies.

Peter held his hand above his eyes to block out the sun until Anthony slapped a floppy bush hat over his head. The railhead team—a crowd of at least twenty Indians and mestizos, dressed in white trousers and baggy white shirts—smiled and shook hands with the new arrivals. They gestured at the waiting trucks, and Billie and the four pilots, now drivers, inspected the big muddy vehicles with critical eyes, exchanging questions and comments.

Peter looked up and saw a large wooden crane newly erected by the side of the tracks. Besides the crane and three shacks roofed with palm leaves and one ramshackle building covered with corrugated steel, the railhead was a void butted against thick forest.

The only sour note was the appearance of a short, stocky Army officer and three of his men. Their uniforms were rumpled and their broad belts and black shoes scuffed and covered with specks of mud and mold. Two of the soldiers wore dusty, dented helmets. The third went bareheaded. The officer waved papers with their orders. They were to verify that the visitors were all legitimate, authorized by the government in Caracas. The Indian and mestizo workers seemed to make them nervous. Shellabarger told the officer politely enough that he could verify all he wanted, they could not stop now or the animals would suffer.

"Would you want the animals to die and everybody around the world to know it was you that made them die?" he asked the stocky officer coldly.

The man drew himself up, took a deep breath, and said, "*Señor,* I am a mild man, but the *colonel* is most irritable. He is on Pico Poco now. I please him, not history. Nevertheless, I will do my best to hurry."

The tarps were removed from the cages, and the animals got their first clear sight of El Grande. Blinking in the sun, they made quite an uproar. Dagger slapped his tail against the cage, making it rattle alarmingly. One by one, the roustabouts poured water from drums into their drinking troughs. The Indians gathered around, their faces filled with fear and reverence.

"The muse calls," Anthony said, lifting his camera. He smiled at Peter and ran off to take more pictures.

Peter wondered what he was supposed to do. Shellabarger hadn't called for him, and he did not want to be in the way. He decided to climb up on the flatbed car beside Sammy and keep him company.

Wetherford and Ray walked by, talking about the trees. "Hundreds of species of hardwoods," Wetherford said, "and figs and of course the lianas, the creepers . . . " The Englishman looked up, shading his eyes against the sun. His eyes met Peter's. "Take a walk down to the river?" he asked. Peter looked for OBie. The film crew was unloading the camera cases again and OBie was already heading down the trail.

"We're going to scout," Ray said.

"I'll stay here," Peter said. He felt the dinosaurs might need him—Shellabarger might call for him. Or he might see something else he could do.

"All right," Wetherford said. Ray tipped his hat and they followed OBie.

"Peter!" Shellabarger called. Peter answered and the trainer came up to the car, frowning and squinting at the jungle. "The animals can eat some of this stuff," he said. "Sammy can eat just about anything and survive. Fill his cage with creepers and leaves. Give him a small log if you find one. He won't eat what he can't tolerate. Fresh food will do the herbivores a lot of good."

"What about Dagger?" Peter asked.

"Last side of beef until El Grande," Shellabarger said. Keller and Kasem walked up beside him.

"Real ripe." The head roustabout pinched his nose. "Just the way he likes it."

"If you find any bugs, give 'em to the struthios," Shellabarger added. "A couple more days on the river, and then we're at Washington Falls. Where's your father?"

"Taking pictures."

"He needs to sign some chits. Find him, then help pick foliage."

Peter picked vegetation and piled it in the cage for Sammy. He found a few impressive-looking beetles and cockroaches, but Dip and Casso took little interest in them.

After he was done, he walked with his father, Ray, and Wetherford down to the water. OBie stood at the river's edge, stamping his feet to test the ground. The Indian foreman of the crew that had erected the crane stamped his foot also and smiled at OBie. He spoke in a language none of them knew, and OBie kept shaking his head. "You speak Indian?" he asked Wetherford.

"Sorry, no, but it sounds like Camaracotas."

"Well, my Spanish is poor, and my Indian is nonexistent," OBie said.

Shellabarger and Billie came down the trail last. Billie stepped in to interpret. "This man's name is Jorge," he said. "He is the *jefe* here."

"I gathered as much," Shellabarger said, lighting up another terrible cigar.

"He speaks Camaracotas and a little Spanish and Portuguese. He came here from Roraima in Brazil when he heard there was work. He is an expert woodworker, and he says not to worry about the mud, because there will be a log road by the end of the day."

"Well, I see how we'll lift the boats off the train cars," Shellabarger said, "but how will we get them down here?"

Billie spoke to Jorge and listened with his head cocked to one side. "With ropes and log rollers. He says it is no problem. They loaded the trucks onto motorized rafts two weeks ago and it worked fine, but the river rose and floated the log road away. So they will build it again." Jorge spoke again, and Billie added, "There has been much rain on El Grande. He says the falls will be spectacular."

"Has he seen them?" Shellabarger asked.

"Oh, yes. His father took him there when he was a boy. That is why his name—because of the falls, and because of Professor Challenger. His father remembers you, *señor,* and also *Señor* Gluck."

Jorge smiled proudly and stepped forward to offer his hand. Shellabarger took the hand and shook it firmly. "Tell him the crane looks like good work. His men are fine *obreros.* I expect the road will be rebuilt just fine."

Billie told Jorge, who nodded vigorously, then went off to instruct his men.

"What about the cages?" OBie asked. "How can we load them on the boats down here?"

"We can't," Shellabarger said, clamping his cigar and chewing its end. A trail of smoke stung Peter's eyes. "We use the crane to unload the boats, we lift the cages and swing them out onto the boats, and then we roll them together right into the water."

Wetherford whistled.

"Yeah," Shellabarger said, "well, if anybody else comes up with something better . . ." He looked up the river. "What about using the radio and finding out how things are up there? Maybe we can talk to the Mendezes, or whatever their name is."

"Our radio is not working, *señor,*" Billie said. "The air, the mountain . . . a storm somewhere north." He shrugged.

"Yeah, well," Shellabarger said, "that's just fine." He looked at Peter and decided the word he really wanted to use was perhaps too strong for this company. "Hell," he muttered, and blew smoke at a cloud of enthusiastic flies.

Wetherford pointed to the soldiers, standing unhappily to one side. "Not too tough to see their problem," he said. "So few of them, and so many Indians."

"The Indians came here to work," Peter said.

"That was just the beginning," Wetherford said. He rubbed the three-day growth of beard on his chin. "El Grande holds them together. Take our friend Billie, for example. An upright, well-educated lad." Wetherford gave Peter a knowing look. "And here we are with all these very interesting animals. Our troubles are not over, young fellow."

The workers had already cut and stacked long, straight white logs in a clearing not far from the railhead. They now hauled the logs down to trackside and began to reconstruct the road, laying them perpendicular to the tracks. Billie watched the workers intently. Peter stood close beside him, hoping to clear up his thinking about what Wetherford had said. Billie frowned as the logs passed.

"To some of the families, the tribes, those trees are sacred," he said to Peter. "They agree to cut them only for the Challenger."

Shellabarger took Peter by the shoulder and kept him close, "For luck," he said, as they tested the crane on a boat. Anthony snapped pictures and Wetherford stayed to one side, keeping his mouth shut for once. Ray recorded the scene.

"OBie told me to stand by here in case something goes wrong," he told Peter as their paths crossed. "I feel like a vulture."

The crane was strong enough to lift the boat clear of the car, and its steel bearings let it swing smoothly over to the log rollers already in place. Workers tied ropes to the boat and put chocks under the supporting rollers.

The struthios went first, silent in their cage. Peter wondered if they were all screeched out, or if they were just fascinated by the constant din of monkeys and macaws. Large black caciques flew around the clearing and the road, looking for scraps. One of them blundered into the venator's cage and the carnivore gulped it down like a fly. After that the other birds stayed away.

When the struthios' cage had been secured, the workers, instructed by Shellabarger through Billie and Jorge, gradually unrolled the long ropes and guided the boat with log poles and frequent stops and readjustments and much shouting down to the water. The boat stuck briefly on the mud, but with twenty men poling and wedging it farther, it floated free. They tethered it to trees on the bank.

"One down," Shellabarger said.

Shellabarger saved the venator cage for the last boat. He had changed the loading scheme and was going to put the venator alone on his own boat. They let the avisaurs out of their cage for exercise, and the bird-lizards rode on the trainer's and Peter's arms, shoulders, and head, down to the water.

Shellabarger and Peter were hidden beneath flapping wings and snapping beaks. None of the birds bit them, however. "They know I taste awful," he said. With the birds under Peter's charge, tied down with ropes around their talons, Anthony, Ray, and three of the workers carried their cage.

When the birds had been shut up once again, Shellabarger retrieved his cigar from Billie and relit it. Billie refused to smoke. His mother was Colombian, he said, and she used to smoke cigarettes and cigars with the burning end in her mouth. "They made her very sick, after a while," Billie said. "Maybe they killed her."

The venator stood in his cage, his forearm claws locked firmly on the steel water trough. As the cage swung out to rest on the boat, a chock beneath the forward roller splintered and the boat slipped sideways with a hollow rumble. Workmen scrambled to get out of the way. Peter jumped aside as the bow swung about. The boat's pilot shack struck the suspended cage with a mighty whack, tumbling the venator about. With a scream of rage, Dagger kicked and snapped, swinging the cage even more wildly. The crane made an ominous groaning noise.

Shellabarger leaped onto the cage with a rope and clung to the bars. Peter's throat seized; he expected the venator to grab the trainer through the bars and crush or claw him to death then and there. But Dagger could not right himself in time, and Shellabarger made it to the top, where the animal could only snap at him. From the top of the cage, the trainer swung the rope over the crane's boom and tied it to the cage on the other side, in case the crane's main cable snapped.

Peter and Anthony joined the film crew and roustabouts in chocking the boat with bits of log, rocks, even palm fronds, so it would not roll any farther. The roustabouts and workers began laboriously wrestling the boat back into position, pulling with ropes attached to log-drum winches. They lost two hours. Noon was almost upon them by the time the boat had been levered back onto its rolling logs.

Shellabarger remained on top of the cage the whole time, yelling instructions and checking the ropes. The cage swung a few inches back and forth and twisted slowly first one way, then the other. The venator stood within, motionless except for his neck and head, examining the top of the cage and the trainer's feet like a bird hoping to peck a piece of fruit. He made low grunting noises deep in his throat and flexed his claws against the bars.

Peter thought he had never seen anyone as brave as Vince Shellabarger.

Anthony had finished two rolls of film by this time and was loading another in the shade of a black cloth. He grimaced and clicked the camera back shut. "I wonder he's survived this long," he said under his breath.

With the boat secure, the crane operator lowered the cage onto the boat and it was locked down. The workmen maneuvered warily around the steel bars, keeping their eyes on the animal, ready to shout a warning to jump clear if he made a move. But Dagger kept his attention on the trainer, and Peter realized Shellabarger was not just checking the ropes: he was also distracting the dinosaur.

"Stand clear," Shellabarger said when the work was finished. "And put down some branches. I'm going to jump."

Billie took branches and palm fronds from the workmen and laid them in cross-thatch on the deck, and for good measure, put the pilot's seat cushion on top. Shellabarger jumped, landed on his feet, fell back onto his butt, and let out a groan. But he got up unhurt and brushed off his pants with his hat. The workmen cheered.

The venator leaned forward slightly, measuring the distance between the bars of the cage and Shellabarger: eight feet. Out of reach.

The workmen rolled the last boat down to the water, picking up the logs behind and carrying them around to the front. By one o'clock, the venator's boat was in the water, and all the boats strained against their ropes as the Caroní tried to push them downstream.

OBie and Ray finished filming with the big cameras and packed them up. Shawmut and Osborne carried them through the shallows to their boat. OBie took charge of the small camera. As the expedition prepared to continue upriver, Ray sat on the bow of the boat carrying the struthios and avisaurs, sketchpad in hand.

Peter thought he could tell without looking what Ray was drawing: *Venator Escapes!*

Billie showed them a chart of the river up the side branch to Challenger Canyon and the Jorge Washington Falls. Shellabarger, OBie, Anthony, Peter, and Wetherford crowded around him, listening intently.

"There are three sets of rapids," Billie said. "The first two, they are okay. These boats, no problem, so long as the engines keep going. There are channels right up the middle, between big split boulders. But here . . . the rapids are worse. I don't know how bad yet, because the water is still high, but we may have trouble."

Shellabarger removed his hat and wiped his head with a red kerchief.

"We will not know until we try, true, *señor?*" Billie said.

"Let's do it," the trainer said. He patted his pockets, made a face, and said, "We'll have to get there soon. I'm out of smokes."

Wetherford pulled a cigarette from his shirt pocket and handed it to Shellabarger. "Held one back for you," he said.

Shellabarger took it with thanks, looked at it, made another face, and handed it back.

"Something wrong?" Wetherford asked.

"Thinking about Billie's mother smoking with the burning end in her mouth . . . "

"Does put one off, doesn't it?" Wetherford agreed. He flipped the cigarette into the water. One of the workmen waded out and retrieved it. He raised it high and grinned triumphantly.

The disheveled officer and his three subordinates approached the shore at the last minute. "The radios are not talking with each other, *señors*," he said. "I can only assume you are who you say you are. Will you take a word of warning, kindly, *señors?*"

"Surely," OBie said.

"What we last heard, *el Presidente* Gallegos and my generals are very unhappy with each other. I do not know the mood of my colonel at Pico Poco, but he will not be content, for the radios must be silent up there, too. We are isolated. Do you understand?"

"We understand," OBie said. "*Gracias.*"

"*¡Adiós!*" the officer said, and waved his hat.

The workmen cheered again as the boats switched on their engines and cast loose. Shellabarger and OBie shouted their thanks and Billie translated. The waving and shouting continued as the boats pushed out against the current, now making less than a mile an hour headway.

Peter stared up at the sheer flanks of El Grande. High up there, he thought, were animals even fiercer than the venator. He wondered if any of them ever ventured close to the edge, to peer down at the other, newer world below.

Chapter Eleven

———◆———

After a week on the river, the thunder of the falls sounded like heaven to Peter. It meant they had made it this far with only scrapes and bruises, and that soon they would be riding in trucks, climbing the road to Pico Poco.

The boats crept up the dark waters, surrounded on both sides by escarpments of a thousand feet and more. Fly and mosquito bites covered Peter's body and he itched all the time; his arms and legs ached from tugging on ropes on the rugged banks to guide the barges through the open channels in the rapids, one at a time.

The last set of rapids almost did them in. The third boat, carrying the centrosaur, was almost through the middle section of smooth high water when it fetched up against a submerged rock, and the shock pitched Anthony into the water. Sammy's cage swung forward, squealing on its blocks and straining against the tie-downs.

"Get him a rope!" Kasem shouted from the bank. His voice was almost lost in the roar of rushing water. Ray and OBie, on the fourth barge, threw a line forward into the white roil, and Anthony made a grab. A sudden undercurrent drew him down and he bobbed up in a whirlpool. The line was pushed back downriver.

Peter watched from the back of the third barge. He saw clear water between him and the whirlpool and rapids, and without thinking, he grabbed the loose towline and jumped over the side. He had always been a fair swimmer, and now he worked his way with the river current toward his father. Anthony's head bobbed above the surface and was lost again in foam. Something seemed to wrap around Peter's leg and he dipped under the water himself, then shook his foot loose from a vine tangled in the streambed rocks. Half drowned, spitting and coughing water, he bobbed up, still gripping the towline. He paddled to rotate himself, saw his father's hand a few feet away, and grabbed for it with his right hand. Anthony gripped the hand tightly and nearly pulled him down. Peter felt a tug on the towrope; Shellabarger was trying to reel them both in and the venator's barge was closing, less than a dozen yards away. Anthony came up and spit water and shouted, "The rocks! Grab a rock!"

Peter felt all the air go out of him as he slammed into a boulder. Water slid over his head and he tried to crawl up onto the algae-slick rock without letting go of Anthony. The towrope slithered from his grasp. Water sluiced around his arms and knees and a sudden surge almost shoved him off, but Anthony held on to his hand and arm and balanced him against the pressure. They both clambered into the broad flat rock.

Anthony grabbed Peter by the ribs and squeezed hard. "That was too damned close!" he shouted over the river.

Peter gave Anthony a woozy grin. His ribs throbbed and he felt as if he had swallowed gallons of water.

The third barge was almost back to the beginning of the rapids. The pilot of the fourth boat cut her engines to avoid a collision. Keller, Kasem, and the roustabouts tugged from one side; the other towline was back in Shellabarger's hands. He tossed it toward them. Peter reached out and missed, lost his balance, and landed on his butt, then slid right off the rock into the water. Green and white bubbles surrounded him. No matter how hard he thrashed and paddled, there did not seem to be air anywhere. He felt something kick him in one leg, and then a hand closed around his head, grabbed his hair, yanked him painfully to the surface. Anthony had snatched the rope with one hand and Peter's head with the other. He wrapped his legs around his son and Shellabarger hauled them hand over hand to the barge. Billie powered up the engine and they began to pull away from the rapids.

Peter and Anthony lay on the rear deck behind the pilot house. Peter tried to sit up but couldn't. Anthony rolled to his side, hair in wet slick lines down his forehead, and said, "My God, what a swim! What a *genteel* afternoon dip!"

"Never again," Peter coughed.

"I owe you one," Anthony said.

Peter shook his head. He didn't know what to say. Only now did the fear catch up and make him shiver. He thought he might throw up.

"Quick thinking, Peter," Shellabarger said.

"I *wasn't* thinking," Peter said.

Billie leaned out of the pilothouse and wiped his brow dramatically.

A shaft of sunlight broke through the clouds and painted the whole river. Anthony held up his wet camera in disgust. In all the struggle, it had not slipped its strap from around his neck.

They stopped for a rest a mile upriver, taking advantage of a broad calm pool wide enough and deep enough to hold all five barges. The trainer changed barges and Ray joined them on the third barge.

OBie and Anthony exchanged disgruntled advice over the still dark water. The Leica could be dried out and oiled again; Anthony's film, however, was getting moldy in the cans, and Anthony had been scrounging 35 millimeter stock from OBie, cutting and rolling it at night by feel in an unlighted tent. "Everything's wet," OBie said philosophically. *"Everything's* moldy."

Clothes still damp, Peter seemed to hear their voices from a great distance. The sound of the rapids and the falls seemed much closer. He wondered if what he had done was a brave thing. What was the difference between a brave act and a dangerous but necessary act? His father was not going to make a big deal out of it; but Peter had saved Anthony's life, and then Anthony had saved his.

Ray settled beside Peter when he had finished helping Anthony clean his camera. Peter came out of a light doze and blinked up at him. Ray's angular, affable features stood out against the darkness of the eastern cliffs. "What do you think of adventure now?" Ray asked.

"It's all right," Peter said.

Ray laughed.

"Want your own adventure?" Peter asked.

Ray suddenly went serious. "Lord, no," he said. "I'd like to get out of this alive."

"Why are you here, if you don't want adventure?" Peter asked.

"Bit of a cruel question, don't you think?" Ray asked.

"My father thought I should be here," Peter said. "He thinks I'm too bookish. And to tell the truth, I want to be here, I really do . . ." Their eyes met. "As long as I survive. I'd still like to read another book sometime."

Ray grinned. "Why am I here? OBie is from the old school. He thinks he's rough and tough, and he is. He's certainly a survivor. So many disappointments and tragedies . . . real sadness, though he doesn't show it much. But he's never been through the kind of action Monte and Coop saw. I think he envies them."

"What kind of sadness?" Peter asked.

"His son was killed," Ray said.

"In the war?"

"No. When he was just a boy." Ray seem reluctant to give details. "OBie took me under his wing, gave me a break. Looked at my films—things I put together in my garage—taught me what he knows. Got me work. I owe him a lot."

"He wants to be a father to you?" Peter asked.

"No . . . My own dad suits me fine. But OBie has a heart as big as a mountain. The point of my wandering monologue is, if he wants to be here, and he wants me here with him, then so be it." Ray shrugged and peered downriver. "Maybe he's right. Maybe you need to dip your hand into the fire now and then, just for perspective."

"Which hand?" Peter asked.

"Not my drawing hand!" Ray said.

● ● ●

The barges set out again in the late afternoon. OBie came over to Sammy's barge to join Anthony, Peter, and Ray, jumping as the boats came within a yard of each other.

"Another mile," Shellabarger shouted from the venator's boat. Here, the river became ominously smooth, running smoothly north through shelves of forest snugged close to the canyon walls. The barges pushed steadily against the current. Anthony estimated they were making about two miles an hour; Billie concurred.

An hour passed before Ray spotted a long yellow *curiara* stationed beside a half submerged log near the left bank of the river. Three men in wide plaited grass hats sat motionless in the dugout canoe, faces hidden in shadow. OBie waved from the barge's blunt bow, but the men did not wave back.

"There are more," Billie called from the pilot house. More *curiaras* had been pulled up to the narrow shore, under the thick overhang of trees; dozens of them, on both sides of the river. Ray squatted beside OBie on the bow, panning the smaller movie camera, and Anthony lifted his Leica, twisting focus and exposure swiftly to take a panoramic series.

Peter stood beside Billie, not sure whether to worry. "Who are they?"

"They are Indians and mestizos," Billie said. "Workers from south of El Grande." Peter saw them in the jungle now, stepping forward. Some stood in the river shallows where the water did not run too swiftly. Others sat in the crotches of tree limbs, and all watched silently. Then, acting as one, they scrambled into the *curiaras* and padded quickly to surround the barges. With little apparent effort, they kept up against the river's currents, saying nothing, staring at the animals in their cages. They paid particular attention to the venator, who stood high above the river in his tall thick-barred cage, erect on his big three-toed feet, and the venator observed them, moving his head with oiled grace to keep both eyes focused on the left rank of canoes, then suddenly spinning it around to observe those on his right. Where his gaze swept, the Indians drew back on their haunches, wincing as if hit by a blast of hot air.

"They have not seen the Challenger before," Billie said. "The

Army will never allow them to climb Kahu Hidi, to meet him there. So they come to open the road for him."

They were passing the last of the dozens of men and canoes, and Peter walked aft. The Indians paddled quickly downriver, vanishing around a curve. In minutes, it was as if they had never been.

Anthony stood beside Peter, and OBie beside him. "They must have come from hundreds of miles," OBie said. His voice sounded like the buzzing of a gnat against the roar of Jorge Washington Falls. Peter could no longer hear the cries of birds or the howls and squeals of monkeys; only the falls, tossed out into space from holes a hundred feet below the lip of El Grande, plunging six thousand feet to the huge pool below.

The spray drifted across the jungle and reached them even a mile away, soaking their clothes, bedewing the boats and the cages.

Everyone was wet, aching, exhausted, and happy. Even the animals seemed to sense the journey was almost over. The struthios craned their long necks and gave out high-pitched shrieks of hunger and excitement. Sammy had stopped eating but appeared healthy. He rocked from one side to the other, lifting his head and blowing through his nostrils, then inhaling great drafts of the damp, cooler air.

The venator now crouched in his cage on barge number two. His eyes grew wide and his throat pulsed and blushed.

A constant downdraft from the plateau dropped the temperature by ten degrees, to around eighty. The night before, OBie had said that up on El Grande itself the temperature at this time of year would be about sixty, no more than sixty-five.

The animals smelled home, a place they had not seen in decades and almost certainly could not remember, except in their flesh and blood: smells and sounds.

The barges motored slowly around the last bend at twilight. The half mile-wide pool at the base of Jorge Washington Falls stretched before them, water almost black in the shadows. Peter stared up and up, from the bottom of the falls, lost in billows of gray mist, up until his neck bones popped, to the top of the sky: a cataract of moonbright white water, gleaming against the wet lacquered blackness of the cliffside, falling forever as if in slow motion, breaking, misting, and finally smacking into the pool with a sound like all the world's hurricanes, a howling roaring hissing blowing noise full of immense power and peace.

Peter thought Forever might sound like Jorge Washington Falls.

No human could survive the force of water at the base of the falls, OBie said, and no dinosaur either. Thousands of tons struck the pool every minute at over a hundred miles an hour. "We'd be mush in an instant," he said, voice full of awe and admiration.

Ray and Peter sat on the bow of the third barge, which had pulled ahead of the others under Billie's direction. Ray had put away his sketch pad; the light was too dim for good camera shots, and he now sat with arms across his drawn-up knees, brows pulled together, contemplating the wonder.

Peter surveyed the shores of the pool. He spotted a light in the gloom. "There!" he shouted to Ray. Ray squinted and nodded.

"Must be the camp," he said. Wetherford came forward on barge four with a flashlight and waved it. Billie turned their boat toward the lights, about a quarter mile from the falls, and the others followed.

The single light that had greeted them was held by a compact, wrinkled old Indian named José Esteban Miguel. He had come down to the shore to await their arrival and had pitched a single tent under a stunted tree. As they stepped off the boats and tied them to rocks on the shore, José Esteban Miguel greeted them indi-

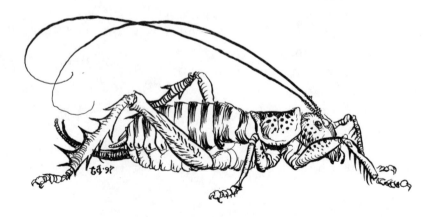

vidually with a hearty handshake and words of Spanish or broken English. To Peter he said: *"Muy bien,* pleased to have you, *bienvenido,* is well-come!"

The shore campsite was a wet mess, inundated by spray, slick with moss and algae and covered with a variety of wet, creeping bugs that Peter stepped over carefully, more for his sake than theirs.

José Esteban Miguel was a So'oto Indian from the west. He never told them his Indian name, never used less than all three of his first names, and never revealed a last name. He informed them gleefully that the trucks and the rest of the workers were at a site about a mile away, where it was drier and less plagued by insects. *"El Colonel* is here," he added, and nodded up the road to Pico Poco, now obscured by night.

Shellabarger and the roustabouts slipped tarps over the cages to keep mist off the animals. Only the avisaurs seemed to enjoy the moisture, spreading their wings, fanning their tails and preening as the drifts of spray drooped down around them.

Anthony and Ray examined the bugs. Anthony showed Peter a fierce-looking six-legged creature about five inches long, with powerful legs, a thick, black abdomen, and large shining yellow and black eyes. "I think it's a kind of cricket," he said. "Biggest I've ever seen."

"Bigger than the wetas in New Zealand," Wetherford marveled.

Shellabarger collected as many of the aquatic crickets as he could in an empty tin and offered them to the struthios, the avisaurs, and the *Aepyornis.* They found them very acceptable and ate all the trainer had gathered. Peter reluctantly acquiesced to Shellabarger's order to pick up more of the fat insects. He did not like the way they squirmed and prickled in his hands.

Dark turned the shore camp into a noisy, wet black void, relieved only by glimpses of stars through the drifting vaults of spray and the flash of lights on and around the boats. The air smelled of jungle—thick and green and damp, with the heavy, musty wet-basement odor of soil and jungle rot. Some of the odors reminded Peter of the piss-wet hallways in the brownstone in New York.

José Esteban Miguel volunteered to walk to the second camp and bring a truck, but Shellabarger and OBie agreed that was probably not a good idea. "We'll wait until morning," they said.

Peter regretted that. José Esteban Miguel showed them how to arrange their tents so that the insects would not bother them—the crickets avoided higher ground, frequenting the low sandy spots near the pool—but the night was still wet and miserable, and in the morning, for the first time in weeks, Peter felt chilly. J.E.M. (as Keller began calling him) tended a fitful fire and served them passable coffee, but soon ran out of dry wood.

Without breakfast, Anthony, Peter, Billie, Ray, and J.E.M. walked up the steeply inclined gravel road to the second camp. There, four big trucks were parked beside five tents, and a few yards away, an army jeep and two more small tents. Smoke rose from four fires.

Two soldiers carrying rifles were the first to greet them. They emerged from their tents and jogged down to the banks of the pond. There, Shellabarger and Anthony spoke with them briefly. The soldiers seemed concerned; by their gestures, Peter understood they were talking about not being able to communicate by radio. Anthony, using Billie as an interpreter, told them all was going smoothly and that their papers and permissions were in order as of a few days ago. That seemed to mollify them, but again Peter heard the words *el Colonel,* uttered reverently or fearfully.

Peter was a little surprised to see Jorge and his workers cooking over the largest of the fires. Jorge offered them cassava cakes and fried crocodile tail.

"Try it!" Billie suggested, seeing Peter's expression. "It is very good."

Peter took the tin plate of cake and crocodile and sat beside the fire to eat and dry out. Anthony sat beside him, carrying his own plate. Ray took the cake but declined the crocodile. Billie ate and spoke with the men around the second fire.

"It's pretty tasty," Anthony said, lifting a bite of crocodile meat.

"I hear the real delicacy around here is tapir," Ray said. "Best cooked the native way." He shuddered. "Makes me long for a hamburger and a Coke."

Billie joined them a few minutes later. "Trucks all ready. The men walked here from the other camp. Walk faster than we boated, obviously. They like your pay, *Señor* Belzoni."

"Glad to have them," Anthony said. "Tell them we need to move the animals up to Pico Poco by nightfall, if possible."

"Some good late afternoon shots would be nice," Ray said.

Billie doubted they would be on the top of Pico Poco before dark. "It is eight miles to the top and the bridge. Jorge says the roads are good after all these years, except for jungle growth, and he sent word to workers on this side of El Grande, friends from other tribes. They met us on the river . . . in their *curiaras*. They have cleared enough of the thick growth for the trucks to pass."

"There must be lots of Indians here now," Anthony said.

"A great many," Billie agreed.

"How long will the trucks take to get from here to the bridge?" Anthony asked.

Billie asked Jorge, and the Indian shrugged his shoulders and replied. "Three, four hours," Billie translated. "If you are cautious."

OBie and Wetherford came up the trail. "Film is still good, miraculously," OBie told Ray. "But I'm not going to load our cameras anywhere near those falls. Shellabarger wants us to get the trucks down there and start hauling animals and equipment now. Still have film in the mini?"

Ray said he did.

"Use it sparingly and shoot the falls and the first camp."

"Right," Ray said.

"Jorge says nothing about how the bridge is," Billie said. "He has not been up there yet. Too close to *el Colonel* for him. The men from this side of the mountain say the bridge is still there, but they do not understand machinery."

OBie mulled that over, then smirked mischievously.

"Don't say it!" Ray warned.

"Say what?" OBie asked.

"Not a word about crossing that bridge when we come to it."

OBie feigned complete innocence. "Let's shoot what we can, but conserve stock. I'm sure Vince is going to take his own sweet time carrying his babies."

• • •

The loading actually went fairly quickly. By the pool, they fed the animals what was left of the food stored in the drums. Four trucks grumbled down the road to the pond. For a few minutes, Peter watched the roustabouts confer with Jorge and Billie about how to transfer the cages to the back of the trucks. Sammy and the venator would each ride on one truck; the other cages would be divided between two trucks.

"There's going to be some overhang," Shellabarger said, measuring the truck beds with his eye. "But it'll work if we don't jostle them too much."

Ray and Anthony shot footage and pictures of the discussions, and Shellabarger obliged them by waving his hands and grinning broadly. When he turned away, though, his grin faded. He poked his fingers into his empty pockets for cigarettes. Peter thought Shellabarger seemed more nervous than he had been at any point on the trip, and he could guess why: so close, and still so many things that could go wrong.

Shellabarger asked Peter to stay beside Sammy. "He likes you. You seem to keep him calm." Shawmut and Osborne carried the black boxes of equipment from the first barge through the shallows on their backs, with help from a few of J.E.M.'s workers.

The shore of the pool was sand spread thin over solid rock, and could easily stand the weight of the trucks. Peter wondered how the cages were going to be transferred, then saw the large ramps on the back of the first truck. All of the trucks had winches mounted behind the front bumpers.

The barge carrying Sammy was brought up to the center of the beach and moored securely to trees, rocks, and the nearest truck. Ten men rolled and carried the ramps one at a time across to the boat and locked them down side by side. The ramps had big steel wheels along their lengths.

Shellabarger, Kasem, and Keller waded around the boat in the shallows to see how far it would dip on one side when the weight was shifted. "Two feet, then she'll hit bottom," Keller said.

Anthony eyed the ramps, the truck, the boat, and shook his head. "It might work," he said.

"Why won't it work?" Shellabarger asked grumpily. He turned on Anthony, hands on hips, clearly agitated by Anthony's doubts.

"All right," Anthony gave in. "It'll work." Then, to Peter, standing beside Sammy on the boat, he said in an undertone, "It'll have to."

Sammy knew something was up and nosed the cage until Peter turned and reached between the bars to pat the centrosaur's beak. He couldn't see how Sammy could feel anything there, since it was nothing but horny material, but the big animal seemed to like his touch anyway.

Ropes were tied to the forward and side rings on the cage, then men scrambled past Peter and applied pry bars, first to one side, and then to the other. The bars dug into the boat's deck and there was much swearing and grunting, but eventually they managed to place wedges and chocks and blocks under the cage and lift it eight inches off the deck. Then the ramps were unfastened and extended under it.

"This isn't going to work," Shellabarger murmured, standing in the water beside the ramp. "Rob, bring out the logs." Keller unpacked foot-thick logs of varying lengths from barge number two and the roustabouts propped them in place under the big steel ramps, making a kind of bridge.

Ray filmed this in brief economic clips. He even lifted the camera to bring Peter into frame. Peter felt acutely embarrassed but tried to act naturally. He got out of the way as the blocks under Sammy's cage were knocked aside. It settled onto its bottom steel plate, jerking Sammy a little and making him grunt forlornly. He lifted his beak and let out a series of bellows that rose above the thunder of the falls. Then the winch on the second truck began to reel in the cable attached to the ropes, and the cage—all four tons of it, including Sammy—rolled down the ramps, shuddering and jerking, onto the bed of the truck. The boat hardly dipped, so stable were the logs, but Shellabarger had all the workmen brace the sides of the ramps with poles, in case the logs decided to lean or sway, or worst of all, split.

By noon all the cages had been loaded—even the venator's. The big carnivore endured the transfer stoically, crouched on his stomach, eyes half closed like a cat trying to nap.

Peter let out a big sigh when the cages were all locked down and the trucks were ready to roll. He walked past the caged animals and talked to them soothingly. Even the venator received a visit. "That was pretty brave," Peter said, unsure how to speak to this monster. Dagger stared at him with both eyes forward, unblinking, then lifted his upper lip in a fair imitation of a sneer and stretched wide his mouth, as if yawning. His teeth gleamed like old ivory and his breath smelled of rotten meat.

Peter's stomach twitched. He backed away and fetched up against his father. Anthony took his shoulders and gripped them. That grip felt familiar, as if his father were going to lecture him about something. Instead, Anthony looked down at his son with a peculiar, tight expression, nostrils flared, and lifted his eyes to the beast.

"He should never have been brought down," Anthony said.

Wetherford, a few yards away, said, "Amen to that."

Anthony and Peter rode in the cab of the first truck with the driver, a large, solemn Carib named Julio, from the Karina tribe in the north. The other Indians held Julio in great regard. They claimed his forefathers had eaten their forefathers, or so Billie said. "Many of our fathers ate each other, once," he added. "Some still eat men of other tribes, deep in the forest." To Peter, the Carib seemed nice enough, though quiet. Julio waited for instructions from Shellabarger, who rode with Sammy on the back of the first truck.

"It is tough road," Julio said. "But we do it."

Shellabarger swung his arm and the big diesels roared to life, coughing black smoke from vertical exhaust pipes.

"Just a few more hours," Anthony said.

Peter's heart felt like a nervous pigeon. The trucks lurched up the rugged machete-cut path, their fat, alligator-tread tires digging into the loose branches, stumps and roots, rocks and gravel.

The old road up Pico Poco followed green-walled ridges or cut-in switchbacks. It rose on a steep but constant grade, one mile up in eight miles of driving. At first they managed about a mile and a half each hour, stopping twice to water the animals and once to remove a fallen tree. The heat for most of the journey was still tropically intense. Only in the last couple of miles did they come under the cooling umbrella of clouds embracing the shoulders of El Grande.

By the time they reached an ant-chewed wooden marker that read 11 KM, dusk was falling rapidly. Shellabarger walked along the convoy, spoke with the drivers using Billie as interpreter, and returned to the first truck, face grim. "Push on," he ordered.

The trucks switched on their lights in the gloom. Rain began to fall and they rode the last half mile over rivulets that gathered to form creeks, and past mossy falls of water that spilled on the road and cut muddy ruts. Their truck got stuck in mud in the last quarter mile and had to be pulled out using its winch to reel in a steel cable attached to the truck ahead. Julio arranged the cables and switched on the winch from within the cab, leaning out of the door in the pouring rain to judge the progress. The windshield wipers cleared small arcs and only intermittently at that. They could barely see. The winch snarled and the cable twanged taut like a giant's guitar string. The truck rolled forward a foot. Peter wiped fog from inside the window. The truck rolled back, pulling the truck ahead with it, slamming him against the hard rear of the seat.

Julio grimly released the winch clutch and glanced at Peter, then let it out again. The winch motor groaned under the load and their truck rolled forward a foot, then another foot. Without warning, the truck fishtailed, its end swerving down a muddy incline toward the edge of the road. Peter grabbed the door handle, ready to jump if Julio did, but the Carib stared fixedly ahead, tongue poked between tense lips, nursing the winch clutch, pulling them steadily forward. Still, the truck continued to slide sideways, and from the rear, Peter heard Sammy honking and bawling. He opened the door and jumped out, almost over the edge. Shellabarger caught his arm and they trudged through the hacked brush and mud to examine the right rear tires, now just inches from the steep slide to complete destruction. They shinnied around the truck bed and stood behind.

"What can we do?" Peter shouted over the rain's hiss.

"His cage has too much weight on the wood blocks this side," Shellabarger said. Keller and Kasem joined them behind the truck. "If that Carib—"

"Julio!" Peter said.

"If Julio doesn't pull 'er out soon, we'll have to rig more rope on the opposite side."

The main blocks on the right ground against the truck bed. Sammy's cage was slipping sideways, only a few inches, but the blocks were under tremendous pressure. Peter turned and saw Ray and OBie, hats pulled low against the downpour. "Anything we can do?" Ray asked.

Shellabarger shook his head helplessly. "We're losing him!"

Peter ran around to the driver's side. Anthony was already there, holding the door open as Julio craned to look around the fogged and useless windshield.

"We have to hurry!" Peter shouted. Julio grinned and shook his head, but caught Peter's tone. Working both the winch and the main motor alternately, he stopped the slide and pulled them forward another foot.

The roustabouts cut long, woody branches on the left side of the road and Ray, Obie, and Shellabarger slipped them under the rear tires.

"Go!" Peter yelled, wiping his eyes. "Go!"

Julio fed power to the truck's rear wheels. The branches were pulled into the mud by the tread. Several pulverized sticks shot out behind the truck, one taking OBie across the face, knocking him backward and bloodying his chin. Ray helped him to his feet.

The truck shuddered and began to slip again. "Go!" Peter and Anthony yelled together. Julio hunkered down behind the windshield and let the winch clutch out completely. The rear bed of the truck ahead jerked under the sudden strain and the struthio cage rattled and banged. Sammy's truck began to move, however, and Julio applied power to the rear tires once more. The truck leaped ahead, the winch screamed as it reeled in cable, and suddenly the cable parted with a sound like a small cannon. Peter and Anthony jumped aside. The cable lashed back and shattered the truck's windshield. Glass sprayed down on Julio in tiny shards.

The rear wheels continued to turn and grab, pushing the truck up the road until Julio kicked in the clutch and applied the brakes. The truck rocked slowly back and forth and Sammy bawled hoarsely.

Peter got up from the mud and reached the truck cab in time to see Julio calmly brush glass out of his hair. Anthony stepped forward to help him. Peter ran to the back. Ray and OBie and Shellabarger inspected the cage. The roustabouts and camera crew stood ready with more branches and rocks.

"All right," Shellabarger said. "Give that driver a medal."

"Julio," Peter said.

"Give Julio a medal and let's get some more rocks in that muddy area. We have to keep moving."

In the last hundred yards, with visibility down to zero, Anthony, OBie, Ray, and Peter walked with the trainer ahead of the trucks, swinging flashlights to make sure the way was clear of thick limbs and boulders. Yard by yard, the trucks advanced in pitch darkness, headlights flaring, flashlight beams fishing at the dark, and brilliant sheets of lightning painting everything icy white.

Peter pulled his hat down tight as a gust of wind tried to lift it from his head. The rain pounded. He could hear the animals complaining—all but the venator, who kept his grim silence, beyond all outrage.

The rain stopped abruptly, as if someone had cranked a tap shut. The trucks roared their way onto a grassy clearing with flat stretches of rock beyond. They covered the distance to the edge of Pico Poco in a few minutes. The trucks formed a line and Shellabarger called for them to cut their engines.

After so many hours of the belching roar of the diesels and the hiss of rain and the crack-rumble of thunder, Peter felt stunned by the sudden quiet. The animals had fallen silent, all but the avisaurs, who made small whistling sounds as they flapped their wings in their cage. A waning quarter moon cast a mottled glow through parting clouds in the west.

Everyone swung down from the cabs or leaped from the backs of the trucks. They followed OBie and Shellabarger across the flat, weathered sandstone to the ghostly outline of the old steel swinging bridge. Years before, this had been the outside world's gateway to El Tepui Grande.

Beside the bridge, five large tents had been pitched. Near the tents squatted two jeeps, one Army green, the other white. Beyond the jeeps lurked the shadows of several canvas-backed Army trucks.

Three men strolled out of the darkness beyond the tents, two soldiers in steel helmets and a broad-shouldered, heavy-bellied man with a thick black mustache. From other tents came dozens more soldiers, all armed with holstered pistols and slung rifles.

The mustachioed man's tailored khaki uniform strained over his shoulders and paunch. He wore a stiff-brimmed, high-peaked officer's hat and carried a small, thin-barreled pistol in one beefy hand. This, Peter thought, must be *el Colonel*.

Two almost identical men and a woman emerged from the closest tent, all dressed in tough hiking pants and wearing leather jackets. The woman was tall, with long black hair and a face more severe than Peter liked, young but with the air of a stern teacher. The men were short and balding. Peter wondered if they were twins.

Catalina Mendez

"Welcome, *Señor* Shellabarger, and congratulations," the woman said, walking ahead of the colonel. She obviously wanted to stake a claim to the visitors. "I am Catalina Mendez. I represent the Office of Natural Resources in Ciudad Bolívar. May I present Colonel Juan de Badajoz, commander of the security of this region?"

"Pleased to make your acquaintance," Shellabarger said. He shook the colonel's hand firmly, then turned and shook hers.

The colonel's two adjutants also wore khakis, with a yellow handkerchief pushed beneath one epaulet. The taller of the two advanced and offered his hand. "On behalf of the Army of Venezuela, *Colonel* de Badajoz welcomes all to the region of El Tepui Grande." The colonel smiled briefly and gave them a curt nod. Soon there was a flurry of hand-shaking and congratulations.

Catalina Mendez was a naturalist assigned by the Betancourt government to oversee the return of the animals. Peter quickly realized that she was the only representative of the government; she and her two brothers, the bald-headed men. They were construction engineers and as Peter had surmised, they were identical twins. There seemed no love lost between them and *el Colonel*.

Tin cups were brought out, and OBie rummaged through the camera supplies to find two bottles of red wine. Everyone drank a toast. The colonel stood to one side and downed his wine quickly, then tossed the cup to the taller adjutant. The colonel still clutched his pistol and stared off into the night as if nervous about what might be lurking out there.

Peter sipped his cup. It tasted like medicine, but not unpleasantly so.

The shorter adjutant, young-faced and beardless, with a shiny nose and forehead, approached Anthony. Peter's father was the darkest, most Hispanic-looking of their party. "The Venezuelan Army is proud to be of assistance," he said. "As you can see, there have been efforts made to bring the bridge back into repair. Colonel de Badajoz has brought Army engineers with him to make sure all is well."

The colonel holstered his pistol and shook hands formally with Anthony, but still said not a word. He snapped to attention, saluted, and gestured to the shorter soldier.

"The colonel apologizes for not speaking English. I will translate for him."

After Colonel de Badajoz returned to his tent, Catalina Mendez took Shellabarger aside and whispered to him for several minutes. The trainer listened with a deepening frown, then shook his head vigorously. "We'll talk about it in the morning," Peter heard him say, and he stalked away from her. She stared after him, arms folded and fingers clutching her forearms.

Peter was very tired and the wine made him ache for sleep, but he followed the others as dry wood was pulled from beneath a tarp and a large fire was kindled to warm them all. Peter looked at his watch with the aid of a flashlight: ten o'clock.

OBie found a third bottle and offered a toast to their hosts and to Vince Shellabarger. "We made it," Peter said to his father and to Ray as they gathered around the fire. Everyone lifted their glasses.

Peter glanced over his shoulder at the animals, still in their cages on the backs of the trucks.

Shellabarger took Anthony and OBie aside for a conference. Peter and Ray followed.

"The Mendez woman says things are getting dicey. The colonel is here to monitor some sort of native uprising. The Betancourt government supports the local tribal alliance, but the Army apparently doesn't agree. *Señora* Mendez represents the government, such as it is; but she's not sure who's going to be in charge in the next few days or weeks. They can't reach anybody with their radio—must be a hell of a lot of interference. Sounds like the Army junta is pulling back from Betancourt and Gallegos and they're going to install their own new man, someone by the name of Pérez Jiménez.

"They've flown engineers from the airport at Uruyen and landed them here on Pico Poco. They looked over the bridge and flew back. The Army engineers think the bridge won't hold more than a few hundred pounds—that it might collapse any minute of its own weight. The Mendez brothers think the bridge is sound enough to hold about four tons, and they've been working to get the motor running, but they haven't got many resources. The Army wouldn't let them bring more than their jeep up here. Besides that, everybody's in complete agreement."

"That's the way things are in this part of the world," OBie said. "So, do we go or not?"

The trainer shrugged. "I'll look at the bridgeworks tomorrow—Anthony, you've had some engineering training, haven't you?"

Anthony nodded.

"We'll see what's what in the morning."

The conference broke up. Peter and Anthony walked away from the fire toward the steel bridge. It was as big as a covered bridge across a stream, but completely open, mounted on a large motorized pivot sunk into the rock, with girder-hung concrete counterweights slung on both sides behind the pivot. To Peter it resembled a big, thick construction crane, with a roadway built down its center. Its girders were rusty and the engine house had not been painted in years, but tools and oil cans and drums of fuel were lying about;

work had been done recently. Anthony peered into the engine house, wrinkled his nose, and walked to the edge with Peter.

Ray joined them. "Eager?" he asked.

Anthony nodded. "Yeah," Peter said.

OBie's footsteps sounded behind them, and he lined up beside Ray. "It's been a long time," he said quietly.

They stood on the rim of the cleft between Pico Poco and El Grande. Peter felt dizzy, looking into the windy darkness below. He moved back a step.

"A mile deep," Ray said, leaning over the abyss. The fringe of hair around his high forehead rose and fluttered in an updraft.

They all stared across the gap of one hundred feet at the starlit cliff face opposite, the southern edge of the greatest of all the tepuis. Atop the plateau, beyond a clearing about fifty yards wide, rose the shadows of thick round sandstone shapes, weathered into weird faces and the broken battlements of old fortresses.

For the first time, they looked upon the ancient landscape that Professor George Edward Challenger and Sir Arthur Conan Doyle had called the Lost World.

Chapter Twelve

OBie and Ray and the camera crew woke before dawn. Peter had been too excited to sleep—or so he thought—but Anthony roused him before sunrise. For breakfast they ate beans and cassava bread and dried apricots. The air smelled of woodsmoke and steaming coffee and stony damp. The clouds had broken up during the night, leaving clear air still sprinkled with the brightest stars.

Jorge's workers crowded around a smoky fire near their camp. They drank coffee and waved cheerfully as Peter and Anthony walked past. Billie and the river pilots and drivers sat around another fire. Billie leaped up to join them.

"Today or tomorrow will be the big day," he said.

"Looks that way," Anthony said, lifting his camera to check the composition for a sunrise shot. The cages were outlined by skyglow to the east.

Shawmut and Osborne had placed the heavy camera and dolly on their tracks near the bridge. They were making sure the tracks were level and wouldn't wobble as the dolly passed over.

Shellabarger was nowhere to be seen. Catalina Mendez stood with her brothers near the bridge. The bridge motor was being tested. As they neared the engine house, Shellabarger and the taller adjutant emerged, their hands black with grease. The colonel followed. His hands were immaculate.

Anthony

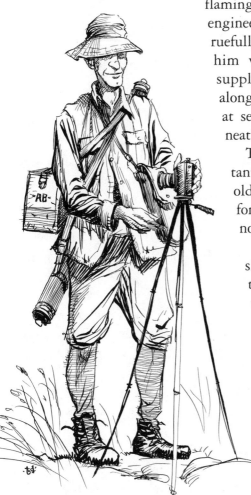

The trainer glanced at Anthony, face orange and eyes glinting in the flaming sunrise. "Looks like all the engineers need a little help," he said ruefully. Kasem and Keller joined him with more tools from the supply crates. Anthony walked along the length of the bridge, and at several points crawled underneath to inspect it.

The young-faced Army adjutant said, "The bridge is very old and has had no maintenance for almost twenty years. We do not think it is safe."

Wetherford stood to one side, picking his teeth with a twig. He seemed disinclined to get involved in the brewing dispute.

Shellabarger approached the colonel as if he would tower over him.

"We were told this bridge would be fixed and ready to go," he said.

"Apparently, Caracas did not know it was so bad," the adjutant said with a half pleading look at Doña Mendez. "The engineers have come and gone. Their report is final."

"We have made our conclusions known to Colonel de Badajoz," Catalina told Shellabarger, "but he tells me his engineers are more informed than my brothers."

Shellabarger pointed at the steel-girdered span in disgust. "I've gotten eleven tons of animals and cages and equipment this far. The bridge will hold until they cross. I don't give a damn what happens after that."

Colonel de Badajoz understood enough English to get the gist of the trainer's words. He spoke in a low voice to the adjutant and cast dark looks at Shellabarger. The adjutant, uncomfortable at being caught between these two, said, "The Army engineers say the bridge's main weight-bearing girders have rusted badly across the center span . . . It cannot support a truck and a big animal. Crossing would be disastrous."

Catalina rolled her eyes and turned to Anthony, just back from his inspection. "My brothers are good engineers," she said. "There may be some concern about a truck carrying an animal crossing together, but the bridge is sound enough to bear at least three tons."

"Our heaviest animal weighs three tons," Anthony said. "We can change our plans and keep the trucks off the bridge. We push the animals across the bridge, let them go free, one at a time, and after that . . ." He smiled at her. "We're done. Nothing over three tons."

"We don't expect to crash a truck into it," Shellabarger snapped at the adjutant.

The adjutants and the colonel drew back and conferred for a few moments. The taller adjutant returned and said to Shellabarger and OBie, "We are here to ensure your safety. There is also another matter—that of quarantine inspection. The animals must be inspected before being released back into the wild. We apologize that our livestock inspectors have not yet arrived. They will be flown out of Uruyen within three or four days. Perhaps by then we will have resolved this controversy—"

"None of this was brought up before," Shellabarger said. His face was growing dangerously red. He turned toward the colonel, hands raised to heaven. "The animals will be dead in three or four days! We don't have the proper food—they have to be returned to the wild—"

He advanced on the colonel, who fingered the strap of his pistol's holster. The adjutants tried to push between their superior officer and the beet-faced trainer. Catalina intervened, taking the trainer's arm.

"*Señor* Shellabarger, come with me, please." She nodded for Anthony and Wetherford to follow as well.

Peter tagged along with them to the concrete pad surrounding the bridge's engine house. OBie and Ray listened from a few yards away.

"Can't you just order them to stand aside?" the trainer asked.

"It is not so simple," she said, sighing deeply. "None of us knows what may happen next between the junta and the president. May I make a suggestion?" She stood with hands on hips, taller than the trainer, glaring down at him.

Shellabarger drew up one side of his lips in an acquiescing grimace. "Sure," he said.

"You do not have to worry about the inspectors. They are civilians and under my authority. I can waive the inspection, which I did not ask for in the first place."

"Our animals are healthy," Shellabarger grumbled.

"I see that," Catalina said. "I suggest that we test the bridge to learn what sort of weight it might bear. We can drive an unloaded truck across first. If the bridge survives that, and my brothers are certain it will, we can then send the animals across. The Army cannot object reasonably under those circumstances."

"What about unreasonably?" OBie asked.

Catalina looked to the sky. This was the best she could offer.

"All right," Shellabarger said. "Let's try it."

Catalina and her brothers spoke with the adjutants and *el Colonel,* voices rising several times. The colonel finally gave in, with some sharply worded provisos. Catalina agreed.

She returned to the concrete platform. "They will allow testing."

Shellabarger softened a little and his face lost its reddish hue. "We appreciate the help," he said gruffly, and returned to work in the engine house, where the motor had begun to roughen its idle. Keller and Kasem entered after him, and then Billie.

Wetherford pulled the twig out of his mouth and tossed it aside, then stuck his hands in his pockets and ambled over to the weed-grown, sun-cracked macadam roadway leading to the bridge.

Anthony looked at Peter and gave him a wan smile. "That bridge cost a lot of money in 1914," he said.

"Is it really solid?" Peter asked.

"It'll hold at least four tons for now. In another couple of years, who knows?" He made his left hand into the edge of the cliff and sailed the right over it and down.

A crowd of J.E.M.'s workers began to cut at the brush and trees on the edge of Pico Poco. Ray filmed them briefly, then joined OBie near the bridge. Peter watched the two framing shots with their hands and looking through little sighting scopes. The film crew began measuring and marking distances to points near the bridge from the dolly and tracks.

Shellabarger called for Peter and he joined the trainer near Sammy's cage, still on the back of its truck. "He's our main problem. The venator's only two tons; Sammy's three. All the other animals put together weigh less than either of them. Poor Sheila was five tons." He shook his head sadly. "She might not have made it anyway. If your father and the Mendez brothers are right, the bridge will still hang together." He sighed. "But we don't want any *excitement.*"

Peter nodded.

"We're going to build a stockade to hold all the animals except Dagger. He stays in his cage and goes last. We'll dismantle the other cages and use the ramps to make a run for him directly from his cage to the bridge. I trust he'll have sense enough to go straight home." Shellabarger walked over to the venator's cage, Peter by his side. The tarp had been raised and tied back, giving the animal a clear view of the proceedings but shielding him from the direct sun.

"For twenty years I've watched him, and he's watched me," Shellabarger said. "I've never made a false move . . . and he's never had a chance to show us what he can really do."

Still crouched on his belly, the venator viewed them with a half shut eye. Simply being near the beast made Peter's insides twist. Every cell in his body knew that here was swift death: ivory teeth and shining claws.

"I worked in an abattoir in Chicago when I was a kid," Shellabarger said. "Hauled slops from the drainage floor to make sausage and fertilizer. He stinks worse than anything I ever hauled." But the trainer's expression and tone revealed no disgust; rather, admiration, and something like regret.

The sound of axes and machetes reached them from the edge of the mountain forest. Shellabarger walked around the cage, rubbing the thick gray stubble on his jaw with one hand. "They all wanted to come close to him. Men, women, kids . . . hundreds of thousands of them. They all wanted to look death in the face. Caged death. We didn't bother telling them there were bigger, meaner, swifter animals on El Grande."

"The death eagles?"

"Yeah," Shellabarger said. "I saw one on my last trip. We didn't even bother trying to catch it. Twenty feet tall and thirty long, with a wicked hooked beak and teeth to boot . . . a big dish of white feathers around its neck, and brown and white feathers hanging from its arms and fanning out from its tail." The trainer hung his fist in front of his abdomen. "Center of gravity *here,* not back *here,* with a shorter, thicker tail, like one of the avisaurs but really"—he sucked his breath in—"*big.*" Shellabarger looked at Peter and smiled. "Dagger isn't the meanest son of a bitch in the valley of the shadow of death." They walked a few yards back from the truck. "We'll send him back where he belongs. He'll be on his own then."

"Do you think he'll find a mate?" Peter asked.

"I don't know," Shellabarger said. He surveyed Peter critically. "You've put on some muscle, son, don't you think?"

Peter smiled. "Hauling Sammy's alfalfa," he said.

"There wasn't time to tell you back on the river," Shellabarger said, "but that was a hell of a thing you did, jumping into the river after your father. Quick thinking." The trainer tapped his head.

Peter did not know what to say. The trainer was not prone to sentiment, but he was clearly focused on speaking his mind about Peter, and Peter was embarrassed and pleased at once.

"You've learned a lot about the animals."

"I wish we could have saved Sheila," Peter said, glancing back down the road, as if she might be thumping along to join them even now.

"If the circus was still a going concern, I'd hire you in a minute," Shellabarger said. "Tell your dad that."

Peter watched the trainer as he crossed the sandstone flats to the engine house.

After lunch, the workers began carrying the fruits of their toil up to the flats—long straight logs, creepers, branches, palm fronds. With OBie and Ray filming, and Anthony and Shellabarger and Billie supervising, they started work on the stockade.

The soldiers and *el Colonel* stayed out of their way. The Army and the Indians behaved like oil and water, refusing to mix or even to come too close together.

It was hard to believe this would all be over soon, and they'd take the trucks back down the trail, ride the boats downriver to the towns on the Caroní and the Orinoco, and then catch a ship back to the States—to home, wherever that would be. OBie and Ray would have their movie film, and he and his father would have their still pictures and their memories.

He did not know what Shellabarger and Lotto Gluck would have. Memories as well, he supposed.

Peter opened his notebook and wrote:

Until now, I've never understood my father's need to find excitement and go to interesting places. I always felt safest going places in my head. Now that we're here on Pico Poco and the animals are going home soon, I wonder if I'll ever have another adventure again. I'm pretty sure that if another opportunity like this comes my way, I won't turn it down. So now I know more about why my father behaves the way he does—and why my mother could not stand it.

Mrs. Birdqueen

Chapter Thirteen

❖

By three o'clock that afternoon, the stockade was finished. The walls stood eight feet high. The five separate enclosures within the irregular construction gave the animals ample room to turn around. They would not be in the stockade for more than a few hours, but they would be much happier than they were in the cages, Peter thought.

Sammy was the first to move in. The centrosaur's truck was driven a few dozen yards to the side where his entrance lay open. The roustabouts hauled out the ramps and hooked them to the back of the truck.

Sammy was facing forward, and the tricky part was backing him down the ramps. Shellabarger unhooked the watering trough and slid in through the narrow slot. Sammy watched this with interest, and nosed the trainer forcefully once he stood up in the cage. Shellabarger pushed his beak back.

"Open the door before he thinks this is a game," he shouted, and Keller and Kasem unhooked the cage door and swung it wide with a grating squeak. Shellabarger prodded Sammy back slowly, talking to soothe him.

"Peter, stand by the side and tell him it's okay," Shellabarger ordered. Peter did so, and they both coaxed the centrosaur backward step by step until he was out of the cage and on the ramp. Sammy looked down, then raised his beak skyward, trilling and honking in concern. Animals as heavy as the centrosaur did not enjoy heights. Shellabarger renewed his efforts and Peter patted Sammy's thick ankles and then his pebble-skinned haunch. When Sammy stood on solid rock, he turned around slowly, sniffed the air, and then sidestepped, almost treading on Peter's feet. Peter jumped aside. Anthony took a picture of this, but gave his son a fatherly grimace and said, "Watch yourself!"

Shellabarger and Peter led the centrosaur to the enclosure. Beyond Sammy's wide door lay a pile of fresh-cut leaves, ferns, even some flowers. Sammy looked back, as if regretting a decision to commit himself to a cage again, however green and leafy, and waddled in with several resigned *whuffs*.

Once he was inside, the struthios and *Aepyornis* were unloaded into their enclosures. The avisaurs remained in their cage.

The colonel and his soldiers stood by their tents, watching the preparations. The colonel was never without his thin-barreled pistol. He wore MacArthur sunglasses now and his expression was unreadable. The bridge motor was running as smoothly as could be expected, and the Mendez twins had finished yet another inspection of the bridge.

With OBie's cameras set up, the bridge swung slowly and with much groaning and grinding of gears across the abyss, finally *chunking* into place over the concrete and steel pad on the opposite side. Rust and dirt sifted down from the bridge's girders. The engine coughed and kicked out thick smoke from within its ramshackle house. As a precaution, Shellabarger ordered the engine shut down.

"I would be privileged to drive the truck across," Billie told the trainer, standing before him with face lowered but eyes looking up expectantly. Shellabarger glared down at Billie, then turned to OBie.

"What about that Julio fellow?" he asked, looking among the drivers for the Carib. Julio stepped forward, but nodded at Billie. A murmur arose among the Indians. Peter watched them closely.

The colonel's translator walked from the tents to the truck and approached Shellabarger. Catalina also stepped forward.

"*El Colonel* would prefer that no Indians be involved with this," the adjutant said. "There is concern . . . of injury."

Billie did not look at the adjutant, but kept his eyes focused on the trainer.

"I'll drive it across myself," Shellabarger said, and strode toward the truck cab. Billie blocked his way with a lithe sidestep.

"*Señor,* we have drawn lots, and I have won the draw. It is a privilege to risk one's life for the return of the Challenger to his home."

Catalina questioned Billie quickly in Spanish. Billie responded in another language Peter was not familiar with. Wetherford, standing between Peter and Anthony, said, "That's Makritare, I think."

Catalina struggled to respond in kind. With a minimum of words and gestures, Billie answered her questions, his meek attitude betrayed by the stiffness of his posture and the darting of his eyes.

Catalina turned to Shellabarger. "Billie tells me the Indians have chosen him to prepare the Challenger's road."

"What's the colonel worried about?" OBie asked her.

"The Army is concerned about any Indian acquiring special status from stepping on El Grande."

"I see that," OBie said. "But what can they do about it? Surely some Indian is going to swing across someday and return."

"That is why Colonel de Badajoz is here with his troops," Catalina said. "They kill any who try."

Peter stared at Billie. The young mestizo did not seem very heroic.

"Then the hell with the colonel," Shellabarger said. "Billie, you go. You'll drive the truck across, then back it up and return it to where it is now." He faced the adjutant. "No special privileges. Just a little truck driving."

The adjutant returned to the colonel. He studied the faces on the Indian and mestizo workers, his mustache twitching nervously. His hand strayed once more to the butt of his pistol. Clearly, he sensed the tension here, and with the radio still useless, calling for reinforcements was out of the question. He nodded.

The adjutant shuttled back to Shellabarger and OBie. "That is okay. But the truck and its driver must not stay on the other side for more than a few minutes. We must protect the natural habitat against intrusion." His expression practically pleaded for them to believe this excuse.

The colonel barked orders in Spanish and three soldiers with rifles positioned themselves near the bridge.

Shellabarger stepped up on the bridge and stamped his foot, then grinned over his shoulder.

"If there should be an accident," the adjutant told Catalina, "you will absolve the Army and Colonel de Badajoz of all blame."

Billie got into the truck that had carried Sammy's cage, the one with the shattered windshield. He started the engine and looked toward Shellabarger. "Go," the trainer said.

Billie turned the truck slightly and aligned it with the bridge. He crept up the concrete ramp and onto the metal deck. Peter held his breath. The bridge took the truck's weight with a silence that surprised him. He had half expected dramatic groans of straining metal, stressed rivets popping, warning signs of real danger. Instead, the bridge seemed solid as a rock.

The truck rolled slowly along the span. Ray followed its progress with the portable camera. Anthony took several pictures, then stood behind the soldiers, his Leica held ready.

The truck reached the opposite side of the bridge. Its weight brought the bridge down with a heavy clang against the concrete on the opposite side, but the girders held. Billie drove onto the cracked and weathered macadam roadway beyond.

The workers watched with solemn expressions. Shellabarger nodded his satisfaction and glanced at the soldiers and the colonel. "All right," the trainer shouted across the chasm. "Bring 'er back."

Billie reversed the truck's gears and backed onto the bridge, leaning out of the window to gauge his progress. The truck returned to Pico Poco without causing any apparent damage. Billie stopped the truck and turned off the engine. The workers seemed to relax as one. Grinning, Billie stepped down from the cab.

"What's the colonel going to object to now?" OBie asked in an undertone.

Catalina spoke to the adjutants. The debate seemed heated; arms waved vigorously, but somehow, the *Doña* Mendez prevailed.

Colonel de Badajoz threw up his hands in disgust and stood by his personal tent as the shorter adjutant unfolded a camp chair.

Catalina smiled broadly and walked toward the stockade. "You may send the animals across," she said to Shellabarger.

"Are we permitted to set foot on El Grande?" Shellabarger asked Catalina. She asked why he would want to do this.

"Because I expect things to go wrong," the trainer replied. "We may need to escort some of the animals. I've always planned to help the avisaurs across personally. I don't want the colonel's soldiers getting itchy trigger fingers."

Doña Mendez referred to her attaché case and withdrew a folder filled with papers. "The edict of 1927 and amendments for 1929 instruct that for scientific purposes, brief footfalls on the Great Tepui, as occasion requires, are permitted for a few unarmed members of an authorized expedition," she said.

Wetherford grinned.

Catalina caught Wetherford's expression and added, "We interpret this liberally to mean that you may stand on the opposite side to help return the animals. But for the sake of peace with the colonel, *por favor,* no Indians."

"Good," Shellabarger said.

The trainer clapped Billie on the shoulder. Billie took a place beside Ray and Peter as Keller and Kasem made their preparations.

Kasem and Keller led Sammy from his enclosure to the bridge, following the marks established by OBie and the film crew.

Shellabarger stood beside Sammy for a moment. He whispered to the centrosaur. Sammy shook his shield vigorously and sniffed the air.

"Go, fella," Shellabarger said, poking Sammy in the rear with his prod. Sammy resisted, turned, and headed back to the enclosure. The trainer ran to bar his way.

"After all this, he doesn't want to go," Wetherford observed. "He doesn't want to give up his meal ticket."

Shellabarger prodded the centrosaur into a tight turn and managed to guide him back to the bridge. Again, Sammy reversed, gently butted Shellabarger aside, and pushed at him all the way back to the enclosure. Inside the fence, he snuffled the remaining fronds and leaves and started eating.

Shellabarger and Keller removed him again, with infinite patience and gentle words, and aimed him toward the bridge. A dim idea of what was expected of him seemed to enter the centrosaur's mind.

Sammy stepped up reluctantly onto the concrete, then advanced a few feet onto the bridge itself. He stopped to peer down through the thick iron grating at the chasm below. The fear of heights struck him and he bellowed miserably.

"Peter!"

Peter came forward at the trainer's call.

"We're going to have to baby him all the way," Shellabarger said.

"All the way to El Grande?" Peter asked, looking across at the forbidden plateau. The broken battlements and faces appeared less ominous in bright daylight, but the landscape still seemed to deny and reject human presence.

"He won't go by himself," Shellabarger said.

Peter looked over his shoulder at his father. The unspoken question passed between them, and the answer returned the same way. Anthony met his son's gaze and said not a word.

Peter did not know whether to feel terrified or privileged.

They flanked the centrosaur. Shellabarger poked him gently in the withers. Sammy seemed to finally make his own decision; he began to move. Together, Peter behind and Shellabarger in front, they accompanied Sammy across the old steel span.

The dinosaur snuffled at the air with each step, then quickened his pace until Peter had to trot behind him. Shellabarger stepped to one side and flattened himself against the rail, letting the dinosaur pass. The bridge banged against the concrete abutment again as Sammy's weight reached the opposite side, shivering wisps of dirt and rust from the beams.

Sammy broke into a gallop and leaped onto the broken roadway beyond. His feet thundered on the weed-grown surface for two dozen yards and then he stopped abruptly, shield swinging forward with its own momentum, his haunches and withers tensing beneath the thick, scaly skin. Peter joined Shellabarger at the end of the bridge.

Across the abyss, on Pico Poco, OBie sat behind the dolly-mounted camera, filming steadily. Ray stood beside him.

"It's all yours," Shellabarger said, shooing the animal with his hands. "Go on! Git! Before we send Dagger across."

Sammy swiveled his long beaked snout and peered at them with his left eye. A rope of saliva swung from his mouth and his sides heaved with thick, deep breaths.

"He drools when he's excited," Shellabarger said to Peter, as if confiding the dark secret of a family member. "Git!"

Sammy spun about with a swiftness that startled Peter. For a second, Peter thought the centrosaur was going to double back and charge them. He lowered his head like a bull and made throaty clucking sounds, then stared over the broken macadam at Shellabarger and Peter. He lifted and twisted his head, stretching his neck skin into taut wrinkles, and his eyes showed their yellow sclera.

"He's going to do it," Shellabarger said in a whisper, as if for Peter's benefit alone. "He doesn't remember—it's been too long for his little walnut brain—but he *knows* the place." The trainer's face contorted. Peter could not tell whether Shellabarger was going to laugh or cry.

Peter watched the centrosaur, his own chest and throat tight. "Go on," he encouraged Sammy. He waved his hands as Shellabarger had done.

Sammy turned more slowly this time, and with great dignity stumped across the field of green grass. With a shiver of his rump, he squeezed between two high rounded lumps of sandstone, and vanished.

The wind blew across the empty plateau. Peter looked down at his feet. He was standing on the Lost World. Beyond the rocks, just miles or maybe only yards away, were hundreds, even thousands of dinosaurs and other animals, some much bigger than Sammy.

Shellabarger put his hand on Peter's shoulder. "We're not done," he said.

Peter could not immediately break the spell.

"Come on," the trainer said.

They walked back over the bridge to Pico Poco.

The roustabouts and workers were making progress breaking down the steel cages. They had paused to watch Sammy's liberation;

now they were back at work, hauling the sections of cage and stacking them beside the bridge, preparing for the venator's release. In the meantime, however, there were the struthios, the *Aepyornis,* and the avisaurs.

Ray approached the enclosure with the portable camera on his shoulder. One of the film crew carried a lightweight tripod and set it down on an X marked with black tape. Ray mounted the camera on the tripod and looked over the viewer, grinning radiantly. "What was it like, standing over there?" he asked Peter.

Peter smiled. "You should try it," he said.

"I'll do my best," Ray said.

Anthony nodded to Peter, his face solemn.

The struthios came next. Shellabarger released them from the enclosure and they took dancing steps past him, swayed their heads back and forth on their long necks, gawked at the mestizos, the film crew, Ray and his camera, and the bridge. Their eyes locked on the bridge and the plateau beyond.

"Come on, pretties," Shellabarger said. He tapped them on their upper thighs with his prod. They looked at him with affronted dignity, then loped ahead, weaving across each other's path, stopping on the roadway just before the ramp to the bridge.

OBie's crew pushed the dolly forward to the end of its rails. The shiny black eye of the camera lens followed the struthios closely. Ray carried his camera to another mark, just out of OBie's shot. Anthony waited until OBie gave him the signal, then moved in closer.

Billie stood with hat in hand, ten yards from the bridge, brow deeply wrinkled. He scratched behind his jaw with a persistent finger. *Doña* Mendez and her twin brothers stood beside Billie. Again, the workers and roustabouts had stopped their labor. The colonel and his soldiers came no closer than the front of their tent.

The struthios showed little sentiment for their past. Shellabarger, the circus, the captivity, had no hold on them. As soon as they figured out that the bridge would return them to El Grande, they leaped forward, running as fast as their long legs could take them, over the bridge and down the road. They veered sharply right, skirting the boulders, and blended into a wind-ragged stand of trees and bushes where the old plateau road had once passed, on the east side.

Shellabarger beat his hat against his pants, replaced it on his wispy gray hair, and said, "Next."

The *Aepyornis* had watched the other animals over the wall of her enclosure. As soon as Shellabarger opened her gate, she leaped out, knocking him on his rear, and dashed for the bridge. Then, abruptly, she turned and emitted a heartfelt screech of alarm. She ran back, stopped by the enclosure, then tried to run south. The roustabouts gave chase and caught up with her only because she hesitated before the soldiers and the tents. Colonel de Badajoz remained seated, but gripped the arms of his camp chair firmly.

Waving their hats, Keller and Kasem herded her back toward Shellabarger. She looked at him indignantly, as if betrayed.

"It's your home, dammit," Shellabarger said to her. "You have to go home."

Mrs. Birdqueen lifted her left foot as if to strike out at the trainer, but then lowered it, and dropped her head as well. She squawked plaintively, then gave several melodious, fluting calls.

Shellabarger approached slowly. She lifted her long neck and ruffled her body feathers. Shellabarger gave a signal and she dropped her head down from its queenly altitude of twelve feet. She stared him straight in the eye with her round, blinking orb, beak agape.

Then she shook herself vigorously and backed away. With great dignity, head held high and neck curved like the body of a question mark, she walked with elegant, high steps up to the bridge, stopped, and called again, sounding like the alto pipes on a pump organ.

The avisaurs trilled back at her from their cage.

Shellabarger ran past Peter and said, "I'm changing my plans. Help me grab the avisaurs. They'll hang around here all day if we let them loose by themselves, but they'll follow Mrs. Birdqueen anywhere."

Peter helped Shellabarger remove the toothed birds from their cages. The trainer handed Keller and Peter leather pads to protect their skin from flexing talons. The trainer carried two of them on his shoulders, where they flapped and screeched loudly. Peter held two more, feeling their sharps claws dig in even through the leather, and Keller the remaining two.

Mrs. Birdqueen had waited patiently for her circus mates. Now, she started across the bridge. Released directly behind her, the avisaurs hopped and ran along the bridge, alternating between roadrunner gait and bird gait, tail feathers spread wide, wings extended. For a moment, Peter was afraid one of the toothed birds might jump off the bridge, but for all their clownish darting, they stayed on the span.

Mrs. Birdqueen reached El Grande, turned, and rose to her full height. She stretched her stubby flightless wings. Two of the avisaurs ran around her and flapped a dozen yards across the grass and broken macadam. One made it to the top of a wind-polished rock and called to the others from its perch. The *Aepyornis* shook her body and head one final time and followed the same route the struthios had taken, into the brush.

One avisaur stayed on its rock perch, watching them. The other toothed birds disappeared without a backward glance.

Shellabarger walked slowly away from the bridge. He idly patted his pockets for nonexistent cigarettes, then looked at Peter and gave him a smirk. One animal remained: the venator.

Catalina said to the trainer, "Congratulations, *señor.* Your big animals have made it."

"One more to go. The venator's no lightweight," Shellabarger said.

The woman turned to Anthony. He raised his camera and took her picture. She smiled. Everyone's spirits seemed raised by the sight of the animals set free. Peter was too exhilarated to feel even a twinge of concern.

"Sammy's going to miss us," he told Shellabarger, following him toward the venator's cage.

Shellabarger grunted and told Billie to bring Dagger's truck around to the bridge. The venator lurched a few inches as the truck started, but remained squatting. "I hope he hasn't got sores and blood poisoning, sitting like that," the trainer said.

The truck rolled to within ten feet of the concrete ramp.

"All right, let's get that runway built," Shellabarger said. The workers and roustabouts gathered around the pieces of cage and began to move them into place.

Catalina and her brothers approached OBie and Ray. "You may shoot from the other side, if you wish," she said. "It is permitted for a brief time." She gave Anthony a look that Peter was all too familiar with. His father attracted the looks of many women. "You should get pictures from El Grande, too."

OBie looked up from the big camera to Ray. "You go," he said. "I've been on the plateau before."

Ray and Anthony moved toward the bridge. Peter looked at Shellabarger. The trainer cocked his head to one side. "Your work's done here," he said. "Go on across and get your fill. It may be the last time for any of us."

Peter ran, then caught himself, slowed, and walked quickly to the ramp to join his father and Ray on the ramp before the bridge. "May I go, too?" Peter asked.

Anthony faced the length of the bridge, one hand on his Leica, the other stuck firmly in his pocket. "Looks pretty safe from here. We'll only be there for a few minutes."

Peter grinned.

"It'll look better in the magazine, with your picture, standing on El Grande," Anthony added. They started across the bridge.

Ray carried the portable camera on his shoulder. "A few panicky shots to complete the effect," he said. "Lord, my hands are trembling."

They walked down the ramp on the opposite side. Black clouds flowed overhead, threatening more rain. Across the chasm, on Pico Poco, the milling people seemed incredibly far away. The rushing updraft muffled the clanging and hammering of the cage pieces being assembled for Dagger's runway.

They stopped. Peter scuffed his boot in the loose gravel and mud covering the sandstone surface.

"It feels pretty sacred, doesn't it?" Anthony asked.

Peter nodded. His palms were sweaty even in the cool air.

"Glad you came?"

He nodded again. Words would not come easily.

Ray dutifully recorded the people on the opposite side, then framed the venator. "I'd love to get a shot of him walking right by here," he said, swinging his hand to the foot of the ramp.

"Pretty expensive shot," Peter said.

"No doubt," Ray murmured, one eye in the viewfinder, panning the camera slowly, the other eye half open and unfocused. "Nooo-o-ooo doubt."

Peter studied the rocky mounds. This end of El Grande sank slowly into a shallow bowl filled with rock-strewn jungle. The rocks between the edge of the chasm and the bowl formed a difficult maze almost a mile wide, with some open areas of as much as an acre; but mostly the maze consisted of tight little passageways, wandering in twisted confusion for hundreds of yards. Unless one knew a secret path or hacked through the thick patch of jungle growing over the old road on the eastern side, it could take days to get to the bowl.

Not that Peter was considering such a thing.

He looked across the chasm at the workers. They had erected the cage runway and were now wiring and cabling it to the bridge. Shellabarger stood with his back to them. OBie and the film crew were rearranging the tracks and dolly.

Peter wondered what it would be like to be alone on the Grand Tepui, on Kahu Hidi, as Billie's father had been.

Ray set the camera down and flexed his shoulders. "All my life, this place has haunted me. Nobody wanted my space creatures and mythical beings . . . They kept saying, 'Look, we have all the monsters we want right here and now. Why make 'em up?'" He shook his head. "For OBie and me, El Grande has been the bane of our existence. But you know what?"

He gazed across the rocks. A few drops of rain spattered on the sandstone around them.

"I forgive it," Ray said. "Just being here, I forgive everything."

"Time to come back," Shellabarger called over the wind. "We're going to hook 'er up." Already they had fastened one side of the runway to the cage and slung the ramps from the bed of the venator's truck.

The workers clustered around the cage. Soldiers milled a few yards from the edge of the chasm, rifles slung. Peter saw *el Colonel* standing with his adjutants near the truck with the broken windshield. He did not understand why he could be here and the Indians could not. It seemed manifestly unfair.

"Let's not overstay our welcome," Anthony said. "Wouldn't want to have to explain to your mom why you were eaten."

Peter saw a man running from the middle of the workers. It was Billie. He jumped through the gap in the cage runway and sprinted across the bridge. The Indians and mestizos scattered in all directions from the bridge, as if to create a diversion. Before the three of them could move, Billie was across. Shots rang out over the chasm.

"Get down!" Anthony shouted, pushing Peter's shoulder. They dropped. Bullets ricocheted from the bridge and pocked the ground around Billie, who passed less than twenty feet from where they lay on the rock. Peter heard voices shouting in Spanish, loudest among them the colonel's. He rolled and twisted to see if Billie would be hit.

Bullets sprayed chips from the grotesque mounds ahead of Billie and the sandstone at his feet, but he seemed to have a charm. Peter started to get up, but Anthony slammed him down again, pressing his cheek into the mud.

"Stay down!" his father ordered. The soldiers on the edge were joined by their comrades, and a forest of rifle barrels contended in the crowd for open space to shoot. Smoke rose in thick puffs as if from a shooting gallery.

In seconds, Billie darted across the macadam and grass and plunged behind a tall pillar wind-carved into the profile of an old man. "He made it!" Peter said.

"Down!" Anthony repeated harshly.

OBie and the camera crew had trained the camera on Billie as he made his break. Now OBie turned the lens on the soldiers. The workers who had scattered had come to a stop well behind the commotion, dropping to their knees or lying flat on their stomachs, as if expecting to be shot at as well. Some soldiers turned as if to do just that, aiming their rifles back toward the end of the road to Pico Poco, but the tall adjutant waved his arm, shouting orders not to fire.

The Mendezes stood in the way. Shellabarger remained by Dagger's cage, but Wetherford, Keller, and Kasem were crawling and running bent over toward the trucks.

"Stop shooting!" Anthony called. "For God's sake, stop shooting!"

Shellabarger walked toward the soldiers near the edge, holding out his hand. They had emptied their clips and now there was nothing worth shooting at. They stood like exhilarated children, some solemnly reloading, others smiling and laughing.

"He must come back!" the tall adjutant cried, his voice dulled by the rising wind. *El Colonel* was furious. He screamed at the Mendezes. Catalina ignored him and resolutely stalked toward the bridge. Her brothers followed with less conviction. She pushed through the gap between the unfastened side of the runway and the bridge girders, intent apparently on retrieving Billie single-handedly.

Out of the corner of his eye, Peter saw the venator rise from his crouch. Shellabarger turned at the noise.

The venator swung his tail against the cage and tucked his forearms against his chest. With his full weight he slammed into one side, and then back against the other. The truck wobbled. The soldiers crouched, rifles down by their sides, uncertain what to do. Nothing had prepared them for this.

The Mendezes stopped halfway across the bridge. The soldiers on the lip of the chasm crouched and backed away.

Shellabarger approached the cage. Peter could not see his face. The venator slammed back and forth again, making the truck's springs squeal. Part of the cage snapped and sent a piece of metal whizzing.

"Jesus," Anthony said. Peter's father never swore that way.

Ray lifted the camera from the ground with a look of focused concentration. Everything seemed to happen in slow motion. The Mendezes stopped on the bridge and turned around, as if Billie were no longer important.

The venator's assault skewed its cage on the truck bed. Jorge, who had replaced Billie behind the wheel of the truck, leaped from the cab and stood a few feet from Shellabarger, holding up his hands as if trying to calm the beast. The venator let out a painful, rasping shriek. Jorge, too, broke and ran.

Shellabarger stood his ground.

The cage leaned. The venator made a querulous clucking noise, then shrieked again as the cage slid on its bottom plate, caught once more, and toppled from the side of the truck, torquing the runway. Bolts snapped sharply.

Peter opened his mouth, but there was no time to scream.

Shellabarger held up his hands. The cage fell on him with a resounding clangor. The full weight of the cage and the venator covered the trainer and Peter could not see him. He felt his father wrap his arms around him but shook loose, crying out.

The venator kicked at the ruined cage with all the might of his powerful feet, snapping more bolts. The beast screamed like a huge woman, voice as big as the sky. The remaining soldiers darted back and forth like frightened mice, then ran for the road.

"My God," Ray said, still filming. "What can we do?"

Anthony looked at the rocks and the brush.

"Nothing," he said. "Not yet." To Catalina and her brothers, he waved and shouted, "Get off the bridge! Come over to this side!"

But the trio seemed frozen, gripping the rails beside the bridge roadway. Anthony snapped two pictures of the mayhem, then handed the Leica to Peter and ran for the bridge.

Dagger

The venator broke through the top of the cage. He rolled and grunted and kicked free of the entangling bars.

The Mendezes suddenly made their move. They ran for Pico Poco.

"No!" Anthony and Ray cried out simultaneously. "Come back!" Anthony reached the bridge but did not cross.

The woman looked back at them, then darted between the broken pieces of runway, followed by her brothers. They dashed all-out for the closest truck. The workers, Wetherford, the roustabouts, the film crew, all had scattered, leaving only OBie standing by the side of the cliff and Shellabarger beneath the ruins of the cage.

The venator rolled from side to side, kicking out with one leg and then the other, until he came upright, legs drawn up, feet flat against the ground. He pushed with his forelimbs, which hardly seemed strong enough to hold a quarter of his weight, and stood in delicate balance, muscles quivering, tail jerking down behind. He lifted his head to the sky.

The ground shook with his triumphant roar. All of twenty years of rage and confinement, of being enslaved, blew loose in that roar and echoed from the rocks behind them. If ever a sound had a color, that one did, and the color was blood.

OBie backed toward the edge of the cliff. For a moment, Peter thought he might step off.

Catalina and her brothers crowded into the truck's cab. The truck's engine started and thick black smoke shot from its stacks. Gears ground and the truck spun its rear tires and jerked ahead. The venator leaned forward, pivoting on its hind legs, nose pointed straight out at the truck. With a grunt and a deep *chirrup,* he covered the ground between in four great bounds, claws digging up showers of dust and gravel. With another *chirrup* Dagger leaped onto the back of the truck. He butted his head against the rear of the cab, denting the metal on one side and shattering the rear window. The truck veered left and then right and Dagger lost his balance and toppled off.

The venator landed on his side and thigh with an awful thump, two tons of flesh hitting hard. He crumpled and lay still for long seconds. From their position, Peter could not see if the animal was breathing.

"He's dead," Ray said.

"He's knocked the wind out," Anthony said. The truck rumbled down the road and below the rise.

Except for OBie, the staging area before the bridge was now deserted. OBie turned. He seemed stunned, his jaw hanging open, arms half extended, as if he expected someone to take his hand.

"Quick—come on across!" Ray shouted.

OBie jerked as if shocked. "What the hell good will that do?" he called. "We'll be stuck. God only knows what's on that side!" He approached the collapsed cage. Rubbing his hands on his pants, as if expecting some very unpleasant work, he bent and peered at Shellabarger.

"Is he alive?" Anthony shouted.

The venator's upper leg rotated a few degrees in its hip socket. His chest shuddered and rose and fell; dirt fanned from his nostrils.

"He ain't moving," OBie said. "He's pressed pretty tight under there . . . lots of blood on his head."

Peter felt sick. He had never been so afraid; all he wanted was someplace to go where he could throw up. Anthony stepped out onto the bridge. "Peter," he said. "If the venator gets up again, get some pictures. I'm going across to help OBie."

"I'll go, too," Peter said.

"You stay here. Nobody knows how fast that animal can move."

Ray put his hand on Peter's shoulder. "He's right," he said. "If they need help, they'll let us know."

"What can they do?"

"Get that cage off Vince, maybe," Ray said.

OBie found a pry bar left by the workmen. Anthony stepped off the far end of the bridge, surveyed the venator where he lay about fifty yards away, and jogged to help OBie lift the edge of the cage.

"They'll need our help," Peter said, and he started for the bridge.

The venator lifted his head, snorted and growled loudly, and rolled onto his back, stretching his legs and arms slowly into the air as if waking from a long, leisurely nap.

"Hold it!" Ray shouted.

Peter stopped, eyes wide. Anthony and OBie worked even more

frantically on the cage and wrenched away one side, leaving Shellabarger still pinned beneath.

The venator turned his head and stared with both eyes directly at them. "Dad!" Peter called.

The animal turned to the sound of Peter's voice and rolled on his side like a playful dog. He rolled back and forth twice, flexed his legs, and with one amazing swing, flung himself over and up onto his feet. He was off balance, however, and teetered, falling again with a slam onto the rocky ground. The venator groaned and blinked, then kicked his legs out and began all over again.

Anthony said something to OBie and they got up from their crouch. Ray joined Peter at the bridge and grabbed his shoulders firmly. Peter tried to jerk loose. "Stay here," Ray said. "He knows what to do."

Dagger swung up again onto his feet, leaning forward on his long, wiry arms. With another jerk of his tail, he regained his upright stance and shook his head vigorously. Then he pivoted, brought his head low and level with his body and extended tail, and stomped toward OBie and Anthony.

The two men broke into a run—taking opposite directions. Dagger made a quick decision and veered toward OBie. Anthony saw this and darted across his path, taking a shortcut toward the bridge. The venator leaned to one side and snapped at Anthony's head, jaws meeting inches from his whipped-back hair. Anthony flung the pry bar with a sidearm swing that struck the venator full in the snout. Dagger drew back and shook his head, blinking in pain, but slowed only for an instant. This gave OBie time to swerve like a broken-field runner in football. He swung around behind the venator. Dagger's tail lashed out and clipped his arm, nearly knocking him down; he stumbled onto one hand, legs still churning, and knelt briefly before getting to his feet. Scrabbling, the venator dug his claws into the gravel and rock.

It seemed impossible for such a large animal to change course so quickly, but there was no arguing with reality; Dagger was within yards of the bridge before OBie joined Anthony near the broken runway. They pushed through the dismantled cages and started across.

Peter ran out onto the bridge to meet his father before he consciously knew his legs were moving. Ray ran beside him, trying to grab his arm. "Peter! For God's sake!"

OBie and Anthony made it about a third of the way across while Dagger tore apart the runway. Sections of steel bars flew as he lifted one broad foot and clawed and kicked.

Anthony shouted for Peter to go back. Peter stopped and Ray ran into and over him, and both fell onto the deck of the bridge. Through the metal plating, Peter could see the bottom of the chasm between Pico Poco and El Grande, thousands of feet below, and a curious tiny curve of white water like a silver snake. Anthony yanked him up by his left arm; OBie did the same with Ray, whose nose streamed blood.

Peter looked back and suddenly understood the glare of the basilisk, the hypnotic gaze of the cobra before its prey. Dagger stood before the bridge and drew back to leap. Anthony jerked on Peter's arm, nearly unsocketing it. The end of the bridge on El Grande seemed very far away; the distance to Pico Poco seemed little more than a step or two, telescoped, the view closing into a tunnel of shock around the gaping mouth of the venator, still drawing back, back, legs splayed, all his muscles tensing like steel bands beneath his gleaming skin. The sun caught the animal's eyes like twin arcs on a welding torch; he lowered his head and the eyes became pits of night.

Dagger's arms pushed out first, and then the venator sprang forward. His leap took him a good five yards over the bridge. Peter felt the pain in his arm, and another pain as Anthony jerked him forward again. They were less than three running strides from El Grande, but that was little relief; the venator would be on them in seconds.

The shock of Dagger's landing knocked them off their feet and slammed the bridge on both sides with a hideous groan and a deep ringing bell-tone on the concrete abutments. Peter nearly slipped through the wide-spaced iron bars of the railing. He hung on grimly with both hands and saw once more the cleft's distant bottom. Showers of rust and flakes of corrosion fell like a ghostly russet curtain into the abyss.

He could not help looking back over his shoulder once more, though he was convinced Dagger's jaws would be wrapped around him in an instant; but the dinosaur had hesitated.

The bridge swayed several feet back and forth on its rotating foundation. It swung away from the concrete abutment on the El Grande side, scraping and flinging sparks, and the ramp dropped, slamming hard against dirt and rock.

Anthony fell back on his hands and knees. "Crawl!" he shouted to Peter, but the bridge shuddered violently beneath them and they all fell on their stomachs, fingers clinging to narrow gaps in the deck.

The venator made a querulous grumble, then screeched with alarm as the bridge slid sideways. His head cracked into the support beams and his two-ton weight strained the pivot even more severely. The concrete crumbled and bolts gave way.

Hand over hand, Peter reached the end of the bridge. His fingers touched dirt and sandstone; he felt the rough, painful grit beneath his fingernails and bloodied the tips of his fingers as the bridge swung again. He heard OBie cough behind him, and wondered where his father was, and saw Ray crawling with a determined frown to his right, as if looking for something he had dropped.

Once again, as he kicked forward, Peter looked back. The venator took a step in their direction and the bridge dropped several feet below the swinging foundation. A cloud of rust gathered at that end and rust fell from the girders and support beams all around.

"It's going! Get clear!" That was Anthony shouting hoarsely. Somehow, everyone had gotten around Peter and was now ahead of him.

Dagger hesitated again, nostrils twitching. Fury gave way to instinct. The venator pushed back one step, then two, miraculously staying on his feet as the bridge slipped another few inches and swayed, all its weight now resting on the support girders where they had shoved into the rock. The roadbed girders grated against the cliff's face; the bridge was held by little more than two sticks of iron and its wedged position.

Pebbles flew off into the chasm and the bridge slipped another foot.

The venator turned and kicked. The bridge made a tooth-grinding, tortured-metal roar and fell away beneath the animal. OBie and Ray rolled onto the rock of El Grande and Anthony grabbed Peter's arm once more, his fingers hard as steel. Peter suddenly hung in space and slapped against the cliff face, mashing his side and cheek. He cried out in pain. He was sure he was falling, but Anthony's grip tightened and Ray and OBie held Anthony's waist, and all together, with a pig-grunt heave, they pulled him over the edge.

As it fell, the bridge made a terrible grinding and screeching, the sound echoing and diminishing, until a final distant tinny bang ended it all.

Peter lay on his back, wrapped in pain, and stared up at the sky.

"Mary Mother of God," OBie said reverently.

"Amen," Anthony said.

Ray sat with knees drawn up, rubbing his bloody lip and nose. He drew his hand away, stared at the smear of blood, and then focused his attention across the chasm, to Pico Poco.

"I'll be damned," he said, and shook his head once as if to scare off a mosquito.

Peter, still dazed, turned and saw Dagger standing by the shattered foundation of the bridge. The venator's ribs rose and fell rapidly, and his tongue peeked purplish pink between his long narrow teeth like a piece of raw beef. His feet and thighs were bloody from numerous deep gouges, and blood streamed from his nose and the side of his head. One eye was swollen shut. Dagger turned his massive head and surveyed them with the remaining eye like a battered prizefighter.

"He made it," Anthony said in disbelief.

Peter sat up, cradling his wrenched left arm in his right hand.

The bridge was gone.

"We're stuck," he said.

"At least until the crew comes back and shoots that son of a bitch," OBie said passionately. "They can rig a rope bridge and we'll swing across, and then, by God . . . " He stood and brushed off his pants. "By God, I'm going back to Los Angeles and take a long hot shower and never go any goddamned place again in my life."

Anthony shook his head and gave his son a wide, almost maniacal smile. "You all right?" he asked.

"Yeah," Peter said.

"Let me look at you."

Anthony touched his son's arm solicitously. Peter made a face and said, "It's all right, really," and they all froze. Through the whispering harshness of the wind they listened to something, not the venator; something on *their* side of the chasm, a sound Peter had never heard before . . .

Like the cry of a huge eagle.

BOOK

TWO

Chapter One

O Bie stared north at the wind-sculpted rocks of El Grande's maze. "It's been a long time since I've heard that cry," he said, "and I don't welcome it."

"What is it?" Anthony asked.

"Could be a small avisaur trying to scare us," OBie said. "But I don't think so." He turned in a circle, clearly uneasy, scrutinizing the plateau, the maze, the deeply overgrown road reaching around the eastern side of the maze. "We're out in the open here. All the noise could have attracted something . . . We should wait in the rocks for our people to get back."

"Doesn't look like they're coming back," Anthony said grimly.

"It takes more than a dinosaur to scare off motion picture folks," OBie said. He gave Peter a wink. "I'll be charitable and suppose the circus fellows will come back, too."

The venator paced restlessly on the edge of Pico Poco, grunting and grumbling like an old man fretting over some overdue debt. He had perked up at the eagle shriek, as well, but now seemed unconcerned.

A truck motor rumbled from the south, out of sight below the top of Pico Poco.

"That's probably them now," Anthony said, patting Peter's head.

He hadn't done that to his son for at least three years—at Peter's request. Peter did not complain. He was relieved just to hear the truck. The roustabouts might bring more guns. They would have to shoot the venator, unfortunately—he didn't think they'd be able to capture him alive. They probably would not want to, after what had happened to Shellabarger.

"Is Vince dead?" Peter asked.

"He was mighty still," OBie said. "I didn't have time to check his pulse."

Peter thought that when the venator got hungry, it would forget them long enough to lift the bars and pry Shellabarger loose. End of a long story.

Ray pointed. "Look!" Two men were climbing over the rise onto the top of Pico Poco, about two hundred yards south of where they stood. Peter could not see them clearly enough to identify them, but Anthony said, "It's Arnie Kasem and one of the Mendez brothers." A third appeared. "And there's Rob Keller."

"Nobody from our crew?" OBie asked, disappointed. He shielded his eyes and squinted.

"Not yet," Anthony said. Keller waved at them but did nothing to attract the attention of the venator. He slowly and dramatically flapped his hands up and down, as if trying to fly. Then he swooped his arm out.

"What's he trying to say?" Ray asked.

OBie shook his head. "Do they have guns?"

"No," Anthony said.

"There's some of our crew, and some of the Indians, too," Anthony said. Four more men came up over the rise, and again they heard the truck.

The truck ascended the trail slowly, smoke belching from its stacks. Soldiers crowded the truck bed. The venator turned at the diesel noise and faced the truck, long tail switching stiffly back and forth.

With a swing of his head and a backward glance at his intended prey, still inaccessible across the chasm, Dagger took one step away from the edge, then another, and leveled himself head to tail before breaking into a swift trot. He was going to confront this renewed threat immediately and head-on. The thump of his feet on the rocky surface and the sound of his grunting breaths increased as he picked up speed. Peter watched the play of muscles in his thighs and back with a shiver of admiration.

"They'll shoot him now," OBie said. He did not appear particularly convinced or even happy about that. The truck bed became a haze of smoky bursts pierced by brief muzzle flashes. A bullet struck the rock next to Ray, and another whizzed past Peter's head.

They all dropped as more bullets flew by. The venator's speed increased to fifteen, eighteen, twenty miles an hour. The slender muscular legs pounded faster. Peter heard a steady *crack-crack-crack* of rifles and pistols. Whether any of the bullets hit the animal, he couldn't tell—but none slowed him down.

They heard shouting and then screams as the venator closed on the men. Kasem and Keller ran for the truck and hoisted themselves on, as did Mendez. The other workers retreated and scattered. The truck backed down the grade, and still the venator ran faster and faster.

"My God, my God," OBie said, getting to his knees. Anthony lifted himself as if doing a push-up and peered across the chasm and plateau.

All the men and the truck had retreated. The venator stopped at the far side of the rise. Distant pops rang out, more desultory gunfire. Dagger shook his head, as if bothered by flies.

They stood. OBie looked disgusted enough to spit. "We'll have to take care of ourselves. We can cut some strong vines in the jungle beyond these rocks, north of the maze," he said. "Maybe we can hook up with Billie, wherever he's got to. You'd think all this noise would bring that Indian back—unless he kept on running."

The venator swiveled quickly on his big three-toed feet.

"He doesn't look hurt," Ray said.

Dagger returned at a steady gait to the rim to assume his vigil once more. Peter's heart sank. Even across the chasm, the venator's appearance made Peter want to run—or just lie down and wait to die.

Anthony raised his camera and took a picture.

"They *must* have hit him," Ray said, and took a deep, shuddering breath in frustration.

"I doubt that anybody over there is a crack shot," Anthony said.

"If you'd had a gun—" Peter began.

"Yeah," Anthony said peevishly. "Well, none of us has a gun."

Nostrils twitching, the venator leaned over the chasm. His eyes remained focused on the four of them and the long tail made an audible *swoosh* with each swing back and forth. Bright bloody spots on his breast and muzzle marked fresh wounds.

"They *did* get him," Peter said, awed.

"Looks that way," OBie said, "but it hasn't slowed him any."

Clouds of flies buzzed around the animal. Dagger paid them no mind. He squatted on his belly and twisted his head to lick at blood on his flank. He couldn't quite reach the wound. With a patient, resigned look, like a cat about to take a nap, he snapped his jaw shut and blinked slowly.

"We could be here all night before the crews regroup and think of a plan," Ray said.

"I hope they're in radio contact with somebody," Anthony said.

"Peter, you forgot our sleeping bags," OBie said.

"Sorry," Peter said.

"And dinner," Ray said. The cameraman gave Peter a lopsided grin. Everybody was trying to act brave, but their faces were ashen with concern.

"Nobody said they wanted a picnic," Peter said. He thought of Shellabarger. The contrast between their forced banter and the trainer lying under the collapsed cage made his eyes well up with tears. Peter went to his father and Anthony put his arms around him.

OBie looked at them with a funny expression, as if a knife had just been twisted in him. He said, "It'll be dark shortly. We might get our chance if Dagger there bleeds a little more and gets woozy. Maybe we should scout out some vines in case we can cross in the morning."

"A hundred feet of vines?" Anthony said dubiously. "I don't know if that will work."

"There are vines in the forest three times as long as that, and tough as leather," OBie said. "The Indians call them *mamure*."

Again came the horrible, high-pitched *skreee* from farther north in El Grande. It did not seem close, but it was loud.

"That isn't anything small," Ray said. He rubbed his hand back from his high forehead through his hair to his neck.

OBie's eyes were wide with large dark pupils. "Yeah," he agreed, voice shaky.

"Could it be a death eagle?" Peter asked, his mouth suddenly parched. *Maybe OBie doesn't want to scare us—but I'd sure rather know.*

OBie didn't answer. He picked up a pebble and flung it at the ground. "The hell with waiting here," he said. "That bastard has no intention of dying. Let's go hide in the rocks."

Peter followed Anthony and Ray across the clearing. OBie lingered for a moment, hands stuffed deep in his pockets, shaking his head regretfully. Then he jogged to catch up with them.

The rocks in the tumult of the maze seemed even more gnomish and unnatural as the day ended. Tortured dark clouds hurried above the tepui again, frantic with rain, swooping sunset shadows over the outlines of faces and creatures Peter kept seeing in the rocks. A cool breeze and thick cold drops quickly followed.

"This could have gone a lot better," OBie said, squeezing into a narrow passage.

Anthony tucked the Leica in his jacket. Ray still carried the portable movie camera.

"I've got about two minutes of film left," Ray said to Anthony. "How about you?"

"Ten shots," Anthony said.

Peter followed his father between two pillars. Moisture dripped down the granular face of the rock. A few lichens hung like green beards from a jutting stone chin. Looking up, he saw a small slate-black frog staring down at them from a crevice. It blinked shiny black eyes and retreated out of sight.

"It won't be long now," OBie said with no confidence whatsoever.

The *skreeee* sounded again, followed by another cry, a heart-stopping bellow of pain and terror. They instinctively backed up against the walls of the narrow passage. Peter's shirtback was soaked by the dripping moisture and he trembled both from chill and fear.

The cry of pain returned, weaker and sadder, subsiding into resigned groans and then black silence. Rain pattered. A mournful whistle rose between the rocks. The sky overhead gloomed charcoal with flinty details. Everything smelled of water and earth and something else—a faint scent of the cages in the circus, a cloying blunt bird smell.

"No lanterns, no coats, no food," OBie said. "We are the prize chumps of all time."

Peter fingered the clasp knife in his pocket. Night came quickly and they huddled between the rocks. Peter thought it would be impossible to sleep, but he underestimated how tired he was. He jerked himself out of a troubled doze to see thin rips of dawn spreading over a clearing sky. He pushed himself out of a clump of lichen and branches, brushing scraps of moss from his hair, and realized someone had made a pillow for him. He rubbed his eyes and saw Ray and OBie standing farther back in the maze, talking softly.

"We could get lost in here really easy," Ray said, voice clear in the quiet.

"I've been through here before, twice," OBie said. "I should recognize the key landmarks. But everything's grown. I'd swear even the rocks have changed."

"You don't see anything familiar?" Ray asked.

"Not yet, damn it," OBie replied. "There's faces all over, and animals, too. Somewhere around here there's an old Indian with a hooked nose . . . " He tapped his own nose with his finger. "I know the main side route to the east around the maze, where we used to bring out the animals, but it's completely overgrown now. Still, we might try it—if we had a couple of machetes."

Anthony pushed into the gap between the pillars, returning from the edge of the chasm. "How's it going?" he asked Peter.

"I feel a lot better," Peter said. "But thirsty . . . and really hungry."

"We do get used to three squares a day, don't we?" Anthony said. "Dagger's still on patrol. Doesn't look like anybody's planning to come back soon. Maybe they're waiting for Sears Roebuck to deliver a howitzer."

Ray and OBie joined them. "I can't find an easy path through these rocks," OBie said. "I know there is one. Billie ran right through somewhere . . . "

"No sign of him, either," Ray said. "And nothing to eat."

"We might find some fruit in the jungle," OBie said. "Bananas, *bijiguao* fruit."

"How big's the maze?" Anthony asked.

"About two miles across. There are a few small streams and there might still be a swamp somewhere in the middle."

"I'm really thirsty," Peter repeated.

"Lick the rock," Anthony suggested.

Peter made a face.

"Really. It works."

"There's water pooled on top of some of these rocks, if you don't mind a little scum and frog spawn," OBie said. Peter cupped his hand against a rivulet of water still dribbling down the side of a rock and gathered enough liquid in his palm to wet his tongue and throat.

"We should agree on a plan," Anthony suggested. "We might be here awhile. Is there any way to climb down on this end?"

"Not that any Indian or white man has found in a couple of thousand years of searching," OBie said. "It's a mile or more straight down, along stretches of rock smooth as a baby's bottom, but no diaper pins to tie our rope to, even if we had any rope."

Peter saw a shape flit across the gap between the pillars. For a second, he thought the venator had somehow crossed the chasm and found them, but the shape had seemed shorter, smaller, darker. He grabbed Anthony and Ray and pulled them back into the passage.

"Something's out there," he said.

"Maybe it's Billie," OBie said.

"No. An animal."

"Sammy, then."

"Not that big."

"Someone's going to have to peek out," Ray said.

"You volunteering?" Peter asked.

Ray shook his head.

They heard a scrabbling on the rocks above. Peter and Anthony looked up in time to see a dark green and brown animal finish its leap over the passage. They discerned stumpy hind legs and a long tail, and then it was gone.

"It's as big as a dog," Anthony said.

OBie started pushing them. "We'll take our chances deeper in," he said. "Grab a stick, a rock, anything you can find." They walked and slithered and climbed through the winding cuts and gouges and passages, stooping beneath ledges like jutting noses, sinking up to their ankles in marshy pits. After venturing fifty yards or more into the maze, Anthony called a halt in an open space about four yards wide.

They listened and looked all around.

"What do you think it was?" Ray asked OBie.

"I didn't see it clearly," OBie said. "Don't think I'm an expert here, either. There's lots of animals we've never seen, much less captured."

"Stay close. Don't get separated," Anthony said. He reached for Peter's arm. They were both winded from clambering over the rocks. Peter had skinned his knuckles and torn his pants. One knee was bleeding. He could still smell the bird odor. He felt very exposed.

"Are you sorry I brought you with me?" Anthony asked. Peter did not know what to say.

"Into danger," Anthony said, eyes searching Peter's face.

Peter said, "It depends on whether I get eaten or not."

Ray laughed and Anthony responded with a faint smile.

OBie hadn't heard. "What was that?" he asked.

"The success of our expedition," Ray said dramatically, "depends on whether or not we get consumed by the locals."

OBie glowered. "I have never felt so naked and helpless in my life, and I've lived longer than any of you."

"My father was in Italy," Peter said, awkwardly and unexpectedly defensive.

OBie turned his lips down and raised his brows in acknowledgment. "I was too old for the war," he said. "Where would you rather be?" he asked Anthony.

"Italy or here?" Anthony chuckled. "No contest. Italy."

"Battle or here," OBie specified.

Anthony shrugged. "We don't have to kill somebody else to stay alive."

His eyes fixed on something over Peter's head. Peter turned and lifted his gaze to the top of a rock shaped like a pile of pancakes. Ray and OBie looked up as well. A sleek mottled brown and green head watched them intently through large almond-colored eyes. The animal's body was slender and long and bluish-black with white spots. It stood on four legs and was bigger than a cat and smaller than a beagle. It did not look particularly fierce. It turned its long head sideways and opened its curving mandible, revealing small sharp teeth.

"Don't ask me what it is," OBie murmured. "I've never seen it before. May be one of the northern animals come south."

"Look at the canines," Ray said. Peter examined the dog-like head. It resembled a squat, bowlegged, hairless collie wrapped in lizard skin.

"I think it's a kind of therapsid," Ray said.

Another rose up, and a third, surrounding them in a precise triangle. None seemed in any hurry. Peter judged the distance across the open space. The animals could leap down on them easily.

The first animal raised its snout and gave a whistle. The whistle ended in a hoarse, guttural howl.

OBie raised his stick. Peter and Anthony clutched sharp-edged rocks in their hands. Ray seemed ready to use the movie camera as a club. All three animals backed off with a quick but awkward-looking side-legged gait until they were no longer visible.

"Damn," Anthony said. "I didn't get a picture."

Swift as a snake striking, something leaped from a hole between two boulders and streaked into OBie's side. He fell on his back with a grunt. Anthony caught a second animal on the side of its head with his rock and it gave a hoarse yip. Peter saw the third running up beside him, head cocked, and raised his rock; the animal scuttled sideways like a crab, jerking its gaze from Peter's knees to his head, sizing him up.

OBie's attacker rolled away, then doubled back and leaped again, catching OBie's arm in its jaws. OBie brought the stick down hard on its head, jamming its upper teeth through his shirt into his skin but stunning the animal before it could clamp down. OBie cried out. Peter's animal moved in and nipped at his legs, pushing him away from Anthony. Ray alone seemed free of an adversary. He kicked at OBie's stunned attacker and both of them retreated as two new animals rushed in.

Peter concentrated on the therapsid following him. The animal seemed content to snap and jump in quick feints, leaping sideways just in time to avoid a kick or the rock. Peter reached for a second rock and lobbed it at the animal's head. The rock bounced from the top of its skull and it stopped for a moment, shaking itself all over.

"Go away!" Peter yelled. The therapsid had forced him around several turns into a narrow ravine. He could not see any of the others, but he heard Ray and OBie shouting.

He stooped over, head up, hands out, backing into the ravine. "What do you want?" he asked the animal. He did not really expect to be told; it just seemed better to engage the beast in some sort of conversation. The therapsid was clearly a pack animal. There must be others around; it was probably herding Peter toward another group and together they would bring him down.

The therapsid rolled its yellow eyes. All of the noises it made—whines, growls, a short high noise like *keuf, keuf*—sounded gravelly, rough, *old*. Peter tried to remember his reading about El Grande. He thought the therapsids might be older than dinosaurs; he recalled them being related to mammals, somehow.

"You're one of us," Peter said, "a cousin." The animal was not impressed. It rushed in again, snapping its jaws in a quick blur, claws ticking on the rocks. Pebbles skittered beneath Peter's shoes and he slipped and nearly fell.

"You're not going to push me any farther," Peter vowed, and backed up against a gouge in the sandstone face, rock raised. The animal had been hurt once—its scaly, puffy-looking scalp oozed blood—and it seemed unwilling to move in too close. It suddenly dropped down on its stomach, legs crooked on all sides, and lowered its head. It flattened its jaw against the dirt and rock. It seemed to be listening.

Peter could no longer hear the others. He felt a stab of panic at being separated from Anthony and got to his feet, kicking out. The therapsid calmly watched Peter's foot sail harmlessly over its head, moving only its eyes. Then it lifted its head and snapped casually at the air.

"You'd make a dandy pet," Peter said breathlessly. He wondered why he felt better talking to the animal; it would be just as effective, he thought, trying to strike up a conversation with an alligator.

"You and your friends want to crowd in here and strip me down to my bones, don't you?"

The therapsid whistled faintly.

Peter looked quickly to both sides to find the best escape route. "I can't wait around," he said. With a grimace and a yell, he jumped away from the rock and brought his left boot hard against the animal's snout and then its side, catching it by surprise.

He wanted to rejoin the others, but all the rocks looked alike. He jumped down a long, reasonably straight fissure and heard claws ticking and scratching and *keuf, keuf* right behind. He did not slow to look. With feet and heart pounding, hands deflecting him from jutting rocks, Peter half ran, half tumbled down this lane.

He veered to the left, rounded a pillar rising from thick tufts of yellow grass, saw a broad open stretch at least twenty yards across, and ran like hell, head back, arms pumping, filling his lungs with a whoop, tears streaming from his eyes. He knew the therapsids were going to catch him in the open, surround him; he knew he had made the wrong move. He had seen the exhibit in the American Museum of Natural History of an elk surrounded by wolves, with dead and dying wolves scattered all around; he did not think he would avenge his death so well.

Something snagged his ankle and he pitched forward on his face. An animal ran right over him. Peter caught its rear leg in his hands before it could turn, and with unexpected strength, he lifted the animal, rolled, and swung it back over his body. It thumped down on another therapsid and both screamed like jackals. Peter's arm hurt like hell at the effort, but he shouted triumphantly in spite of the pain and got to his feet. "Come get me, you little bastards! Come here and get me!"

He felt the spirit of Shellabarger at that moment, and the force of his father's defiance and strength all rolled together, and he knew beyond any doubt he would be with the trainer in a few minutes, and he didn't really care. He would just do as much damage as he could in that short time, like the elk.

Five of the therapsids skulked with heads low and shoulders hunched. Two boulders flanked Peter; he saw with some amazement that he had actually chosen a pretty good place to make a stand. He bent to pick up the rock he had dropped and rotated it in his palm, sharp side foremost.

"Come on," he muttered to the animals. His face was scratched and muddy and his clothing was soaked through.

None of the dog-lizards seemed ready to do more than stalk back and forth, weaving in and out of one another's paths, yellow eyes fixed on Peter. They opened their long jaws and snapped them with distinct toothy *clops.* Two of the animals bore spiny crests that rose from their backs like hog bristles.

"You're *cute,*" Peter said through clenched teeth. "You really are."

The animal that he had flung walked with a slight limp and whistled plaintively, jaw open and thick forked purple tongue thrust limply out. It shook its head woozily and licked both sides of its upper jaw at once.

"I can't tell which of you are boys and which are girls," Peter said. He did not feel as brave as his words, did not feel anything in particular, but it still seemed better—even necessary—to keep talking. When he talked he felt less alone, and he hoped some-body—his father, OBie, Ray—would hear him and come running.

Or maybe Peter was appealing directly to the dog-lizards, showing them that he was a pack hunter, too, and it wouldn't be right to eat him. He had heard that wolves regarded humans as fellow hunters.

That's stupid. Wolves are a lot closer cousins to me than these fellows.

It was time to do something besides talk. He saw three more good-sized chunks of rock and bent to pry them from the muck. The dog-lizards closed in. He stood erect with the rocks cradled in his arms.

The first rock he threw missed. It landed in the middle of the pack, however, and disrupted their pattern. Two of the animals bumped into each other and snapped warnings, and a third—the limping one—actually retreated, licking its thick-whiskered chops and blinking rapidly. Peter threw another rock and caught the animal with the highest fringe of bristles right across its muzzle. It screeched and hunched backward, nose bloody.

"YeaAAAHHH!" Peter shouted, waving the last two rocks and jumping at them.

As if making an instant committee decision, all five of the dog-lizards turned and ran, bumping into one another, snarling and whining as they lined up to dash back into the fissure single-file.

Peter stood alone, breath ragged, a rock in each hand, too stunned to make a move.

I scared them off, he thought. Then, *They're going back to get the others. They're going to join up with the rest of the pack and overwhelm Anthony and OBie and Ray.*

Peter chased after them, down the lane, hoping the dog-lizards would guide him back to his father and friends; hoping he might be some help in the battle.

Chapter Two

The wind picked up, blowing shrubs and small trees back and forth with a sound like whispering crowds. Peter climbed up one rock alley and down another, listening for voices; but all he heard were ghosts: wind, blowing leaves, and once, a drawn-out *thrum* like the croak of a huge frog. Muttering in frustration, arms and legs burning with exertion and his chest heaving, Peter found one of his own footprints in a muddy patch and realized he had come full circle through the maze.

"Father!" he called. "OBie! Ray!"

No response. The wind subsided. A front of cloud settled over the plateau in billows and streamers. Cloud filled the alleys and passageways between the rocks. Peter looked up and saw the late afternoon sun surrounded by millions of water-drop sparkles; then the sun was shut out and a gray uniformity enveloped him. Water condensed on his clothes and soaked him through. He sneezed. He wiped his face and beaded hair with his fingers, then sucked on the wet fingers for moisture.

Finally, too exhausted to go on, unable to see more than a couple of feet ahead or behind, Peter stepped into a muddy pool and knelt to get a drink. He pushed aside grass and algae, hesitated, then thought of making a kind of grass filter to screen the larger pieces of muck. He sucked up the water through a mesh of grass blades and had his first good drink in hours.

Something wriggled in his cheek. Tonguing the wriggler to his lips, he plucked an insect larva from his mouth and flung it aside.

After a few minutes of rest, Peter began to twitch. He had to do something, keep searching at least until dark or he thought he would go crazy. He wondered what his mother would think, seeing him in this situation; he could hardly believe where he was himself. Too tired to be afraid, his body tingled at the obscene prospect of ending up in some animal's stomach.

Peter felt his way through the cloud by hand. He advanced a few dozen yards down a series of zigs and zags between boulders. His neck hair prickled. He sniffed a colder kind of air. Something was different. Something had changed. Up ahead, the dense cloud seemed to swirl.

He took a tentative step—

And his foot came down on nothingness. With a surprised *yawp,* Peter tumbled out into space. He grabbed a tree branch and hung for a dizzying moment with one foot braced against rock and one hand slipping slowly along the bunched leaves of a slick green limb. The clouds cleared beneath his feet, showing him with nature's blind perversity just where he was: about a mile above the Gran Sabana, spreading far beneath his kicking foot like a lumpy carpet of bread mold.

Peter did not make a sound. He had to put all his energy into holding on. His grip tightened, yet his hand continued to slide. Clumps of torn leaves fell spinning and whirling past his head. He saw birds wheeling thousands of feet below and realized he must be on the western edge of the tip of the plateau. Had he made it to the eastern side, he would have encountered the overgrown roadway, not this cliff edge.

He brought up his free right hand and tried to grab the branch, but that only made his grip slip faster. His balance shifted, his foot skidded loose, and he whirled about, slamming into the rock with his chest and nose. In a starburst of pain Peter saw a brown creeper hugging the cliff face. He grabbed that with his free hand and prayed it would hold. His numb left hand slid to the thin tip of the branch and tore more leaves free as it slipped completely off.

His feet skipped down the rock and one boot's tip fetched up against a small ledge. Peter closed his eyes, certain he was going to sail out into space, but the creeper held. He dug both boot toes into the ledge. His eyes opened again and he scooted himself up a few inches, saw a crack in the rock, reached up and jammed his fingers into the crack, propped his toe against a knob, shimmied his hand up the creeper . . . Pulled with his left arm, causing more pain in his shoulder. And again . . .

Every muscle tense with the certainty he was about to lose his grip and fall, his fingers clawed against sandy rock, he pulled on the creeper, pulled and clawed, dug in the toe of his boot and hung, and minutes later he slung his leg over the edge and rolled away from the cliff face.

His heart hammered, but he did not care about being hungry or thirsty or about his bleeding hands and bruised face and knees and chest. He was alive and that was more than enough.

The cloud flowed aside for a moment and Peter saw the sun setting over distant tepuis, limning their silhouettes like the hulks of ancient ships carved from dirty ice. They appeared frozen in the golden light, floating in a rough dusky sea of jungle and plains.

He could not believe an entire day had passed. It seemed only a few minutes since he had scared off the dog-lizards.

His left shoulder throbbed. The ache grew as he watched the sunset until he cradled his arm and moaned. His father had jerked that arm hard, saving his life the day before. Peter had jerked it again falling over the edge. Now the abused limb was taking the opportunity to complain.

The sweetness of simply being alive passed too quickly. In a few minutes, as dark closed and cloud damply blanketed everything once more, Peter felt himself wrapped in fire. He crawled into a narrow space between two rocks, made sure it was empty of vermin—scaring away a large brown spider with a mouse in its mandibles—and curled up. Body throbbing, forehead hot as a furnace, he closed his eyes. He envied the spider. At least it knew where it was and had food. He should have fought it for the mouse.

Half delirious, he dreamed of challenging spiders and scorpions with a stick and a rock. Finally, he ran into a nest of wasps shaped like a huge flower, and a delicate, buzzing voice invited him into the nest for nectar and roast tapir. *Wachedi,* the buzzing voice said.

He jerked himself awake before the queen wasp could sink her sting into his shoulder. It was so dark he could not tell he had his eyes open.

He called out weakly for his father, then fell back into troubled sleep. This time he dreamed of maggots burrowing in the Earth. He was one of them. It was so comforting to be surrounded by his fellows, so soothing not to be completely alone.

Chapter Three

Peter heard a voice.

"You are lost, Peter Belzoni! I walked almost to the jungle, past the swamp, but I hear all these noises. So I come back."

Peter sat up and rubbed sleep from his eyes. Someone had a hand on his shoulder and the shoulder burned. He shrugged the hand away and moaned.

Billie squatted in front of him, brown face sympathetic, rich black eyes watching him intently. He wore a woven reed vest tied with pieces of cloth, muddy torn pants, and a hat plaited from palm leaves. His machete stuck out of his belt to one side.

"Real glad to see you," Peter croaked. "I'm a stupid gringo white kid . . . I'll die out here."

"I see where you scared away the dog hunters. You did that right. But you can't find food here, that's sure."

"Have you found my father and the others?"

Billie shrugged. "Footprints, but not as clear as yours. So I find you and wait to go after them. There are three—but who?"

"OBie, my father, Ray. We came across . . . "

Peter coughed and Billie offered him a cupped leaf filled with water. He drank it greedily. Billie pasted the leaf with a piece of gummy sap up against a rivulet snaking down the rock and it filled quickly. He gave it to Peter again to drink.

"I saw the bridge is gone, and the cages broken," Billie said. "And the old devil. He knows he should be over here to help challenge me. Why did you come?"

"To get pictures. Just to stand here."

Billie thought for a while, then wrinkled his forehead and looked at Peter. "Did you have a jaguar dream?"

"No," Peter said. "Wasps."

Billie whistled. "Not good. What else?"

"I became a maggot," Peter said.

Billie raised his eyebrows. "Better. In meat?"

"In the Earth," Peter said.

"I think such a dream may be good enough to make up for the wasps. White people have different dreams. It is the way your mind is made, out of radios and newspapers since you were born. Maggots . . . that is good. Big, juicy maggots?"

"Big as people," Peter said.

Billie smacked his lips and shifted from one leg to another. "I could eat some right now. Roast them in a fire."

Peter's stomach, empty as it was, did not appreciate this.

"Did you see anybody on the other side, on Pico Poco?" he asked, pushing himself up against the rock. The leaf had filled again and Billie passed it to him.

Billie said, "There is nobody there, not even the soldiers. But I hear noises down below. And trucks. They will bring big guns. Only white men would shoot the Challenger."

"Dagger, you mean."

"Yes. That is what they will try to do. I do not know what it will mean to kill the Challenger with guns. No one of any people or any of the families has ever killed the Challenger."

"Why did you run away?" Peter asked. "To become a hero?"

Billie swung his arms out like wings, fingers spread. "It is what I have dreamed of," he said. "I feel my father's spirit here. This is where the *wiriki* comes from, that flows down the rivers, and that my ancestors traded for iron with the *Fanuru*. It is Kahu Hidi, the

Heaven Mountain of the gods." Billie looked up and squinted, though the sky was not bright. "My father found a door into Odosha's country," he said, "where the dead go, other side the Nona, the Moon. It does him honor if I find the door, too."

"I don't understand," Peter said. Billie's whole manner had changed, even his way of speaking. His voice now was lower-pitched and husky, with a different accent. He would not look Peter directly in the eye. His perpetual light smile was gone, too, replaced by a neutral mask. "This isn't like you at all . . . the way you were on the boats, before we got here."

"This is me when I am in Kahu Hidi. You are lucky to be here, but you are not ready, I see. You do not know what to eat or where to drink."

"I'm very hungry," Peter admitted.

"There are things you can eat and stay who you are. Eat some things only if you want to see Kahu Hidi the way it thinks it is. I will show you those, even though you are white, because you probably want to avoid them."

"Okay," Peter said.

Billie

Billie rested his hands on his knees. "We should find your father and the others so you can be together."

"Yes," Peter said.

"I can't stay with you long. I have important jobs." He looked around Peter and patted his pants legs, concerned. "You have no machete."

Peter searched his pocket. The folding knife was gone. It must have fallen out while he dangled from the cliff. He didn't even think to use it on the dog-lizards. Suddenly, he felt very weak and incompetent and ashamed.

"Funny," Billie said. "I am glad to find you. Being in Kahu Hidi alone isn't easy."

He stood and pointed their way. Peter got to his feet slowly and went after him. They followed a seemingly endless series of curved fissures and turned dozens of corners, until Peter had no idea which side of his body was facing east or west, north or south. At one point, Billie paused over a muddy stretch and pointed out fresh prints. Peter bent to examine them: boots, too big to be his own.

"They are past the swamp by now, maybe into the forest. All this is Kahu Hidi's lips and tongue." Billie puckered his own lips and stuck out his tongue. "They do not know where they are going. They should wait for your people and the *Fanuru*."

"Who are the *Fanuru?*" Peter asked.

"The Spanish in the cities," Billie said. "The Army. The Army is evil *Fanuru*. They do not know why to kill."

"The dog-lizards didn't get them—my father? Ray and OBie?"

Billie made a quick face of disdain. "These are little lizards, *makako*. They scare you, but if you are brave, you chase them away. They are nothing like the Challenger."

Peter felt relief. "But the Challenger—Dagger—is across the chasm."

"There is Challenger wherever you go in Kahu Hidi," Billie said. He walked on and added over his shoulder, "He is a good friend of Odosha. Some say he is Odosha's brother."

A half hour later, the sun came out and they stood on the margin of a wet, dreary bog filled with the gray moss-hung skeletons of dead trees. Billie squatted by the rocks for a few minutes, tossing pebbles into a finger of still, murky water. "The three others went around, I think," he said. "This is where a really big lizard lives, like the crocodiles in the river, but bigger than the barges are long. I saw her yesterday, covered with her young. She was not happy, so I did not say hello." He flashed a smile at Peter, then returned to his neutral mask. "She is not of the Challenger, but strong enough, I guess."

"Why are they going to the forest?" Peter asked, a tightness in his chest.

"I don't know," Billie said. "To get away from the *makako,* the dog-lizards, maybe."

"Maybe they know where a landing field is. That's it. OBie knows where Jimmie Angel cracked up, and they're going there." His eyes brightened and his head felt hot and he almost forgot his hunger. He thought of the roustabout waving his arms, as if signaling an airplane was coming. "They know a plane is going to land and pick us up."

Billie said nothing.

"Let's find them."

"I try to show you where they are, and then I go," Billie said.

"I'm grateful," Peter said.

"It is what my father would do."

They walked around the swamp, staying close to the rocky mounds. Peter heard something big thrashing among the dead trees, and a cloud of black and white birds with long pink legs ascended, blotting out the sun. He realized he did not know the name of anything and he was too ashamed to ask Billie. Billie behaved as if he had been born here, but maybe that was just his own kind of bravado.

The swamp was beginning to harbor a few living trees on grassy islands. Peter got his bearings from the sun and realized they were walking north, to the broad bowl-shaped depression and the forest.

"You're sure the others are going this way?" Peter asked Billie.

Billie, five yards ahead, stood on a low lump of sandstone surrounded by brilliant green marsh grass. He shrugged. "They leave little things behind, broken twigs, footprints. I suppose it is them. Who else?"

Peter felt his chest tighten even more. He did not want them to go this way, even if OBie did know where a landing site might be; he wanted to go back and stand by the chasm. Billie waited for him to catch up, then confided, "This Kahu Hidi, it is like a big body, and when it swallows you, you are pressed into the belly. No going back up to the lips."

"Oh," Peter said. He began to feel despondent again. This wasn't adventure; it was horrible.

Billie climbed a wall of grotesque ridges and prominences, like a jumble of old stone men with deep-set blind eyes and pouting lips. Peter followed, his left arm protesting with each tug and pull, and stood beside him. They looked north from their vantage, level with the upper canopy, over thick forest dotted with tors of yellow and brown rock. Several miles away, a small lake glistened brilliant blue in the afternoon sun. Just beyond, past the opposite side of the bowl, Peter saw a thin line of more blue: perhaps the south-central lake.

"I've lost their trail," Billie said. "But they must have come here. They did not go back."

Peter tried to spot any sign of them. He couldn't. Then he saw something about a mile northeast, a clearing in the forest. Beside the clearing rose a massive, artificial-looking structure, like a step pyramid in Mexico, though cruder in outline.

"What's that?" Peter asked, pointing. Such a formation had not been on any of the maps, nor had it been mentioned in the books he had read.

"I don't know," Billie said.

"Did people ever live here?"

"Not our kind of people," Billie said.

"More friends of Odosha?"

Billie cocked his head to one side. "Odosha is death and your devil and the power of night. He would invite all his friends here if he could. He is master of the Challenger. He takes the shape of *Dinoshi*, the biggest Challenger."

Peter had had just about enough of this new Billie. "Do you believe all that?" he asked.

"Do you believe in Jesus and Mary?" Billie asked sternly.

Peter's face reddened. "I've never spent much time in church."

Billie shrugged. "Who knows what is real here? Nothing the whites or *Fanuru* can imagine."

Billie climbed down the other side of the jumble, to the edge of a wall of green. Peter looked behind him regretfully. Still, he did not want to face the dog-lizards again, even if Billie held them in contempt. There might be something to eat in the forest. He would eat leaves pretty soon if he did not find something. He could always find his way back, if Billie did not lead him too deeply into the forest.

Peter used all these excuses, but really, he had no option but to follow Billie. Billie had a machete and knew something, if not everything; Peter had nothing and knew nothing.

Over the jungle, from some distance away, came a low rattling squawk, like a parrot melded with a snare drum and spun on a slow record player. Other sounds—chirping yips, a dismal hooting, and the wheeling reedy cries of a rising pink cloud of birds near the lake, were the jungle's answers.

Peter scrambled down the rough slope and into the green.

Chapter Four

———◆———

Billie did very little hacking at first. Beneath the thick canopy, the jungle was relatively clear, with huge tree trunks spaced every four or five meters, some wrapped in iron-hard black vines. There was little understory save tiny patches of white flowers rising from pale thick leaves. Peter's feet sank into a thick loam topped with moist dead leaves and bits of bark. Insects, mostly small black ants, scampered across the leaves. Very little sunlight leaked through the high green roof of this shadowy world.

Gradually, the canopy let in more slanting beams of sun and the understory grew thicker as the big trees were spaced farther apart. Huge fallen logs nursed a profusion of orchids and young saplings, as well as fungal shelves hard as wood, orange and brown and black.

"Do you know the names of all these plants and things?" Peter asked.

Billie shook his head. "Some I know from stories. There are big grubs here good to eat—some birds are familiar. Some frogs. A few trees. Not much else. It is different here, like we are fleas going from the body of a man to the body of a god."

Peter chuckled despite his hunger. "I'd hate to be a flea on a god," he said.

"Yes! The flea doesn't know where to bite. And when he bites, he gets sick, or has strong dreams."

"If I don't bite something soon, I'll die," Peter said.

"No, you have maybe four, five days before that," Billie said.

"Well, I'm a white," Peter said, trying to mix a little irony with a real message of hunger. "I'm used to three square meals a day."

"I had square bread once," Billie said. "They called it white bread and it was pale. Whites make square meals out of it."

Peter could not tell if he was joking.

After a time, Billie stopped beside a thick clump of bushes beneath a hole in the canopy. He made several signs with his hands, smiled and waved as if saying hello to something in the treetops, and then pulled up a bush. At the end of the bush hung a thick root, like a long potato.

"Here," he said, offering it to Peter. "It is yuca. South it is called manioc."

"That's poisonous until it's fixed," Peter said.

"This is sweet yuca. It is wild here. Some say it was brought down from Kahu Hidi long ago, in the beginning. I will taste it first if you like."

"No, I believe you," Peter said.

"There must not be many animals like Sammy around here," Billie said as Peter bit into the dirty skin and hit a starchy, crisp pulp inside.

"They'd like these, wouldn't they?" Peter asked, chewing.

"Probably. I think there will be small bananas ahead."

"No monkeys?"

"Only us," Billie said.

He picked as many roots as he could carry and forged ahead. Peter took several of Billie's discards and followed. The going was getting tougher and Billie wielded his machete frequently to hack a pathway.

"I don't see how big animals could get through here," Peter said, still eating. The root tasted wonderful, though the starch made his mouth dry. Billie said nothing but stopped and listened. Peter heard a chorus of high-pitched chirping, like big crickets, and then a rattling buzz. "Insects?" he asked, stopping beside Billie.

Billie shook his head. Through the trees, they saw rustling leaves and shooting green forms in the canopy, about thirty yards away. It was a troop of animals the size of howler monkeys, but green.

Billie lowered himself to his haunches. He looked at Peter. "Do you know what those are?" he asked.

"No," Peter said.

The troop pushed overhead, the chirping and buzzing suddenly very loud. They had sleek green bodies with long tails and long scaly heads, long wiry legs with four grasping toes, and bright red eyes; Peter wished that one would be still for a moment so he could see it more clearly.

Four of the animals scampered down the trunk of a huge old tree, upside down like squirrels in Central Park. They were about five feet from nose to tip of tail, with snake-like snouts and eyes, beautifully dappled green and bright yellow. They stared at Peter and Billie, righted themselves, and craned their lizard heads on sinuous necks. He noticed they had very long arms, with a flexible membrane folded between the arms and the ribs and hips.

"Tree lizards," Peter said, transfixed by the animals' red gaze. "Flying, too, maybe."

Billie made hand gestures at the animals. They blinked with lazy nonchalance, tensed themselves with heads and eyes focusing straight up the trunk, and then climbed rapidly back to join their fellows in the upper branches. The troop moved on, dropping bits of leaves and branches in its wake.

"Snakes who eat monkeys become this on Kahu Hidi," Billie said.

"Snake monkeys. Friends of Odosha?" Peter asked, only half in jest.

"Yes," Billie said, and smiled quickly at Peter.

"I can't tell if you are joking or serious," Peter said.

Billie frowned for the first time. "I have to leave you soon. I teach you what I can, then you're alone, unless you find your father."

"I'm sorry," Peter said.

"I am not your damned clown Indian, making jokes and telling children's stories. I know how you whites think, even when you try not to."

"Sorry," Peter said again, more quietly.

Billie lifted the roots and the machete. "We will not go hungry for now, no?"

Peter nodded.

Billie seemed suddenly sad. "Everything here is not what I expected. I thought it would be glowing, like a jaguar dream, but it is just another mountain, with different animals and plants. It is not a ghost place."

Peter stood, confused by Billie's sudden change in mood.

"My mother was Colombian. I have too much of others in me, whites and *Fanuru,* and I do not see with the right eyes. It is still Kahu Hidi," Billie concluded.

"Where are you going?" Peter asked. "I mean, do you know where your father went—where he traveled?"

"He followed the Spirit Path and that is all I know."

"Where does the Spirit Path go?" Peter asked.

"From the maze, around Lake Akuena to the northern end, the Cloud Desert and Warrior's Shield. There are many ways between."

"What will you do if you meet a Challenger?" Peter asked.

"There is only one Challenger, in many forms. Odosha is the master and comes as *Dinoshi,* the death eagle."

"Yeah, but what will you do?"

Billie shrugged. "Dance or die."

As they proceeded, they soon crossed small streams, shallow at first, meandering between the trees along shifting beds, leaving many islands separated by ten or twelve feet of glistening clear water. They were descending, and the ground was getting wetter and the vegetation thicker until it presented a wall of green splashed with red-tipped leaves, beautiful flowers yellow and white and violet, and intensely green knobby vines hanging from tree limbs like pea-beaded curtains. Peter had seen none of these plants in the jungle below the plateau, and could not remember seeing them in the books his father had brought.

New plants, new animals; he thought of the Charles Knight paintings he had seen in New York and tried to imagine them come to life. The forest was not static; it had changed, evolved, in the tens of millions of years since its isolation.

How many naturalists had come here, desperate to make their reputations by charting and collecting and classifying? Peter thought there had to be thousands of new species waiting to be discovered. Then, looking at Billie's back as the Indian hacked a path through the growth, he understood what Billie meant. *I'm thinking like a white man—which is what I am, of course, and there's no shame in that, I hope. But can I really see the forest for what it is?*

"How do Indians think?" Peter asked as they rested beside a small waterfall. Brilliant green and red butterflies played around them, bigger than Peter's hands put together.

"Like people," Billie said. He sniffed the air and leaned back on folded arms. A hummingbird the size of a pigeon flapped ponderously around their heads before flexing and buzzing off through the jungle.

"Whites think like people, too, I suppose," Peter said. He looked up at the vine-draped trees rising over them like the nave of a green cathedral.

"We think like *my* people," Billie said, clearly not comfortable with this talk.

"That's what I want to know. How do you think differently from me?"

"When I find Odosha's foot and eat it . . . Then I will think differently. Like my ancestors when the best of them, the heroes, came here."

"Odosha again," Peter said. He sniffed. "What's his foot?"

"Hard . . . " Billie held his hands out flat beside his ribs. "On a tree, blue as moonlight, wide as arms wide." Billie showed his teeth and gave a shiver of his head. "Not for whites. Kill you if you eat it."

Peter wondered if he meant a giant tree fungus. "But it won't kill *you?*"

"Hope not," Billie said.

"I always thought people were pretty much alike, deep down," Peter said, and then was embarrassed by his presumption.

"Um," Billie said.

Twilight was coming and the forest was getting very dark. Peter got up to walk a few steps and pee. He was unzipping his pants when he saw something pale glisten under a broad, spiky-leafed succulent. When he was finished, he zipped up and knelt to look, but still couldn't make out the object in the gloom. He reached beneath the plant and touched something hard and pointed, grasped it, and pulled it easily from the loam. Clumps of dirt fell away. It was bigger than he expected.

Peter stood and turned it in his hands, realizing it was a bone, the jaw of some animal. He touched the teeth and then froze. It was human. With a shocked cry, he dropped it.

A few yards away, Billie stooped and pulled a mold-encrusted cloth belt from the dirt. At the end of the belt dangled a brass buckle green with tarnish.

"Probably white," Billie said. "Not my father. Not yours, either."

Chapter Five

Rain pattered down through the forest all night. Something large passed within a few yards of them, but Peter, wide awake in the blackness, could see nothing and smell nothing. Whatever it was, it was not interested in fresh meat. As light filtered through the canopy and a thick fog broke, Peter rose and stretched. He had slept little. His bones popped like firecrackers and every muscle in his body ached. Billie was nowhere to be seen.

Nearby he found trampled bushes and deep, broad tracks in the earth, but the mucky damp soil had filled in behind the creature, obliterating details.

Billie returned a few minutes later. "Sammy went by last night," he said. "He does not know how to live in the forest. He is as lost as you and I."

Peter wished they could find the centrosaur. It would be like finding an old friend—not as good as finding Anthony, Ray, and OBie, but to come so close . . .

"Maybe he's not far."

"I found a trail maybe from your father," Billie said. "I show where I think they go."

They ate more yuca and Billie led Peter toward a broader stream, where three creeks joined. There, on a sandy bank by the water, he showed Peter bootprints. "They are going north, like us," Billie said.

Peter touched the prints. "We can follow them."

"They go along this river. You follow. I will go another way."

Peter thought about arguing with Billie and decided that would be entirely too white a thing to do. "If you have to," Peter said.

Billie nodded. "You find your father and the others and go back. You do not belong here."

"Don't I know it," Peter said.

"I will learn whether I belong," Billie said, looking down at the stream swirling beyond the mud and sand bank. "You take this. I go naked to steal Odosha's magic."

He passed the machete to Peter, and two yuca roots. Peter did not know what to say. Billie smiled and they shook hands. Billie ran away from the stream, back into the forest. In a few minutes, Peter could hear nothing but the forest sounds and his own breathing.

For the moment, he felt a crushing unwillingness to move. The forest seemed to float around him, filled with strange life, thick and suffocating. Thousands of insects hovered above the stream. Ants swarmed up a nearby tree trunk, hanging from leaves and vines. Unknown animals near and far made their cryptic squawks, screeches, chitterings, even a new sound, a musical brassy series of notes, like the practice of an expert trumpeter.

Peter closed his eyes. He took a deep breath, smelled rotting vegetation, water, greenery, hints of lemony sweetness. He had never felt so out of place and alien; he could hardly believe he was in the forest at all. Part of him felt as if he were back in New York, and he would wake up at any moment, Doyle's book cradled in his lap, Anthony coming through the kitchen door with an onion and noodle casserole . . .

He opened his eyes to see a butterfly with a body as big as his thumb, broad wings striped blue and white, pumping and soaring over the stream's glittering surface. An ant carrying a lump of mold crawled up the toe of his boot, hesitated, crawled off again.

He took another breath. The lassitude passed. The forest was not going to go away. If anything, the forest was dreaming *him*, and not the other way around. Even if he was going to die, which

seemed likely, he could explore and discover a few things before the end.

He wondered about the man whose jaw and belt they had found. What was the last thing he saw? Was it worth dying for?

Peter felt calmer than he had in days. Whether that was resignation, courage, or simple exhaustion, he could not say—but he decided to follow the stream, search for the others, and stay alive as long as he could.

He saw no more bootprints as he walked along the stream bank, now confined in a channel of stones and pebbles. Using Billie's machete, he cut his way through thick vines and branches, then jumped on several rocks to the other side of the stream, where the path appeared easier. After walking beside the flow for several dozen yards, he found another tree crawling with ants. He stopped for a moment to watch the glistening blanket of small brown insects.

"Myrmecology," he muttered. "The study of ants." It was one thing to know the words from a dictionary—quite another to understand what they represented. He had seen so many different kinds of insects since the journey began, and at least two dozen varieties of ants, enough for a whole university full of professors to study—yet to him, and the people who wrote about the plateau, El Grande had always been a land of dinosaurs and other big, ancient creatures suitable for newsreels and circuses. Trophies. How narrow a view! The little things were important, too—and perhaps just as strange and isolated as the dinosaurs.

He thought he saw a banana tree peeking out a few yards from the stream. He was about to cut through to see if it bore fruit when he heard a distinct cow-like bellow and the sound of brush being trampled. He froze. It was on the other side of the stream, whatever *it* was. A log had fallen across the stream and knocked down small trees and brush, affording a better and higher view. He climbed onto the log and craned his neck to see a lumbering green and brown shape some yards west in the forest. The shape raised its large head, showing a parrot-like beak munching on leaves, a forward-curved nose horn, and a broad crest.

"Sammy!" Peter called. He crossed the log quickly and hacked and snapped away a few black creepers, then plunged through a glade covered with thick green grass. In the middle of the glade, chewing at the leaves on a tree, a centrosaur stood with its left side turned toward Peter. Its jaws worked for a second, then stopped. The huge head turned slowly.

Peter wanted only to touch the animal, to reacquaint himself with an old friend. He smiled broadly and held out his hands. From behind the animal, two smaller centrosaurs emerged, also chewing leaves.

"Sammy!" Peter exclaimed. "Where did you find babies?"

The realization came almost too late. Peter examined the shield and the eyes and the shape of the nose horn, saw that this animal was several feet longer than Sammy, and realized this was a female, *not* Sammy. With a snort, the mother centrosaur swung around to face him. She thrust her horn into the air.

"Babies," Peter said under his breath. He walked backward. "Sorry." His foot fell into a hole and he stumbled.

With an angry *snark,* the mother centrosaur took a run at him, head twisted to one side and nose horn pointing straight at him. Peter picked himself up and stumbled toward the forest. "I'm sorry!" he shouted. "I'm sorry!"

But the mother was having none of that. He was back in the forest and tangled in vines before he realized he had dropped the machete. The mother was ten yards behind, trotting steadily, when one of her babies emitted a high, pig-parrot squeal. With amazing adroitness, she stopped dead and reversed course.

Peter found himself halfway up a large tree trunk, grabbing at creepers and branches for support. The centrosaur babies had moved away from the center of the glade. On three sides they were being stalked by what Peter at first mistook for bald bears. They were the size of grizzlies and dark, but they had scaly wolf snouts and tiny ears. Peter had seen their pictures in books: these were *Lycognathus,* wolf-jaws, fast, strong carnivores, much larger cousins of the dog-lizards. Though a ruff of red-tipped black fur covered their shoulders, and patches of smooth short pelt mottled their flanks, on their heads and forelimbs they had no fur at all.

At the mother's charge, two lycos scattered, leaving one imme-

diately behind the bigger of the two babies. The mother *Centrosaurus* could not attack this animal without running over her baby, so she stopped and swung her head and tail, complaining in a braying, bawling succession of honks.

Peter heard something below and felt a breath on his ankle. He looked down and saw the onyx-black eyes of a fourth lyco directly beneath him. The animal's jaws opened and it sniffed audibly at this strange prey, broad forked tongue lolling. Peter scrambled higher into the tree just as the beast decided to lunge. The lyco's teeth sank into a branch inches below his foot and it shook its head and backed away with a sneeze.

"Good of you to visit," said a voice above him. As Peter climbed up a few more branches, he looked up and saw Ray three yards above him. The cameraman squatted casually on a thick limb.

Below, the lyco leaned its foreclaws against the trunk and fixed its eyes on Peter.

Peter was too scared and out of breath to say anything immediately. The first words he managed were, "Where's my father? Where's OBie?"

"I wish I knew. We're in the wolf's wood now. The lycos are thick around here. They surprised us and we took off in three different directions."

The three big hunters had reestablished their posts around the centrosaur family. One lyco rushed in sideways, jaws wide, and snapped at the rear of the smaller baby. The baby gave a high squall and wheeled, shoving its nose and smaller shield instinctively, though it lacked any nose horn for defense.

The lycos sat on their haunches, mouths open, and serenely surveyed the glade. One idly snapped at a dragonfly buzzing through the bright sunlight. The mother centrosaur kept close to her babies but could not surround them. A fifth lyco rose from hiding in the high grass suddenly and lunged, taking another chunk from the baby's hide. The baby writhed and screamed. The mother bounded out and swiped her horn at this latest attacker, but the lyco scuttled out of the way and again its opposites attacked the babies, bringing the mother back.

Peter wiped sweat from his forehead and eyes with a sleeve.

"We've been trying to get back to the maze for a day and a half now," Ray said. "We thought we'd lost you for good."

"The lizard-dogs, dog-lizards, whatever . . ."

"Therapsids," Ray said. "Like these guys."

"They chased me until I scared them away. I found Billie," Peter continued. "Or rather, he found me. He's on a spirit quest. He found some food and gave me a machete."

"Good of him," Ray said. "Where's the machete?"

"Out there, somewhere," Peter said, pointing to where the natural drama was unfolding.

The lyco below them maintained its station but seemed more interested in the action in the glade than in the two humans.

"How long have you been in the forest?" Peter asked.

"Since yesterday afternoon. We found some bananas and I snared a fish with a basket of twigs. Savage little thing, tried to nip my finger off, but it tasted good."

"We saw snake monkeys," Peter said. They watched the drama in the glade for a few moments. Peter pointed to the centrosaur. "I thought she was Sammy."

"Easy mistake," Ray said. He seemed relaxed and amiable on his high perch. Peter decided the limb was strong enough for both of them and climbed to sit beside him.

"I've drawn fighting dinosaurs since I was a boy," Ray said. "But I've never actually seen it before. It's brutal."

"They don't just attack, do they?"

"Nope." Ray shook his head, watching the mother centrosaur run a quick circle around her babies. "They're waiting for her to tire. They don't like her horn or her feet. She could inflict real damage, and a predator is dead if it can't run fast or bite hard."

"How long will they wait?"

"As long as it takes, I suppose," Ray said. "Want to lay bets?"

Peter settled on the branch and offered Ray a chunk of sweet yuca from his shirt. Ray bit into it, made a surprised face, and ate it quickly. "Not bad," he said.

"Where did you last see my father and OBie?"

"I didn't. One minute we were together, walking along a nice stream trying to find some high ground to see where we were . . ."

He paused as a lyco made another attack on the larger baby. The noise drowned out everything for a few minutes as the mother stamped around her young, trying to gore the carnivores, who always managed to bound out of reach.

"And then the lycos attacked us, and we fled our separate ways."

"You don't know if they're alive or dead, then," Peter said, a lump rising in his throat.

"No, but we're alive, and that's a small miracle."

"What are we going to do?" Peter asked.

Ray shook his head and took another bite of root. "I feel like a spectator in a bullring," he said. "But I'm getting damned tired of these seats." He peered down at the lyco guarding them. It was still paying more attention to the action in the glade.

"Do you see that branch?" Ray pointed to a slender offshoot from a main branch near the one on which they perched, and a couple of yards higher up the tree. "I've been looking at that branch for almost a day now. See how it gets real close to that next tree?"

Peter examined the branches. "We could climb over."

"You might. I don't think it would hold my weight."

"What will you do, then?"

Ray shrugged. "If we're in two trees, our wolf-jaw friend here might drop his guard long enough to let one of us get away."

Peter looked dubious. "I don't know," he said.

"My butt is getting very, very tired," Ray said with a pained expression. "What little I can feel of it."

"We should try something," Peter agreed. He stood on their branch, reached up to the higher branch, and swung out onto it. Then he crawled carefully to the offshoot, tested it with half his weight, and looked back at Ray.

Ray nodded.

The lycos in the glade had finally worn the mother centrosaur to a frazzle. She seemed to make some instinctive strategic choice, and nuzzled in close to the larger baby. In a flash, a lyco savaged the flank of the smaller and now more vulnerable baby, bringing it to its knees. The mother nudged the larger baby and they pushed through the perimeter paced by the lycos, toward the forest, away from the tree in which Peter and Ray were perched.

The lyco guarding them suddenly became restive, harrumphing and swinging its head at the smell of blood from the glade. It glanced up at Ray and let out a frustrated bellow.

Peter was halfway out along the thinner limb when it snapped. He reached out with his sore arm to grab another branch, caught a handful of leaves, and fell.

Ray shouted. Peter heard the shout, and then landed on something moving, knocking the wind out of himself. He tumbled to one side into grass, on the edge of the glade.

He couldn't move. Something nearby groaned. Peter turned his head, managed to catch his own breath, and saw the lyco barely five feet away, leaning to one side with its right leg splayed. Peter could smell its rank breath and see the insects buzzing around its big shoulders and neck pelt. He also heard somebody making a great commotion up in the tree.

The lyco righted itself, swung its head, and glared in stupid surprise at what had hit it. It lifted its heavy-jawed head. The oddly shaped pupils in its eyes flexed, and the eyes grew even blacker, with tiny glints of blue.

Peter pushed to his feet.

Ray was still trying to distract the lyco by whooping and screaming.

"Damn," Peter said.

The lyco took a step forward. Peter raised his arms and shouted, "You're nothing but a big old horny toad!" Then he stamped his foot and waved his arms.

The lyco took a step backward, clearly unsure what to do with this strange bipedal animal now that it was within reach.

Peter jumped and the lyco scuttled a couple of yards to the rear again, growling and whining. It lifted its head and opened its jaws to their fullest extent, and very impressive they were, boasting long rows of sharp teeth culminating in huge canines. The forked tongue dangled.

Ray landed beside Peter with a thump. Peter did not expect this and jumped away, startled, and the lyco also jumped. It seemed for a moment as if all three were waiting for the others to be spooked and run. Instead, Ray waved his arms and shouted, "We're tough and stringy! Get out of here!"

The lyco circled around them and the trunks of the two trees, then looked longingly at the glade. The other lycos had brought the baby centrosaur down on its side and were ripping at its abdomen. The baby's screams had stopped and the forest and the glade seemed very quiet.

"Go get your share!" Ray shouted, standing beside Peter. "On your mark . . . " He crouched and looked at Peter. "Get set! GO!" They both leaped toward the lyco, shouting nonsense at the top of their lungs. This was too much for the big animal and it turned decisively and loped to the glade to join its fellows around a more familiar kill. The growling and bickering rose to a crescendo as dominance was reestablished, and Peter and Ray ran back to the stream, away from the glade and its grim scene of feasting.

"We won't be that lucky again," Ray said as they hid in the shadow of a fallen log.

Peter nodded agreement. "I hope the others have been as lucky."

"Me, too."

They caught their breaths and listened for the sounds of more big animals. Far off, they heard roars and hisses and growls, like the mixed voices of lizards and lions.

"Poor thing," Ray said. "Mama left it behind."

Peter felt in his shirt for the remaining root. It had fallen out— not surprisingly.

"She knew she couldn't save both," Ray said.

"What a choice," Peter said. Missing the root reminded him of the machete. "Do you think it would be safe to go back?"

"Why?" Ray asked

"The machete," Peter said.

"Oh." Ray slumped back into his seat beside Peter and crossed his arms around his knees. "Could be useful. I wouldn't try it now, though."

They stared at each other.

"We're both pretty dopey, aren't we?" Peter said.

"Yup," Ray acknowledged. He coughed and shook his head. "I need some water."

Ray got up and went to the stream to drink. He scooped great handfuls of water to his eager lips. "Tastes like fine wine," he said between swallows. He returned to the tree trunk's shadow.

"How long can we last out here?" Peter asked.

"Depends on whether we catch our second wind. I haven't had any sleep for a day and a half. I've got to take a nap."

"Maybe the lycos will be done by then," Peter said.

But Ray had already dropped his chin to his chest. Peter listened to the jungle and smelled the air. *I'm becoming like a wild animal myself,* he thought hopefully.

While Ray slept, Peter walked cautiously back to the glade, trying to be as alert and quiet as possible. The lycos were still feeding, but the fighting seemed to have stopped. There were six of the big carnivores and they had almost stripped the small centrosaur. Peter saw a few small green heads pop up in the grass, and then he saw an avisaur like the ones in the circus land in a tree near the carcass. More scavengers and opportunists showed up, keeping a respectful distance from the lycos. Peter hid behind the trunk of the same tree he had fallen out of, his heart racing.

We don't know where my father and OBie are. We can't just stay in one place—we'll starve, or something will finally call our bluff and eat us. Tears welled up in his eyes at the next thought. *There is no place for an airplane to land. The soldiers on Pico Poco must have killed Dagger by now. Father would tell me to go on without them, to try to get back . . .*

Then he remembered what Billie had said: that El Grande, Kahu Hidi as he called it—the Heaven Mountain—swallowed you.

When you're swallowed, you don't just crawl back up the throat. But we have to try. We won't last more than a few days here.

The lycos growled over a few last scraps of tough skin. Two of the animals grabbed the centrosaur's head and tugged and another two grabbed the remains of the tail. They pulled each other around in a circle, their feet kicking up great divots of dirt and grass. After a few minutes, they dropped the carcass, sniffed around, made a few tentative attempts to snag an avisaur, and finally wandered back into the woods.

Peter waited a little longer. His tongue stuck to the roof of his mouth and his lips had split painfully. The sky had been cloudless and the wind light all day and it was now at least eighty degrees, warm for the plateau. A few smaller dinosaurs—two-legged theropods, he thought, though he saw none of them clearly—bobbed out of the tall grass and chased or nipped at avisaurs who had settled on the carcass. Peter looked at the trampled area where the mother centrosaur had defended her children, then walked across to see if he could find the machete.

The grass formed a thick mat and the ground had been thoroughly pounded. He got as close as he dared to the carcass and squinted at the dashing green heads and feathered wings, the lashing tails. They paid him no attention.

Back and forth he walked in the sun, the smell of the baby dinosaur's blood thick in the air. He stared at the grass until his eyes crossed, almost dead from exhaustion but unwilling to give up. Without some sort of tool, Peter knew they didn't have a chance of getting back.

A red and brown snake at least seven feet long slithered to one side of the trampled area, lifted its head, and stuck out its tongue at Peter. He waited for it to pass—there were far too many poisonous snakes for him to take any chances—and resumed his search. Flies big and small circled the carcass and bit Peter as a consolation prize. His neck and cheeks burned with stinging welts. He thought of a long hot shower and an ice cream soda and his mouth made a dry sucking sound when he tried to open it.

Muttering, he got down on his knees and spread the grass blades. His chest hitched whenever he sucked in air, and he felt as if he might strangle. His vision started to swim. The grass melted together into a yellow-green field. In the middle of the field floated something dark. *Another skull,* he thought, and a sudden picture of finding his father's head made him shudder. *This is an awful place. When you read about such a place, it seems wonderful—but up close it is just awful.*

He tried to focus on the dark thing in the grass. He reached out with one hand and touched it. The coolness of steel and the sharpness of a cutting edge gave him strength. He pulled the machete from the dirt and grass, wiped it on his pants leg, and stumbled back across the glade to the tree. From there, he did not remember the trip to the fallen log. He dropped to the ground beside the stream and drank greedily, stopping only when his stomach protested and he began to gag.

Thirst quenched, he lay down beside Ray, who was still asleep, and leaned back on a mossy bit of rock.

Chapter Six

Peter came awake in darkness. Ray shook his shoulder. "Almost a half moon and clear skies tonight," he said. "Let's get moving."

"We're going back?" Peter asked.

"We need to find some high ground first. One of these tors might be suitable. We could thrash our way through this forest and never know which way to turn. Right now, which way is south?"

"We can tell by the stars," Peter said.

Ray chuckled. "We could, if you know how to do it. I don't."

Peter felt his face burn.

"Next time, we'll have to remember to bring our Boy Scout manuals. If we learn a few landmarks we can keep a good sense of direction."

The tors dotted the jungle every few hundred yards.

"What about nocturnal hunters?" Peter asked.

"Are they any worse than day hunters?"

"At least we can see better in the daytime."

"So we see them before they eat us. Any other arguments?" Ray sounded testy.

"No," Peter said. "I'd rather be doing something than just sitting here, waiting to die."

"Amen," Ray said.

Ambition was easier than accomplishment. They stumbled through the velvety-dark forest for half an hour before deciding to follow the stream again. Ray did not remember any tors south of where they were; Peter could not visualize their location well at all.

They went north along the stream, more to be doing something than with any plan in mind. Following the stream was not easy; tree trunks and leaves thrust out over the banks until they had to walk in the stream itself, which Ray did not enjoy. "I remember the teeth on that fish," he said. "Let's stay to the shallows."

The moonlight was less help than Ray had anticipated and after a while he began to get discouraged. "I don't know why we're even trying," he grumbled. He plunged up to his knees into a hole in the streambed.

A cloud of stinging gnats enveloped them before Peter could take his turn to give a pep talk. Swatting and swearing, they splashed half blindly in the stream and on the bank. Finally, Peter ducked himself completely underwater and swam a few yards, until he bumped against a submerged rock. He stood and saw Ray splashing along the surface close behind.

"Jesus, Jesus," Ray swore with each stroke. Peter expected to feel fish mouths nibbling at him and scrambled up onto the shore. He crawled along a tilted tree trunk and grabbed at dead, rock-hard creepers.

The river curved in such a way that moonlight now fell full between the halves of parted forest, painting a shimmering band of white on the stream. Ray was surrounded by a carpet of diamonds as he splashed ashore. He stopped in the shallows, body tensed, standing in only a few inches of water, staring downstream at something hidden from Peter by the dense overhang of foliage. He seemed transfixed.

"What is it?" Peter asked.

"A salamander," Ray said.

Peter wiped water from his eyes. "*What?* Come on!"

"No," Ray said, eyes still locked on the unseen animal. "It's a kind of amphibian, I'm sure."

"Ray, get out of the water!"

Ray held out his hand with fingers spread toward Peter. "I've never seen anything like it. Not even fossils. It doesn't look like a *Diplocaulus*."

Peter made a face and screwed up his courage. He walked out into the stream and stood beside Ray on the pebbly bed.

"Quiet," Ray said. "Who knows what it eats, or how fast it moves?"

"Great!" Peter whispered, and stared downstream. The moonlight shone on a still pool set aside from the stream's flow. Trees surrounded the pool on three sides. On a patch of sloping shore stretched a nightmare length of shiny dark flesh, eight or nine feet from its yard-wide, scythe-shaped head to its thick, wrinkled, partly submerged tail. The creature raised its wide blade of a head, eyes mounted on the extreme ends of the scythe, and blinked lazily.

"It's like a shark," Peter whispered, all his misery temporarily forgotten.

"A hammerhead Axolotl," Ray agreed, boyish enthusiasm in his subdued voice. "Look at the gills."

Behind the creature's jaw puffed faint flowers of paler color against the dark flesh. The amphibian cheeped. None of the three moved.

"Dawn of time stuff," Ray said. "Why such a broad head? Think of the stereo vision—"

A thick bank of cloud covered the moon and dropped them into pure black ink. Peter felt the darkness as a viscous resistance. Disoriented, he reached out for Ray, touched his arm, and said, "Let's get out of here."

"I want to see it again," Ray said.

"Ray—"

Something big splashed in the pool.

"Ray, *let's get out of here!*"

Gripping Ray's forearm, Peter dragged him to the unseen bank of the stream. They collided with an overhanging limb and almost lost their balance, but managed to blindly creep onto the leaning tree trunk and squat there like frogs.

"What a *wonderful* monster," Ray said. The clouds parted briefly, allowing a final shaft of crystalline moonlight to sparkle on the flowing water and the shimmering leaves. Darkness closed in again. Peter couldn't see his hand in front of his face.

It began to rain. Hard.

Chapter Seven

The upper and middle canopy of the forest sounded like the rhythm section in a big band: fat drops of rain hit the leaves like brush sizzles on a snare drum, drips landed on the lower leaves and floor like taps on a hi-hat. "Damn," Ray said. "We forgot our bumbershoots."

There was nowhere to go in the darkness so they sat blind on the tilted trunk. Peter nursed his sore shoulder and arm, rubbing his joints and grimacing. He licked at the drops that fell from his hair. He was suddenly very hungry again.

"Where's your camera?" Peter asked. The question had just popped into his head.

"I threw it at a dog-lizard," Ray said. "How's that for dedication to my craft?" Silence between them for a moment, listening to the rain's music, then, "You went back and got your machete, didn't you?"

"Yeah."

"Still have it?"

"Yeah." It seemed glued to Peter's hand, his grip on the tape-wrapped handle was so tight. He couldn't remember swimming with it, but he must have—and without slicing his legs off, either.

"We're not helpless, then. We can whack something."

"We could find more edible roots."

"I'll eat tree bark and ants pretty soon," Ray said.

Peter wondered what ants did in the wet.

"It's going to be dawn in a few minutes," Ray said. "Isn't it getting a little brighter?"

Peter couldn't tell at first, but after a while, he could make out pieces of wet sky through gaps in the trees. The rain continued unabated, however, and soon a fork of lightning cast a ghoulish glare over the forest. Ray came and went in a flash before Peter, squatting like a gargoyle on the tree. The rain suddenly doubled and the music became a steady pounding roar so loud they could barely hear each other.

"I don't like this," Ray shouted. "We're down in a little gully here—about two yards below the—"

Upstream, they heard a sharp crack, a splintering, and a deeper rumble. There was not enough light to see more than vague shadows but Peter felt Ray's foot on his arm and reached out to grab a knee. "What?" he called.

"We should get to higher ground. This might be an arroyo—a flood channel!"

"Right," Peter said. He slithered down the tree onto the spongy forest floor and felt rather than heard Ray close behind. Walking any farther was difficult. Branches and vines reached out to grab, and Ray collided with him. "We've got to get to an open space," Ray shouted.

"There isn't any until we—"

Peter heard the roar suddenly reach a crescendo. The flood hit them first at their knees, knocking them over backward, then a second wall struck, engulfing them. Peter struggled to keep to his feet, but the water dug dirt out from beneath his boots, and the third wall spun him like a child's ball. His head poked briefly into air and then submerged again. Something hit his shoulder, poked sharply at his ear, and slammed against the back of his neck.

He could not move or breathe. Eyes wide open, he flopped and rolled and swirled down the channel cut by the stream, bumping into tree trunks, sliding over rocks, helpless.

• • •

When Peter came back to himself—and it seemed he had been on a long, long journey through a confused landscape of painful dreams—he was walking on the shore of a small lake. The trees on this shore were spaced far apart and the forest floor was almost free of growth. Warm sun fell on him and the pebbly beach around him. His fingers tightened around a wooden handle. Somehow he had managed once again to keep a grip on the machete.

He was walking toward a body tangled in debris a few yards away. He knew the person was dead. "Ray," he said.

The body stirred and an arm reached dramatically for the sky.

"Yes, what is it?" the body replied.

"You all right?"

"Hell, no."

"I think I made it."

"What about me? Did I make it?"

"I wasn't sure at first, but you're talking." This idiotic conversation felt perfectly natural. All Peter's fear and pain seemed suspended. He might have been on vacation, trying to find a friend.

He unwrapped creepers and branches from Ray's body and head. Ray raised his eyes to Peter's face, winced, and said, "Just my head?"

"I think the rest of you is here, too."

Ray struggled out of the mud and debris. His eyes stared from a face painted with swipes of half dried dirt. Peter looked down at himself. He was covered with mud.

"You're a mess," Ray said.

"So are you."

"Anything broken?"

"I don't think so."

"Me, neither. I think." Ray took a tentative step. "A true, honest to God miracle."

"Where are we?" Peter asked.

The lake stretched for about a quarter of a mile, bounded on most of its shore by thick forest. They could not see around the bend of shore to determine if it met up with a larger body of water. Peter found the sun, at its ten o'clock position, he estimated, and decided they were on the southern shore. He looked due east and saw a white prominence rising just above the tops of the trees: a tor.

"We can climb that and get a look around," he said, pointing.

"I'm not climbing anything," Ray said, falling back on his butt on the sandy shore and sinking his head between his knees. Peter felt too tired to argue or do much more than stand. Still, he thought fuzzily, they had to do something. He turned slowly, stumbling because of a weakness in one leg, recovered, and looked west. Debris had spilled from the stream mouth into the lake, forming a raft—a *camelote*—of foliage, small logs, branches, and scum. In the debris floated a small green body.

Peter struggled through the wrack a few yards east to see the green body more clearly. It was a reptile or dinosaur, about three feet long. He couldn't tell more than that. He walked back to Ray and asked in a flat voice, "How hungry are you?"

Ray looked up, irritated by the obvious question. "Enough," he said. "Not polite to talk about it."

"All right," Peter said, and meticulously waded out to the debris raft.

The green body was fresh and Peter figured it weighed about twenty or twenty-five pounds, a good-sized turkey. It resembled a small struthio, but with large eyes and no feathery scales. He dropped it in front of Ray and they both stared at it. The head flopped on its long neck, half open red eye fixed dully on nothing in particular.

Ray lifted his face to squint at Peter. A light mist had settled over the small lake.

"I've been thinking," Ray said.

"About what?" Peter asked.

"How long we can last here."

"Not very long, without food."

"This is food?" Ray asked.

"Yeah," Peter said with a sigh. He lifted the machete.

"Raw," Ray said.

"I suppose," Peter said.

Peter squatted by the carcass and lifted one limp leg. Then he brought the machete down on the hip joint and split the skin. Pale pink muscle and yellowish fat showed through the slice. He hacked again. Ten or eleven hacks and some sawing removed the leg, and Peter tried using the machete to cut away the thin, tough skin. The work was tiring, but he managed to rip off a strip of thigh and handed it to Ray. Ray took it, examined it with narrowed eyes, and bit into it.

Peter cut himself a piece and was surprised to find he had no qualms about putting it in his mouth. He was too hungry to care how it tasted or felt.

After they had eaten both legs to the bone, leaving only the horny skin around the clawed toes, they lay back on the beach and stared up at the golden fog surrounding them. "Amazing," Ray said.

"What, having food?"

"I ache all over, I've got bruises and welts on every square inch of my body, there's a good chance I'll be dead in a day or two . . . but I feel pretty good."

"A full belly," Peter said. He didn't feel *good,* but he didn't feel bad, either.

They heard a low droning noise. Peter tried to locate the direction, but it seemed to come from everywhere.

"That's an airplane," Ray said, sitting up on his elbows.

The mist was starting to thin above them, and they saw patches of blue sky and higher puffy clouds with gray bellies. They both scanned the patches. Suddenly, the drone turned into a coughing roar and a big high-winged scout plane passed over the forest and the lake at about a hundred feet. They both stood and waved frantically, but the plane continued on a straight course until it was out of sight behind the wall of mist.

"Didn't see us," Peter said.

"At least they're looking."

"Who?" Peter said.

"They must be flying out of San Pedro or Uruyen," Ray said.

"Where can they land? Are they going to find us, or will we find them?" He suddenly felt very excited. "I was thinking earlier about finding the place where Jimmie Angel crashed, maybe that would be a landing field, and—"

Ray shook his head. "He *crashed*, Pete. Must not be a very good place to land if an ace pilot crashes."

"But maybe they would know how to find the plane—"

"If it isn't covered with forest by now."

Peter would not give up. The food made all the difference in the world; his spirits started to soar at the multitude of plans frantically crowding into his head. "But if they can see the plane, maybe they'll fly over it, and if we're there, they'll see us!"

"We'd have to find the plane first," Ray said.

"Then we climb a tor and look around."

Ray shrugged, then smiled. "All right." He stared dubiously at the small, dismembered dinosaur torso. "We can't waste food."

Peter began enthusiastically cutting up the rest of the carcass. He disemboweled it with astonishing objectivity, for a boy who had felt faint dissecting frogs in school, and washed the well-hacked body parts in the lake water. "Do we want to save the liver and stuff?" he asked Ray.

"Let's not carry this too far. How do we know parts of these animals aren't poisonous?"

Peter agreed and looked around for something to carry the chunks of meat in. A broad, tough leaf about two feet wide served the purpose, and he tied it with a fern stem.

As they were about to head east, into the forest, something slopped in the lake shallows. The scythe-headed amphibian, or one very much like it, swam sinuously through the water and crawled up onshore. Its slick wrinkled skin was patterned in dark green and black spots with touches of yellow and red along its back. With a slow hunch of its upper body and twist of its broad head, it gobbled the small dinosaur's innards. When it finished, it turned its widespread golden-brown eyes on them, then padded around and slithered back to the lake.

Peter shivered. Ray watched it depart with fascination. "What a *monster*," he said again, as if a nine foot long salamander were any more monstrous than a pack of bear-sized lycos.

"How far from the chasm do you think we are now?" Peter asked as they hiked between the tall trees toward the distant outcrop.

"This part of the forest looks different," Ray said. "Less undergrowth. We could be a couple of miles farther north. That would make it three or four miles."

Peter tried to imagine the flood carrying them a mile or more, and couldn't. "If we'd been swept that far, wouldn't we be dead?"

"We should be dead by now anyway," Ray said. The package of dinosaur meat attracted flies and Peter kept having to brush them away. The biting flies were fewer, at least, and for that they were grateful.

They traversed about two hundred yards with fair speed, avoiding a swampy hollow and an odd outcrop of low, flat stones free of vegetation. They skirted this barren area with an instinctive unease. It curved behind an intrusion of forest, and as the obscured reach gradually came into view, they saw a series of low sandy mounds, surrounded by a thick U of trees. Ray stopped and put his hands on his hips. "The ground is moving out there," he said.

Peter looked at the low, flat rocks. A tan and orange mass crawled over the distant stones like opaque honey. This honey, however, seemed made of millions of discreet parts. "Ants," he said. "Those must be ant mounds." He walked carefully to the edge of the barren stretch and knelt. Across the rocks scuttled dozens of golden insects the size of his thumb, with wicked-looking pincers and glistening abdomens. Their eyes were black, and no matter which direction they moved, they seemed to be looking straight at *him.* He backed away in a hurry, scanning the forest loam for more of the big ants.

"Nothing goes in there, right?" Ray said.

"I wouldn't," Peter said. "They look big enough to cut away trees."

"Maybe that's what they've done," Ray said. They were about to move on when a high, melodic *skree* froze them in their tracks. They looked around slowly, afraid to even move. Peter stared across the barren rocks at the forest beyond. He felt like falling on his belly to hide.

Emerging from the forest on two muscular pillars of legs,

pushing aside trees with a stealth and grace astonishing for its bulk, its broad, long tail sweeping behind, twenty-five feet high from tip of saber-clawed toes to glittering white feathery crest, white- and yellow-plumed head sporting a long snout with both a scimitar beak and long rows of knife-like teeth, two long black-feathered arms bobbing gently before it, *Stratoraptor velox,* the *Totenadler,* the death eagle, stepped out onto the denuded territory of the golden ants and surveyed the situation with dark-rimmed green eyes.

Peter stood rooted to the ground by the sight, even though a hundred yards separated them. His only thought was that it was after them, that they had to flee, but his legs would not take instructions from his brain. Ray's mouth worked, but no words issued forth. They did not move or make a sound; the beast so quickly and unexpectedly revealed to them, descendant of the first lines of birds, monstrous cousin to the avisaurs and ancient *Archaeopteryx,* fixed them like deer caught in the headlights of an oncoming car.

The *Stratoraptor* strode slowly to the flat barren area west of the ant mounds, cocked its head as if to inspect the ground and the mounds, and slowly hunkered down with arms folded by its sides. It settled itself, making deep drumming noises, and closed its eyes as if about to go to sleep.

Peter let out his breath slowly. They quietly backed into the cover of the trees.

"It didn't see us," Peter said.

Ray lifted his eyebrows and sighed in relief.

"We should get away from here as fast as we can."

"I wonder how fast it can travel in these trees," Ray said, peering around a trunk to observe the animal. It perched unmoving on the ant field.

"I don't want to find out," Peter said.

"We might be able to outrun it in the forest," Ray said, a gleam in his eyes. His brow furrowed. "More curious, though, is why is it sitting on an ant nest?"

Peter shrugged his shoulders.

Ray sat on a low rock with a good view of the ant mounds, as if preparing for a vigil.

"Are we staying?"

"I want to see this," Ray said. "It's very odd. What I'd give to have my camera right now . . ."

Peter leaned against the trunk, heart racing. He was curious, too, but more concerned about staying alive.

"I'll take some of that meat," Peter said, and Ray handed him the package.

"Make sure we're upwind," Ray suggested.

"It would have smelled us by now," Peter said. He chewed on a tough strip of tail meat. The less hungry he was, the less palatable the raw flesh tasted, but he did not want to waste it, and soon it would be spoiled or flyblown. *Of course, Anthony says maggots are high in protein,* he reminded himself.

The *Stratoraptor* drummed again, like a huge prairie chicken. It opened its eyes and blinked calmly, twisting and tilting its head.

"Look at its legs," Ray said. Peter focused on the thick thighs, pooched out in its squatting position. Their color seemed to be slowly changing from dark yellow to greenish gold; furthermore, the color was creeping from the ground up. Closer to the dirt, the *Stratoraptor*'s hues had changed to dark gold.

Peter sucked in his breath. "It's letting the ants crawl on it!"

Ray nodded. "Looks that way."

"Maybe it's old and sick . . . it's come here to die."

Ray shook his head. "This isn't a graveyard for monsters."

They watched in silence. Within ten minutes, the *Stratoraptor* was completely covered by a glittering carpet of golden insects. Despite Peter's qualms, curiosity now gripped him, as well. He could not imagine why such a huge animal would let itself be covered by *ants.* Unless . . .

"Tick birds," Peter said.

"Cleaner shrimp," Ray said simultaneously. They stared at each other in amazement.

"It's letting the ants *clean* it!" Peter said.

"What else?" Ray said, his face bright with discovery. For a moment, they forgot their predicament, watching the *Stratoraptor* sit quietly for its ant bath. "Even big animals have lice, ticks, fleas

. . . The ants feed on its pests, remove dead skin and scales . . . and in return, the animals stay away from the mounds."

"Or maybe the ants clean up bloodstains, remains of prey," Peter suggested.

"Plausible," Ray said. "I don't think anyone's ever seen this before!"

Peter thought of his father and OBie, a sudden sharp image that obscured the delight of discovery and reminded him of their danger. "We don't have much time," he said softly.

Ray kept watching the ant field and the huge, quiescent *Stratoraptor*. With a jerk, he diverted his attention and grinned sheepishly at Peter. "You're right, of course," he said. "But maybe we can wait and see where the old bird's going next. We should stay out of its path."

"If we leave now, we'll get a head start," Peter said.

Ray couldn't argue with this. He agreed with a clamp of his jaw muscles and a sharp nod. "Let's go."

They kept glancing over their shoulders as they moved deeper into the forest and east once more. With the *Stratoraptor* almost out of sight—and still squatted contentedly, tended by a honey-like sheen of the big golden ants—they heard the airplane's drone again. They had no clear view of the sky, nor the sky of them, but certainly did not want to appear out in the open with the *Stratoraptor* so close. They halted and listened. Through the trees, they saw the same high-wing plane fly low over the northern forest. With a roar of its engine, it circled and dove a few yards lower to buzz the *Stratoraptor* at an altitude of less than fifty feet. The beast shook itself free with a quick shower of ants, got to its feet, and stretched straight out, screaming its surprise and rage. The scream hurt Peter's ears and made his knees rubbery: it was the same *skreee* they had heard on the southern end of the plateau, only much louder.

The pilot angled the plane over them, above the forest, turned due south, and continued on until the drone subsided.

"Thanks for nothing!" Ray said angrily.

The *Stratoraptor* continued to shriek its defiance, and Peter and Ray hurried deeper into the forest, toward the tor.

Chapter Eight

———— ❡ ————

The trees here were younger and spaced more closely together. Overall, the canopy had dropped by twenty or thirty feet and was thin enough that sunlight speckled the floor and undergrowth. Ghostly white vines covered with lacy, pale leaves twined around an old log and spread out in a lumpy wave across the floor, pouring up against other, living trees and wrapping their trunks in tight spirals, like string wound around a spool. A few dozen yards ahead, Peter and Ray could occasionally see through the forest the yellow-brown mass of their goal brightly illuminated by the sun. Peter had given his machete to Ray, who opened the path for their fairly rapid progress. Peter's left arm continued to hurt with each step, but less so than a few hours before.

They had just walked around a particularly impressive tree, with a trunk almost fifteen feet across, when Peter saw a gray shape crawling overhead. He jumped aside. "Ray!"

Ray turned and Peter pointed up. Standing on a branch, a cluster of leaves clamped in its mouth, was a gray, heavily wrinkled, sausage-shaped animal, tiny black eyes prominent on a rounded head. It had a short snout and a stumpy tail and was no more than a yard long. The animal watched them quietly, not moving. Peter saw that its snout was actually a kind of horny beak, the apexes of the upper and lower halves divided into two flat cutting edges, like a rat's incisors.

"Do you know what that is?" Peter asked.

"Looks like a big mole," Ray said.

"It has scales," Peter said. "I think it's a reptile."

"A mole-reptile, then," Ray said.

The animal turned deftly and wriggled along the branch toward the trunk. Three-clawed feet gripped the trunk tightly and it lifted itself with a grunt. They watched it until it vanished in the tree's thick crown.

Ray glanced at Peter and lifted his shoulders. What to make of so many wonders?

As they came to the edge of the forest, they discovered that a clearing surrounded the supposed tor, and that the formation was much broader than they had thought.

"It's the step pyramid," Peter said. He remembered the step pyramid had not been far from an open space, which must have been the ant field.

"We saw it, too," Ray said. "OBie says it wasn't there the last time he came to El Grande."

They stepped out of the abrupt edge of the forest onto a pebble-strewn causeway that flanked the stepped mound. "Looks as if the forest has been manicured," Ray observed, looking back at the sculpted topsoil and neatly chewed root ends, the lopped limbs and pruned branches.

The pyramid rose about two hundred feet and covered an area twice that in width. The walls were made of thick, dried, irregular masses of fine-chopped leaves, branches, and mud or clay, like a crazy pattern of brickwork. These masses were held together by a dark brown mortar with a faint, viscous sheen, like dried snail slime. Overall, the pyramid was pale brown or dirty yellow, graying and brightening alternately beneath the cloud-mottled afternoon sun.

"Listen," Ray said. From within the pyramid came a subdued, whiny skirling. They approached the base and placed their hands against it.

Peter realized what might be responsible for the mound.

"Ants," he said, and backed away quickly. Ray leaped back as well, then squinted dubiously at the high mound.

"This big? It doesn't look like an ant or even a termite mound."

"What else, then?" Peter said. "Giant bees?"

"I'd hate to meet one," Ray said. "There don't seem to be any openings on this side. We came here to climb up and look around. Won't be hard to scale these walls . . . "

Peter shook his head. "We should find out what made it first."

"Yeah," Ray agreed. "No sense being reckless. Let's walk around."

The causeway made for easy hiking, level and almost as smooth as a gravel road. They rounded the first corner. "It isn't square," Ray observed.

"A pentagon, or hexagon?" Peter suggested.

"Pentagon, maybe—or irregular."

Beyond the second corner, the forest opened up into hummocky grassland, dotted with low, flat mounds each about fifty feet across and made of the same irregular mud bricks. Long elevated dikes connected the small mounds with the central step pyramid. Ray climbed over the first dike, about five feet high, and Peter followed—then froze at the sight of a bootprint.

"Did you step over here?" he asked Ray.

"No."

"Somebody did."

"Billie?"

"He wore sandals."

"Maybe OBie or your father, then."

Peter smiled broadly. "Yeah! They're probably around here doing just what we're doing—trying to see where they are, and how to get back."

They walked on to the next dike and found more prints in the finer patches of gravel and grit. "Looks like one pair of boots to me," Ray said. "Big, too." At Peter's concerned expression, he added hastily, "But I'm no tracker."

Peter looked around in the dirt. He bent down and touched a mark apparently made by a heel, looked a pace beyond, and saw a clearer print. This one was smaller than the other, somewhat smaller than Peter's, and the tread seemed markedly different from that on his own boot, which matched his father's. He tried to remember OBie's feet. They had not been very large, but larger than this print.

"Here's another," he said. "There are two sets, but I don't think they belong to my father or OBie."

Ray knelt beside him. "You're right. Who, then?"

They continued to the third side of the mound. The clouds were building again and a high pale haze softened the sun's glare. The high-pitched skirling within the larger mound continued. Ray wiped sweat from his brow. They rounded the next corner and saw a long ramp reaching to the top of the mound's first step. Ray pushed Peter back and they peered cautiously around the corner. Several wrinkled gray mole-reptiles climbed the ramp. They made sharp *whuk whuk* noises to one another, accompanied by a continuous low chittering.

Peter smelled vinegar and held his nose.

"Smells like a tossed salad," Ray observed softly. The gray animals ignored them and waddled up the ramp to the first step. More followed.

One of the animals appeared half again as large as its companions, its pebbly gray hide marked with white stripes, and its longer tail forked into two large, vertical horny spikes. This forked tip twitched upward sharply several times as the animal walked.

"Same species?" Peter asked.

"I don't know," Ray said. "Did you see the front claws?"

"Yeah. Long and blunt."

"They're diggers," Ray said. "*They* made this mound."

That conclusion seemed obvious enough, but it was still startling. "You mean, they build like beavers . . . or prairie dogs?" Peter asked.

"Or like bees."

Peter and Ray stared at each other for a moment. "This *is* a hive, then?" Peter asked.

Ray shrugged.

They waited for the ramp to clear, then walked to the top of the first step.

"Maybe they're nocturnal, and there are just a few guards or workers out and about," Ray said. "They look pretty pale to be out in the bright sun."

The wall of the second level was marked by regular round indentations, like large mouse holes. These were covered with a flexible flap made of some compressed and chewed vegetable matter. Peter lifted one of the thick, papery flaps and peered down a long tunnel. The skirling noise, like dozens of ghostly bagpipes, floated with greater intensity from the tunnel. Peter held the flap up while Ray knelt and inspected the opening. Ray then stood and brushed his hands on his pants, sniffing at the air. "More tossed salad," he commented. "Too heavy on the vinegar."

Peter turned northeast and heard a faint sound, like an abrupt shout. "Did you hear that?"

"Another animal," Ray said. They heard it again.

"No animal!" Peter said excitedly. "That's a voice!" They ran along the top of the first step toward the northern face of the mound. Cast in late afternoon sunlight, the northern face was covered with quietly scurrying gray creatures. They came in at least four different varieties, the largest almost eight feet long, all of them low-slung, with wide-spread legs and intent, beady, round black eyes. The two larger varieties had horny upturned forks on the ends of their tails and heavier forelimbs with long claws. For the moment, clambering up the walls and along steep ramps leading from step to step, the mole-reptiles paid no attention to Ray and Peter.

Peter heard the shout again and looked up at the top of the mound. "It's Wetherford!" he cried, and Ray looked up as well. The Englishman stood about a hundred and sixty feet above them, waving a machete and shouting, "Halloa! All you ratty types, up here! Halloa!" In his other hand he carried a rifle.

Peter called out, "Mr. Wetherford! James Wetherford!" Ray waved his arms as well, but Wetherford did not hear them. He abruptly backed away from the edge just as a group of five large fork-tails started up the wall of the top step.

To compound the confusion, an airplane approached from the east, flying low over the jungle. It was a flying boat, Peter saw—a big, beautiful gray PBY, its motors singing a low throaty song. The plane banked to the north and rose a few dozen feet to pass directly in front of the mound. Ray and Peter waved frantically, and the plane waggled its wings as it completed its turn. The fork-tails and "ratty types" broke into confused scampering. Some brushed past their legs and leaped from the upper step, landing with heavy thumps thirty feet below. Peter peered down and saw three broken bodies; one whimpered and skirled shrilly.

"Lake Akuena!" Ray shouted. "That plane can land on the south-central lake!"

"What about the small lake?" Peter asked. "That's closer."

"Too short to land on, is my guess," Ray said.

"The central lake is miles from here!" Peter said.

Only now did they realize they had the attention of a good number of the mole-reptiles. Five, six, and then eight, nine, ten of the animals circled them, clacking their divided rodent-tooth beaks and hissing alarmingly. Three large fork-tails approached and the others parted to let them through.

Peter and Ray turned. Three other fork-tails crawled over the lip of the step and piped like teakettles.

The animals surrounding them suddenly sidled to the north, forcing Ray and Peter to walk to their right to keep in the middle of a confining circle.

"We're corralled," Peter said.

Ray glanced down at Peter's machete. "We could carve our way out."

Peter examined the larger animals and shook his head. "They could whack us pretty good."

"If we don't, we might end up mole food," Ray warned.

Peter made a fierce face and raised his machete. Behind them, an even more threatening hiss sounded, and they turned to face a true giant among the mole-reptiles—a dusky orange brute almost as big as a lyco, beak parted into two canine-like fangs separated by a middle row of horny serrations. Its small black eyes glared at them and it bobbed its head like a giant chuckwalla, piping and hissing steadily.

Peter let out his breath and lowered his machete. The cordon moved them efficiently to the northern side of the mound, where all the animals stopped together. The air was thick with vinegar and other smells, some of them disgustingly foul. The vapors stung their eyes.

"They're as bad as skunks," Ray said, holding his hand up to his nose and blinking.

The wall beside them collapsed in a cloud of debris and a second lyco-sized creature poked its snout out, scooping rubble aside with heavy claws. The cordon parted and Ray and Peter were herded up to the large hole. The digger withdrew.

Peter hesitated. All the animals hissed at once, and Ray held up his hands as if surrendering. "All right!" he cried. "All right!"

He shot a panicked look at Peter, but they knew instinctively they could not survive a fight with the biggest reptiles.

Peter glanced north at the PBY, barely a dot above the green horizon of El Grande. They both bent over and a mole-reptile butted them through the fresh opening in the wall.

Chapter Nine

Peter did not enjoy enclosed spaces. In Chicago and New York, he had, for no reason he could understand, tortured himself at night, before sleep, with thoughts of being enclosed in a small sewer pipe, trying to crawl through darkness and damp to a spot of light very far away.

And then something had plugged up the light.

The tunnel into the mound was not so small, but it was dark and smelled of skunk and vinegar and foul, beery burps, and beneath all those smells, the now-familiar parrot-cage odor—making him want to vomit. He swallowed hard as Ray jostled him from behind. "They're pushing me!" Ray explained, by way of apology, and they stooped and stumbled down the shoulder-high passage.

Behind and in front of them, tremendous thumps shook the walls. Peter closed his eyes and held his nose and tried to breathe just through his mouth, but the smell still filled his head, and the pounding, and the skirling.

We're going to die, he thought. *This is it. We were being swallowed. Now we're in the stomach.*

He thought of his mother, so lovely and always a little distant, reserved, puzzled and even stymied by her son's need for affection. He thought of Anthony, hating to not be someplace doing something, shunning inactivity and normality, hustling his son from city to city, trying to encourage Peter to see the world through curious, active eyes, to take part in anything and everything.

And he thought of Peter Belzoni, caught in emotional makeup somewhere between his parents, more passionate and curious than his mother and more sensible and cautious than his father. And what did it matter? The mole-reptiles would put them into a food pile and all his work at growing up and finding out who he was would come to nothing, except that he would become reptile chow.

"Communisaurs," he murmured over his shoulder to Ray. The name popped into his head.

"What?"

"Communisaurs," Peter repeated.

"Workers of the world, unite," Ray said.

Peter saw a fuzzy glow ahead. He imagined phosphorescent moss and a scene out of H. G. Wells or Jules Verne, vast caverns with multihued pillars and a huge chamber filled with servile gray creatures, and governing it all, something like the Grand Lunar. The imagined scene almost scared him witless and he felt his face tighten into a terrified mask. Not dead yet, he reminded himself. *Not dead yet!*

The tunnel widened into a bigger place. A few particles of light escaped from somewhere ahead, enough to see hulking shadows. The skirling had become clearer, though fortunately not louder. The thumps were now behind them.

"Smells like bad cheese," Ray said.

"Smells like a sour stomach," Peter said.

They were pushed through a curtain of long vegetal strands and the scene brightened enough for them to see an even larger space, filled with moving black lumps. Peter stopped, unwilling to step into that hip-high welter of shifting bodies. He looked up and saw shafts of light slanting down from several holes overhead. Some drifts of fresh air wafted down and Peter took a deep breath. In the middle of his inhale, a wave of farty-sweet and skunky odors washed around them and he gagged. Ray shoved up behind him and they both tumbled into the mass of chittering, squirming bodies.

Peter pushed up on his elbows and got to his knees. Something scratched his ribs and the top of his head and he screamed and kicked out. "Ow!" Ray shouted. "Watch it!"

Peter swallowed again and stood. There was no spit left in his mouth and his stomach felt full of dry clods. The bodies had parted around them. His eyes were adapting to the dingy light and he could see rounded brick walls, hanging strands of vegetable matter like tattered fabric, small dark bodies on either side, and a clear passageway between to an even brighter chamber. Bodies pushed them from behind and Ray said, "It's getting tight back here."

Peter walked forward, glad that he could at least stand up.

"Now I know how a pig feels going to slaughter," Ray muttered.

Peter shook his head. "Don't say that." It was bad enough for *him* to think such things, worse still to know they agreed as to their probable fate.

"I'll never eat bacon again," Ray added.

Half seen gray bodies shoved them around a corner. Peter made

Communisaur soldier

out that they actually walked between two walls, and that a vaulted roof pierced with small bright holes rose high over them. Tiers of walkways surrounded this large chamber, which had to be somewhere near the middle of the mound. Small and medium-sized dark communisaurs scampered along the walkways.

The parrot smell overcame all others. Peter looked around and saw two of the biggest fork-tails lurching behind them. Their tails rose and they whacked them simultaneously on the chamber floor, making a single sharp, loud thump. Then they withdrew.

The way ahead was clear. All around, the skirling rose to terrifying intensity, hundreds if not thousands of communisaurs raising a ruckus, their chatter filling the chamber with a painful din.

Suddenly, the ruckus subsided. The chamber fell silent.

Peter heard someone quietly swearing, not Ray.

"OBie!" Ray called.

"Who's there?"

That was Anthony's voice! "Father!" Peter shouted.

A yeasty cloud of scent billowed over them. Peter looked up in time to see the silhouette of a huge pair of limbs reach over the wall. Long, curving, blunt claws surrounded his midriff and lifted him into the air like a baby.

Chapter Ten

Every bone in his body seemed to rattle and his teeth clacked together painfully as claws and horny pads clamped and abraded his chest. Peter could hardly breathe. Something dry and cool thrust into his face and snuffled. Whatever held him was immensely strong, at least the size of the big fork-tails, and smelled like parrot and fresh bread and drunken burps. He tried to cry out but couldn't suck in enough air. His head swam and he felt as if he would black out. Suddenly, he was released and fell on his feet, immediately collapsing to his hands and knees.

Anthony called his name.

Peter's head hung low. He dropped to his elbows and side, and finally managed to draw in enough of the thick air to let out a gasp. His vision returned but what he saw made little sense: thick hard mud ridges radiating from a central pile of irregular bricks, topped by a bristling clump of sticks and logs, all dimly illuminated by the bright holes overhead. He rolled on his back, too weak to do anything but feel his chest heave. An orange outline passed nearby—hunched ridge of spine supporting porcupine-like bristles, suggestions of rippling fat, slow, splayed limbs, and then the flat crown of an immense head, mouth a dark crescent beneath. The mouth seemed at least a yard wide, but it was very close and he could not yet judge distance and size.

He heard his father yelling for him to be still. And then another word, perhaps spoken by OBie—it sounded like "expectation." Peter closed his eyes and concentrated on breathing. He felt as if his ribs had been crushed, but decided the pain wasn't sharp enough to prove that. He could move his hands and feet, so his back hadn't been broken. The beast near him brushed past Peter's left side and lifted itself with a casual moan up the curved wall, arms spread wide like a lizard's, claws scraping against the hard mud surface. It reached over the wall and Peter saw Ray lifted into the air, kicking and shouting. The arms contracted and pulled Ray up against the beast's muzzle, and again Peter heard the snuffing sound. A miasma of choking civet smell sank around him.

The arms dropped Ray on the other side of the pit, behind the pile. Peter turned his head and caught a glimpse of more large, dark shapes, surrounded by smaller pale forms that skirled and scurried over the ridges, climbing in and out of the central clump of sticks and logs. He heard mewling whistles.

This is a nest, he thought. His eyes had adapted to the dark enough to show more details: dust drifting in puffs above the nest, dozens of small gray communisaurs, mouths stuffed with leaves and branches, moving in orderly lines on a ramp overlooking the nest, and the biggest of them all—a great, orange shape mottled with black spots, lying with both ends slopping over the sides of the nest, vast flanks rising and falling slowly. This behemoth was three times the size of the large fork-tails. Peter could barely see the top of its head.

He tried to stand. A fork-tail leaped out of nowhere, backed around, and thumped him with its tail-horns. He sprawled forward against the nest and barely missed poking an eye out on a jutting stick. "Stop it!" he shouted. Blood flowed from a gouge on his cheek, darkening his questing fingers.

Ray crawled on his hands and knees around the nest. The behemoth above them rolled its head lazily, watching. He stopped beside Peter, slumped against the pile of bricks, and raised the machete. "You dropped this," he said, and wiped blood from his lips.

"Are you all right?" Peter asked.

"I don't know," Ray said. "You?"

Peter shook his head. "Father!" he called out as loudly as he could manage, barely a croak.

"Peter!"

"We're in a pit."

"The big one's a *queen,* Peter," Anthony shouted. "She inspected us and then the workers put us over here. We've been here for hours."

"Wetherford's outside," Ray said. "We saw him on top of the mound."

Gray communisaur attendants slunk around them with obsequious, breathy skirls. They snuffled at Peter's boots. He raised the machete defensively, but they did not seem to notice or care. The behemoth queen groaned like a giant steam boiler and shifted her weight, showering broken twigs from around the edge of the nest and bringing her tail to bear. Attendants became frantic. Two of them climbed over Peter and Ray and raised their heads to cushion the fall of a brownish egg six inches long. The egg rolled from their snouts into Peter's lap. He lifted it and presented it to them. "Here," he said. The attendants took it gingerly in their mouths, cooperating with delicacy to carry it away. Another egg plopped down from the queen's tail and landed on Ray's shoulder, slipping between the two of them. More attendants appeared and nosed up to the egg, then retrieved it, nodding as if thanking the humans for their help.

"What do they want with us?" Ray asked Peter softly. "Why bring us here?"

"I was going to ask you that," Peter said.

Her egg-laying finished, the queen swung around again and dipped her immense snout to within inches of Ray's head. His hair lifted as she inhaled. At least a cupful of saliva dribbled onto his lap. He grunted and swung his head away from the sour-smelling fluid. "Makes you hate nature, doesn't it?" he said in disgust. "What do they want with us?" he called out.

"How in hell should we know?" OBie called back. "You stay there and tell us. Was anybody with Wetherford?"

"We didn't see anybody," Peter said. "Dad, there's an airplane— a flying boat. It flew north."

The queen showered more sticks on them and rolled to snuff at Peter's head. Then she lifted and extended her snout, casting a shadow over them, and gave a resonant belching roar. The roar seemed to end in hiccups. Civet smell descended in almost visible waves. Peter swung his arms to clear the stench and looked up directly into her tiny black eye. Her head stretched a full four feet from wrinkled, bunched yellowish neck to tip of blunt nose, and she was colored a uniform dusty orange, with blue rings around her eyes and red along her finely scaled lips. She looked like a heavily made-up floozy. She blinked down at him, mouth gaping. Her jaws bore small, wide-spaced teeth, no larger than those of her attendants.

Two medium-sized fork-tails lumbered to attention a few feet from Ray and Peter. They sucked in the hideous vapors, eyes closed and jaws slack in ecstasy. The queen withdrew her head.

"They must think it's awful cozy in here," Ray muttered. "Maybe we can crawl out." He made a move to get up and the fork-tails rotated and presented their persuaders again.

Peter knew he would suffocate if he didn't get some fresh air. He kicked out, booting the forked spikes of the nearest guard. The tail and fork were stiff as stone and did not move on receiving the blow. His toe ached, however.

The ground trembled. Peter looked up to see if the queen had rolled again, but she was not visible. "Did you feel that?" he asked Ray.

"Yeah," Ray said. "Earthquake?"

The nest fell silent. All the communisaurs seemed to be listening. A louder thump shook the bricks, and dust sifted from the chamber ceiling. The fork-tails spun in confusion like dancing bears.

The queen belched and roared and screeched all at once.

The attendants scrambled. The fork-tails rushed to the wall and clawed their way over.

"That's dynamite!" Anthony shouted from behind the wall. Peter and Ray pushed to their feet. The pit was in an uproar. Gray worker communisaurs flocked over the nest and queen. Defenders and guards, big and medium-sized fork-tails, rushed for the ramps and walls to move to the outside of the mound.

Peter slipped the machete under his belt and said, "We'd better get out while we can."

Ray seemed dazzled by the uproar.

"Over the wall, join my father and OBie," Peter suggested, nodding in that general direction.

"Christ," Ray said. "I'd give anything to—"

But there was no time to finish.

Chapter Eleven

Jostling, tumbling, flowing in lemming waves up to and around the nest in the pit and all around the ramps, workers and defenders shoved each other in no pattern discernible from the pit's floor. Ray and Peter had as much as they could do to stay upright. Still, their general progress was toward the outside of the pit, though not toward the voices of their friends.

A few yards of gray communisaur crowd separated Ray and Peter as they approached the surrounding wall. The air stunk of civet, belch, and vinegar, and vibrated with ear-ringing skirls. Peter could not shout loudly enough for Ray to hear. Peter was spun about by the mass and saw the nest and the queen, her head and tail upthrust like a contorting earwig. An egg fell from the base of her thick tail into the crowd. That did not seem to matter.

Peter faced the wall again and jumped. He could not keep a hold on the irregular brick surface, however, and fell back onto the animals, which squealed like pigs. Somehow he got to his feet again, closer to the wall, and reached up, fingers slipping into the chinks between the bricks. Ray was right beside him, a little higher up the barrier. Peter found a hold for one foot, then another, and with sweat-stung eyes and the vinegar smell burning in his nose and throat, he hoisted himself to the top. Ray helped him and they stood above the confusion.

"Where?" Peter gasped.

"There, I think," Ray said, and pointed to a spot halfway around the pit's circumference, directly opposite where they stood. A defender vaulted up beside them, glanced at them with tiny black eyes, and leaped into the shadows on the other side of the wall.

"Look!" Ray shouted. Peter turned and saw two men on the wall, arms held out, balancing precariously.

"Over here!" Peter shouted.

OBie and Anthony walked along the pit's perimeter, arms out for balance, swaying like acrobats on a tightrope. The top of the wall was almost as wide as a sidewalk but not as flat, and the confusion on either side made balancing difficult.

There was little time for rejoicing when they joined. Anthony seemed to know where they all needed to go, and that was not back along the furrow between walls, but around the perimeter a few more yards, to where they could climb onto a ramp.

Once on the ramp, Anthony kicked aside a few gray workers, which gnashed out with their beaks and ripped at the humans' pants legs before conceding, hissing, and moving on.

Anthony grinned like a fiend at Peter. "Anything for clean air!" he cried as if yelling a Musketeer oath, and led them to a hole in the wall. A tunnel, empty but for two uncertain, blinking workers, led into darkness.

"Are you sure this is it?" Ray asked, his voice cracking. The tunnel smelled fetid.

"Positive," Anthony replied. They skirted past the workers, who stood in a shivering daze, and bent over to creep down the tunnel. Peter pulled the machete from his pants to keep from emasculating himself in this posture.

About twenty yards in, the tunnel sloped down at a thirty degree angle. They had to turn and back down to keep from tumbling forward. This seemed a final fillip in a mixed up nightmare: reunited, but descending backward into an unknown, rank-smelling darkness, their hands and feet sinking into a spongy dryness that might have been fungus or moss or dung, their boots sliding over the fingers of those behind.

"Watch it!" Anthony called up to Peter as boot treads rolled over knuckles.

They came into another chamber, where they could stand. Clustering together, they examined the place in the dim light of two vent holes. The floor seemed lumpy. The air smelled sickly sweet. The lumps began to move.

"Babies!" OBie exclaimed. He stooped and picked up a squirming, piglet-sized infant communisaur. Its eyes had not yet opened and it mewed in his hands and snapped its small beak. OBie hoisted it for their inspection. Ray patted its bald, finely scaled head. Anthony grimaced.

"Where are the nurses?" OBie asked, replacing the infant gently on the floor.

"Is this the way out?" Peter asked his father.

Anthony shook his head. "Beats me. I was sure—"

A shadow moved from the darkness and a forked tail swung out sideways, whacking OBie in the gut. He toppled with an oof and landed in a pile of babies crawling over mounds of moldy leaves. The floor came alive with squeaks and hisses. The tail swung again, taking Anthony across his back and staggering him into Peter. They both fell.

"Nurse!" OBie said weakly. Ray danced away from another sweep, and then they faced the head and beak of the hissing beast. They retreated toward the light of a vent hole. "On my shoulders!" Anthony told Peter, and hoisted him quickly to the hole. Peter's shoulders barely fit. Anthony shoved him like a cork into a bottle, and his head poked up into sunlight and air. He dropped the machete. Anthony shoved him again and he wrenched his arms free and pushed down from the top.

His legs finally emerged and he knelt beside the hole. Anthony tossed the machete up. Peter caught it deftly. "Dig it out—make it wider!" his father shouted from below.

Peter hacked at the hole furiously. The bricks rang like stone at first, but the surface gradually crazed, revealing straw-like fibers in a mud matrix, and the hole got a little larger. He dropped the machete into the hole and Anthony began hacking from below, standing on somebody's back.

Ray came up next, and then OBie, who could barely fit through. Ray and Peter pulled on his arms until his belly compressed and he groaned. Out he came with an almost audible pop. Ray held on to Peter as he dropped back into the hole and offered himself as a human rope. Anthony clung to his legs and now it was Peter's turn to be stretched; Ray and OBie lifted Anthony up by hauling on Peter's arms and trunk. Peter gritted his teeth at the pain in his shoulder.

When they all stood in the open, Anthony whooped like a drunken soldier on liberty. "My God, that air breathes sweet!"

OBie did a quick jig, grinning like a fool, an unraveled strand swinging from the rude strip of cloth that bandaged his chewed arm.

They all sobered and took their bearings. They stood on the eastern side of the mound, on the second step. Fewer than a dozen communisaurs were visible from their vantage. A dissipating cloud of dust blew to the south from the opposite side of the mound.

"Wetherford," Ray said.

"He's not the type to come here alone," Anthony said.

"We'll never know unless we go look," OBie said. They walked to the corner and Anthony peered around, then Peter and Ray. OBie hung back, sitting and nursing his leg.

A hole had been blown out of the mound thirty feet away. Dazed and injured communisaurs, including some big fork-tails, crept slowly or dragged themselves around the hole. Peter smelled the unmistakable acrid, powdery odor of dynamite.

"Somebody brought some security with them," Anthony said. "I don't see Wetherford or anybody else. Hope they haven't blown themselves up."

Small communisaurs began removing the injured and a kind of order returned to the damaged side of the mound. A steady stream of animals clambered down the walls, claws digging in to the steep slopes as they descended tail-first. More animals appeared bearing clumps of masticated leafy matter, and some communisaur

Communisaur diggers

"masons" began pushing muddy balls over the edge of the hole, mixing the leaf matter in, and patting them into irregular bricks with stolid dedication.

"For the time being, we're being ignored," Anthony said, "but if we stay here much longer, the queen's minions are going to grab us again and take us below for her amusement. Only this time, I don't think she's going to be very amused. We must smell a lot like the folks who did this damage."

"Where are they?" OBie asked, grimacing as he got to his feet.

"They'd have no reason to blow a hole in this mound unless they knew we were inside and wanted to get us out," Anthony said. "They're probably looking for us or getting ready to cause more damage."

"Well," OBie said, "let's save our gracious host the queen any more grief and find them before these creatures do."

Ray helped OBie by letting him lean on one shoulder. They half climbed, half slid down the wall to the first level, then took a ramp to the base of the mound. A few communisaurs stood aside with sheep-like expressions of uncertainty as they passed. "The fight's been taken out of them," OBie commented.

"Maybe they have other things on their mind," Anthony said. "There has to be some reason—"

Another explosion shook the ground. A billow of dust and debris flew from the western side of the mound. They ran around the corner, OBie hopping beside Ray, just in time to see a corner of the mound collapse, a gaping hole opening in two levels.

"Halloa!" a voice shouted from the forest. Wetherford stepped into the clearing, and then another figure. Peter's jaw dropped in shock. Vince Shellabarger stood behind Wetherford, a bandage wrapped loosely around the crown of his head.

"We thought we could distract them while you escaped," said the Englishman, still waving. "If they hadn't turned you into infant formula, that is."

"My God, Vince!" OBie called out, and they met in the clearing, shaking hands and slapping shoulders to the strident skirling of hundreds of communisaurs. "I was sure you'd been killed."

Vince stared at them with little expression, touched the side of his head, and said, "Not yet."

"Dagger gave it his best shot," Wetherford said. "He was prying old Vincent from under the cage when el Colonel's soldiers brought him down with a bazooka flown in from Uruyen."

"Dagger's dead?" Peter asked.

Vince turned to Peter and regarded him as if he were the only sane one in the group. The trainer's steady gaze discomfited Peter. It seemed as if Vince had died, and his ghost now stared at him. "The Indians fought the Army to save him," Vince said. "They considered it sacrilege to kill the Challenger. A lot of people died."

"My God," OBie said.

Wetherford's grin faded. "Yes, and Mr. Shellabarger's had a nasty time of it. He insisted he come with me, however. And he it was who suggested a few sticks of dynamite would come in handy."

Shellabarger shook his head, face creased with sorrow. "I swear I did not have it in for that animal. I did not want him to die."

"Unpleasant situation back there now," Wetherford said. "They've pushed out the Indians and insisted on closing the tepui completely. Wouldn't even consider a rescue expedition. El Colonel is beside himself. The radio's working again, but the government in Caracas doesn't dare face up to the Army in the middle of an Indian uprising. Mr. Shellabarger knows his vines, however . . . We found some *mamure* in the forest and used bars from the cages to hammer out a grappling hook. Threw the vines across—"

Shellabarger took Peter's shoulder and seemed to derive some strength from the contact. "If you had died, boy, I would have never forgiven myself. How in hell did you get this far north?"

"Yes, well," Wetherford said, "I was about to describe our remarkable feat with the vines—"

"Billie said El Grande swallows people," Peter said.

"That's true enough," OBie said. "The inside of that mound smelled like the very bowels."

Anthony had said little until now. He seemed agitated, even angry. "Peter and Ray saw a seaplane fly over."

"We've heard it, but we haven't seen it," Wetherford said. "The Army's chartered someone from Uruyen to inspect the area, with strict instructions not to land, but it isn't a seaplane."

"We saw that one, too," Peter said. "It buzzed the *Stratoraptor*."

As if summoned by name, a ringing *skreee* cut through the forest and echoed from the mound. The communisaurs investigating the fresh hole froze, then hurriedly retreated inside. A few reluctant fork-tails stayed in place, bouncing back and forth on their husky forelimbs.

"It was getting itself cleaned by golden ants in an open space, an ant field," Peter added.

"That's less than a half a mile from here," Shellabarger said.

"Cleaned—by *ants?*" Wetherford asked.

Anthony grabbed Peter's shoulder. "You didn't stick with us," he said, glaring at his son. "I was sure you were dead."

"Father—" Peter began, but there was no time.

The fresh hole was suddenly mobbed by burly fork-tails, heads swinging as they scrambled from within the mound. They seemed in a mood to attack anything—and several focused their attention on the humans. Shellabarger looked back into the forest. "Let's get the hell out of here." They ran from the open space around the mound, leaping onto the clean-cut edge of forest bed. Looking behind, Peter saw two of the biggest fork-tails following, tails erect, double-fanged beaked jaws gaping. He doubted they'd be taken back to the queen for examination this time.

That was what he had heard his father saying. Not "expectation," but "examination." This thought sprang into his head for no good reason just before Shellabarger came to an abrupt halt.

"Good Christ," Shellabarger said under his breath, then grimaced and stumbled to one side as both Ray and Peter bumped into him. Peter landed on his back and Ray dropped on his knees beside him.

A thick yellow tree trunk dropped to the floor of the forest just yards away. Peter pushed himself into a crouch and stared at the trunk in disbelief.

Shellabarger, Anthony, and OBie lay on their stomachs, hands covering their heads. Peter turned in time to see the fork-tails stumping through the forest, barely four yards behind. One of the fork-tails spotted Peter and veered in his direction.

The tree-trunk shivered and moved again, pulling up long glistening roots. Peter saw thick scales on the trunk, black foliage higher up—

A wickedly curved beak lanced down from the canopy and split the spine of the closest fork-tail like a butcher's cleaver. Peter heard the bones crack and snap and saw the fork-tail fall, a sudden ton of dead meat.

He still could not make sense of what was happening. Another tree moved, and his eyes and brain seemed to focus at once. He looked up—and up—

What caught his eye next in the gloom beneath the canopy was a radiance of brilliant white feathers. Out of the mane of feathers poked a massive head, like the head of a griffin. The wickedly sharp beak plunged again and scissored the side of the second fork-tail. The communisaur fell with a heavy *whump* and skidded in the litter of the forest floor, snout plowing up a cluster of seedlings.

The fork-tail's head stopped within a foot of Peter's knee. Blood sprayed down on Peter and Ray and the animal's side rose into the air, at least three hundred pounds of meat and bone and hide. Blood fountained from the fork-tail's open thorax. It spasmed and its tail thumped furiously against a tree.

The beak plunged again and again, snatching away more meat and bone. The air filled with the snapping of bones and the leathery wet sound of tearing meat.

Ray took hold of Peter's shoulder and pulled him back. They

frog-marched backward several meters, and Peter suddenly made sense of it all.

Dinoshi. The death eagle had crept up to the vicinity of the mound through the forest. Its head reached higher than the canopy when it stood upright, but now it stalked with head and tail at a level, like the venator. Its wicked dark-rimmed green eyes, as big as baseballs, blinked against the spatters of blood from its victims. It jerked back huge pieces of meat and swallowed them with only two or three knife-whispering champs of the big serrated teeth behind its beak.

The death eagle lifted to its full height to swallow, its throat expanding alarmingly and feathers sticking out like quills. The head vanished in the canopy and then dropped a few meters. The animal spread its fan of neck feathers and stared down at Anthony and OBie and Shellabarger. The glittering eyes blinked and focused directly on Peter and Ray. Wetherford was nowhere to be seen.

The fork-tails lay dead. The forest was quiet except for the commotion on the communisaur mound.

"We're next," Ray said softly.

"Yeah," Peter said.

The death eagle swung about gracefully between the trees, its huge lean body like smoke; it hardly disturbed the forest at all as it turned, legs swiftly planting themselves beside the fork-tails. It leaned over Peter and Ray, open beak bloody, and cocked its head with a very aquiline expression, intent on these new animals.

"Be still," Peter told Ray. They froze.

"Does it really matter?" Ray asked. His face shone ghostly pale in the forest gloom. Peter thought they both looked dead already. They had been dead ever since they walked across the bridge, just as a mouse is dead the minute a snake swallows it. It still kicks, tries to breathe, maybe it blinks and struggles against the clutching throat muscles, but it's dead, sure as hell.

The death eagle was beautiful. Its eyes and face seemed almost friendly, with that feathery sunburst focusing sound back to its flapless ears, its beady-eyed expression coldly quizzical. Its yellow legs were as big across as trees. The startling fan of feathers spread at least seven feet wide. Standing erect, weighing in at four or five tons, its black crown towered twenty-five feet above the forest floor. The body feathers seemed black as smoke in the gloom, but in the sun they would glitter like jewels, like a peacock's fan. This was swift death wrapped in glory, hypnotic, the kind of death that could enjoy a bath in honey-colored ants, a loony lovely end to everything.

All it had to do—

Dinoshi dropped its head with a quick jerk and its sunburst of feathers quivered. It scrutinized Peter and Ray from just a couple of yards, feathers rustling stiffly. It was listening to their breathing, to their heartbeats, and it was very interested, but uncertain what to do next.

The death eagle switched its gaze to the three prone men before it—OBie, Peter's father, and Shellabarger. None of them moved; all kept their hands over their heads and necks, like prisoners. For Peter, time moved like cold syrup. Sweat crawled down his forehead in honey-thick rivulets and dripped from his brows. He heard nothing. Sound in the forest seemed muffled, suffocated.

Then the death eagle shifted its weight and sticks snapped beneath its huge talons. *Dinoshi* lifted one leg and slapped its foot down on the broken-backed fork-tail. Bones crunched beneath the avisaur's weight and blood oozed from the fork-tail's mouth, along with a ghastly groan.

The death eagle raised its head and swung toward the mound. The noise of the communisaurs—raucous skirling, scrabbling claws—returned to Peter's sphere of awareness and he wondered why he had not heard it earlier.

The death eagle dropped its head, its Elizabethan feather gorget dished forward to gather sound from the mound. It leveled its back and took a step away from the dead fork-tails, away from the frozen humans. Its glittering eyes seemed to see sights in another universe, one no longer occupied by Peter and his companions.

The death eagle stalked silently east through the trees. *Dinoshi* had more familiar prey in mind, abundant, unaware prey that it had doubtless eaten often before and found tasty. They were not going to die—not yet.

Only at the last minute did it leap, crashing through the thicket into the clearing. From Peter's vantage, he could see only broken pieces of the destruction, but this was more than enough. The death eagle's cry cracked the air into painful pieces. The communisaurs tried to defend themselves, but with their fortress-home already violated by blasts of dynamite, they had little or no protection.

Through the screen of trunks and creepers and leaves, Peter saw *Dinoshi*'s talons kick in the mud walls. Gray bodies rushed out in a flood, sacrificing themselves for the good of the hive. Blood spattered against the mound. With lightning-swift flicks of the griffin head, bodies large and small flew about like stuffed animals on the bed of an angry child.

Wetherford sneaked up behind them. "God help me, I've wet my pants," he said to Ray and Peter. "We had best move our asses before Herr *Totenadler* decides we taste good after all."

Anthony got to his feet first, hugged Peter with painful strength, then helped OBie. The older man's face was dreadfully pale and his arms shook. He clutched his shoulder and grimaced at a sharp pain. "I'm all right," he said as Shellabarger got to his feet. The trainer rearranged the bandage on his head, but the cloth's slip had revealed a deep blood-caked crease in his scalp.

Ray went to OBie and once again lent his arm for support.

"The only place a big seaplane can touch down is the south-central lake," OBie said, voice shaky. Anthony nodded agreement.

"It saw us and waggled its wings," Peter said.

"How do we know it's going to touch down?" Anthony asked.

"Call it a hunch," OBie said. "A PBY doesn't come cheap, and there aren't any local planes of that type. Someone's behind it— someone who doesn't give a damn what the Army or any tinhorn dictator says." He drew himself up and squared his shoulders, but his face was still white with pain. "The lake's about eight or ten miles from here. Maybe we'll meet somebody halfway—guns, food, medicine . . ."

"We can't go back," Shellabarger said. He waved his arms decisively and commanded, "Move!" and they walked north.

The death eagle's screams and the sounds of dying communisaurs echoed behind them.

Chapter Twelve

———◆———

They walked through a stretch of dense forest north of the mound and east of the ant field. Hiking for the rest of the afternoon in weary single-file, they stopped by a narrow, deep creek and drank, then picked clusters of hard purple berries and ate what they could of the raw fruit. OBie pointed out trees filled with another spiky fruit and they ate some of those, but Shellabarger, ever the expert on the diets of creatures away from home, warned that too much wouldn't do them any good. "We need meat," he said, and he and Wetherford walked ahead while the others rested.

Anthony sat beside Peter on a fallen log. Something was bothering him, but for the time being he was keeping himself in check—waiting, Peter thought, for when they were alone. Peter could always feel a good fatherly bawling-out when it was coming. Sometimes it took days to emerge into the open—a delay he always hated.

Anthony rubbed his finger along a series of deep furrows chewed out of the log. "Some of Sammy's cousins might have done this," he said. Peter pulled up a patch of bark. A few thumb-sized yellow grubs crawled beneath, black heads rising indignantly at the glare.

"Yum," Peter said, thinking of Billie's comment on his dream.

Anthony looked down on the larvae with a furrowed brow. He

plucked up one of the grubs, examined it, suddenly narrowed his eyes as if daring Peter to do something, then popped it in his mouth and chewed quickly. He swallowed and his face shifted expressions with comic swiftness. "I *ate* it," he said.

"Tastes like butter, does it?" OBie asked from where he and Ray sat, a few meters along the log.

"Tastes like bug," Anthony said.

"Better cooked, but we don't have a fire," OBie said.

"It's all right raw," Anthony said, but he did not appear convinced. "Your turn," he told Peter, a little too sharply.

Peter smiled suavely, picked up the second grub, and swiftly bit and swallowed. He wasn't going to be outdone by his father, not this time, not in this way. "Nutty," he said.

Ray stepped forward, bent to examine the revealed larvae, and stood again with hands on hips. "I've eaten raw lizard. I can eat anything." He picked up the grub and lifted it to his mouth, then stopped.

"He who hesitates is lost," Anthony suggested.

Ray ate the grub. "Tastes bitter," he said, and looked back at OBie.

"Meat and potatoes," OBie said, shaking his head. "Strictly meat and potatoes."

Wetherford and Shellabarger returned just before dusk, empty-handed. "The river's in a deep gully right to the edge of the plateau," Wetherford said. "Shoots out into space for about half a mile straight down. No place to stop and drink along the way."

"There's a flat grassland about two miles north," Shellabarger said. "According to the old maps, it stretches from the south-central lake to the plateau's eastern edge. We can make better time if we cross the plain. Of course, we'll also expose ourselves to more danger."

Wetherford put on a fatalistic face and shrugged. "Nothing we haven't faced already," he said.

"The grassland is where Jimmie Angel came down in '35," OBie said. "We might find his aircraft."

"There's five or six crash sites up here," Wetherford said. "Hotshots from the mining companies always want to take their girlfriends over the tepuis. One went down on El Grande last year."

"If that bush pilot sees us on the plain," Shellabarger said, "he might decide to land and rescue us, dictator or no. There's bound to be reward money."

Wetherford pursed his lips. "Not bloody likely. The Army has slammed the gate hard on El Grande. No pilot wants to be clapped in irons."

"It's the PBY or nothing," OBie said.

"I wouldn't put too much faith in your producers in New York, either," Wetherford said.

OBie lifted his eyebrows and rubbed his arm: each to his own comforts.

They spent a hungry but dry night beneath the forest canopy, listening to the passage of monkey-sized animals through the trees and the gentle cheeping of small night birds. Anthony found more grubs in the morning, and this time OBie ate several. They washed away the experience with slices of half green spiky fruit. Peter had a stomachache throughout the morning.

They emerged from the forest onto the grassland at noon. Shellabarger kept his rifle ready as they waded through the hip-high green grass. In boggy swales, the grass sometimes grew over their heads, topped with feathery fronds that swayed and rustled in the steady northerly breeze.

After two miles, they sat beneath the spreading boughs of a thick, gnarly-trunked tree none of them could identify. Its leaves formed tight curls in shadow, but spread into six- or seven-lobed fans in sunlight. Dozens of the same kind of trees dotted the grassland.

Peter watched Anthony carefully. Today, he seemed perfectly calm, the storm clouds gone.

After a brief doze, they continued. According to Wetherford's watch, they encountered their first herd of sauropods at one o'clock, browsing among the broad-leaf trees: imposing saltasaurs, the biggest almost forty feet long, with serpentine necks and tails and spike-armored backs. The herd numbered about twenty, and half grown young stayed close to the center.

"Not many of these left now," Shellabarger said. "They're ancient beasts, like Sammy's kind. The death eagles are going to have them all in a few decades. The lycos don't mess with them."

Peter watched the graceful browsers work over a forty-foot-high tree. They pulled and chewed the leaves and branches with the steady deliberation of hungry caterpillars. In a few hours, judging from the condition of trees nearby, they would leave it a denuded skeleton.

"Worse than elephants," Shellabarger said. "Things have to grow fast around here just to keep up."

Peter thought of the death eagles and venators and the animals they preyed upon, and the delicate balances between plants and animals. He wasn't just a city boy anymore. Kahu Hidi was creeping into his personality.

They resumed their walk.

Anthony kept close to Peter. They veered off ten or fifteen yards from the broken line of their companions. Peter kept his eyes on the horizon, trying to see any hunting animals before they saw him—and also to avoid provoking his father. Despite the earlier calm, perhaps because of it, he knew that the storm was about to break.

Anthony stepped ahead of him, head lowered. "I thought you were dead," he said.

Peter smiled nervously. "I was sure you were—" he began.

"You ran away."

"I did *not*," Peter said.

"You knew we should have stayed together, but you *ran*."

Peter faced his father, stunned by this. "I was chased by an animal," he said.

Anthony dismissed this with a wave of his hand. "You should have done everything you could to stay with us. Together, we had a much better chance."

"I tried to find you."

"That was a little too late, wasn't it?" Anthony said, his face very dark.

"I did not run away," Peter said again. They stood in the tall grass, less than two feet from each other. All else seemed to fade. Anthony stared at him with eyes like coals—accusing, furious.

"Christ, I've never . . . felt so miserable in my entire life. I thought I'd lost you—but you, my son . . . seeing you *run*."

"You think I'm a coward?" Peter demanded. This was something he would not take even from his own father.

"Actions, my lad," Anthony growled. "Louder than any words."

Peter felt the tears welling up, the helpless rage he always felt when confronting this force of nature who happened to be his father, this unreasonable and unpredictable man who walked like a cheetah and carved rude poems on the wall and got drunk just when things might be getting dangerous and attracted all the beautiful women in the world—and who stuck with none of them. Peter held back the tears but not the ill-chosen words, meant to sting his father—just as his mother would have stung him. "I thought you were dead. You didn't come and find me!"

"We looked all over *hell* for you."

"Billie found me. You could have!"

"I certainly tried," Anthony said, a little of the glow fading from his eyes. But now it was Peter's turn for the rage to peak.

"You always think I'm a coward," he said, his voice low. "You always expect more from me. And no matter what I do, I always disappoint you. How long have you been waiting to drag me into some awful adventure, just to make me prove myself to you?"

"That's a lie," Anthony said. "You wanted this as much as I did."

"I am not a liar, and I am not a coward!" Peter shouted. "Damn you, I am as good as you, but . . . " He did not know how to say what needed to be said: in his mind, the words appeared, *I am not you. I am not like you.* But all he could manage was to shake his head, hold up his fist, and shout, "I survived! I didn't die! And I did not run because I was afraid!"

Anthony held out his hand to touch Peter, and his eyes were flat now, listless, drained. "Peter, I'm—"

Suddenly there was OBie weighing in, standing with feet spread beside them and poking at Anthony's shoulder. "Pardon an old man for butting into a family affair, but *leave the boy alone!* My God, man, he's a fine boy!"

Anthony retreated but OBie stayed with him, poking, poking.

"You don't know what it's like not having so fine a boy! Why, if

I could go back, if I could take away the years and have my own son here, with me—"

"I'm sorry," Anthony said. "I couldn't stand the thought of losing him. It's been eating at me."

OBie stood with his chest rising and falling, his cheeks apple-red, finger still extended. The finger curled now, less accusing. "He's a strong and brave boy and he did what he had to. No blaming him, and no blaming yourself. We're all in this. We're all men. It shouldn't turn sour this way."

"You're right," Anthony said. He raised his hands, placating. "I was way off base."

Peter saw his father was about to apologize, but his own heat was still too intense to allow that. He stalked away through the grass. Ray watched him, sad and silent, and Shellabarger stood facing north, away from the scene. Wetherford plucked at a thick blade of grass.

Ten minutes later, they took up the hike again, by silent agreement spread out across the flat ground, and the sun rose high overhead. Peter stumped steadily through the grass, paying little attention to where he was going. The minutes passed. His head filled with dark thoughts.

When they had reunited, he had felt a surge of hope and a deep sense of the nature of true adventure. They had beaten the odds; they had all survived. They seemed enchanted, this little group . . .

Now he did not care how far from the group he strayed.

It seemed hours later, he looked up and saw the others were several dozen yards to his right.

Anthony called for him to rejoin them. Peter stopped dead, his arms hanging, still feeling the burn. He stared at the ground, at his feet, more to avoid looking at Anthony than for any other reason.

He peered between the blades of grass. Shiny black bodies welled up from holes in the earth. His boots were covered with them.

Ants. Half an inch to over an inch long.

Peter froze. For a fraction of a second, he thought of the ant field and the death eagle getting cleaned. If he just stayed still, he thought, they might not bite. But a deep shuddering horror collided with his anger and exhaustion, and before he could stop himself he jumped and stamped his boots and brushed ants from his pants legs and lifted the pants and scooped them from his ankles. Ants clung to his fingers. He ran toward Anthony, shaking his hands as if trying to fly. *"Veintecuatros!"* he shouted. "Oh, Jesus, Father, ants, ants!"

A knife blade seemed to stab his ankle and another his hand. Anthony caught his son in his arms and quickly smashed ants with sharp palm slaps on his hands, arms, and back. They danced like frantic scarecrows in the grass, and Peter howled.

He saw a cloud rush over the land black as tar. In the middle of the cloud his father's face appeared, screwed up in anguish. Ray and OBie called out his name but it did not seem familiar and the pain was too much. He saw it would be easy to just fall up to the sky, into the darkness.

It sucked him in like a well of thick crude oil.

Chapter Thirteen

All the things that happened next were as real as could be. He lay in dark dirt. His body hurt all over and he thought his skin would split open. Then it did split open, but he felt much better and he saw himself emerge from the split skin like the white meat of a baked potato, but his white stuff was not fluffy; he was a very large maggot, bigger than a mountain.

Boy, he told himself, *no wonder it hurt, with all of that inside me.*

The maggot was alone. Peter did not know whether that was because he had eaten all the other maggots, or they had been scared away. Either way, he hoped they were not offended.

He crawled for a while over the earth and the jungle felt like sand beneath him, the trees were so small. His skin began to hurt again and he wondered if he would become a butterfly or a beetle, but when his neck split, neither butterfly nor beetle crawled from the giant, shriveled casing. Instead, Peter saw he was a very large cat covered with spots, a jaguar. This was okay. He knew he had a name at last—*Mado*—and his skin did not hurt.

Jaguar/Peter lay on the Earth for a long time, waiting for his wet slick fur to dry, but it rained incessantly and the Earth was covered with mud. This irritated *Mado* and in his anger he swelled and again his skin began to hurt. He opened his jaws as wide as he could and out between tongue and teeth crawled a huge boy, all strong and brown. But this boy could not talk, nor could he eat, because he had left his tongue and teeth inside the jaguar skin.

The huge boy was happy at first because his skin did not hurt. But soon he became hungry. Because he had no tongue he could not complain and there were no animals or plants large enough to be worth eating anyway, so he moaned and rolled in the mud. With his face so close to the Earth, he saw the ground was covered with tiny plants and animals. All of them were male.

Obviously nothing was going to happen on the Earth until all the plants and animals had wives. So he opened up the mud with his big toe and out came wives for the males: females of all shapes and sizes. Babies and seedlings began to appear.

Mado—Jaguar/Peter—waited for someone to come along who would be big enough to eat. But then he remembered he did not have teeth. He hoped for something soft, but most of the animals had bones and shells and he actually did not want to eat slugs.

In his fresh anger, Mado stamped through the mud and wore a deep path over all of the Earth except for the mountains. He looked down between his pounding feet and saw that he had made the tepuis, Roraima and Kahu Hidi and all the other sky-places, and that some animals had hidden on these mountains who still did not have wives.

For a while, Mado contemplated leaving these animals alone to suffer. Nothing he had done so far had relieved his hunger or made him happy. But he could not be a jaguar, even a hungry human boy-jaguar, without clawing, and his nails itched. There were no trees big enough to use as scratching posts. So he reached up and clawed the sky, opening great gashes in the clouds with his long jaguar-nails. From the gashes fell females, but they were all older types of female, like crocodiles and lizards. They landed on Kahu Hidi and on no other mountain, no other tepui.

The older lizard-females mated with the lonely males on Kahu Hidi, with dogs and wolves and jaguars, with bears and birds, and with frogs and salamanders; with possums and anteaters and armadillos, with howler monkeys, but not with humans, for there were no humans there.

A long time passed and Mado grew hungrier and hungrier. He shrank from starvation and walked among the strange old-looking animals of Kahu Hidi. He was not much bigger than a man, but much stronger. He saw that the lizard-wives had mated with eagles and produced feathered monsters, *Dinoshi,* handsome but very hungry. He stole the mouth from a *Dinoshi* but did not like the beak, so he left it in the forest. Then he stole the mouth from a dog-lizard but it was too small and he did not like the snout. Then he stole the mouth of a wolf-jaw. He was able to eat again, but he could not chew his food well enough for his human stomach, so he continued to shrink until he was the size of an ant—a large ant, an *iyako.*

He crawled around between the insects and saw they did not need wives. They had brought their own females to Kahu Hidi. Insects always know what to do. They fed him sweet nectar and honey to honor him for making all the big animals that could die and then be eaten, or whose bodies could harbor eggs that became maggots. He ate a maggot given to him by the ants, and suddenly he was a maggot again, as big as the world—

It was this maggot that heard the tones of Odosha, calling from deep in the ground, below all living things. Odosha said, "You will come see me soon, but not today."

Peter heard Billie's voice. "Come back from there," Billie said. "You should walk for yourself. We have carried you a long way."

"I don't have any legs," Peter said.

"It's good to be a maggot, but you need legs to walk."

Peter thought about that. He was a boy again but not a jaguar-boy. "Did you find your father?"

"Yes. His door was death and I was too afraid to go there."

"He might be around here someplace. Should I look for him?"

"No, he came and went long before you. Just wake up and remember you have legs. Your father needs you. Mine is past needing me."

Peter opened his eyes. He was in a forest and sun came down in small, star-like speckles through the canopy. His skin and muscles hurt and so did his bones, but he remembered he had arms and legs and he moved them.

"I chewed some leaves and made paste and spit it on your bites," Billie said, "and then brought you blue water from the lake. You will get better quickly now, but your father is still ill."

"Are we near a lake?"

"Yes, Lake Akuena."

He saw Billie's face in the forest gloom, eyes dark as night. The Indian's hair was all awry and he had scratches on his forehead and cheeks. Ray came into his view next and his face, too, was dark and scratched. He looked very tired.

"Good to have you back, Peter," Ray said. "You've been out for two days."

"Where's my father?"

OBie and Wetherford hovered above him. He looked down and saw they were standing. That seemed convincing enough; they weren't ghosts. Ray and Billie were kneeling beside him.

"He's still sick, Peter," OBie said.

"We've had quite a time carrying you both," Wetherford said. "Glad you'll be on your feet soon."

Billie felt Peter's forehead. "Did you become a jaguar?" he asked.

Peter turned his head, looking for his father, but it was too gloomy to see much. His eyes hurt. "Is he going to be all right?" he asked.

"I think he will be all right," Billie said. "He was only bitten once and you were bitten twice, but he got sicker. Did you dream of being a jaguar?"

"I think so," Peter said.

"Good," Billie said. "I will stay close to you. Kahu Hidi doesn't like jaguars. It refuses to swallow them. I think we will be spit up soon."

Chapter Fourteen

In a couple of hours, as afternoon became evening and the forest got even darker, Peter was well enough to crawl over to where his father lay. Anthony sprawled on the ground on a sling woven of grass. His normally swarthy face was pale and sweaty. Shellabarger and OBie had woven dry reeds into slings on the grassland to carry Anthony and Peter. All of their friends had carried them to Lake Akuena, not knowing whether they would live or die. Billie had met them at the edge of the forest around the lake. He had already been to the lake.

Peter wiped his father's face with his fingers. Anthony stirred but did not make a sound. His breath came rough and irregular. Peter wondered why he had been bitten by two ants and was already getting better, but his father had been bitten by only one and was still sick. Billie did not know the answer. He had applied leaf paste to both of them.

Billie seemed discouraged. Peter was too tired to ask many questions. They had fish to eat, caught in the lake. OBie built a fire and the smoke drifted up into the dark canopy. Wetherford and Shellabarger had brought matches to light the sticks of dynamite and make fires. They had two sticks of dynamite left and a whole box of matches. The fire was made of damp wood kindled with dry leaves and was very smoky.

Peter felt differently about everything. In the dark, Billie lay beside him. Peter stared up at a single star visible through the dense canopy. A leaf made it wink at him. He felt well enough to talk a little now.

"Why did you come back to us?" he asked Billie.

"I learned what I needed to learn," Billie said. "I ate part of Odosha's foot. It made me sick. Odosha came and told me that he had killed my friends and I was selfish and foolish to come to Kahu Hidi and try to become a warrior. The time was past. I knew he lied, but he also told me I would be a great leader when I got back. I knew that was a lie, too. But it was a good lie."

Billie looked off into the night.

"I'm sorry," Peter said.

"I knew you would get in trouble," Billie continued. "I was having a tough time staying alive, and I know a lot of things. I thought you would probably all die without me."

Peter thought about that and lay quiet for a while, feeling the food in his stomach. The white, flaky flesh of the lake fish had tasted very good.

"What happened to your father?" Peter asked.

Billie did not answer for a time. "Something ate him, or he died and then something ate him. I found his bones and a string of beads he carried, but not his head."

"I'm sorry," Peter said.

"He would have come back and been a leader, but I think Odosha sent some animals to eat him."

"Yeah," Peter said. "We almost got eaten."

"Odosha doesn't want you. You are like a jaguar."

"I dreamed a lot, too."

"Yes." Billie sounded resentful. "I didn't think of letting *iyako* bite me."

"I heard that word in my dream," Peter said. "*Iyako.*"

"Maybe I told you the word before," Billie said.

"I don't remember. Can you tell me what the dream meant?"

"I don't think I can," Billie said. "Except for the part about becoming a jaguar."

"It felt like an Indian dream," Peter said.

"You are not an Indian."

"Are you angry?"

"Yes," said Billie, and rolled over to go to sleep.

In the morning, OBie and Ray told Peter that Anthony's fever had broken and he was whispering words. Peter sat by his father and held his hand, wiping sweat from his forehead.

Ray hunkered down beside them and Billie stood a few yards away. "Will you tell me if he has dreams?" Billie asked.

"I'll ask," Peter said.

"I didn't think about *iyako*," Billie repeated.

Anthony opened his eyes. "My lad," he murmured, and smiled at Peter. "I hear Billie. Does that mean we're all dead?"

"He's alive. We're alive," Peter said.

"Where are we?"

"South-central lake," Ray said. "Lake Akuena."

"That's the lake in the middle of *Kahuna*," Wetherford said. Then, with a touch of sarcasm, "We might as well be in heaven." He brought a cup of water and a piece of fish for Anthony. "Billie saved both of you."

"Tell him thank you," Anthony said. Billie had wandered away.

"It was stupid of me to walk into an ant nest," Peter said.

OBie

"Didn't know," Anthony said.

"We heard the plane again this morning at dawn," OBie said. "We built a fire by the lake. We're hoping they'll land and send a raft for us. I'm sure it's Monte and Coop."

Shellabarger walked over and knelt beside Anthony, feeling his pulse. "You're going to be fine," he said. "We'll keep those ant bites bandaged until a doctor can see to them."

"A doctor," Anthony said, chuckling. "Everybody's so optimistic."

"Well, I've been thinking," Wetherford said. "A PBY is damned expensive and rare around here, just as Mr. O'Brien says. And I saw it again this morning. Maybe your producers do have consciences."

"If a cynic like you believes it," Anthony said, "then I should believe it, too."

Wetherford smiled ruefully. "It's a fair cop. But there's nothing less reliable than a converted cynic." He watched Anthony and Peter for a moment, a deep sadness in his eyes. "Is it the right time for a little confession?"

Shellabarger regarded him sourly. "You a Catholic?"

"No, it's not a faith matter, but I've been converted, nonetheless," Wetherford said. "Anybody care to hear why?"

"Sure," OBie said. "I've always been a little curious about you, Mr. Wetherford."

"Well you might be. I'm in the employ of two masters—your Monte and Coop, through their intermediary in Caracas . . . and Creole Oil, through the same intermediary."

Shellabarger adjusted his bandage, and then, as if he hadn't heard Wetherford clearly, said, "What?"

"Creole Oil. You fellows have upset quite a few apple carts down here. Bringing these animals back, getting the Indians riled, causing the Army trouble. The Lords of Black Crude in Caracas, they like nice political balances, and they hate upsets. So . . . they told me to keep watch on you."

"Did they tell you to stop us?" OBie asked, lips tight.

"Yes, in fact, they did—if it seemed things were getting out of hand. And things did get out of hand, didn't they?"

"Yeah," Shellabarger said. "But I've suspected something from the beginning. I watched you, and you didn't do anything. No sabotage. Why didn't you try to stop us?"

"On the train, and when you were loading the animals on the boats . . . I started thinking. I told myself, 'James, you're a miserable little squint. All your life you've danced to the tune of money, but you're poor as a church-mouse. All your little schemes and double deals, what have they got you?'" He snapped his fingers. "That much. Just that much and not a penny more."

"We gave you religion, then," OBie said quietly.

"Not religion, Mr. O'Brien. Adventure. Before, when I thought I was having an adventure, it was just running from creditors or stumbling on the stairs, too drunk to see straight. But you and the animals—how could I miss such a chance? You've given me the only opportunity to have a real adventure, to accompany some fine and decent fellows and do something wonderful and foolish and brave."

He turned to Anthony. "You're a brave man, Mr. Belzoni, and not because you come here and face danger. You're brave to take someone as valuable to you as your son, and give him this adventure. If my father, the old fist-flinging and ever-drunken sodding bastard, had ever done such a thing for me, I might be a decent man this very day."

They sat in silence for a bit, with only the crackling of the fire and the soughing of the wind through the trees.

"Well, pardon me my sentiments," Wetherford said.

Shellabarger shook his head and with his finger made a weary cross in the air before Wetherford. "You're absolved," he said.

"Thank you, Father," Wetherford said, and grinned.

Chapter Fifteen

There was no sign of the plane that day. Peter was well enough to walk about and even to go to the lake with Ray and Shellabarger while his father slept peacefully.

Lake Akuena was ten miles long and six miles across. No one had ever measured how deep it was in the middle, but Professor Challenger had found it was full of fish and carried a fine population of fish-eating monsters—crocodiles, mesotherm reptiles, and aquatic therapsids.

"We haven't seen any big beasts in the water yet," Ray said as they stared across the misty surface. "But I can feel them out there."

Shellabarger seemed pensive. "I took a walk a little west of here yesterday," he said.

"What did you see?" Peter asked.

Shellabarger lifted his rifle. "Something pretty sad. Doesn't look like Dagger would have had much to come back to. Feel up for a little hike?"

"Yeah," Peter said, though his legs were still shaky and the bites on his hand and ankle were still swollen and painful. "My father's probably going to be asleep for a couple of hours."

"It's not far," the trainer said. He led them out of the forest toward a green bank that sloped into the lake. Mist covered most of the lake today, and clouds blew rapidly overhead. Several small islands thrust up a few hundred yards offshore, all capped with scrubby growth. Vines hung into the blue water on all sides, giving the islands the appearance of hairy men submerged up to their necks.

"Nobody's going to land a plane until the fog is clear," Shellabarger said. "Who knows when that will be?" The land west of the slope was lightly forested and the shore was mostly open, pebbly and grassy inclines where the waters lapped with soft slurping sounds. Promontories of rock jutted into the lake.

Ray seemed more concerned with what the trainer was going to show them. "We've got fish, we have Billie to show us the ropes," he said. "If Anthony responds as well as Peter here, we could all survive for a couple of weeks."

He clapped Peter on the shoulder. Peter concentrated on walking. His muscles hurt abominably and he was starting to sweat and they had only gone a few hundred yards. "Funny what just a little bit of poison can do to you," he said, though it didn't feel funny at all. The dream haunted him. Some of the visions had seemed to come from outside—images and words and ideas he could not remember having encountered before. If Billie was right, El Grande itself—Kahu Hidi—had spoken to him, and he wasn't ready to accept that. "Billie deserved it, not me," he murmured.

"What, getting ant-bit?" Shellabarger asked, scowling dubiously.

"No," Peter said. "Not what I meant." He looked sheepishly between Ray and the trainer. "How much farther?"

"Not far," Shellabarger said.

The lakeshore flattened out. Low brush crept up to the margin of the lake's deep blue water; behind the brush, tumbled boulders and sandy patches vied with copses of tall, shaft-like trees to define a field of about a hundred acres.

They heard growls and querying chirps, followed by low bass rumbles. Shellabarger stopped and held up his hand.

"Scavengers," he said. "Let's go slow."

They climbed a low bluff overlooking the field and the edge of the lake. Ray reached out to Peter and gave him a hand to the top.

In the southeastern corner of the field, half hidden by clumps of ferns and two trees, sprawled the body of a large animal—a dinosaur, Peter saw. It had been thoroughly chewed over. Five animals like nightmare seals were still hard at work—brown and gray, long-jawed, with bulky cylindrical bodies and heavy flippers. Their stomachs and hindquarters were still wet and shiny. They jerked at the thorax and hip of the big animal, tearing off sections of scaly hide and stringy brownish flesh.

The air smelled of death. Ray covered his nose and mouth. The wind blew the smell right past them and it was fierce. Clouds of flies buzzed over the carcass and its five tormentors.

"They look like pliosaurs," Ray said.

"They do indeed," Shellabarger said. "But they're probably some of Professor Challenger's lake-devils, aquatic therapsids more closely related to the wolf-jaws and dog-lizards. They've lucked upon a large free meal. I doubt that they crawl this far inland very often. They're clumsier than seals out of water."

Two of the lake-devils tugged mightily on a forelimb and jerked the beast's head halfway off the ground. Peter sucked in his breath. The dead animal was a venator—very much like Dagger.

Ray swallowed and rubbed his jaw. "What killed it—disease?"

"No," Shellabarger said. "Something stronger and swifter. I took a look at the carcass yesterday before these scavengers moved in. Just some small avisaurs and birds pecking on it then. Shooed them away with a branch. It's a male. Judging from the wounds on the head and shoulders, and claw marks along the ribs and legs, he got into a fight with a death eagle and lost." Shellabarger reached into his pocket and pulled out a long, brown-stained yellow tooth, freshly broken at the base. "The death eagle took a few minor losses." He passed the tooth to Peter, who inspected its bloody length and handed it to Ray.

"There may not be more than two or three venators left on the plateau," Shellabarger said. "This one may have been the last—though judging from the tracks along the beach, I suspect his mate is nearby."

He took them down to the sandy lakefront and showed them sets of tracks—the three-toed marks of the venator and the bigger

marks of the death eagle stalking him, three front tarsals digging deep enough in the sand to show the dew claw marks in the rear. He gestured west and said, "A second set of venator tracks joins the first about a hundred yards west. The death eagle stops and waits here—it doesn't want to tangle with two venators. The male venator comes back—he smells the death eagle and instinct tells him to protect the nest. The death eagle weighs in. Judging from the blood around the battle scene, it took a few injuries besides losing a tooth. It hates the venators with a real passion."

"Out with the old," Ray said softly, lifting the tooth.

"Extinction's an old story," Shellabarger said. "It's not always our fault. Humans only caught a few venators, and didn't ever go for a death eagle, except for crazy Lowell Thomas—and he died trying. The death eagles are larger, faster, more efficient—and meaner." He glanced at Ray and Peter. "We were lucky."

The trainer got a distant look in his eye. "Dagger shouldn't have been put up for show. He should have stayed here with the last of his kind. It wasn't his fault. It was my fault. I deserve everything he wanted to do to me."

He drew up his shoulders and hitched his pants, then tightened his belt. "This one will be bones by tomorrow. Anybody want to look for the nest?"

"The venator's nest?" Ray asked.

"Yeah," Shellabarger said.

"Why?"

"Pay our respects, I suppose," Shellabarger said.

Neither Peter nor Ray answered. Peter had had just about enough adventure. He wanted to go back to the camp in the forest and lie down beside his father and sleep.

"Peter's pooped," Ray said awkwardly, not at all enthusiastic about getting close to another large carnivore.

"Yeah," Shellabarger said. "Maybe tomorrow."

When they returned, Anthony was sitting up and eating. Wetherford and OBie had broiled more fish for supper. Billie had headed northeast to find better fishing and had collected several bundles of yuca, which OBie was baking whole in the embers of the first fire.

Peter sat beside his father. "How are you feeling?" he asked.

"Weak as a kitten. And you?"

"Okay," Peter said. He grinned at his father and Anthony shook his head.

"Ants," he said wryly.

"Ants," Peter responded. He had been thinking the same thing: *It wasn't the big beasts that got us.*

They lay down beside each other and closed their eyes. It was time for a nap, even though it was barely past noon. Anthony slung his arm across his son's ribs and drew him close.

"I'm glad we're both here," he murmured. "Alive, I mean."

Chapter Sixteen

They slept through that day and into the next morning. The smell of more fish cooking woke Peter. He sat up and examined his wrist and ankle. The swelling had gone down considerably. He checked his father's bite and found it much improved. Anthony cracked open one eye and groaned. "I'm stiff all over," he said, sitting up on one elbow. "What time is it?"

"It's morning," Ray said, bringing them a tin cup from Wetherford's pack. It contained a hot, savory liquid. "Billie found a tasty herb. Says it will do us good. Pep us up."

Peter took a sip from the cup. He made a face at the bitterness. Anthony drank as well, but wondered out loud what else Billie's herbs might do. "They eat and drink a lot of things down here that I'd be careful with."

As they were eating, Wetherford and OBie came back from the lake. OBie had made a long stick into a fishing pole and hammered a safety pin from the first-aid kit into a passable hook. "Used some of those big crickets for bait," he said, and proudly lifted a creel of three fat fish. "Don't know what they are, but they taste good."

"Vince is out in the bush again," Ray said. "With Billie this time. Billie says he wants to see the Challenger."

"All I want to see is that flying boat," OBie said. "We've been through hell and not a single foot of film to show for it."

Anthony lifted his battered Leica and shook it. It rattled inside. The lens was cracked and the case had sprung, ruining a roll of film, but he had kept it with him through everything.

"It's almost pleasant here," Wetherford said. "Like a scouting trip. I trust the ant bites are improving?"

Anthony showed them his hand. "Peter seems fit."

"I'm much better," Peter said. "Ray—"

He stopped. They all heard the drone of airplane engines at the same time.

"Twin engine," Anthony said. "Big plane. Where is it flying from?"

"From the coast, or maybe Uruyen," Wetherford said. "More likely, it's taking off from a stretch of the Paragua or Orinoco—refueling at Puerto Ordaz."

Anthony agreed. "PBY has a long cruising range." They walked to the edge of the forest and kept their eyes on the overcast skies. Breaks in the clouds showed pale blue.

"I'd be happier if Vince didn't keep wandering off," OBie said. "We should stick together. Hate to get on board the plane and then be trapped for a week because of weather!"

Anthony stood. "I'd like to see the lake," he said.

"Let's all go," OBie said. "Not much reason to come back here."

"There it is!" Wetherford pointed east. The PBY dropped in low and slow, barely a hundred feet above the forest. The smoke from the remaining fire formed a slanted column in the wind, clear enough to be seen for miles beneath the broken cloud deck, and the pilot of the PBY saw it. The wings waggled as the plane flew over them, and Peter grinned like a fool as the roar of the engines and the wash of the props hit them. There were stars on the fuselage and under the wings; it was from the United States. The trees jostled and the slant of smoke from their fire twisted into vortices. Anthony clutched his son's arm and they danced. Anthony almost fell over and nearly took Peter with him.

"Using our smoke for a windsock!" OBie exulted. "I know who they are! I know who they are!"

Wetherford patted his pocket for nonexistent cigarettes. "Shall I fetch Vince and Billie?"

"No—we all stick together. They'll come back when they hear the plane."

They hurried through the scrub toward the lake. Peter helped his father and Ray helped OBie.

"Ain't we a sorry sight!" OBie said, grinning.

The PBY banked and turned north, then made a half circle and came into the wind. They reached the shore of the lake. Peter looked west to see if he could spot Billie and Shellabarger. They were still out of sight.

The wing pontoons unfolded and the plane skimmed the waters as delicately as a goose, then dropped its hull into the lake. For a moment, it vanished behind an island, just as spray rooster-tailed behind it, then emerged into view, wings heeled over slightly as it turned toward the smoke and the shore. They waved wildly. The PBY was about a mile away. Peter saw a man poke through a hatch in the right fuselage blister and wave back, but couldn't see who it was.

They squatted by the shore and waited as the plane approached as near as it dared—about thirty yards from the shore. Peter could hardly take his eyes off the big gray airplane, its wide thick wing mounted high over the fuselage on a graceful central support.

The PBY cut its engines and dropped an anchor. The man who had poked his head up was now clearly recognizable. "OBie!" he shouted.

"Monte, you bastard!" OBie yelled back. "What took you so damned long!"

Ernest Schoedsack waved wildly and grinned. "Everybody in good spirits? Did you get the film?"

"Lost it all! Ray threw the camera at a dinosaur!"

"Well, Ray, damn it all to hell," Schoedsack chastised.

"I'll go back and find it," Ray said.

"No such thing!" Schoedsack yelled.

Another head poked through the hatch in the Plexiglas. "At this rate, we'll never get that monkey picture made!" Merian Cooper called. "There's going to be hell to pay! You'd better climb aboard and let's vamoose!"

"It's the Army and Betancourt," Schoedsack said. "They're fighting again, madder'n hornets and not much smarter."

"You expect us to swim?" OBie yelled, hopping along with one arm on Ray's shoulder.

"Break out that raft!" Cooper ordered. A limp yellow life raft poked through the side door and two men in fatigues quickly inflated it with a compressed gas canister.

"Is this everybody?" Schoedsack asked.

"Vince Shellabarger and an Indian named Billie aren't with us yet," Peter said.

Wetherford swore under his breath. "I'll go get them."

"Stay here!" OBie insisted. "They can't miss seeing the plane. Vince can take care of himself, especially with Billie along."

The flying boat bobbed lazily in the rippling blue water. Peter was sure now that he had never seen anything so beautiful in his life.

The raft rounded out nicely and finally popped into shape. The two men in fatigues broke out oars and climbed in. They were about to push away when Cooper leaned through the door. "Hey, let me go with you! I want to set foot on the plateau one more time."

"All right," one of the men said, and shrugged. "It's a nine man raft." Cooper raised his leg, holding on to the upper rim of the hatch, and crawled out. They handed him a paddle.

The three had rowed ten yards from the flying boat when a chorus of roars and shrieks came over the western promontory. A rifle shot cracked, making Anthony jerk and drop. Peter's reactions were well-honed now, too, and he dropped beside his father without a thought.

Wetherford ducked as well, hitting the ground on all fours and lying flat. Anthony looked at him from the same level. Wetherford seemed immensely pleased with himself.

"I'm not a bit afraid!" he said brightly to Anthony. "I'm a brave man after all!"

"Good for you," Anthony said.

"What in hell has Vince got himself into now?" OBie asked, hopping on his good leg. He picked up his fishing stick and used it as a cane. Ray had run to the top of the promontory, and Peter followed not far behind.

They looked across the low, lightly forested southern shore of

Lake Akuena. Clouds of morpho butterflies scattered from the bushes and trees like blue smoke. Anthony and Wetherford joined them but OBie stayed behind, waiting for the raft to come ashore. Peter did not catch what Cooper and OBie were saying to each other; he was intent on the trees and scrub, and on two objects bobbing beyond a copse of slender light green trees just south of the shore. One object was white: Peter recognized the spray of a death eagle's neck feathers. The other was dark: a venator's head!

"What do we do, lads?" Wetherford asked. He looked at Anthony, Ray, and Peter.

"They need help," Peter said.

"Righto," Wetherford said. "Here's my chance, at least."

Wetherford ran ahead of them, then thought better of so much extra valor and slowed a bit. Ray caught up with him.

"Are you up to this, Father?" Peter whispered to Anthony as they tried to keep up with the pair.

Anthony snorted. "Are you?" he said, his face flushed with exertion and something else—pride, determination, and sheer curiosity—but also a flashing emptiness that took Peter by surprise, and both saddened him and made him proud.

That look summed up Anthony perfectly and his son felt an inner twinge. Peter was concerned about Vince and Billie, but if they hadn't been out there somewhere, possibly in danger, he would have preferred to wait for the raft.

Anthony would have gone anyway.

They climbed down from the promontory and followed the shore for a hundred yards, until they saw the trainer's boot prints and Billie's sandal prints leave the sandy margin and point into the grass.

Peter stayed close to his father, realizing—convinced—for the first time in his life that to be different from Anthony was not to be inferior. He was as brave as his father; he was as willing to risk his neck to help friends.

But Peter had a stronger sense than his father of who he was and where he belonged; he was not a feather that would blow with the breeze directly into any fire.

They helped each other over a thick grassy hummock. The copse lay ahead. They heard another rifle shot, an aquiline shriek, the

t·Diterliz·

avalanche-like pounding of heavy feet. The trees swayed as half seen monsters pushed against them from the other side.

The men picked their steps with care now, skirting the tall slender trees. They were thirty yards from the animals and not even Anthony was going to rush into this scene willy-nilly.

"Do you see them?" Ray asked Peter.

"No," Peter said, and then he caught sight of Billie's head of smooth black hair. The Indian was running out of the path of a huge venator. This was the female, Peter reasoned—taller and bulkier than a male, a close match in sheer muscle power and lethal weapons for the death eagle, which was still half hidden behind the trees.

The female was paying no attention to Billie. Neither animal seemed concerned with the humans, even as another shot was fired. Billie had no rifle.

"That's Shellabarger," Anthony said. "But where is he?"

Billie ran toward them, short powerful legs fairly flying him over the grass and ferns. The death eagle raced from behind the tall trees toward him and Billie dove into a thick patch of ferns. The huge avisaur turned at the last moment, lifted its gorget and gaping beak, and spread its forearms like outstretched wings.

The venator leaped forward, making the ground tremble, and snapped at the death eagle's side, scraping its hide with her teeth and snatching a mouthful of feathers, but gaining little real satisfaction. The venator shook her head, sending feathers flying. The animals circled, heads level with their outstretched tails, the venator's long tail lean and stiff, moving only a little side to side, the death eagle's broad tail half as long and dressed with a fan of thick black and green feathers. The death eagle jerked its tail up, then dropped it, and the feathers made a sound like scrub brushes as they spread wide.

Billie crawled from the ferns, leaped to his feet, and ran.

Anthony and Ray saw Shellabarger simultaneously. Anthony pointed him out for Peter. The trainer lay on top of a broad, low pile of rocks southwest of the trees, about fifty yards from them. He had assumed a sharpshooter's position with his rifle pointing at the animals.

"What in hell is he doing?" Ray asked. Billie reached them and dropped to his knees. "They are trying to kill each other!" he gasped. "Two Challengers—very bad!"

"What happened?" Anthony asked.

The animals paid as much attention to the humans as two sparring bulls might have to toy poodles.

"Shellabarger, he went to the venator's nest," Billie said. "He does not tell me why. The female is not there, but the eggs are buried—under straw and shit!"

"To keep them warm," Ray said.

"He wants to take an egg. He says the venator will be dead soon, with no mate, but the eggs can be saved."

"By whom?" Wetherford asked, dumfounded. "Who wants one?"

"Then we hear the female coming back, and behind her, from behind the trees, he has been hiding, we see *Dinoshi!*"

Anthony started forward, but Ray and Wetherford grabbed his arms.

"Hold on," Wetherford said. "We need a plan."

"I'm going to help Vince!"

"Help him do what?" Wetherford asked.

"Get away."

Wetherford narrowed his eyes and lifted his mouth into a dubious half sneer. "He's where he wants to be, for some reason. He could have followed Billie if he wanted to."

"He's trying to help the venator," Peter said.

Wetherford's scowl deepened as he swiveled to face Peter. "Why, for Christ's sake?"

Peter knew, but clear expression in words did not seem possible. "Because of Dagger," he said. "Because we screwed up getting Dagger here . . . to his home."

Wetherford seemed ready to spit. "Vince Shellabarger, the grand old man of dinosaur exploitation, who's pulled more bloody beasts off this plateau than anybody, you mean Shellabarger takes all this show-business-return-the-dinosaurs, save-the-plateau crap seriously?"

"I'd say he does," Ray said.

Wetherford laughed. "He's trying to shoot a *death eagle!*" he hooted in disbelief.

"Distracting it, is my guess," Anthony said. "And I'd keep my voice down, if I were you, just in case the animals decide it's a draw and break for a snack."

Anthony grabbed Peter by the shoulder. "Whatever Vince wants to do, he's crazy not to leave now and come with us. We may have to pull him out of there—or help him."

Wetherford stamped his foot. "Bloody hell!"

Peter saw someone walking toward them from the corner of his eye and turned. Merian Cooper carted a camera on a wooden tripod up to where they stood, planted it, put his eye to the viewfinder, and said, "Ray, you know this place better than me. Tell me when I should pack up and get the hell out of here." The camera began to whir.

Ray steadied the tripod.

"We *all* should get the hell out of here," Wetherford said. Peter agreed but saw his father's point. If the trainer wanted to die here, that was his concern—but if he wanted to do something as crazy as save a venator's egg, save a desperate species from extinction—even something as dangerous, as terrifying, as ancient and gory-breathed as *Altovenator ferox*—that was different.

Peter felt dizzied by this reversal of emotion, a sudden irrational resolve. He was not like his father, but—

This was something that had to be done.

"Is that the venator's nest?" Anthony asked Billie.

"Where Shellabarger is? Yes. It is filled with straw and shit and bones."

Anthony disregarded that. "Did you go in there with him?"

"Not all the way," Billie said.

"Are there eggs in there?"

"I did not see."

"Young?"

"I did not see."

The beasts lunged at each other. The venator female took the death eagle by its right forelimb and jerked her head sideways, ripping the limb off at the shoulder. Peter expected the death eagle to lift its head and scream with rage and pain, as it might have done in a movie, but it silently sank its beak into the venator's shoulder and shook furiously, slicing loose a chunk of flesh and bone the size of a human torso. It did not swallow this, but tossed it high in the air. The piece of venator shoulder landed barely ten feet from them. This was finally enough for Wetherford. He turned and passed OBie as he came up from the beach.

"There's a rain squall moving in," OBie called. He carried a heavy hunting rifle—an elephant gun, by its looks. "Pilot wants us in the plane now!"

Cooper grunted and kept on filming. OBie grimly sized up the situation. "Boys, we're all going to end up guano if we don't leave now."

"Here's the plan," Anthony said.

Peter and Ray hunched over like football players to listen.

"Run to the nest. Ray and I grab Vince and haul him out of there. Peter, you find an egg—two if they're not too large—and don't take more than a few seconds in the nest!"

OBie lifted the rifle. "I'll try to cover you."

"Peter," Anthony said as they prepared to make the dash to the nest. "You are my son and I am proud of you and I love you with all my heart."

"Dad, we're crazy as loons. I love you, too."

"My lad!" Anthony said. He lifted his finger to his lips and smiled. "Don't tell your mom."

Anthony jumped through a brake of ferns and Ray and Peter followed. Despite his father's weakness of an hour before, they had a hard time keeping up with him. He dashed back and forth as if dodging bullets.

He's back on Sicily, Peter realized. The lumbering shapes to the east seemed right on top of them, but they were still thirty or forty yards away.

They jumped over humps of grass and bush and ferns, skirted low tree saplings bent by the wind, and ran up the mound onto the edge of the pile of rocks and sticks. The trainer lay beside a green and brown mound of debris that smelled fearsomely bad.

Shellabarger rolled over on his back and glared at them. His right pants leg showed a fresh bloody stain just above the knee.

"I've broken my leg in these rocks," he said. "Bone's punched through."

"Lift him," Anthony said. He and Ray stepped over the boulders carefully and bent to grab the trainer's arms.

"Peter, there are eggs in the middle of the shit," Shellabarger said. "Under the leaves and sticks and——"

"He knows," Ray grunted.

They brought Shellabarger up sharply. His broken leg dangled and he gritted his teeth, stifling a scream. Peter picked his way over the clumps of dried whitened feces and bones—a femur half as tall as he was, a rack of two-inch-thick ribs still coated with hide and bumpy diamond-shaped armor plates—and dug his hands deep into the gray-crusted mound in the center. The black and slippery dung beneath had been piled at least three feet high.

He reached in up to his elbow, feeling the steaming warmth of fermentation. His stomach began to do flips. His fingers caught something sharp and he grimaced, pushed sideways. They jammed against something hard. He fumbled around the shape quickly—rounded, about ten inches long. Nose held high, he dug furiously and pulled a brown ovoid out of the hot muck. In the hole, he saw another, somewhat smaller egg, and reached for that as well.

"PETER!" Anthony shouted.

He pulled out the second egg, looked up, and his foot skidded. Peter fell up to his shoulders in the mess. Shit spattered one side of his face and got into his mouth, but that did not concern him.

The venator had seen her nest being disturbed. The death eagle had moved a dozen yards away from her to reassess the battle, and she took the opportunity to aim directly for the nest—and for Peter. She lowered her head and ran over the rocks and scrub with a weakened, hobbling gait—at less than the speed of a well-bred horse trotting. Her shoulder was a broad patch of red; she was bleeding to death, but she would not allow herself to die before defending her nest.

The venator seemed taller than any tree, bigger than a PBY, all teeth and dripping blood and black, looming shadow. Peter froze. Rain hit his face like small wet hammers.

He stood up with painful slowness and saw that he had pulled both of the brown spotted eggs up to his chest. He clutched them in his arms. Together they weighed about thirty pounds. They steamed in the cold rain.

Irrationally, he thought, *They will die if we don't keep them warm.*

Eggs held firmly, he jumped from rock to rock and down the side of the nest. The air seemed to sizzle with rain and a trilling roar vibrated his chest.

He saw Cooper with the camera, OBie and Billie standing behind, then he glanced to the left and saw his father and Ray carrying Shellabarger. Peter streaked over the ground, faster than he had ever run in his life, and was within twenty feet of the three when a branch tripped him and he sprawled.

His forehead whacked the dirt hard and he almost blacked out. The eggs flew and landed in a thick stand of grass. The world spun; he caught a blurred glimpse of Shellabarger tossing Ray and Anthony like a circus strongman throwing off shill wrestlers. The trainer bounced on one leg and raised his hands to the sky—

A three-toed foot trampled a bush and dug into the dirt not five feet from where Peter lay. The air smelled of stale parrot and butcher shop.

Peter rolled. The female venator's snout and rows of long yellow teeth plunged through the sheets of rain like a speeding truck and her jaws opened to show a horny black tongue and a throat like a purple tunnel.

A rifle butt cracked her in the side of the head and broke in two. Shellabarger stood over Peter on one leg; how he had come this far, Peter did not know. The venator jerked to one side and diverted her downward swoop just enough to wrap her teeth around the trainer's arm and ribs. She lifted him like a high-speed elevator. Shellabarger grabbed her head with his arms and she bit down with the fresh wood snap of splintering bones.

Peter saw Shellabarger's face as he was lifted, saw the trainer's eyes fixed on his own, his lips set tight and turned down at the

sides, and then Vince Shellabarger's jaw hung loose as if he were already dead but passing on a final message—something words would never convey.

Peter pushed himself up, grabbed one egg and then the other in the stumbling start of his dash, and sensed rather than saw the venator toss the trainer's lifeless body in the air.

She drew back to grab for Peter. A white-rimmed darkness rose behind her and filled with two gleaming green eyes and a bloody beak—

And the death eagle dropped on her like a truckload of knives. Its wide white-gorgeted griffin's head thrust again and again, beak stripping skin into ribbons, shredding tendons, and exposing pale fat and pink muscle and snow-white bone. The venator's other arm spasmed and drooped.

Peter saw these things as if in a dream, many views at once—the ground beneath him, the animals to one side, his father and Ray up ahead, on their knees, with Cooper still behind the camera and OBie firing the rifle furiously, *crack-crack-crack.*

The venator was weakening. Truly the time of her kind had come; *Dinoshi* could outlast even the largest and swiftest carnosaur. The death eagle drew back, neck arched, lower jaw withdrawn into the wattles above its breast, and rose to its full height. It lifted the spread yellow talons of one foot and raked the back of the venator's leg, hamstringing her. She gave an agonized squeal and toppled to her side with a thump that nearly knocked Peter off his feet.

The eggs felt like a ton of rocks as he reached his father and Ray. Peter twisted around and stood beside Merian Cooper's whirring camera. Rain drummed on them all and formed a thick scrim over the gray silhouette of the death eagle, talons swiping again and again at the prostrate venator as if carving a turkey, cutting away ribs and thigh, ripping open her abdomen and spilling intestines in twisted sausage jumbles. The female gaped up at her murderer, alive but unable to move or fight.

Peter could not look. Cooper gave a whoop and continued to shoot film. Ray snatched one leg of the tripod. "Time to go!" he shouted.

Anthony grabbed Peter's shoulder and they ran through the rain for the lake.

Chapter Seventeen

---◆---

Peter clutched the eggs so tightly he feared they would break. They all ran like silent-movie comedians: legs pumping high, hair soaked into skullcaps, rain splashing from their faces and water streaming from elbows, noses, and chins.

He saw the yellow raft through the downpour. Anchored in the lake beyond, the PBY floated like some serene giant seabird. The wind had come up and whitecaps laced the beach with froth. The two men in fatigues stood by the raft, soaked and miserable, but when they saw the runners they waved their arms wildly.

And then they crouched, jaws dropping, staring over the heads of the fleeing men. Anthony darted a look backward and suddenly shoved Peter to one side. A great toothed beak and gleaming green eye swept past with hardly a sound but for a thunderclap *snap*. Peter rolled and came to rest face up, still clutching the eggs. The brush of *Dinoshi*'s gorget had left a vivid scrape on his cheek and temple.

The death eagle reared over them, blood streaming from its breast and head, rain washing bloody rivulets down its feathers. It straightened and lifted its beak to the sky, *skreeing* triumphantly despite its pain, totally assured of dominance and power.

Ray threw the camera into the raft and grabbed a thick straight tree limb from the shore. Anthony, on the other side of the death eagle, did likewise. OBie limped along, winded, barely able to make the last few steps. Cooper grabbed him and dragged him by his shoulders over the pebbles and sand.

From out of nowhere, Billie appeared with a machete. He darted in behind the huge avisaur and slapped its leg with the flat of the blade, ducking immediately. One foot kicked back, its talons missing Billie's head by inches, and the beast turned, spraying dirt. The black tail feathers brushed Anthony's hair.

Ray poked the death eagle from one side with his branch and Anthony poked it from the other.

The avisaur did not know which audacious little creature to strike first. It took a step forward, toward Billie; the Indian was back on his feet and his face betrayed no fear. The death eagle leveled, and Ray and Anthony poked it again simultaneously.

Peter stood up less than two yards from *Dinoshi's* stamping, plunging feet.

The avisaur thrust first at Ray, who whacked it sharply on the side of its beak with his stick. It reared back, growling with indignation, and turned on Anthony. Billie chose this moment to expertly throw a rock into its open jaws. The animal hesitated, raised and flexed its neck, gulped the rock down, and faced Peter's father.

Billie threw another rock and hit it squarely in its left eye.

The death eagle seemed to explode. From Peter's perspective, it became all talons and massive pumping legs and swinging tail. The tail caught Ray across his chest and sent him sprawling. Anthony threw his branch at the beast, but it was paying none of them any attention for the moment.

"Go!" Anthony shouted to Peter. The raft had been pushed into shallow water. Cooper and OBie waved to him and he ran to the raft and gave the eggs to OBie. One of the men in fatigues tried to grab Peter, but he jumped clear and splashed back to the sand and pebbles. He would not leave without his father and friends.

Anthony could not get around the thrashing, half blind, and wholly enraged death eagle. Peter ran to Ray, who lay in the grass, the breath knocked out of him, barely able to lift his head. Peter grabbed Ray's arm and tugged him up and over on his hands and knees. Ray rose up, suddenly whooped as he inhaled a lungful of air, then groaned and fell back on all fours.

The death eagle seemed to have recovered from Billie's rock, but Billie flung several more in rapid succession, striking it on its breast, the side of its head just forward of the flared gorget, and again on its beak.

Without a sound, the beast swooped. Billie had no time to think; it seemed impossible for any animal so large to move so fast. And Anthony appeared beside Billie just as quickly, holding up a short, stout stick.

The avisaur jammed its right eye directly on the stick. Its open jaw flattened both of them, but snapped shut only as the animal reared yet again.

Ray had recovered enough to stand. He and Peter dodged crab-wise around the trampled grass and spraying sand and rocks, toward Billie and Anthony. Billie lay on his side, eyes glazed, blood dribbling from his nose and mouth. Anthony was already on his feet. Together, they lifted Billie like a limp doll and ran for the beach.

The death eagle, now almost blind, fluffed its dish of neck feathers forward and turned its head, listening for their footsteps. It put one foot down, talons flexing, and then another.

They waded to the raft. Billie mumbled something, spit a little blood, and grabbed a rope to haul himself onto the rubber gunwale. Anthony and Ray pushed him in the rest of the way.

The death eagle stood in the lake shallows, making deep drum thumps topped by querying hums like strokes on a cello. It was uncomfortable with the feeling of water on its legs, but its anger, its pain, its pure dominant hatred, drove it to follow the humans. It splashed to within fifteen feet of the raft and cocked its crown toward the sound of oars. It hummed again, its eyes swollen shut, pointing its beak first at Anthony, then at Peter and Ray as they pushed the raft into deeper water.

Anthony picked Peter up bodily and threw him into the raft, then vaulted himself up on stiff arms, lifting one leg to swing it over the gunwale. Wetherford grabbed his shoulder to help.

The death eagle spread its tail, tensed its neck, and lunged.

The beak closed on Anthony's right leg just below the knee. With a sound like huge scissors snicking shut, it removed the lower leg and foot as neatly as a surgeon. Anthony dropped heavily into the boat bottom and blood spurted from the stump. The leg and foot fell into the lake and sank. Wetherford cried out and shielded his face; OBie took aim with the rifle and shot at the beast's head. Stung by the bullet, it pulled back.

Peter grabbed his father's shoulders and held him close. Ray unhitched his belt and pushed it through the loops on his pants.

The death eagle stepped into a hole in the lake bottom and skidded, then lost its balance completely. With a hiss, it toppled into Lake Akuena. The wash from its fall almost swamped the raft, but also pushed them farther from shore.

Peter thought he could still hear the beast's angry hiss despite the fact that the bird's head lay in the water. Then Wetherford reached past him and said, "We're holed."

The raft sank in the rear. The two men in fatigues rowed as fast as they could. The raft only had three oars. OBie grabbed the third oar and Wetherford and Cooper used their hands as paddles.

His father's blood filled the bottom of the raft. Ray wrapped his belt high on the stump, near Anthony's groin, and drew it very tight. It was at this point that Peter's father felt the pain and opened his eyes wide and screamed. Peter held him down as best he could. Rainwater, lake water, and blood swirled in the bottom of the raft.

If I live, Peter thought. *If we live—*

But he could not finish the thought. There was too much going on and he doubted very much any of them would live.

Over the loud, dull roar of rain on the raft and the harsh scrub of the rain on the lake, Peter heard the PBY's engines cough, turn over, catch, and then bellow to life. They drowned out all other sounds.

He looked up and behind them, but with rain and blood in his eyes, he could only see blurs. *Dinoshi* flopped and thrashed in the deeper water.

Peter wiped his eyes with his sleeve and spoke into his father's ear. "Hold still, Father. *Please hold still.*"

OBie shielded his face against the rain and stared out over the water. "Look at that!" he cried and pointed.

Cooper allowed himself a single "Gawww—awww-d-dammmnn!"

Peering through the stinging rain, Peter thought they must all be dreaming. Three giant hooded cobras rose from the water around the death eagle. Jaws wide and hoods spread like sails, the sinuous beasts began to tear at the avisaur, heads striking again and again.

"More lake devils!" Wetherford shouted.

The oars splashed even more frantically. Ray tried to bail water, pushing it over the side with cupped hands.

Anthony slumped in Peter's arms. "Jesus and Mary and all the saints," he said, and his eyes closed.

A long glistening hump swam past the raft with powerful vertical strokes of paddle-like flippers. A head appeared some ten feet from the hump, as if a second animal had joined the first, but the head rose higher and a long neck connected the two. The sleek, broad-jawed head turned in their direction, bright yellow eyes wrapped in translucent membranes. It spread wide its boldly patterned hood. The head swung out over the raft, less than a foot from Peter.

"That's it," Ray said. He covered his face.

OBie whipped up his oar but did not connect. With lightning reflexes, the lake devil jerked its head out of range. The back submerged and the neck and head went with it. The lake devil—a kind of plesiosaur, Peter thought, or something new entirely—swam to join its fellows around the death eagle.

By this time, kicking itself into even deeper water, *Dinoshi* had managed to get its legs under its body and stand. It defended itself with resounding snaps of its jaws, then turned and waded with some dignity toward shore, even as the lake devils nipped and slashed at its tail and legs.

The raft was awash aft. Ray and Cooper slipped into the lake and hung on to ropes. Cooper lifted the camera barely above water. Peter saw the eggs roll toward the rear, where they fetched up against his father's left leg.

A shadow fell over them, something huge and insurmountable, and Peter hunched his shoulders, hugging his father tight, waiting to die.

But they had made it.

The wing of the PBY sheltered them from the rain. Men reached through the open fuselage hatch. Peter saw Monte Schoedsack's thick glasses. Arms reached out and passed Anthony along, moaning and kicking feebly, and lifted him by the shoulders into the airplane. Cooper hefted the camera by a tripod leg and Schoedsack grabbed it. Wetherford, Billie, and OBie went next, then Peter. Ray clung to the sinking boat.

"Hey! Don't forget me!" he called.

Cooper and OBie grabbed him and hauled him through the hatch.

Peter crawled forward and collapsed at the foot of the cot on which Anthony was laid. Someone covered him with a blanket and patted his wet clothes. He was almost too exhausted to blink. Legs in brown fatigues stepped over canvas-wrapped parcels and steel drums, moving to the rear. Peter saw a flash of red cross on white field as a first-aid kit was carried past.

Whitecaps thumped on the other side of the hull just inches from his face. The plane was moving, taking off. Light from a port streamed diffuse and gray through the plane's interior.

His father screamed again. Peter gathered all his remaining strength, tossed his blanket aside, and knelt beside him.

Chapter Eighteen

Several cots had been rigged forward of the PBY's blisters and slender tail. Anthony lay on the port side. Two men cut away his pants while a third gave him an injection. The third man glanced at Peter as he stepped around him. He wore a wet blood-stained khaki shirt and a fringe of crisp white hair circled his immense and dignified square pate of tanned skin. His nose hooked sharply and his eyes were small and close together.

"Peter," Anthony said between clenched teeth, and he reached out with his left arm. Peter knelt and took his hand. Anthony's grip felt weak. "You're all right," Anthony said.

His father looked very pale, even *old*. The realization that his father might actually die made Peter's stomach tighten and his head swim.

"Alive," Peter said. He had become quite hoarse.

"I'm Dr. Tannenbaum," the bald-headed man said. "Coop tells me this is your father."

The plane bounced, fell, hit the lake surface hard, and shuddered; then the thud of waves ceased and the roar of the engines took on a steady, reassuring drone.

"I've given your father morphine. He'll be asleep in a little while. You all need to rest."

"What about his leg?" Peter asked.

"We're working on that now."

"Is he going to live?"

"We'll do our best," Tannenbaum said.

A bottle of plasma was hung from a hook over Anthony's cot. The doctor blocked Peter's view of Anthony's legs. Gauze and surgical instruments were passed from hand to hand, and a caged workshop light was suspended from another hook and switched on, silhouetting the doctor and his assistants.

Peter looked down at the other cots. Billie lay on his side, strapped in, with a blanket over him. Blood from his nose stained the white pillow. His eyes were closed. "He's asleep," a young woman said. Peter stared at her in surprise. He hadn't noticed her before. She wore a white blouse and slacks. Drops of blood stained her slacks. Blood seemed to be everywhere. "He's had quite a blow on the head, but no concussion."

Billie moaned and opened his eyes. Peter hunkered down beside the Indian. "Where are we?" Billie asked.

"We're flying to safety," Peter said.

"Did I face the Challenger?"

"You sure did," Peter said.

"And we are not dead?"

"No."

Billie smiled. "I am dreaming of jaguar," he said, and closed his eyes again.

OBie sat up forward of Billie's cot, arguing with Schoedsack and a very young-looking man in a dark uniform. The plane was crowded. Ray maneuvered between the cots and around the medical team and crouched beside Peter.

"OBie has a wrenched shoulder and a fractured tibia," he said. "I have a lot of cuts and bruises and a sprained wrist. It's amazing we got as far as we did. How's your father?"

Peter looked down at Anthony's face. His father's expression was dreamy and he smacked his mouth as if trying to say something. His head rolled to one side. Peter felt a new kind of fear now: fear of going on without this strange, difficult, wonderful man.

"He'll make it," Peter said.

The plane continued to climb through grayness and white clouds. Rain beat against the fuselage and transparent blisters. A gust of wind struck and they slipped sideways and down, then recovered.

Peter suddenly remembered. "What happened to the eggs?" he asked Ray.

"The raft," the cameraman answered.

Peter thought he meant the eggs were lost.

"I picked them out of the raft before it sank and gave them to someone in the plane. They should be here somewhere. Good Christ," Ray Harryhausen said, wiping his face with his hands. He shook his head and slumped against a crate, drawing up his knees. "I never want to see another dinosaur as long as I live."

The young female nurse stepped forward and smiled at Peter. "Your father's lost a lot of blood . . . but he's tough as nails. They're suturing his vessels now and cleaning his leg and getting ready to sew it shut. He's going to be OK." She looked at Peter's bruises and his bloody arm.

"I'm fine," he said.

"I'll tend to those scrapes," she insisted. "You, too," she said to Ray.

As Peter and Ray submitted to her treatment, Cooper and Schoedsack came aft and huddled beside Ray and Peter. Schoedsack goggled at them through his thick glasses. Cooper wiped his forehead with a handkerchief.

"This is the damnedest mess I've ever seen, and I've seen more than my share," Cooper said. "We've been trying to fly due north, but the storm's too thick. Now we're flying southwest to find some clear air. We'll have to circle—"

Peter jumped at a loud sound, like popcorn popping.

Cooper and Schoedsack instantly covered their crotches with their hands. The nurse, Ray, and Peter stared at them, dumfounded.

"Those are *bullets!*" Cooper shouted. "Who in hell is shooting at us?" He jumped up and ran forward. Magically, a hole opened in the floor of the airplane between Peter's feet. The nurse grunted; the loose part of her sleeve had been pierced. Two holes showed as she flexed her arm and stared at her elbow.

"I'll be damned," she said.

The plane made a sudden quick bank. Ray and Peter grabbed for something to hold on to, then looked at each other and reached down to cover their own crotches.

One of the oarsmen from the raft came forward, face white but grinning. "Back in '44, we sat on our helmets! Hands ain't any good."

The nurse returned to her work, wrapping gauze and clipping tape around their wounds.

Cooper returned a few moments later. "Must have been some of the army troops below Pico Poco or on the Caroní. We've ticked off the Army generals for sure—but now they've gone too far. Damned if they'll get any good press from us!"

"You couldn't get permission?" Peter asked. "I mean, to fly in?"

"Hell, no!" Schoedsack stormed, waving one arm. "They told us to leave you *estupido* gringos there to rot!" He motioned for Ray and Peter to follow him forward. "OBie's worn out. You're going to have to explain what happened."

In the space behind the cockpit, Ray and Peter took cups of hot cocoa from the young radioman and sat across the aisle from Schoedsack. Cooper had resumed his place at the controls, with a smooth-faced young Navy lieutenant as his co-pilot.

"Merian called in every favor he did during the war," Schoedsack said. "So did I. So did John Ford. We got this beauty on loan from Pensacola the day after we heard on the radio . . . Flew down from New York and took off the next evening."

Cooper pulled aside his earphones and leaned his head back over the chair. "Nothing but jungle and savanna from here to the coast. We'll be over Guyana soon. I reckon we have enough fuel to make it to Trinidad . . . If we don't get hasty."

"Tannenbaum says our wounded are stable. They'll be okay for a few more hours," Schoedsack said.

Cooper clamped his lips, nodded, and turned forward again.

"Now—the whole story," Schoedsack said to Ray and Peter. "Start at the bridge." He looked somber, eyes goggling behind the thick lenses. "Tell us about Vince. And Ray, what in *hell* happened to your camera?"

One of the oarsmen poked forward. His eyes lit on Peter. "You the kid that brought those eggs on board?"

Peter blushed, as if caught doing something bad. "Yeah," he said.

"Well, one of them's starting to hatch!"

Chapter Nineteen

B right sun filled the courtyard in front of the archway leading to Circus Lothar's Tampa headquarters. Dozens of reporters paced or lounged or puffed on cigarettes in the open-air training ring. Lotto Gluck, magnanimous with the resources of a circus he no longer owned, personally served lemonade to the reporters from a pushcart, shielded from the sun by a red-striped umbrella. When asked how the babies were doing, he smiled broadly, lifted his finger to his lips, and said, "That's not my story to tell."

"Lotto, we're running out of time," groused one reporter, a burly fellow with carrot-colored hair. "We got to file before noon or it's lost in tomorrow's puppy carpet. So tell us—you were supposed to send the dinos back, not bring more out. What gives?"

Lothar Gluck smiled and shrugged and said again, "That'sss not my sstory to tell!"

"So who *will* tell?" the burly reporter asked, wiping his forehead with a plaid handkerchief.

"Why, the proud papa, I ssuposse," he said. "Anybody elsse thirsty?" He was enjoying himself. "I'm willing to tell my own story, to anyone who will listen."

"Yeah, yeah, we know," said a skinny fellow from Boston. He wagged his head and singsonged, "Retired to Sarasota, opens up a shop to sell circus memorabilia—"

"A wonderful assortment, all my own, collected over forty years," Lotto said. "Catalogs free to all legitimate enthusiasts."

The reporters grumbled, but lined up for another cup of lemonade.

From behind the sliding door of the equipment barn, Peter Belzoni looked out on the milling reporters clutching their notepads and cameras. Ray stood behind him, resplendent and a little uncomfortable in a new seersucker suit. Behind them, giant arc lights and generators and huge spools of cable sat in the warm shadows. Lazy flies zapped themselves against bare wires running the length of the roof.

OBie sat in a folding camp chair in front of a mobile arc light. He tapped his shoe against one of the carriage's tires. Three men in brownish gray suits, the color of freshly quarried brownstone—two lawyers and a press agent—stood nearby, arms folded.

"When're Coop and Monte going to get here?" OBie asked the RKO press agent. He fanned himself with a straw Panama hat.

"Any minute now," the agent said.

Peter had not seen OBie so nervous since they had wandered into the communisaur nursery. Ray tugged at his shirt collar and picked up a sketchpad and pencil. On the pad was a half finished drawing

of the damnedest creature anyone would hope to see—like a kangaroo with teeth, or a venator covered with fuzz and given the head of a monstrous shrew. With powerful hind legs and puny little forelegs, it was so ugly it was cute.

From outside came the sound of a motorcycle. Peter looked up, all else forgotten.

"That must be your dad," Ray said.

Peter walked toward the rear of the barn and opened the sliding panel door a crack. Anthony had stopped a big, brand new BMW motorbike on the gravel outside and was taking off a leather helmet. "Hey, Peter, help me with this kickstand—I haven't caught the knack yet."

Peter stepped out into the hot sun and helped his father bring down the kickstand and swing off the bike. "I'm impressing the hell out of myself, hauling this machine around the roads," Anthony said. He kicked out his prosthetic leg and wiggled the foot. "Almost as good as new. We got two things in the mail." He held up a letter and the latest issue of *National Geographic*. He was getting much better at walking with the prosthetic leg, but he still limped a little—and Peter suspected he did it for effect. With that bike, that leg, and that limp, his father attracted women like hungry mice to cheese. Anthony gave Peter a big smile, then reached down to scratch.

"Damn!" he said, shaking his head. "Itches like the devil, but there's nothing there! Doesn't that beat anything!"

Peter could not decide whether to open the letter or the magazine first. The letter was from his mother, and in the magazine was his first published piece, accompanying his father's article and photographs. STRANDED ON KAHU HIDI, the cover read, and in smaller type beneath, *Sunset of a Mighty Hunter.*

Peter looked at Anthony, who seemed to be taking his measure by what decision he would make. Not willing to play that sort of game anymore, Peter stuffed the magazine under his arm and opened the letter.

> *Dear Peter,*
>
> *My apologies for taking so long to write. I have been going through chills thinking about what happened, and have tried to find the right words. I am so angry I could spit, and I've already got enough on your father that forgiveness is out of the question. But of course I am so glad you're still alive. I look forward to your visit, but I suppose you are a man now and will only stay a little while. I understand you have a new job and many future prospects. Grandmother sends her love.*

*I know this hasn't been easy on you—though you say it was
an adventure, a mother can read between the lines, and I know
you were scared and miserable. As I said, I could just spit. But
if you've learned anything from your father and me, it should
be that a young man must become his own person. I do love you,
Peter.*

I know it does not make sense, but I am proud of you, too.

Love,

Deirdre
your mother

Peter folded the letter and slipped it back into the envelope. He
suppressed a sigh. She always signed her few letters with that
unnecessary reminder.

"Smells like her old perfume," Anthony said briskly. He pointed
to the magazine "The pictures came out well."

"Peter!" a voice shouted from the small animal barn. The
Ringling Brothers veterinarian, lanky J. Y. "Doc" Henderson,
pulled a rubber-wheeled cart from the barn into the sunlight. On
the cart rested two cages.

Peter handed Anthony the magazine and grinned. Anthony
returned the grin, but shook his head. "Go see your babies," he said.

Peter crossed the gravel and met Doc Henderson halfway. He
knelt down beside the cages. In the first cage, young Stiletto
blinked at Peter and made a plaintive high-pitched squawk.

"Still won't let anybody feed him but you," Henderson said.
Stiletto stood on thick smooth legs, pressing his head against the
wire mesh, his large golden eye blinking at Peter. At the age of four
months, Stiletto stood three feet high, with a mouthful of sharp
teeth as long as the small blade on Peter's new pocketknife. He was
already showing signs of Dagger's cantankerous independence.
Peter took the can of shredded beef and raw egg—mixed with
Vince Shellabarger's secret herbs—and made several meatballs, then

pressed them between the mesh. Stiletto pulled them through with surprisingly agile lips, like a horse's, and swallowed them whole.

"They've both passed inspection," Henderson said. "Healthy as can be. And surprisingly, they seem to like each other. Stiletto gets very upset when Frankie isn't with him."

Frankie was as odd a creature as anyone had ever seen. Ray's drawing barely did her justice. Now a little smaller than Stiletto, who was outgrowing her rapidly, she stood on two four-toed feet, the middle toes prominent and splayed. Her forelimbs were stunted, even smaller in proportion than Stiletto's, with tiny, ineffectual paws. From the tip of her long tail to her pointed, flexible tube of snout, she was covered with fine mousy-brown fur. Her small, piggish eyes blinked rapidly in the sun; she was born to be a creature of night, but had adjusted her waking schedule to her "sibling." Despite her faint resemblance to a kangaroo, Frankie did not hop, but walked on her hind limbs with ballerina grace, using the long, flexible tail as a balance, much as Stiletto did.

Beyond the bipedal gait and long tail, Frankie and Stiletto parted evolutionary pathways radically. As Doc Henderson had confirmed, Frankie was of a line of mammals known only from fossils. No one had ever encountered them before on El Grande; the old plateau was still full of surprises. She had hatched from an egg only slightly smaller than Stiletto's—and she had hatched first. Her delicate long jaws carried sharp canine teeth, for hunting, but she would never outmatch a venator, or even a bobcat.

On Kahu Hidi, had her egg been left in place and the venator survived, Frankie would have hatched first, then killed and eaten her dinosaur siblings. She would then have departed the nest to live as a nocturnal hunter of small animals. Her species, as yet unnamed, relied on dinosaurs to raise their young—like cuckoos. Henderson guessed she would be about eight feet high when fully grown—a true mammalian marvel.

Frankie cooed softly and Peter reached through the mesh to scratch behind her small ears. That was something he would never do to Stiletto, despite the venator's adopting him as Mother. Even young venators were not fond of physical contact.

Shellabarger had failed after all. He had not succeeded in paying back his obligation to Dagger. Peter was not sure what the trainer had meant to do with two eggs in the first place—perhaps raise the hatchlings on El Grande until they could be released . . . But Frankie's egg and the Venezuelan Army had scotched those plans.

A shadow fell on Peter and the cage. For a moment, his neck hair prickled and his eyes moistened. He seemed to feel the presence of Vince Shellabarger, strong and tall behind him.

He turned and saw broad-shouldered, dark Damoo Dhotre, the Ringling Brothers' chief animal trainer.

"Good morning, Peter," Dhotre said. He knelt beside Peter and peered into the cages with wise black eyes. "That one," he said, pointing to Stiletto, "will never be trained. We will build a large paddock for him. Roland Butler will announce that he is the last of his kind, and who knows? Perhaps he is. Many people will come to Tampa to see him." Dhotre smiled at Frankie. "She will be a challenge, but no worse than a tiger, I think. Will you help me with her?"

Dhotre had offered Peter a job last week, and John Ringling North had approved. North had said, "That's what we need to sell dinosaurs again—young blood." But Peter had not yet decided.

"I do not make such offers lightly," Dhotre said.

"I know," Peter said. "I was just thinking of Vince . . ."

"Did he say that what happened was his fault?" Dhotre asked.

Peter frowned in puzzlement. "Yes, but—"

"It is only what I would have expected. Whatever misfortunes come to us who train animals, they are our fault alone. I see you working with the beasts, calm and cool and knowledgeable, not too brave and never stupid. I say that about few men, Peter."

A long black Cadillac limousine drove up between the buildings, grinding gravel beneath its wide white-sidewall tires. The door swung open and Merian C. Cooper and Ernest Schoedsack stepped out. Ray and OBie walked through the door to the equipment barn.

Cooper waved a thick sheaf of papers and smiled. "We got 'em! The sons of bitches went for it. We are now slaves to Republic Pictures. Ford's going to produce. Peter, Anthony! How're the little fellas?" He peered into the cage. "Damoo! great to see you again. How about a guest shot?"

"In what?" Dhotre asked.

"In the biggest epic of all time. Big enough to make Monte and me partners again."

Anthony walked forward, his new leg clicking at the ankle. Cooper stooped to give it a whack with his knuckles. "By God, you look every inch the hero. Jimmy Stewart! A perfect match!"

Schoedsack stood back, glowering, as if nothing would ever quite cheer him up. OBie and Ray sidled around the group, OBie with hands in pants pockets, like Schoedsack unwilling as yet to show any enthusiasm.

"We going back to shoot?" OBie asked warily.

"To El Grande?" Cooper roared. "Not on your life. Truman's got the State Department staring daggers at Betancourt and those bastard generals. No pun intended. All of the U.S. of A. is riled about what happened down there. Looks like they may twist a few arms and get the plateau opened up as a scientific preserve—in a few years. But we're going to make our movie now—strike while the iron is hot."

"We don't have much footage from the plateau itself," Ray observed quietly.

"That's where you two come in," Cooper said, flinging out his arms as if to embrace them. "You've always wanted to build and animate your monsters in a studio. Hell of a lot safer that way. Now's your chance. *Return to the Lost World!* Technicolor! Two million dollar budget! Jimmy Stewart and John Wayne and Mickey Rooney—that's you, Peter! And Sabu, by God! We haven't signed Kate Hepburn yet, but she's interested."

OBie and Ray appeared stunned.

"It's the *publicity,* boys!" Cooper shouted. "You're in all the papers! You're famous!"

Stiletto grumbled threateningly at the loud and active man. Cooper bent over the young venator's cage and stared him down. "Exactly right. We'll *terrify* 'em!"

"And who will play *you,* Mr. Cooper?" Dhotre asked.

Cooper got to his feet and waved away that question.

OBie tugged on the brim of his Panama. "It's on the level?" he asked Cooper.

"Why, OBie, I'm hurt," Cooper said, feigning a sad expression. "Have I ever joked about making pictures?"

"Never," OBie said. "Ray?"

"We'll have work," Ray said. Peter realized that motion picture people like Ray and OBie faced a lot of disappointments and that was why they were reluctant to show enthusiasm.

"We're in," OBie said. He smiled and held out his hand.

Cooper grasped OBie's hand and they shook firmly, and then he grabbed Ray's hand. "Fine, boys, fine!"

Anthony stood beside Peter. "What about you?" he asked, and there was the usual dare in his voice.

"Someday," Peter said, "I'd like to go back."

"Not me," Ray said.

"Until then, I have a lot to learn about animals. Mr. Dhotre, I'd be honored." Peter shook the trainer's hand.

Schoedsack removed his thick glasses and rubbed them with a handkerchief. "It's all show business," he said philosophically. "Craziest goddamn life in the world."

"Going to go visit your mother first?" Anthony asked Peter.

"Of course," Peter said.

"Give her my best," Anthony said.

"Of course."

"Come on!" Cooper shouted, taking the cart by its handle and tugging it toward the equipment barn. "We have to make our entrance!"

Peter followed OBie and Ray, helping Doc Henderson pull the cart with the two cages on it. Frankie settled back on her haunches, long nose twitching. Stiletto paced and whickered restlessly. He kept his eyes on Peter as they passed through the shadowy equipment barn, back under the bright sun and all the eyes of the world.

What's Real, and What's Not

El Grande, of course, does not exist.

Sir Arthur Conan Doyle set his novel *The Lost World* on a tepui in Venezuela, and the tepuis are real, but they are much smaller than either Doyle or I have described them, and none of them has dinosaurs. The little black frog that Peter sees in the maze on El Grande is real, and more typical of the species found on these odd and wonderful plateaus.

Professor George Edward Challenger is Doyle's invention, as is Maple White. Cardozo, Lowell Thomas, Colonel Percy Harrison Fawcett, Sir Walter Raleigh, and Jimmie Angel were all real people. Jimmie Angel actually did crack up an airplane on Auyan Tepui, and may have been the first human of European descent to see the falls that bear his last name. Colonel Fawcett, a true eccentric, disappeared in the Mato Grosso in Brazil in 1925.

Calvin Coolidge, his wife and son, and Herbert Hoover were real, but having no El Grande in their lives, did not do what I have described. The United States of America's proprietary attitude toward Latin America, and the Venezuelan political situation of the time, including Gómez, Betancourt, Gallegos, etc., was roughly as described. *El Colonel* and all other characters are fictional.

The indigenous tribes of the Amazon did not gather around El Grande and use it as a ceremonial site. The tribes named do exist, or existed at the time, in and around the rain forests and the Gran Sabana, and their plight is even more desperate. Billie, who never reveals his Indian name, is fictional.

John Ringling North, J. Y. Henderson, and Damoo Dhotre were all real, as was Gargantua, the giant gorilla. Vince Shellabarger and Lotto Gluck are fictional.

Merian C. Cooper, Ernest Schoedsack, John Ford, Willis O'Brien, and of course Ray Harryhausen are actual people. Cooper, Schoedsack, and O'Brien made a film called *King Kong,* and OBie did indeed animate the dinosaurs in the early silent version of *The Lost World,* based on Doyle's novel.

Released in 1933, without the interference of dinosaur circuses, *King Kong* became a huge hit and inspired generations of young people. One of those youngsters was Ray Harryhausen, who realized his dreams and animated dinosaurs, creatures from Venus, mythical monsters, and quite a few skeletons. Harryhausen in turn inspired later generations of moviemakers—and not just moviemakers, but dinosaur experts and paleontologists around the world. He inspired me, as well.

I owe a debt of gratitude to all of these people, real and imagined, and to the animals.

Altovenator ferox is fictitious, but modeled from varieties of theropod dinosaurs. *Stratoraptor velox* is completely made up, but based on speculation (admittedly my own, for the most part) about what avian precursors might have evolved into, given the opportunity. *Aepyornis titan* lived well into modern times, as did other large flightless birds such as the Moa. *Neostruthiomimus planensis* is based approximately on *Struthiomimus. Centrosaurus, Ankylosaurus,* and avisaurs such as *Archaeopteryx* all lived at one time.

Frankie, the nest-robbing mammal, is loosely based on a real creature as well, *Leptictidium nasutum,* found in the Messel fossil beds in Germany. Frankie's habits and size (and egg) are fictional, however. *Leptictidium nasutum* was a hunter, about as large as a cat, and strangely enough seemed to have been built very much along the lines of theropod dinosaurs like *Tyrannosaurus rex:* long balancing tail, locomotion on two hind limbs adapted for running, not hopping, and small forelimbs not suitable (supposedly) for holding down large prey. It makes an interesting contribution to the controversy about *T. rex*'s tiny arms!

The hammerhead amphibian that so fascinates Ray and Peter is not known in the fossil record, though *Diplocaulus* and *Gerrothorax* might be prototypes.

Therapsids—mammal-like reptiles—existed at one time, but not necessarily as I have described them. The lizard-monkeys and communisaurs are my own invention.

Remember, El Grande was sealed off from the outside world (in three parts, no less!) tens of millions of years ago, and it is my supposition that many species would have evolved to fill vacant ecological niches.